MAN OF MY
Dreams

MAN OF MY Dreams

Sherrilyn Kenyon

Maggie Shayne

Suzanne Forster

Virginia Kantra

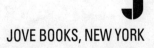

JOVE BOOKS, NEW YORK

THE BERKLEY PUBLISHING GROUP
Published by the Penguin Group
Penguin Group (USA) Inc.
375 Hudson Street, New York, New York 10014, USA
Penguin Group (Canada), 10 Alcorn Avenue, Toronto, Ontario M4V 3B2, Canada
(a division of Pearson Penguin Canada Inc.)
Penguin Books Ltd., 80 Strand, London WC2R 0RL, England
Penguin Group Ireland, 25 St. Stephen's Green, Dublin 2, Ireland
(a division of Penguin Books Ltd.)
Penguin Group (Australia), 250 Camberwell Road, Camberwell, Victoria 3124, Australia
(a division of Pearson Australia Group Pty. Ltd.)
Penguin Books India Pvt. Ltd., 11 Community Centre, Panchsheel Park,
New Delhi—110 017, India
Penguin Group (NZ), Cnr. Airborne and Rosedale Roads, Albany, Auckland 1310,
New Zealand (a division of Pearson New Zealand Ltd.)
Penguin Books (South Africa) (Pty.) Ltd., 24 Sturdee Avenue, Rosebank, Johannesburg 2196,
South Africa

Penguin Books Ltd., Registered Offices: 80 Strand, London WC2R 0RL, England

This is a work of fiction. Names, characters, places, and incidents either are the product of the author's imagination or are used fictitiously, and any resemblance to actual persons, living or dead, business establishments, events, or locales is entirely coincidental.

MAN OF MY DREAMS

A Jove Book / published by arrangement with the author

Copyright © 2004 by The Berkley Publishing Group.
"Fire and Ice" copyright © 2004 by Sherrilyn Kenyon.
"Daydream Believer" copyright © 2004 by Margaret Benson.
"Shocking Lucy" copyright © 2004 by Suzanne Forster.
"Midsummer Night's Magic" copyright © 2004 by Virginia Kantra.
Cover design by Erika Fusari.
Cover photo by Franco Accornero.
Book design **by Kristin del Rosario**.

ISBN: 0-7394-4728-9

JOVE®
Jove Books are published by The Berkley Publishing Group,
a division of Penguin Group (USA) Inc.,
375 Hudson Street, New York, New York 10014.
JOVE is a registered trademark of Penguin Group (USA) Inc.
The "J" design is a trademark belonging to Penguin Group (USA) Inc.

PRINTED IN THE UNITED STATES OF AMERICA

Contents

MAN OF MY
Dreams

Fire and Ice

SHERRILYN KENYON

Chapter One ✑

ADRON Quiakides had never been the type of man one approached recklessly.

Not if one wanted to live, anyway.

And tonight, while he sat alone in a back booth of the Golden Crona nursing a bottle of expensive Grenna alcohol, the last thing he wanted was for anyone to disturb him.

His pleasures in life were minimal, and consuming bucketsful of the yellow-orange liquid gave him the solace his battered soul craved.

Because tonight, more than ever before, his memories hurt.

This very hour marked the fifth anniversary of the night he had made the decision he would spend the rest of his life paying for.

Adron gripped the bottle tight in his right hand, unable to believe it'd been that long since he'd last walked without a pronounced limp. Moved without pain. Spoken without his throat aching from the effort of it.

Five years since he'd experienced any comfort or peace whatsoever.

He'd lain in bed for hours trying to sleep. Trying to forget, and finally he'd realized the only way to silence his demons was to drown them out.

And nothing worked better than Grenna.

Tipping the large bottle to his lips, he let the fire pour down his throat.

"Hey, baby," an attractive redhead said as she sauntered over to him and propped a thin hip against his table. "You want some company?"

"I have company," he said, his raspy voice grating on his ears. "Me, myself, and I."

She raked a hungry look over his body, then leaned across the table to show him her ample breasts. "Well, there's enough of me to make all three of you happy."

There had been a time, once, when he wouldn't have hesitated to take her up on that offer.

But then life was nothing if not ever-changing, and usually it altered on the hairpin of a second.

She licked her lips. "C'mon, handsome, buy me a drink."

Adron glared at her. She wasn't the first woman to proposition him tonight. And in truth it mystified him that any woman would bother, given the vicious scar on his face. But then, the women in the Golden Crona weren't all that discriminating, especially not when they sensed money.

"Sorry," he said coldly. "None of us are interested."

She sighed dramatically. "Well, if any of you change your minds, you let me know." With one last wistful look at him, she headed back into the human and alien crowd that drifted through the packed bar.

Adron shifted uncomfortably in his seat as a bone-deep pain shot through his left leg. Clenching his teeth, he growled low in his throat.

One would think the amount of painkillers he lived on, when combined with the alcohol, would squelch any amount of ache. But it barely numbed his physical torment.

And it did nothing for the burning agony in his heart.

"Damn it to hell," he snarled under his breath, then he threw his head back and finished off his drink.

He grabbed a passing green-fleshed waitress and ordered two more bottles.

As he waited for her to return, he saw another woman headed his way. The fierce glare he narrowed on her sent her scurrying away.

He was through playing around. Tonight he intended to get fully flagged and he pitied the next fool stupid enough to approach him. Unless they came bearing more alcohol.

LIVIA typpa Vista had lived the whole of her life in protective custody. More hostage than princess, she'd long grown weary of everyone's dictates for her behavior, and at age twenty-six, she'd had enough.

She was not a child.

And she was not going to marry Clypper Thoran in two weeks. Not even if he were the last male in the universe!

"You will do as you are told."

She winced at her father's imperious command. High Eminence he might be, but she, not her older brother, had inherited his stubbornness. No matter the cost, she refused to marry a territorial governor sixteen years her father's senior.

Since Clypper had demanded a virgin for his bride, she knew a way to thwart them both.

After tonight, she would be a virgin no more.

Tomorrow, her father would kill her for it. But better to die than to be married to a cruel, goat-faced ancient who groped her with cold hands every time he got near her.

The Golden Crona.

As the cold rain poured over her, Livia stared at the sign above her head. Her maid, Krista, had told her about the club. Inside, it held all manner of heroes and villains, and though she would rather surrender her virginity to a hero, she honestly didn't care. So long as he was passably attractive and gentle, he would be good enough for the night.

Gathering her courage, Livia opened the door and stopped dead in her tracks.

Never had she seen anything like it. A sea of aliens and humans danced and bobbed through the smoky bar that smelled of sweat from many species, and of cheap alcohol. The obnoxious music was so loud, it made her ears throb.

A big, orange reptilian male gave her a frown as she hesitated in the doorway.

"In or out," he snarled.

She took a deep breath to fortify her courage. That, and she mentally conjured an image of Clypper's fat jowls and beady, lust-filled eyes.

Shuddering, she stepped inside and let the door pulse closed behind her.

"Twenty-five credits," the reptile-man demanded.

"Excuse me?"

"Twenty-five credits. You pay or I toss you out on your ass."

Livia arched a brow at him. It was on the tip of her tongue to put him in his place, but then she remembered he had no idea who she was. And she must keep it that way.

If anyone learned she was a Vistan princess, she would be sent back to the hotel where they were staying.

Not to mention the fact that her time was short. She had to find a man before someone missed her and started a search.

Pulling out the money she'd stolen from her brother, she paid the fee.

"Okay," she whispered to herself as she surveyed the bar full of people. "It's time to find him."

She walked through the crowd and flinched as several unwashed humans eyed her with interest.

Livia quickly amended her list of qualifications to include a man who bathed.

A tall, dark human male smiled at her, displaying a set of black teeth.

Okay, she would also add one who knew how to use a toothbrush.

As she crossed the room, she saw a brunet at the bar who looked like a hopeful prospect. She headed for him. But as soon as she drew near, she froze.

It was her father's personal runner.

If she knew how to curse, she would definitely curse at her luck.

Just don't let him see me.

Falling back into the crowd, Livia kept an eye on him while trying to scan the crowd for her target. Surely there was someone here who could . . .

A commotion in the entrance caught her attention.

Livia turned to look.

Oh, no! She panicked at the sight of her father's Royal Guard swarming into the bar. Immediately, the gray-clad soldiers began questioning patrons as they spread out to cover as much of the bar as they could.

She trembled. For them to be here in force and grim meant Krista had volunteered her location and no doubt, her intent as well. Livia groaned at the very thought.

How could Krista betray her? Her maid had been so helpful in the planning and execution of her escape.

But then for some unknown reason, Krista lived in fear of Livia's father and one scowl from him would have easily caused her maid to tell everything.

Right down to the grittiest of details.

Livia cringed at the thought of her father's reaction. But at least Krista, unlike her, would be spared his outrage.

Krista was protected by their laws. Only a male of her family could punish her, and Krista had no living male relative.

Livia was not so fortunate, and there was no telling what her father would do to her for this.

Chastity was one of the highest virtues any woman could possess on her world. In fact, men and women were only allowed to mix during meals, chaste, royal functions, and when married couples performed conjugal duties. For a woman to seek out a man not related to her was strictly forbidden.

And punished severely.

She shook the fear away. She'd known the consequences before she set out. Either way, she was going to pay for her indiscretion, and if she had to pay, then she was going to make sure she completed the deed.

Clenching her teeth, Livia scanned the room for a hiding

place. At the back of the club was a line of booths. She headed for them.

Unfortunately, all of them were occupied.

Drat!

"Hey, babe," a rough-looking man asked her, "you want some company?"

She considered it until he reached out and grabbed her arm. He pulled her toward him, his hand biting fiercely into the flesh of her upper arm. "C'mon," he said with a slick smile as he roughly ran his hand through her wet hair, "what say you and me head to the back?"

She jerked away from him before he hurt her any more. "No, thank you."

Stepping away, she saw the guards heading her way as they skimmed the crowd.

Her heart hammering, she ran to the last booth and sat on the empty bench before the guard saw her.

"What the hell are you doing?"

She shifted her gaze from the guard to the man who sat across from her. Livia's breath caught in her throat.

He was more than passable.

In fact, she'd never in her life seen a man so incredibly handsome. His features were sharp and aristocratically boned. His dark brown eyebrows arched finely over the most piercingly blue eyes she'd ever seen.

Dressed all in black, he had long, white-blond hair tied back into a neat queue. Clean-shaven and washed, he had an air of refinement and power surrounding him.

But his eyes were cold as he watched her. Guarded.

An aura of danger clung to him and by the set of his jaw, she could tell he didn't want company.

He tugged at the black gloves over his hands as he eyed her with malice.

She should get up and leave, especially since he had a fierce scar that ran across his cheekbone, to his hairline, and then down along his jaw. It looked like someone had intentionally carved it there, which made her wonder just what kind of man he was.

What had he done to deserve such a wound?

Biting her lip in indecision, she glanced back to the guard who was steadily headed this way.

What should she do?

Adron arched a brow at the woman who had yet to leave him.

He was drunk, but not so drunk that he didn't realize the wet little mouse sitting across from him didn't belong in this dive. He could smell the innocence on her.

And it turned his stomach.

Her dark brown hair was loose, spilling over her thin shoulders in waves.

She had large, angelic eyes. Green eyes that had no past haunting her. They were completely guileless and honest.

A shiver ran over him. Who in this day and age had eyes like that? And what right did she have, looking at him with them?

"I'm hiding from someone," she confided. "Do you mind?"

"Hell, yes, I mind."

Livia frowned at the stranger. His angry tone set her back, and if it wasn't for the fact that one of the guards was scanning the booths, she would have left.

Think of something!

The guard stopped two booths up and held out a holo-cube to the aliens sitting in it. "Have you seen this woman?"

Her plan in ruins, she only knew one way to thwart her father. She got up from her seat and sat next to the stranger.

He scowled at her.

Before he could say anything, Livia leaned forward and kissed him.

Adron sat in stunned silence as she placed her tightly closed lips over his. It was the most chaste kiss a woman not related to him had ever given him.

By the way she held his head in her hands, he could tell she thought this was the way a kiss should be given.

But worse than the innocence he tasted, he hadn't kissed a woman in over five years and the feel of those plump, full lips on his was more than his drunk mind could handle.

And her smell . . .

Lord, how he'd missed the sweet, intoxicating smell of a woman.

Closing his eyes, he let go of the bottle, and cupped her face in his hands as he took control of the situation.

Livia trembled as he opened her lips and slid his tongue into her mouth. She'd seen people kiss like this in plays and reels, but no one had ever dared such insolence with her before.

She tasted the sweet, fragrant alcohol on his tongue, smelled the warm, clean scent of him as he ran his hands over her back and held her so gently that it made her quiver.

He was definitely the one, she thought as her body burned from his touch. This was the man she would give her virginity to. A man with tormented blue eyes and a tender touch.

A man who made her breathless and weak, and at the same time hot and strangely powerful.

In his arms, she truly felt as if she had control of her life. Her body.

And she liked it.

Adron had never tasted anything better than her mouth. He felt her inexperience as she hesitantly met his tongue with hers. His body roared to life with a long-forgotten throbbing that demanded more than just her lips.

Oh, God, it was heaven and he'd lived in hell for so long that he had forgotten the taste and feel of it.

"Excuse me," a man said as he stopped in front of them. "Have you seen this—"

Adron broke away from the kiss only long enough to pass a lethal glare at the newcomer. "Go away or die."

Fear flickered across the man's eyes. It was a look Adron was used to.

Without another word, the man left them.

Adron returned to her lips.

Livia moaned as he deepened his kiss.

The guards and her fear forgotten, she sighed in pleasure. Foreign emotions tore through her as he buried his lips against her neck and sent white-hot chills through her. His arms tightened around her waist as her breasts swelled.

What was this deep-seated throbbing she felt?

This unbearable ache?

He made her light-headed and breathless. And she wanted him desperately.

"Would you make love to me?"

Adron pulled back in surprise. Had he been sober, he would have sent her away, but there was something about her that called out to him in a way he'd long forgotten.

It'd been an eternity since he last slept with a woman. Years of bitter, aching loneliness and pain.

And here she was offering herself to him.

Send her away.

But he didn't. Instead, he found himself getting up from the booth and leading her through the crowd.

Livia didn't know where they were going, but she made sure none of the guards saw her as they left the bar. In the back of her mind, she was terrified. She didn't know anything about this man.

Not even his name.

Never in her life had she done anything so foolish. And yet she instinctively knew he wouldn't hurt her.

There was pain in his icy blue eyes, but not cruelty.

He kept a possessive arm draped over her. And he walked by leaning heavily on a gold-tipped cane.

She wanted to ask him what had happened to his face and leg, but didn't dare lest it cause him to reconsider.

He led her outside the club, to a transport.

After they got in, they rode three levels down to an upper-scale apartment building.

Livia relaxed a tiny bit as they entered the grand lobby. At least she wouldn't be seduced in a dark, filthy back room somewhere.

Krista had well prepped her on what to expect. Right down to an estimation of how long a man would take before he let her go.

Taking a deep breath for courage, Livia figured she would be back in her hotel room by midnight. There would be questioning, and eventually her father would learn the truth.

God have mercy on her then.

But she had made her decision and once her mind was set on something, that was it. She would not be swayed.

Without a word to each other, they took a lift to the top floor.

He led her into a flat that was almost the size of her palace chambers. And as soon as he closed the door, he pulled her into his arms.

This time his kiss was fierce. Demanding. His kiss stole her breath as he pressed her back against the wall.

Her head swam at the powerful feel of his hands roaming over her.

What are you doing?

Shut up, she shouted at her mind, squelching the guilt and fear.

It was her life and she was going to claim it.

With that thought in mind, she started unbuttoning his shirt.

Adron sucked his breath in sharply at the feel of her hand against his bare chest. Her touch singed him. He could only vaguely recall someone other than doctors, nurses, or therapists touching his flesh.

To her credit, she didn't cringe or comment about the multitude of scars that bisected his body. She didn't even seem to notice them.

That was why he hadn't been with a woman since that long-ago night. He hadn't wanted to explain the scars. To recount where they had come from.

To have to face his lover in the early morning light.

Perhaps that was why he'd chosen a stranger tonight. He owed her no explanation. Owed her nothing at all.

He didn't want to see pity or repugnance on a lover's face.

But there was nothing in her pale green eyes except curiosity and hunger.

Livia had never seen a man's bare chest before, at least nowhere other than on reels.

Fascinated by it, she ran her hands over the smooth, tawny skin that was stretched tight over hard, steely muscles. Like velvet over steel. The contrast amazed her.

"You feel so wonderful," she breathed.

Adron pulled back to look at her. There was a strange note of awe in her voice, a gentle hesitancy in her touch. And in that instant, a feeling of dread consumed him.

He was drunk, but he wasn't *that* drunk. "You're a virgin."

Her face turned bright red.

"Shit!" he snarled as he stepped away from her.

His erection ached and his entire body burned. Leave it to him to find the only virgin he was sure had ever set foot inside the Golden Crona.

Gripping his cane, he limped his way to his bar and poured another drink. But the watered-down alcohol did nothing for him.

Suddenly, she was behind him, leaning up against his back as her slender arms surrounded his waist.

He shook all over from the gesture, from the feel of her small breasts against his spine. And in that moment, he needed her even more.

"I want you to make love to me," she whispered in his ear.

"Are you insane?" He turned to look at her.

She shook her head. "I want to give my virginity away. I don't want it taken from me."

"Taken by whom?"

She dropped her gaze. "Fine. If you don't want me, I'll go find someone who does."

A peculiar wave of jealousy stung him as he thought of someone else inside her.

What do you care?

And yet for some unknown, stupid reason, he did.

He caught her hand as she moved away from him. "What's your name?"

"Livia."

"Livia," he repeated. It suited her and those guileless sea-green eyes. "Why would you give yourself away so cheaply to someone like me?"

Livia paused as she saw the self-deprecation in his icy eyes. He hated himself. It was so obvious and she wondered why. "Because you seem nice."

He laughed bitterly at her answer. "Nice? I'm not nice. There's nothing *nice* about me."

That wasn't true. He had yet to be mean to her. He was hurting, she knew that. And it made him snappish.

But it didn't make him cruel.

"I need to go," she said quietly, regretting that he wouldn't be the one after all. "There's not much time before I have to return, and I have to take care of this by the morning."

"Why?"

Livia bit her lip as she felt her face flush again. In the morning, she'd be inspected by Clypper's doctors.

If she didn't find a man tonight, she was doomed.

"I just do." She let her gaze wander over his lush body. He had broad shoulders and a lean, firmly muscled frame. His white hair contrasted sharply with the black he wore.

He was gorgeous.

But he didn't want her.

Adron saw the steely determination in her eyes. She was going to find herself another man to sleep with her. He knew it.

He should let her and yet . . .

Why not me?

Ever since he'd lost his agility, he'd avoided women. He'd been afraid of embarrassing himself with his stiff clumsiness. But she would have no one to compare him to.

Adron gripped his cane. He remembered a time when he could have scooped her up in his arms and run with her to his bed.

But those days were lost to him forever.

"My bedroom is this way," he said, grabbing a bottle and heading down the hallway.

Livia quivered as she realized he was inviting her to join him.

Excited and terrified, she followed him down the elegant corridor and into a room at the end of it. The master bedroom was every bit as large as her own. A king-sized bed was set against the far wall, looking out over the city below them.

He set his bottle down on the nightstand, then moved to a chair by the bed. His face hard, he sat down slowly.

She saw the pain on his face as he bent his leg and moved to take off his boots.

She wanted to know what had happened to him, but didn't dare ask for fear of making him angry.

So, she went to him and took his foot in her hand.

He looked up at her, his eyes startled as she pulled the boot free.

"You know, I've never done anything like this," she whispered.

"Seeing that you're a virgin, I would think not."

Licking her lips, she removed his other boot.

Adron could feel her nervousness, her uncertainty, and he wanted to soothe her. "I won't hurt you," he assured her.

She smiled a smile that wrenched his gut. How he wished he'd met her before that fateful night. Then, he could have been the lover she deserved. He would have been able to take her all night. Slowly. Teasingly.

He had no idea what he'd be like now. But he would try to pleasure her. Do his damnedest to make sure her first time was a favorable memory.

His groin tight, he pushed himself up and moved to the bed.

Before he knew what she intended, she sat in his lap and kissed him.

Adron inhaled the sweetness of her breath as he ran his hands over her back. He'd never expected a virgin to be so bold. And she was a quick learner. She deepened her kiss and teased his tongue with hers.

Oh, yeah, this could be fun.

He unbuttoned her shirt to expose her small corslet. She moaned as he ran his hand over the satin-covered breasts and squeezed them gently in his hands.

Livia shook all over at the foreign throb between her legs. And when he released the catch behind her back and her corslet fell open, she shivered. No man had ever seen her naked before.

He stared at her bare breasts as he ran his hands over the taut peaks. He traced slow, simmering circles around her, sending chills all over her body.

"You are so beautiful," he breathed. Then, he dipped his head down and took her breast into his mouth.

Livia hissed in pleasure as his tongue swirled around her flesh, teasing, licking.

Never had she felt anything like it.

She leaned forward, cradling his head in her hands. Her body was on fire. He trailed his hands over her back, down her hips, and when he touched her between her legs she groaned.

He looked up at her, his eyes dazed and hungry as he breathed raggedly.

He rolled her over, onto the mattress, and turned the lights off. She heard him remove the rest of his clothes in the darkness, but she couldn't see anything at all.

Adron ached to see her naked, but he didn't want any light for her to see his damaged body.

His groin hot and throbbing for her, he unfastened the stiff, prickly brace on his left leg and let it fall to the floor. Next, he removed the one on his hand.

Then, slowly, carefully, he pulled her clothes from her.

He ran his hand over her smooth, hot skin, delighting in her murmurs of pleasure. He'd never taken a virgin before and the knowledge that he was her first lover added even more excitement to the moment.

No man had ever touched her.

No one but him.

Even with his wings broken and clipped, he soared at that knowledge.

Livia moaned as he covered her with his long, hot body. She'd never felt anything like all that lean, hard strength spread out evenly against her bare flesh.

He kissed her fiercely as he separated her thighs with his knee. Then, he pressed his thigh against the center of her body, the hairs on his leg teasing her intimately.

She ran her hand over his back, feeling the rugged terrain of scars, muscle, and skin.

"My name is Adron," he breathed in her ear a second before he traced the outline of her ear with his tongue.

"Adron," she repeated, testing the syllables. It was a strong name that suited him.

He stroked her with his thigh, his tongue, and his hands. Arching her back, Livia welcomed his touch. It was so wickedly erotic to feel him all over and yet see nothing of him. It was like a dream. A midnight fantasy.

Reaching up, she freed his hair and let it fall around his face, then she buried her hands in the silken strands of it. He leaned down and placed his lips in the crook of her arm, where he suckled her flesh.

Adron swallowed as he pulled back, wanting desperately to see her face. Instead, he lifted his hand to trace the contours of it. He could feel the tiny cleft in her chin, imagine the small oval face overwhelmed by large green eyes that tugged at a heart he had thought was dead.

She was breathtaking. And for tonight, she was his.

All his.

Closing his eyes, he moved himself down her body, then cursed as a wave of fierce pain lanced up his leg and across his back.

She tensed beneath him. "What's wrong?"

Adron couldn't answer. The pain in his leg was so intense that it instantly quelled his desire.

He rolled over onto his back and struggled to breathe.

"Adron?"

The concern in her voice ate at him.

"My leg," he said between clenched teeth. "I need the painkillers on my nightstand."

"Which leg?"

"Dammit, get my medicine."

"Which leg!" she insisted.

"The left one."

Livia took his knee into her hands.

Adron cursed as more pain tore through him. "Stop!" he snarled.

"Shh," she said peacefully as she massaged the joint.

A strange warmth came from her hands, seeping into his skin. Adron frowned as the ache diminished.

Then suddenly, it was gone entirely.

For a full minute, he lay there, tense, waiting for it to return. It didn't.

In fact, nothing hurt. Not his chest, not his arm, not his knee. Nothing.

"What did you do?"

"It's only temporary," she whispered. "But for a few hours, it won't bother you at all."

Adron couldn't believe it. He'd learned to live in a state of constant, unrelenting pain. Physical agony so severe that he couldn't sleep for more than a couple of hours at a time.

Until now.

The absence of it was unbelievable. His heart swelled with joy. He was free. Even if it was only temporary, he still had a moment to remember what he'd been like before his body had been cruelly, vengefully taken from him.

And it was all because of her.

He pulled her into his arms and kissed her precious lips.

Livia felt his heart pounding under her hand and she heard the laughter in his voice. "Thank you."

She smiled. Until he moved down her body with his kisses. Livia moaned as fierce pleasure tore through her. His hands and mouth felt incredible against her bare skin.

This was so much more than she had expected. Krista had told her that a man who didn't know her would be quick with the deed, then let her leave.

But Adron was taking his time. He seemed to actually savor her.

It was as if he was really making love to her. And she wondered, if he was this tender with a stranger how much more so would he be if they actually knew each other?

But tonight was all they would ever know. When it was over she would leave him, and this moment would be nothing more than a treasured memory she would carry with her the rest of her life.

Tonight, there was just the two of them.

And she would revel in it.

Adron drank in the smell and taste of her skin as he nibbled the bare flesh of her hip. The taste of her was addictive, and her smell . . .

He could breathe in the sweet floral scent forever.

Her soft hands caressed his hair and neck in a way that made him burn. He'd never thought to have another night like this.

A night with no demons. No memories.

She engulfed him and he gladly surrendered himself to her.

She was his angel of mercy, delivering him from his sins. Delivering him from his loneliness and solitude. He would treasure this peaceful moment for the rest of his life. It would warm him and keep him company when his body returned to being hateful.

His heart tender for her, he spread her legs and placed his body between them.

Livia bit her lip, expecting him to enter her. He didn't. Instead, he kissed a small path down her thigh while he buried his hand at the center of her body.

She hissed from the pleasure of his touch. It was sweet, pure bliss. And he took his time circling her with his fingers, delving, stroking, caressing.

"That's it," he breathed against her leg as she rubbed herself against his hand. "Don't be embarrassed."

She should be and yet she wasn't.

At least not until he took her into his mouth.

Blind ecstasy ripped her asunder. "Adron?" she asked, her voice husky and strange. "Are you supposed to do that?"

He gave her one long, deep lick. "Does it feel good?"

"Oh, yes."

"Then I'm supposed to be doing it." Without another word, he returned his mouth to her.

Livia writhed in his arms as his tongue tormented her. And when he slid his finger inside her, she thought she would perish from the pleasure.

Krista had told her to expect pain, but there was nothing painful in his touch. Nothing but heaven.

She threw her head back as he swirled his finger inside her, around and around, matching the rhythm of his tongue.

Assaulted by fierce, fiery sensations, Livia felt her body quiver and jerk as if it had a mind of its own.

Her ecstasy mounted until she could stand no more and then just as she was ready to beg him to stop, her body ripped apart.

Livia screamed out as her release came hard and fast.

Still he toyed with her. His finger and tongue pleasured her until the sensitive flesh couldn't bear his touch any longer.

"Please," she cried. "Please, have mercy on me."

Adron laughed at her tone, and was amazed at the sound. He couldn't remember the last time he'd laughed.

He pulled back, but kept his finger inside her for a moment longer. He could feel her maidenhead still intact. His body burned, demanding he take her. But he couldn't do that. They hadn't done any real damage to her yet.

Once he broke that barrier, there would be no going back. No second chances.

It would be like when he decided to . . .

He flinched at the memory. His life had been completely ruined by one impulsive act. He wouldn't let her ruin hers the same way.

She was kind and gentle. A pure heart in a world of corrupt ones.

He wouldn't spoil that.

Closing his eyes, he was mystified by what he felt for her. At the fact that he was able to pull himself back and rein in his treacherous body.

It had been years since he'd done anything noble. Years since he'd *wanted* to do anything noble.

He reached down for the blanket and covered her with it.

Livia paused as he spooned up to her back and held her close. She reveled in the feel of his arms around her, but he didn't seem to be making any move to . . .

"Adron?"

"Yes?"

"We're not through, are we?"

He rubbed his cheek against her shoulder. "I gave you your pleasure, Livia. What more do you want?"

She turned to look at him, but in the darkness all she could see was the vaguest of outlines of his face. "But you didn't . . . You know."

"I know."

"Why?"

"Livia, don't you think you should wait until you find someone you care about?"

"I care about you."

Adron snorted. "You don't even know me."

She turned in his arms and reached up to place her hand against his cheek. "You're right, I don't know you. And yet I've already shared my body with you. I want you to finish."

He pulled away from her. "Livia—"

"Adron. If you don't, then I will be forced into marriage with a man older than my father. I don't want him to touch me the way you have. Please help me."

Her words tore through him. An image of Lia flashed through his mind. He'd been forced by Andarion custom to marry her. And she had shown him a whole new meaning to the word *hell*.

Livia skimmed her hand over his chest, down across his stomach. His gut contracting fiercely at her touch, Adron felt her nails brushing at the hairs between his legs until she held him in her hand.

His groin tightened and swelled even more. In that instant, he knew he was lost.

And when she kissed him, his entire world came undone.

Livia was unprepared for his reaction. He growled low in his throat and rolled her over, pinning her against the mattress.

He was wild and untamed as he kissed her lips, then buried his face against her neck where he licked and teased her flesh, burning her all over.

He reached down between them, stroking her until she lost all reason, all sanity.

Then, he spread her legs wider. She felt the tip of his manhood against her core.

In a sweet gesture, he took her hand in his and held it above her head. He kissed her lightly on the lips, then slid himself deep inside her.

As he filled her, she bit her bottom lip to keep from crying out at the unexpected pain that intruded on her pleasure. He was so large that her body ached at the foreign feel of him.

But at least it was done.

She was a virgin no more.

Adron held himself perfectly still, waiting for her body to adjust to his. The last thing he wanted was to hurt her, but by the fierce grip she had on his hand, he knew what she was hiding.

He also knew better than anyone that a person couldn't feel pleasure and pain at the same time.

And he refused to hurt her tonight.

Reluctantly, he let go of her hand and raised himself up on his arms to look down at her. He was used to the darkness. So much so that he saw her eyes tightly shut.

"Don't be afraid," he whispered, then he skimmed his hand down her body until he touched her between her legs.

Livia sighed as his hand stroked her nub. The pain receded behind a wave of building delight.

"That's it," he said. Then, he slowly started to rock his hips against hers.

Livia arched her back as the pain was washed away by his hot touch. He felt so good inside her and every stroke seemed to reach deeper as she clung to his broad, muscular shoulders. She'd never imagined it could feel so wonderful.

Adron watched her face as she surrendered herself to him. He ground his teeth at the incredible feel of her. She was so wet and hot beneath and around him. He had forgotten the pleasure to be had in a woman's arms.

Had forgotten the incredible feel of someone just holding him in the darkness.

He lowered himself and took her into his arms, where he cradled her head in his hands. Her breath fell against his bare shoulder, burning him.

She turned her head to kiss his neck as she ran her hands over his back.

He growled, scalded by the bliss of it.

Livia wrapped her legs around his lean waist. He held her

so tenderly that it touched her deep inside her heart. Krista had told her he would use her without any feelings for her whatsoever.

But it didn't feel like that.

Not the way he held on to her as if he were afraid of letting her go.

He returned to her lips and she moaned at the taste of his tongue. He stroked her faster. Deeper. Harder.

Livia held him close as her pleasure started building again. Oh, goodness, what was it about him that she would feel like this?

And this time when her release came, he joined her.

He growled low in his throat as he delivered one last, deep stroke, and shuddered in her arms.

Adron collapsed on top of her.

Completely spent, he lay there, holding her as he waited to drift back down from heaven and into his body.

So much for meaningless sex. There had been absolutely nothing meaningless about what they had just shared.

And what terrified him most was the fact that he didn't want her to leave.

He didn't want to return to the vacant emptiness of his life. He'd been alone for so long. Had lived without anyone other than servants and family.

But she had changed that.

He didn't want to go back.

"That was amazing," she breathed against his ear. "Can we do it again?"

He laughed, and was shocked to feel his body already stirring. "Yes, we can."

In fact, he wasn't going to stop until she again begged him for mercy.

Chapter Two

ADRON came awake slowly to the most incredible feeling he'd ever known.

Livia by his side.

She lay nestled in his arms, facing away from him. He wasn't sure what time they had finally fallen asleep. All he knew was that he'd never experienced such peace. Such warmth.

And there was no pain. Neither physical nor mental.

Reveling in the moment, he buried his face in her hair and inhaled the fresh, sweet scent of her.

His body stirred immediately.

How?

After the night they had shared, he should be sated for days to come and yet there he was craving her in a way that was almost inhuman. He didn't understand it.

He pulled away to kiss her shoulder, then he froze as he saw her skin in the faint morning light.

Frowning, he ran his hand over her bare shoulder and the scars that marred her back.

She'd been beaten. Severely by the looks of it.

Was she a runaway slave?

She sighed contentedly and snuggled against him. Adron forgot the scars as her buttocks collided with his erection.

He tightened his arms around her while he nudged her legs apart with his thigh. God help him, but he wanted more of her.

Livia came awake to the sensation of Adron behind her, filling her again. "Oh, my goodness," she breathed as he thrusted himself deep and hard into her body.

Biting her lip, she hissed in pleasure.

"Don't you ever get tired?" she asked with a hint of laughter in her voice.

"Not of you, I don't."

She smiled at that. No one had ever made her feel so treasured. And she had to admit, a woman could get used to waking up like this.

Closing her eyes to savor his long, luscious strokes, she surrendered herself to him.

She came an instant before he did.

Livia rolled over to see a gentle smile on his face as he stared at her.

"Thank you," he said. "For everything."

She returned his smile. "Thank you." She placed her lips against his.

Adron's senses swirled as he cupped her head in his hand. He was definitely going to keep her in his bed for the rest of the day.

"Adron, you're not going to believe—" His father's voice broke off the instant his bedroom door swung open.

Gaping at them lying entwined, his father froze.

Then, all hell was unleashed.

Livia dove beneath the covers at the same time a fetid curse rang out.

Adron looked from her cowering under the covers to the six men surrounding his father. Two of them wore royal Vistan robes, marking them as an emperor and his heir. The other four wore the dark gray uniform of imperial bodyguards.

"I told you it was true!" the elder Vistan snarled. His dark brown eyes were filled with hatred as he tilted his head to look up at Adron's father. At six foot six, and a former League Assassin, his father wasn't the kind of man you addressed in anything except the most reverent of tones.

Not unless you wanted to die, anyway.

"The informant was correct when he said your son left with her."

Adron arched a brow at the contemptuous sneer on the man's face. And it was then he realized the Vistan emperor had hair the same color and hue as the woman cowering in his bed. And as he scanned the younger Vistan, he saw further confirmation of who Livia really was.

Shit.

"You whore!" the younger man said as he threw the covers back and grabbed Livia.

Adron removed the man's hand from Livia's arm and shoved him back. "She didn't do anything wrong." Oblivious to his nudity, Adron left the bed. "You touch her and I'll tear your heart out."

Rage descended on her brother's face, but Adron saw the fear in the man's eyes as he took in Adron's height, build, and vicious scars.

Her father, however, wasn't so easily intimidated. "Take her," he said to his guards.

Livia hung her head as she wrapped the sheet around herself. The guards lifted her from the bed and took her to stand before her father.

Adron ached at the frightened look on her face.

Her father raked her with a scathing glare. "Modesty isn't becoming of a whore who spreads her legs for a man she meets in a filthy bar."

Before Adron knew what he was doing, her father yanked the sheet from her body.

"Take her outside and beat her."

"Damn you to hell," Adron growled as he grabbed the first guard and shoved him away from Livia.

He pulled her behind him and retrieved the sheet from the floor, then wrapped it around both of them. Livia stood so close to his back that he could feel her trembling.

And it made him even angrier.

If her father wanted a fight, he was ready to give him one. No one would hurt her for what she'd done. Not unless they wanted a taste of him first.

"Boy," her father snarled, "this is no concern of yours. You've done enough damage." The man took a step forward.

"Whatever concerns my wife, concerns me."

Livia froze as soon as the words left Adron's lips. Last night, she'd had no idea that he was the Andarion heir. But Emperor Nykyrian Quiakides she knew. They had been introduced a few days ago when she and her family had arrived.

Indeed, it was business with Adron's father that had them on Kirovar to begin with.

Now that the two men were together, she saw the similarities between father and son. Nykyrian had the same white-blond hair, the same firm, sculpted jaw. They also shared an identical height and build.

"Is this true?" her father demanded angrily. "Are you his wife?"

Livia swallowed. If she said yes, Andarion law would recognize them as married.

"Adron," his father said sternly, "do you understand what you're doing?"

Adron turned to face her. He tilted her chin until she looked up into his icy blue eyes. "It's entirely up to you."

Aghast at his offer, she stared at him. She'd never known a man so honorable. He could have left her to her father's wrath and yet here he was offering her sanctuary.

"Are you sure about this?" she whispered.

"No," he said with a hint of a smile. "But then, I've never been sure about much of anything in my life."

She looked to her father's angry face, and her brother's. If she went home, they would have her beaten until she passed out. But if she stayed . . .

She had no idea what that would be like.

The known or the unknown.

"Take her," her father ordered.

Adron put himself between them.

"Nykyrian, tell your son to step aside. He is interfering with royal Vistan business."

For the first time, Livia noticed the deep, angry scars bisecting Adron's body. His back was completely covered by them. It looked as if someone had once carved him into pieces.

Then, her gaze fell to the dragon and dagger tattoo on his left shoulder that marked him as a League Assassin.

She trembled. She knew absolutely nothing about him.

Nothing except for the kindness of his touch. Nothing except for the way he had made her feel when he kissed her. The way he made her feel wanted. Safe.

And in that instant, she made up her mind.

"What happens to me is the business of my husband," she said quietly.

Her father's face turned to stone. "Then your ties to our house are severed." He glanced at her brother. "Come, Prinam."

Her brother's features softened a degree before he caught himself. Without a word, he followed her father from the room.

Nykyrian stepped forward with an amused light in his green eyes. "Some things must run in our blood."

Adron frowned. "I beg your pardon?"

"Ask your mother one day how we ended up married." He looked to Livia. "In the meantime, welcome to our family, Highness."

Adron's frown deepened as he regarded his father suspiciously. "You're being awfully understanding about all this. Should I be afraid?"

Nykyrian laughed. "Probably. I hope this means you'll rejoin the world again. We've missed you."

A tic started in Adron's jaw.

His father's face was kind and not the least bit judgmental as he smiled at Livia. "You know, you'll have to bring your wife to the palace to meet the rest of your wayward siblings."

"And Mom?"

He nodded.

Something strange flickered across Adron's features. Something Livia couldn't define, but it looked as if Adron wanted to avoid his mother. "When?"

"Tonight."

"Will Jayce be there?" Adron asked.

"He is your brother."

Hatred flared in Adron's eyes. "He's your son. He ceased to be my brother the day he refused to uphold the League's Code."

Nykyrian sighed, then looked to Livia. "I hope you know what you've gotten yourself into."

The bad thing was, she didn't.

Nykyrian left them.

Now that they were alone, the reality of what she'd done came crashing down on her.

She was married.

To a stranger.

"Well, isn't this interesting," Adron said, turning to face her. "I don't know about you, but when I went to the Golden Crona last night, I never intended to find a spouse."

She laughed. "Since I was there to avoid one, I can honestly say that never crossed my mind either."

He cupped her face in his hands, and smiled a warm, dimpled smile at her. And when he kissed her, she quivered at the tenderness of his lips.

"God, you taste so good," he said as he nibbled the corner of her mouth. "I could kiss you forever."

Desire stabbed her at his words. "You're not so bad yourself," she said.

He laughed, then scooped her up in his arms.

Livia gasped at the unexpected feel of his strong arms surrounding her. But as he reached the bed, he staggered.

Agony contorted his face as he let go of her and fell to his knees.

"Adron?" she asked, kneeling beside him.

She could tell by his face that he hurt too much to speak. "Here," she said, "lie on the floor."

She helped him to lie down, then she took his knee in her hands. Livia did her best to summon her powers, but they refused to come.

No!

Adron held his hand to his head as if something vile were being plunged into his brain. He writhed in misery and she ached that she couldn't help him.

Her heart hammering, she rushed to the nightstand.

"The injector," he snarled from the floor. "There's a bottle for it in the drawer."

Livia found them and took them to him.

He placed the bottle in the injector, then held it against his stomach and pulled the trigger. Sweat drenched his body as he shook all over.

Livia covered him with the blanket and then held his head in her lap.

Adron tried not to fight the pain. It hurt less when he did and yet it ripped through him with such a torturous fury that it left him weak. Drained.

He stared up at Livia as she brushed her hand through his hair and held him close.

He'd never before allowed anyone near him when he was like this. Not when he had a choice about it, anyway. But there was something about her that soothed his tattered spirit.

Better still, he didn't see contempt or pity on her face. A peaceful calm stared at him from her green eyes.

After a few minutes, his pain ebbed enough to where he could move again.

He sat up slowly, carefully, but it felt as if every muscle in his body had been shredded again. He started to push himself to his feet.

She moved to help him.

"Don't," he said with more rancor than he meant. "I can stand on my own."

She took his angry tone in stride. "Can I get you anything?"

"A bottle of alcohol." He lay back down on the bed.

"Adron, it's morning. Shouldn't you eat something?"

He glared the glare that had never failed to send his family scurrying away from him. "Get me something to drink."

She got dressed, then returned a few minutes later with a glass of milk.

"Dammit, Livia! I'm not a child."

"Then stop acting like one."

Before he could answer, the door chime sounded.

"Should I answer it?" she asked.

"I don't give a damn what you do."

Livia sighed at his hostile tone as he shifted slightly in the bed, then grimaced.

She went to the door and opened it to find a tall, attractive brunette barely dressed. The short red halter top was scooped low and the tight black leather skirt would have given Livia's parents the vapors.

The woman removed her sunglasses so that Livia could see the red irises and white pupils that marked the woman as a full-blooded Andarion.

"You must be Livia," she said cheerfully. "I'm Zarina."

Livia cocked a brow at her.

"Adron's sister," she added. "Dad just told me about the marriage and I had to come meet you."

Unsure what to make of his unconventional sister, Livia let her in.

"You're really cute," Zarina said as she stepped inside and dropped her bag on Adron's couch. "But I wouldn't have pegged you for his type."

"Excuse me?"

"Adron always had a thing for long-legged blondes with the intelligence of a piece of paper. You look like you actually have both a brain and a soul."

Livia arched a brow at her words. "Should I be offended?"

Zarina laughed. "Please don't be. The only people I ever intentionally offend are my brothers. And speaking of, where's Big Bad Angry One? Dad said he was actually up and walking around without his cane."

Before Livia could answer, a loud crash sounded in the bedroom. She ran back to Adron with Zarina one step behind her.

As soon as they entered the room, she saw him leaning with one hand braced against the nightstand. Livia gasped at the sight—blood covered him, and every time he coughed, more blood came up.

"Oh, God," Zarina gasped, running to a communicator.

Terrified, Livia went to her husband.

He opened his mouth to speak, but only coughed up more blood. His entire body shaking, he fell back against the bed, where he writhed in agony.

When she tried to touch him, he pushed her away.

"A med tech unit is on its way," Zarina said the instant she rejoined them.

Livia locked gazes with Adron. She saw the torment and the shame in his eyes. He was embarrassed.

But for her life, she couldn't imagine why.

"He needs his clothes," she said to Zarina over his shoulder.

By the time they'd wiped the blood from him and dressed him, the med tech team had arrived.

"I need to call our parents," Zarina said, leaving Livia to watch as the team worked on her husband.

They inserted a tube down Adron's throat and gave him another injection while they started an IV. He just lay there and his calm acceptance of their actions told her he was well used to things like this.

Dear Lord, what had happened to him?

Could it be because of what they'd done? Could having sex with him kill him?

The thought horrified her.

From the air gurney as it passed her on the team's way out, Adron gave her a tired, sheepish look, then turned away from her.

"C'mon," Zarina said from the doorway. "I'll give you a ride to the hospital."

Livia followed her to a transport and got inside. "What happened to him?"

Zarina winced as if the memory was too painful to even contemplate. "Five years ago, Adron was the League Assassin who was assigned to terminate Kyr Omaindon."

Livia knew the name well. Kyr's bloodthirsty cruelty was the stuff of nightmares. He'd blazed a two-year trail of rape and slaughter through the Brimen sector.

Zarina raked a graceful hand through her hair. "When

Adron entered Kyr's home to execute him, Kyr grabbed one of his servants and locked himself inside his study. The woman was pregnant, and Adron blamed himself for letting her get taken."

Livia remembered the famous standoff. There had been hours of media coverage. And it had ended when one of the League Assassins had allowed his hands to be cuffed behind his back, and then traded for the pregnant woman.

Now she knew the name and face of that assassin.

Worse, she knew his gentle touch.

Zarina drove through the crowded sectors. "Kyr decided to make an example of Adron. He wanted to ensure that the League thought twice about sending another assassin after him. So he tortured Adron for days, then carved him up like a roast. A week after Adron vanished, my brother Jayce found him barely alive inside a Dumpster. There was so little left of Adron that Jayce barely recognized him as a human being, never mind his own brother."

Livia blinked away the tears in her eyes as she imagined what it must have been like for Jayce to find his brother in such a condition. "Why does Adron hate Jayce?"

"Because, according to League Code, when an assassin finds another assassin who has been permanently maimed or disfigured, he's supposed to terminate him. The idea is to die with honor and dignity."

Livia cleared her throat as she ached for her husband and his family. "Jayce couldn't do it."

"No, he couldn't. The two of them were too close. Plus, Jayce would never have been able to face the rest of us if he had killed him, or let him die."

Zarina sighed. "I wish you could have seen Adron back then. He was something else." She smiled. "He was always rushing around at warp speed, joking, laughing. Now there are days when he can't even leave his bed for the pain."

Livia remembered catching a glimpse of that playful Adron last night. "What happened to Kyr?"

Zarina's face tightened. "My father tore him to pieces."

Livia had never condoned violence of any sort, but after seeing Adron and the constant pain he lived in, she understood his father's reaction.

Now, she just wanted to make it better for him.

She just didn't know how.

Chapter Three &

ADRON pushed the oxygen mask off his face.
His doctor gave him a peeved glare. "Would you stop that, you need it."

"I can't breathe with it on."

"You can barely breathe, period." Theo put the oxygen mask back in place.

Adron narrowed his eyes at the man, but as usual, Theo didn't care. Over the last five years, their battle of wills had become legendary in the hospital gossip mill.

Theo brushed a hand through his graying black hair while he scowled at him. "I can't believe you'd even try to have sex in your condition. What were you thinking?"

Adron jerked the mask off. "I'm not a friggin' eunuch."

"No, you're not," Theo said, putting the mask back in place. "You're a man whose internal organs are barely fused together. Their functionality is minimal at best, and any strain on them can kill you. How many times do I have to tell you that you can't put any pressure on your abdomen?"

"Well, if I have to die, I'd rather go out with a good bang."

"You're not funny."

His throat tight, Adron closed his eyes. An image of Livia drifted through his mind, and he cursed it.

Theo checked his IV. "If you'd wear your chest brace—"

"It's hot and it chafes."

"Like it or not, Adron, one misplaced fall and you could break and collapse every bone in your chest."

Adron removed the mask again. "I don't care. I'm not going to wear that monstrosity. It makes me look like a freak."

Theo rolled his eyes. "One day, that stubbornness is going to get you killed."

More roughly than before, Theo replaced the mask. "By the way, there's a reason why I don't give you medicine to completely numb your pain. You need to feel it to know the limitations of your damaged body. Tell your wife it was a nice thought, but in the future you better not let her help you. Not unless you want to become my permanent guest here at Hotel Hell."

Theo stopped at the door and turned back to face him. "And the next time you want to have sex, you better find some way to do it without putting any strain on your chest or abdomen."

"Hey, big brother."

Adron opened his eyes to see Zarina leaning into the room. He tried to muster a smile, but couldn't.

"Theo the Bad just said it was okay to see you. How do you feel?"

Zarina took a hesitant step inside his room, and it was then he saw Livia behind her.

His wife had her long hair braided down her back. The blue pantsuit made her skin glow and those large, catlike eyes held so much tenderness in them that it made him ache.

Adron clenched his teeth as a wave of desire tore through him. He couldn't stand to see her, knowing she belonged to him, and yet he could never again have her.

It was the cruelest blow of all.

"Get out," he said, turning his head away from them.

"Adron?"

The sound of Livia's gentle voice washed over him like a gentle caress and it tore through him like glycerin on glass.

She came forward and when he felt her touch on his arm . . .

"Get away from me!" he snarled, pushing her away. He glared at his sister as his monitors blared. "Take her to a lawyer and get us divorced. Now!"

Theo came running in with two nurses behind him. "Out!" he snapped at the women. "I told you not to upset him."

Livia felt her tears swell at the sight of the doctor forcing Adron to lie down and the sound of Adron cursing them all.

Her throat tight, she looked up at Zarina. "What did I do?"

"It's not you," Zarina said, hugging her to her side as they left the room and headed down the hallway. "Adron is just blaming you for what Lia did."

"Lia?"

"His first wife."

Livia stumbled. "He was married before?"

She nodded. "Yes. And she was one serious bitch. Since she was the Wurish heiress, her father had negotiated a marriage between them when they were both twenty. Lia had only agreed because she wanted a trophy husband and as the youngest commissioned officer in League history and heir to my father's empire, Adron was a choice candidate for her.

"But they never really got along. Three weeks after Adron had been found, my mother, father, and I were in his hospital room, trying to give him reasons to live. All of a sudden, Lia showed up with divorce papers. She handed them to him and told him that she was too young to be some guy's nursemaid."

Livia was aghast. "How could she do such a thing?"

"I have no idea, but if I live an eternity, I will never forget the look on Adron's face. But then, I personally think it's the best thing that could have happened to him. I just wish the ogress had had better timing."

Zarina stopped and leveled a hard look on her. "So, are we going to a lawyer's office?"

Livia bit her lip in indecision. Adron had been through so much that she wondered if he was still mentally sound. His physical scars she knew; it was the ones she couldn't see that scared her.

She searched Zarina's eyes for the truth. "Tell me, is he psychotic or abusive?"

"No. But he is angry and bitter. He was never the type of person to depend on anyone for anything. It humiliates him every time he has to ask for something."

She could understand that. "Then, take me home."

Zarina smiled. "I knew I liked you for a reason."

LIVIA spent as much time as she could learning about Adron while she waited for him to come home.

Zarina and Adron's twin brothers, Taryn and Tiernan, were a fount of information. And that afternoon, they had provided her with a box full of disks for a holo-cube.

Sitting alone in Adron's viewing room, she pulled out a handful of disks and put them in.

The first one was of Adron with a tall, dark-haired man. They appeared to be around the age of twenty. Adron's long blond hair was loose, spilling over his shoulders as the two of them played a board game.

Goodness, but she barely recognized her handsome husband. His face intact, his eyes glowed like blue fire.

"C'mon, Devyn, move."

"Leave me alone, Adron, I'm thinking."

"Yeah, I can see the smoke coming out of your ears from the strain of it."

Devyn smirked at him.

Before Devyn could do or say anything else, water poured down over the two of them.

Adron held his hands out. "What the hell?"

The men looked up to see a young, teenaged Zarina with a hose.

"Oh, Rina," Adron said with a faked snarl. "You're going to die."

Dropping the hose, Zarina shrieked and ran, but Adron caught up to her quickly.

"Get her, Adron!" Livia recognized the voice as Tiernan's. He must have been the one filming them. "Make her pay!"

Adron slung Zarina over his shoulder as he sprinted across the yard with her.

"Put me down, you overgrown bully."

"You got it," he said an instant before he flipped her into a pool.

Zarina came up sputtering. "Oh, that's it! Taryn!"

Taryn came running. Four years younger than Adron, Taryn was all gangly limbs. His dark brown hair was cut short and his eyes glowed with mischief. He grabbed Adron by the waist and the two of them fell into the pool.

Adron broke the water's surface, laughing.

Taryn grabbed him from behind and dunked him.

"No!" Adron's mother, Kiara, shouted as she ran to the pool. Her eyes were wide with fright, and her beautiful face was stern. "No playing like that! One of you could get hurt."

"It's okay, Mom," Adron said.

Kiara shook her head, causing her long mahogany braid to spill over her shoulder. "No, it's not. I couldn't live if I lost one of you. Now, get out of there and stop playing around."

Subdued, the three of them climbed out of the pool.

Subdued, that was, until Taryn snuck up behind Adron and pulled his shorts down.

Livia gaped at the sight of Adron completely exposed.

So, her husband had never worn underwear. She smiled at the knowledge.

Cursing, Adron jerked his pants up and ran after his brother.

"Adron!" Kiara shouted, but the laughter in her voice took the sternness out of her tone. "Don't you hurt him."

"I'm not going to hurt him, I'm going to kill him."

"Mom!" Taryn shouted. He came running back around and put their short mother between them. "Help."

"Adron," she said sharply.

Adron paused as he glared at his brother. "It's all right. You have to sleep sometime."

Livia laughed at their loving play and as she watched more disks, she realized that Zarina had been right. Adron was a kind, fun-loving soul.

Somehow, she was going to find that man and return him to the world.

IT was two weeks, and three more surgeries, before Theo finally allowed Adron to leave the hospital. All he wanted to do was go home and be left alone. He didn't want to see any more pity on his mother's tear-streaked face. See the guilt in his father's eyes.

He just wanted peace.

His brother Tiernan moved to help him from the transport. Adron leveled a scowl that made him shrink back.

"Jeez, you ought to bottle that look. I know armies that would pay a fortune to have something that toxic in their arsenal."

Adron got out even though the strain of it made him sweat. "Why are you still here?"

"Dad wanted me to make sure you got home safely."

"I'm home, now leave."

"Why would I want to do that? I mean, damn, heaven forbid I should be around someone who actually likes me."

Ignoring him, Adron made his way to the lifts and did his best not to remember who had been with him the last time he'd crossed this lobby.

Livia.

Her name and face still haunted him. And in spite of himself, he wondered where she was. How she was doing.

"I don't care."

Tiernan stepped into the lift beside him. "What was that?"

"Nothing."

Adron didn't speak until he was back in his flat. He limped to the bar, and searched for something to drink. But there was nothing there. "Dammit, which one of you did this?" he snarled at Tiernan.

"I did it."

He froze at the sound of Livia's voice behind him. "What are you doing here?"

"I live here."

"The hell you do." He turned on his brother. "I want her out of here."

Tiernan shrugged. "According to your own words, she's your wife."

"Tiernan," he said in warning.

"Adron," he shot back.

Livia came forward and, by all appearances, she didn't look a bit shaken by his anger. "Thank you for bringing him home, Tiernan. I think I can handle it from here."

Tiernan arched a doubtful brow. "I don't know if I feel right leaving you at his mercy. He can let blood with that tongue."

"I'm used to people insulting me." She directed a meaningful stare at Adron. "As well as being unwanted. I promise you, there's nothing Adron can say to make me cry."

And in that moment, Adron felt low. He'd never wanted to hurt her.

Turning away, he headed for the bedroom.

Livia said good-bye to Tiernan, then followed after Adron. In spite of her brave words, she was terrified.

But then, she was used to living in fear, too. At least Adron wouldn't beat her.

He was lying on the bed with his arm over his eyes.

"Are you hungry?"

"No."

"Well, then—"

"I want to be alone."

"It seems to me you've spent far too much time alone."

"Dammit, why are you still here? Why didn't you do what I told you to?"

She took a deep breath and counted for patience. "Because I have nowhere else to go. My father has disowned me."

"If it's a question of money—"

"I don't want money," she said sternly.

"Then what do you want?"

"You."

He removed his arm slowly and looked at her. "You must be deranged."

"Why? Because I want to be with you?"

"Yes."

She moved to sit by the bed. "You know, while we were making love, I felt a connection with you. Did you feel it, too?"

"No."

"I don't believe you. You were too tender. You held me too close. I might be innocent, but I'm not stupid. I know men don't treat women that way."

He gave her a droll stare. "And how do you know that?"

"Zarina told me."

He grimaced at her. "Oh, jeez. You discussed it with my baby sister?"

"She was very informative."

"I can imagine."

"So, are we just going to sit in here all day?"

"No, you're going to leave."

"I'll leave when you do."

He growled at her. "Do you have any idea how much pain I'm in? It hurts to breathe, so if you don't mind, I'd like to just lie here in silence."

"Fine." She got up and pulled a small holo-cube out of his nightstand. "I just wanted to show this to you."

Adron frowned as she handed him the cube and turned it on. Static flickered until the image of a brunette woman and a small blond girl appeared.

"Hi, Commander," the woman said, holding the girl in her arms. "This is my daughter, Alycia. I don't know if you remember me or not, but I'm the woman you saved from Kyr and this is the daughter I had six weeks later. Say, hi, Alycia."

"Hi, Commander." The little girl waved. "Thank you for saving my mommy and me."

Livia watched the agony play across his face as the woman and child talked to him. Then, he snarled and threw the holo-cube against the wall, shattering it.

"Adron!" she snapped, losing patience with him.

He turned on her then with a vicious snarl. "What? Did you think showing me that would make all this okay? Did you think I'd look at them, then cry and say how grateful I am they are alive while I'm trapped like this? What of the children I wanted to have?"

The bitter misery in his eyes scorched her. "Good God, Livia, I'm only twenty-nine years old and all I have to look forward to is a future where I will slowly, painfully disintegrate into an invalid."

His words brought tears to her eyes. She had stupidly thought it would make him feel better.

"I'm sorry," she whispered. "I was just trying to help. But you won't let anyone help you, will you?" She turned and ran from the room.

Livia didn't stop until she reached the sitting room. She curled up into a ball on the couch and bit her lip to hold back the tears. She wouldn't cry.

But inside, she ached for him. Ached for what he'd once been.

Even now she could see him laughing and playing games with his sister and brothers.

How she wished she had known him then.

Suddenly, she felt a hand on her head. Looking up, she found Adron standing beside the couch. His brow was damp and she saw the whiteness of his lips as he struggled with his pain.

"I'm sorry," he said, his voice tense. "I know you were just trying to help. But I passed the point of help a long time ago."

He shifted and winced. "Look, I know about your people and customs, and I know you were raised inside a cage. The last thing you need is to be saddled with a man who can barely walk. Why don't you just go and get your own place and live? I'll be happy to put you on all my accounts. You'll never want for anything."

It was a generous offer he made. But she couldn't accept it. "I can't do that."

"Why not?"

"Because I love you."

Chapter Four ～

ADRON couldn't have been more stunned if she had reached up and slapped him.

"How could you? You don't even know me."

"Yes, I do. You try and hide what you are, but I see it. It shines through."

He scowled at her. "And what is that?"

"You have a good heart."

"I have no heart at all. What I have is a mechanical substitute that pumps blood through a broken body."

She rose from the couch.

Adron flinched as she touched him. God, how he wanted to kiss her.

She took him by the hand and led him into his viewing room. "Zarina said that it's painful at times for you to sit, so I thought I'd make a few modifications."

He stared at the new sofa. It was twice the size of his old one and looked more like a small bed. She'd piled pillows up all over it.

Adron sat down and leaned against the pillows, amazed at just how good it did feel.

Until Livia sat down next to him. His body reacted instantly to her nearness. "You're killing me," he whispered.

"I don't want to kill you." She leaned forward and captured his lips with hers.

Closing his eyes, he savored the taste of her. Over the last two weeks he'd done little except dream of her kiss. Dream of touching her again.

She ran her hands over his body, making him burn even more.

And when she touched his erection, he cursed. "Livia, stop. I can't make love to you."

She smiled patiently at him. "That's okay. I'm making love to you."

He frowned as she started unbuttoning his shirt.

Adron opened his mouth to protest, but then she dipped her head to his neck. He hissed as her tongue gently laved his skin. And as she nibbled and licked his flesh, she unbuttoned his pants, slid her hand down, and took his swollen shaft into her hand.

His head light, he couldn't speak while she caressed him. Couldn't move.

Adron trembled as she blazed a scorching trail down his chest with her mouth. Slowly, carefully. Her touch blistered him and went so much deeper than his skin.

It touched his soul.

His eyes shuttered, he watched her while she licked and nibbled the flesh of his stomach, and when she took him into her mouth, he thought he'd die from the pleasure of it.

Her dark hair was fanned out across his lap and he buried his hand in her soft curls.

Adron ground his teeth as her tongue and mouth massaged him. She was relentless in her tasting.

Never had he felt anything like it. Her actions were so selfless, so kind.

Why would she care?

Why would she do this for him?

I love you.

The words tore through him. No woman had ever said that to him before. Only her.

And for his life, he couldn't understand what about him she could possibly find lovable. Or even desirable.

The woman was insane.

But she touched him on a level that defied explanation. A level he'd never known before.

Throwing his head back against the pillows, Adron growled as he released himself into her mouth.

Still, she didn't pull away. Not until he was completely weak and spent.

He stared at her in awe. "I can't believe you did that for me."

"I told you, Adron, I love you. I would do anything to make you happy."

"Then kiss me."

She did.

Livia moaned as he ran his hand under her shirt and gently squeezed her breast. Bracing her arms on each side of him, she carefully straddled him while making sure not to put any pressure on his chest or abdomen. His doctor's warnings had been explicit.

Adron cupped her head with one hand while he reached around behind her with the other one and released her corslet.

"I love the way you feel in my arms," he whispered against her lips. "I love the way you look when your cheeks are flushed and your eyes are bright."

He skimmed his hand down over her breasts, to her stomach and down to where she ached for him. "And I love the way you look when you come for me." He gave her a tender smile. "You make me feel like a man again, Livia. You make me whole."

Shamelessly, she rubbed herself against him. And when she came, she cried out from it.

Adron smiled at her then, and held her close.

They spent the rest of the day lying naked in each other's arms, caressing and stroking, and just talking about absolutely nothing important.

It was the best day of Adron's life, and he kept her up until the wee hours of the morning for fear of it ending.

* * *

THAT day was followed by three more days of bliss.

Adron was constantly amazed by the woman fate had miraculously dumped into his life. She was funny, intelligent, and so incredibly giving that it made him hurt.

How he wished he was the husband she deserved. It pained him to think of her spending the rest of her vivacious life strapped to him.

"Hi."

He looked up from the book he was reading to see her standing in the doorway. Her hair was still damp from her bath and her eyes glowed mischievously.

"Hi," he said reservedly, unsure of what that look might herald for him.

She walked slowly toward the bed. "Would you like to go out for a bit today?"

Yes, he would. More than she would ever know. "I can't."

"C'mon, Adron. You told me your therapist said you needed more exercise."

"Not today. My leg is too stiff. Why don't you call Zarina?"

"Because I'd rather be with you."

The woman was the biggest fool he'd ever known.

She sat beside him. "Here." She placed her hands on his knee.

Adron tensed as the warmth seeped into his leg. "How do you do that?" he asked as the pain ebbed.

"My mother taught me. She comes from a long line of great healers." She gently massaged his knee and leg. "I wish I could get you to her. She'd be able to heal you in an instant."

"Really?"

She looked askance at him. "You don't believe me?"

"Let's just say I have a hefty dose of skepticism. I only believe what I can see and touch."

She rolled her eyes at him. "Feeling better now?"

"Yes."

"Then join me."

How could he say no to that? Besides, he hated being home all the time.

He left the bed, but didn't go far before she stopped him. "You still have to use your cane. I don't want you back in the hospital."

He growled as she handed it to him. "I hate this thing."

"I know." She wrapped her arms around his and took him outside for the first time since he'd returned from the hospital.

"So, where are we going?" he asked.

She hailed a transport. "I want to go to the park."

"Why?"

"Because, and I know this is a new concept for you, we might actually have fun."

He touched her cheek and watched the way her eyes sparkled with life. "I've never allowed anyone to talk to me the way you do."

"That's what Zarina said last night. She also said she was amazed I was still alive."

He laughed at her as the transport pulled up.

Once they reached the park, he allowed Livia to lead him toward the large pond.

"Want to try a paddleboat?" she asked.

"I'm too old for a paddleboat."

"You're twenty-nine, Adron. Not an ancient by any stretch of the imagination."

"I'm too old for a paddleboat," he reiterated. "And even if I wasn't, I couldn't pedal it anyway."

"I'll do it."

"I'm not helpless."

She glared at him. "I know that. It's okay to let others help you from time to time, Adron. Why are you so afraid of it?"

He clenched his teeth, and looked away.

She took his chin in her hand and turned his head back to where he met her questing gaze. "Answer me."

Rage clouded his vision as agony coiled inside him. "You want to know what I'm afraid of? I'm afraid every morning when I wake up that this will be the day when I can no longer move for myself. I know it's coming. It's just a matter of time until I have no choice but to have someone else clothe me, feed me. Change my diaper. And I can't stand it."

"Then why don't you kill yourself?"

"Because every time I think of doing that, I can hear my family praying over me while I was in the hospital. I hear my mother weeping, my father begging me not to die." He swallowed. "I could never intentionally hurt them that way."

The love in her eyes scorched him. "You are the strongest man I have ever known."

"Weakest fool, you mean."

She shook her head and gave him a tender smile. "Come, husband." She led him to the paddleboats.

Reluctantly, he got inside one and let her take them out to the center of the pond.

"It's a beautiful day, isn't it?" she asked.

Adron leaned back and stared at the sky. The light blue was covered in soft white clouds and the warmth of the sun felt good on his skin. "It's okay."

She rolled her eyes at him. "You're such a pessimist."

In spite of himself, Adron ran a hand down her bare arm that was exposed by her sleeveless tunic. He touched the faint scar on her shoulder and frowned. "Who beat you?"

A hint of sadness flashed on her face, but she quickly recovered. "My father."

"Why?"

She leaned forward and whispered as if imparting a great secret to him. "I tend not to do what other people want me to do."

"I noticed." He laced his hand through her hair. "But I think I like that about you."

She smiled, and instantly the day was brighter.

Livia watched the way Adron leaned back on his elbows as he stared at her. His white shirt was pulled taut over the muscles of his stomach and chest. His broad shoulders were thrown back and his biceps were flexed with the promise of strength and power. The wind teased the white-blond queue.

Goodness, he was gorgeous even with the scar on his cheek.

"Tell me something," she asked as she paused in her pedaling. "Why was a royal heir in the League?"

He sighed. "I wasn't the heir at the time I enlisted."

The knowledge surprised her. "No?"

"I used to have an older sister." The pain on his face was profound and went deeper than the one he wore when his body hurt him.

"I'm sorry. What happened to her?"

"She and my father fought over Thia's choice of a husband. In a fit of anger, she stormed out of the palace and vanished. My father's been trying to find her for years, but we've had no word of her."

Now it all made sense to her. That was the real reason he hadn't killed himself. His family had already lost one child, and he had seen their grief firsthand.

Had felt it himself.

"You miss her," she said, noting the agony in his eyes.

"A lot. She used to arm-wrestle me to the ground."

She smiled at the teasing in his voice.

He sighed. "She was the best confidant I had growing up. I could tell her anything and know it would never reach the ears of my parents."

She reached out and took his hand into hers. "Tell me something, Adron. Something you've never shared with anyone else. Not even Thia."

"I'm the one who glued Zarina to the toilet seat when she was seven."

Livia burst out laughing. "I was serious."

"I am, too. I'd meant to get Jayce, but she made a mad dash for the room and ran into it before he did. Poor Taryn ended up taking the blame for it."

"And you never confessed?"

"If you'd ever seen my father truly angry, you'd know the answer to that. I was only thirteen and my father was a giant to me back then."

"So what happened to Taryn?"

"He was restricted from playing ball for the whole summer season."

Livia frowned. "That doesn't seem so bad a punishment. Why were you afraid to own up to it?"

"Because I knew my father would punish me twice as severely since I not only did it, but I let someone else pay for it. My father is a firm believer in justice." He squeezed her hand. "It was a cowardly thing, I know, and I spent the whole summer staying home with Taryn to make it up to him."

"Did he know you were the one who did it?"

He shook his head. "No. It's always been my guilty secret."

And now it was hers, too.

"What of you?" he asked. "Tell me who you were running from at the Golden Crona."

Her face flamed. "It was horrible. My father was going to marry me to Clypper Thoran."

"The Giradonal governor?"

"Yes."

Adron frowned as he stared at her. "Good Lord, he's what? A hundred and fifty?"

"Eighty-two."

His jaw dropped as he shuddered. "Your father was going to marry you to an eighty-two-year-old man?"

She nodded. "He wants a trade agreement with them, and Clypper wanted a young wife."

"No wonder you didn't mind me," Adron said with a snort. "One way or another, you were bound to end up as some man's nursemaid."

She lost her temper at him then. "You know, I'm tired of your self-pity, Adron. Instead of thinking of all the things you no longer have, you should concentrate on what you do have."

"And what is that?"

"A family who loves you. And though your body is damaged, at least your mind isn't."

"Yeah, well, trapped in an invalid body happens to be my worst nightmare."

Livia glared at him. "I would rather be crippled than mindless. My worst fear is ending up as a vegetable trapped in a whole, sound body. So, from where I'm sitting, you have nothing to complain about."

His frown deepened. "Why would you fear something like that?"

"I saw my grandmother die that way. It was terrible. She lay in a hospital bed, hooked to monitors and machines, for almost a year before they finally let her die."

"Why did they do that?"

"Because they couldn't let her go." Her look intensified. "If your mind was gone, Adron, you couldn't be here with me now. You wouldn't be able to see the sky above us, hear the children laughing or anything else. You would be trapped in cold, awful darkness."

"Okay!" he said, wanting this conversation to end. It was too gruesome even for him to contemplate. "You made a good point." She'd obviously given this a lot of thought. "You're right, I am a self-pitying bastard. But I will endeavor to be a little less so."

"Promise?"

"As long as you're with me, yes."

WEEKS went by as Adron tried to keep his word to her. Some days it was easier than others. And today it was particularly difficult.

"Come on, Adron," his therapist said as she increased the weight on his leg. "You can lift it."

Grinding his teeth against the pain, he hated the patronizing tone Sheena always used. Like a mother coaxing a small child.

"That's it. You're doing fine. Good boy."

"Go to hell," he snarled.

"Adron!" Livia snapped at him as she came forward to stand beside him. "You behave."

Adron curled his lip. This was the first time he'd allowed Livia to come with him to his therapy in the hospital. And if she kept that tone up, it would be the last.

"It's all right," Sheena said. "He says that to me a lot."

Livia reached out and took his hand in hers. Adron's heart pounded at the softness of her touch.

God, he'd gotten so used to her. Had become dependent on her and that terrified him more than anything else.

"Be nice," she said.

Holding her hand over his heart, he nodded. And then he lifted his leg.

"See, I knew you could do it."

He ignored Sheena.

"Okay, let's try some pulls."

Adron let go of Livia and sat up slowly. But no sooner was he upright, than he felt the familiar burning in his chest. Two seconds later, his nose started bleeding and he coughed up blood.

"Dammit," he snarled as Sheena grabbed a towel.

He lay back down while Sheena ran to get Theo.

Livia brushed his hair back from his damp forehead. The tenderness of her touch and look scorched him. And it made him yearn even more for a way to love her like she deserved to be loved.

"Are you okay?" she asked.

"I just damaged another internal organ. Who knows which one. Since they're all pretty much soup, it could be . . ."

His voice trailed off as Theo came in with a gurney and three orderlies.

"You know, Adron," Theo said as the orderlies picked him up and placed him on the gurney, "if you want to spend the night with me, there are easier ways of going about it. You could just ask."

He wasn't amused by Theo's playfulness. "I want to go home."

"Maybe tomorrow." Theo put an oxygen mask on his face.

Adron pulled it off.

Livia put it back on.

Adron met her gaze.

"I'll call your parents." Holding his hand, she walked beside him as Theo pushed him through the familiar hallways.

When they reached the scanning room, Adron reluctantly let go of her.

Livia's heart was heavy as she watched the doors close behind him. How she wished she had her mother's healing powers. Her mother could make him whole again.

So could you.

True, but if she did, she'd lose him forever.

ADRON spent two days in the hospital before Theo let him go home.

While he'd been in the hospital, Livia had stayed with him the entire time and though it was selfish of him, he loved it.

As soon as they were back in his flat, they had gone to bed and hadn't emerged except to attend to basic needs like food and drink.

LIVIA came awake slowly. She blinked open her eyes to find herself lying in bed, wrapped in her husband's arms.

Adron was still asleep, but even so, he had a tight grip on her as if he was afraid she'd vanish.

Smiling, she picked his hand up and placed a kiss over his scarred knuckles.

Then she heard someone in the outer room. At first, she assumed it was the cleaning lady who came twice a week, until she heard Taryn call Adron's name.

"Hey, bud," he said, throwing open the door, "I need—" Taryn took one look at them lying naked in the bed and turned around to give them his back.

"Sorry, Livia," he said. "I assumed by three o'clock in the afternoon the two of you would be up."

Adron rubbed his stubbled cheek against her shoulder as he came awake. "I need to learn to lock my door," he said.

She laughed.

Taryn snorted. "I'm going to go out here and wait until you two get dressed."

Adron brushed his hand over her hair and she felt his erection against her hip. "Why don't you keep walking until you get to the other side of the front door?"

"Ha, ha," Taryn said as he closed the door. "By the way, your wife has a great body."

Heat exploded across her face.

Adron gave her a stern frown. "Say the word, and I'll kill him for you."

She smiled. "It's okay. If you did that, Tiernan would miss him."

Adron rolled over slowly and reached for his injector and medicine on the nightstand.

Livia cringed as he gave himself a shot in the stomach. How she wished he didn't have to do that every few hours. Unfortunately, he would have to do it for the rest of his life.

His features strained, he left the bed and dressed.

While he went to speak to his brother, she headed into the bathroom for a shower.

She took her time, letting the hot water cascade over her, until she felt someone watching her. Turning around, she saw Adron leaning against the wall, staring straight at her.

"You startled me," she said while the hot water slid against her back.

"Sorry, I was just wishing I could join you."

It amazed her how comfortable she'd become around him. Her nudity in front of him had long since ceased to bother her. As did his. In fact, she'd learned every dip and curve of his tawny flesh. Every scar.

She glanced over to the tub a few feet away. "Want me to join you?"

He smiled. "Yes."

Livia turned the shower off, then ran them a tub full of water. Adron got in first, then pulled her in on top of him.

"Careful!" she warned as a wave of panic went through her. "I don't want to hurt you."

"You could never hurt me," he said, then he claimed her lips with his.

Livia moaned. Oh, but she would never get tired of his kiss. His touch.

Pulling back, Adron stared at her in awe. Her lips were swollen from his kiss and her cheeks red from his whiskers. He ran his hand over her ravaged skin.

"I'm sorry," he said, reaching for his razor in the cubbyhole in the wall above his head.

She sat beside him, watching him shave with a frown on her face. "Wouldn't that be easier with a mirror?"

"Probably."

"Then why don't you use one?"

He paused and looked away from her. "I don't like looking in mirrors and I damn sure don't want to do it first thing every morning."

She took the razor from his hand and, to his shock, she shaved the scarred side of his face. "You are incredibly handsome."

Adron stared at her doubtfully. "When I was younger, I was really vain about it. Zarina used to tease me that I looked at my reflection so much that one day the Tourah beast was going to come and steal my face from me." He dropped his gaze to the floor. "I guess she was right. He did."

Livia rinsed the soap from his face. "You know, there is a bright side to all you suffered."

"And that is?"

She hesitated as if gathering her thoughts. "Tell me truthfully, Adron. If Kyr hadn't scarred you, would you have taken me home that night at the Golden Crona? Would you have even looked twice at me?"

Adron opened his mouth to deny it, but he couldn't. She was right. She was beautiful to him now, a vital part of his life, and yet he would never have looked twice at her before Kyr had crippled him.

That thought cut him all the way to his soul.

"I wish I could be whole for you," he whispered. "I wish I could hold you and dance with you, take you in my arms and make love to you the way I want to."

"And I'm just grateful I have you at all. It's not your body or face that I love, Adron. It's your heart, your soul, and your mind."

He trembled at her words, then he pulled her to him and kissed her. She moved carefully into his lap.

Adron nibbled her lips as he felt her sliding her hand over his shoulders, down his arms.

She lifted her hips, then impaled herself on him. They moaned simultaneously.

Bracing her hands on the edge of the tub, she rode him hard and fast, making him blind from the pleasure of her body surrounding his. And for the first time, he was grateful to Kyr. Grateful he'd found Livia.

God help him if anything should happen to her. She was the one thing he could never lose. The one thing that could truly destroy him.

His throat tight, he watched her as she climaxed in his arms. The pleasure on her face tore through him. And as he felt her body tighten around him, he surrendered himself to his own release.

Livia started to collapse against his chest, then barely caught herself before she hurt him.

She smiled at him, but she saw the turmoil in his eyes, felt him go rigid over her action. It always hurt him when he realized the frailness of his body.

She would give anything to remove that look from him forever.

Would you give your life?

"I love you," she said.

As usual, he said nothing as he shifted away from her.

Livia sighed. She hadn't meant to hurt his feelings. But it was too late; he was closed off from her again.

BY the time they dressed, it was nearly dinnertime.

"You want to go out to eat?"

Adron's question startled her. "No, it's okay."

He looked at her skeptically. "C'mon, you can't spend your life locked in this apartment."

"Are you sure you feel up to it?"

"Truthfully? I hate being stuck here all the time. I was never a homebody."

They didn't go far, just a few sectors over to a quaint restaurant.

Adron sat beside her with his arm wrapped around her as they waited for their food.

"I don't believe it."

Adron went rigid at the voice.

Livia looked up to see a man who looked so incredibly similar to her husband that she knew he must be Jayce.

Jayce's green eyes were warm with friendship. He extended a hand to her. "You must be Livia."

Before she could move, Adron knocked his arm away. "You're not welcome here. Why don't you slink off into the hole you crawled out of?"

"Oh, that's real original. Look, can't we just put it behind us?"

Adron's response was so crude that it sent heat over Livia's face.

Jayce went flush with his rage. "Fine, wallow in your self-pity."

He turned to leave.

"That's right," Adron snarled, "turn your back on me, you coward. That's what you were always best at."

Jayce whirled about and grabbed Adron out of his chair. Livia gasped as she rose to her feet.

"Don't you ever call me a coward. You, of all men, know those are fighting words."

"Why not? It's true, isn't it? You dare wear a League uniform yet you betrayed your oath to them and you betrayed your oath to me. You are nothing but a self-righteous coward."

After that, everything happened in a blur.

Jayce bellowed, then swung.

Adron ducked and caught Jayce a staggering blow against his jaw.

Trained and honed as an assassin, Jayce acted on autopilot as he returned the blow with one of his own. A fist straight into Adron's heart.

Livia heard the horrendous sound of bones breaking. The force of the blow knocked Adron back, into the table.

Before he hit the floor, Livia knew he was seriously injured.

"Oh, God, Adron," Jayce gasped as he knelt beside him.

"I'm so sorry. I didn't mean to. It was completely reflexive. Oh, God, I'm sorry."

Adron couldn't answer.

Livia watched, horrified by the paleness of Adron's face as his breath rattled loosely in his chest. She'd never seen panic in Adron's eyes, but she saw it now and that scared her most of all.

Jayce called for a med tech unit, but it was too late. Adron's breathing was growing shallower. He started coughing up blood.

Livia cupped his face in her hands.

Adron touched her arm and tried to memorize her features before he died. He should never have goaded Jayce. His brother had always let his temper get the better of him. But now it was too late. Jayce had finally done the one thing he was supposed to have done when he found him lying in the Dumpster.

He'd killed him.

Adron reached up and placed a hand to Livia's face. His angel of mercy. At a time when he had wanted to die, she alone had given him a reason to live.

He didn't want to leave her. Couldn't stand the thought of not having her with him.

But it wasn't meant to be.

Her face faded from his sight, then everything went black.

"No!" Livia screamed as his hand fell from her face. "Don't you dare leave me!"

Jayce laid him on the floor and prepared to resuscitate him.

"Dammit!" The agonized cry tore through her as Jayce realized he couldn't give him CPR. Adron's body couldn't sustain it.

In that instant, Livia did the only thing she knew to do. She reached down deep inside her and summoned all the power she possessed.

She didn't care what it cost her. She couldn't live without Adron. And if it meant her own life, so be it.

Almost instantly, her hands were hot. Hotter than they'd ever been before. She placed her hands against Adron's chest and willed her life force into him.

Jayce leaned away as an orange halo of healing surrounded Adron's body.

ADRON came awake with a jolt. At first, he thought he was dead. There was no pain anywhere in him.

His body felt strange. Different.

It felt whole.

Then he became aware of Jayce touching his face, and of a strange weight on his chest.

"Adron?" Jayce gasped in disbelief.

Looking down, Adron realized the weight on his chest was Livia.

His heart pounding, he sat straight up with an agility he hadn't possessed in five years.

And in that instant, he knew what she'd done. She'd healed him again.

As he pulled her to his chest, he saw his blood-covered hand. The scars were completely gone from it. Not even the scars on his knuckles remained.

"Livia?" he asked, holding her against him.

She didn't answer. Adron tilted her head and saw the ghostly paleness of her face.

"Livia?" he tried again, shaking her gently.

She didn't respond.

The med techs came in and he released her to their care.

More terrified than he had ever been before, he followed them out of the restaurant.

FOR the first time, Adron was the one sitting in the antiseptic waiting room, while Theo tended Livia. He finally understood some of what his parents had felt while they waited for word of his multiple operations.

The fear and uncertainty tore him apart. And he and Livia had only known each other a short time.

How much worse must this have been for his mother?

"Adron?"

He looked up as his mother and father joined him. Kiara took his face in her hands and stared at his cheek. "What happened to your scar?"

"Livia cured him," Jayce answered. "I don't know how she did it, but one minute he was practically dead and in the next, he was perfectly fine."

"What did the doctor say?" his father asked.

Adron pulled back from his mother's touch. "He wants to do tests on me later." He didn't give a damn about himself.

Livia was all that mattered.

"Did you call her parents?" his mother asked.

His chest tightened at the memory. "I tried. Her father told me she was no longer his concern."

Kiara scowled. "How could he?"

Adron shrugged. He didn't really want to talk at the moment. Then again, Livia was the only person he liked to talk to, period.

His father smiled as he passed a glance from Adron to Jayce. "It's good to see the two of you in the same room without bloodshed."

Adron exchanged a wary, shamed look with Jayce.

Jayce turned away.

His parents went to get something to drink.

"I'm sorry about all this," Jayce said when they were alone.

Adron glared at him. He was tired of Jayce's excuses. "If you'd killed me when you were supposed to, none of this would have happened."

Jayce curled his lip as his eyes blared a cold, harsh rage. "Tell me honestly, could you have killed me if you'd found me lying half-dead and helpless?"

"Rather than see you suffer, yes."

"Then you're a better assassin than I am. Because I would never have been able to live with myself had I killed my own brother."

"Adron?"

He looked up as Theo joined them.

Theo hesitated in front of him. "This is weird, isn't it? I'm not used to having discussions with you while you're dressed and upright."

"You're not amusing."

Theo looked apologetic. "Sorry, nervous humor." He cleared his throat and a feeling of dread washed over Adron.

Theo was avoiding something bad.

"Well?" Adron prompted.

"She's firmly in a coma. Whatever she did, it caused a great deal of neurological damage to her. Honestly, I've never seen anything like it. It's as if she burned up part of her brain."

Adron choked on a sob as he thought of her lying helpless. It was her worst fear.

Why had she done it?

For him. . . .

Oh, God, he couldn't breathe for the agony in his heart. He wanted to scream out at the injustice. Wanted to rail against everyone and everything.

He leveled a fierce stare on Theo. "Will she come out of it?"

"Honestly, no. There's too much damage. She's only alive right now because of the machines." Theo gave him a hard stare. "My professional opinion is that we should turn everything off and let nature take its course."

Adron fell back against the wall as his heart shattered into a thousand pieces. He felt the tears in his eyes, felt the bitter, swelling misery that overwhelmed him.

He couldn't let her go.

But then, he couldn't let her live when he knew she wouldn't want to.

And all he felt was a pain so deep, so profound, that it made a mockery of the one he'd learned to live with.

He grabbed Theo by the shirt. "Don't you dare let her die. You hear me?"

Theo looked aghast. "Her mind is already gone."

"Only half of it, right?"

"Well, yes."

"Then there's a chance." And half a chance was better than none. "You keep her heart beating until I get back."

"I'll do my best."

And so would he.

Releasing Theo, Adron ran from the hospital with a strength and agility he hadn't known in years. Livia had one chance for survival, and no matter what, he was going to give it to her.

"WHAT are you doing here?" Livia's father demanded as Adron forced his way into the throne room where he was overseeing his advisors.

Oblivious to the roomful of men who gaped at him, Adron approached his father-in-law. "I have to see Livia's mother."

"It is forbidden."

"The hell it is. Livia's dying and her mother is the only one who can save her."

Her father's face stoic, he seemed completely immune to the news. "If she dies, so be it. She has disgraced us with her disobedience. I told you and her that she was forever severed from us."

"I need to see her mother."

"Guards!" he called. "Remove him."

Adron knocked the guards back, until they called for reinforcements. Seriously outnumbered, he fought as best he could, but eventually they seized him.

"You can't let her die," Adron said as he struggled against their hold.

"Had you wanted her to live, you should never have shamed her."

"Damn you!"

Against his will, Adron was pulled back from the throne, but as he fought against the guards, he saw a teenaged servant girl watching him with concern and pity on her face.

Adron met her frightened gaze. "Tell her mother, Livia needs her. Please."

"Krista!" Livia's father snapped. "Get out of here."

The girl scampered off, and the guards threw him out of the palace.

Adron struck the closed door with his fast. He bellowed in rage. "So help me, if she dies, I'll see all of you in your graves!"

But no one heard him. Defeated, he turned and headed back to spend as much time with Livia as he could before death stole her completely away from him.

ADRON paused in the doorway of the hospital room as he listened to the familiar monitors beep and hiss. Only this time, they weren't connected to him.

He knew from his own experience that she could hear them. Knew what it felt like to lie there unable to communicate. Alone. Afraid.

He wanted to scream.

His throat tight, he crossed the room and sat on the bed beside her.

"Hey, sweet," he whispered, taking her cold hand into his. He cupped her face with his other hand and leaned over her to brush his lips against her cool cheek.

"Please open your eyes, Livia," he whispered as tears blinded him. "Open your eyes and see what you did. I'm actually sitting here without grimacing. There's no pain at all. But you know that, don't you?"

He traced the outline of her jaw. And then he did something he hadn't done in a long, long time. He prayed.

He prayed and he yearned to feel her sweet arms wrapped around him. To hear the precious sound of her voice saying his name.

Hours went by as Adron stayed with her, talking more than he had ever talked before.

Sitting by her side, he held her hand to his heart and willed her to wake up. "I don't know why you stayed with me, Livia. God knows, I wasn't worth it. But I don't want you to leave me alone anymore. I need you. Please open your eyes and look at me. Please."

"She can hear you."

Adron tensed at the voice behind him.

Assuming it was a nurse, he didn't bother to look. "I know."

"Are you going to unplug her?"

He choked at the thought. And for the first time, he understood exactly how Jayce had felt when he'd pulled him from the Dumpster.

God, he'd been such a fool to hate his brother for loving him.

"I can't let her go," he said between clenched teeth. "Not while there's a chance."

"It's what she wants."

"I know." He knew it in a way no one else ever could. He'd been there.

The nurse came forward and placed a gentle hand on his shoulder. "She wants me to tell you that she is with you. And that you were well worth it."

Frowning, he turned around to see a small woman wearing a cloak that completely shielded her identity from him. "Who are you?"

She lowered the cowl. Her features angelic, he knew her in an instant. She was Livia's mother.

And he saw the silvery green eyes of a race that was more myth than reality. "You're Trisani?"

She nodded.

Adron gaped with the knowledge. The Trisani were legendary for their psychic abilities. So legendary that they had been hunted almost to extinction. Those who survived were very careful to stay hidden away from large populations where they might become enslaved or killed by those who wanted or feared their powers.

She stepped to Livia's side and removed the IV from her arm. Then slowly, piece by piece, she took the monitors off.

"It's time to wake up, little flower," she whispered. She placed a gentle hand on Livia's brow.

Stunned, Adron watched as Livia's eyes fluttered open. "Mama?" she breathed.

Her mother smiled, then kissed her on the forehead. She passed a hand over Livia's body.

Adron felt weak in relief as joy spread through him. Livia was alive!

Her mother took his hand and Livia's and held them joined in hers. Adron's heart pounded at the warmth of a touch he'd thought was lost to him forever.

Livia looked from him to her mother. "You had Krista send me to the Golden Crona, didn't you?"

Her mother nodded. "You two were destined for each other." She looked at Adron. "And to answer your unspoken question, yes, it's permanent. Livia healed you, but . . ." She turned a sharp glare at her daughter. "You are not to call on your powers anymore. Your human half isn't strong enough for them."

"I know, but I couldn't let him die."

Her mother nodded. "Now, I have to return before I'm missed." She paused in the doorway and turned back. "By the way, it's a boy."

Adron frowned. "What's a boy?"

"The baby she carries. Congratulations, Commander. In nine more months, you'll be a father."

Epilogue ❧

One year later

LIVIA paused in the doorway as she watched Adron giving their infant son his three A.M. feeding. Propped against pillows, Adron sat on the bed, wearing nothing except a sheet draped modestly over his lap as he held the bottle and stared adoringly at Caillen.

He laid his cheek against the top of the baby's bald head and held him close. "I've got you, little bit," he whispered. "Yes, I do."

She laughed.

Adron looked up and smiled. "I didn't know you were back."

"I can tell." She moved to sit next to them. Then she leaned against Adron's raised leg to stare at the beautiful baby on his unscarred chest.

Caillen cooed at her as he wrapped his tiny hand around her finger.

Adron brushed a loving hand through Livia's soft, mussed hair. Thanks to her, he'd come a long way from the bitter alcoholic she'd found tossing down drinks in the back of the Golden Crona.

She'd found a broken, bleeding man and she had made him whole again. Not just in body, but in his heart.

She had reunited him with his family and with his soul.

Over the last year, he'd watched her grow ripe with his baby and had held her hand as she struggled to bring Caillen into the world.

Life turned on the hairpin of a second. He'd always known that, but on one rainy, cold night in the backroom of a filthy dive, his life had taken a sharp turn into heaven.

Livia looked up from their son. "What are you thinking about?"

He traced the outline of her lips with his fingertip. "I'm thinking how glad I am that I traded myself for that woman. How glad I am that my brother couldn't kill me. But most of all, I'm thinking just how damn grateful I am that you saw something in me worth saving."

He leaned forward and kissed her gently on the lips. "Thank you for my son, Livia, and for my life. I love you. I always will."

Daydream Believer

MAGGIE SHAYNE

Chapter One

MEGAN sat up in bed, a cold sweat coating her skin, her trembling hands already clutching the telephone. Sure, it was upside down, but that was sort of beyond the point. Obviously, her subconscious thought this was it. The big one. Time to do some good. Her eyes were drawn to the television on the far side of the room. She'd fallen asleep with the set still on, and at the moment, it was showing a photo of the missing woman, Sarah Dresden, smiling at the camera, obviously unaware what the future held for her. Underneath the photo was a telephone number: the Pinedale Police Department's "Tipline."

Bringing the receiver closer, she dialed the number. She had never phoned the police department after one of her episodes before. Never. God knew her visions had never inspired much action up to now. Certainly nothing police-worthy.

"PPD Tipline, can you help us?"

Quaint, she thought. "I, um . . . I need to speak with the chief, please."

"May I ask who's calling?"

She didn't want to answer that. "It's about the missing woman," she said instead. "I know where she is."

"Hold on." The voice betrayed no emotion, but there had been a brief hesitation before the reply.

A second later, a male voice came on the line. "Chief Skinner speaking."

"Good," she said. "Look, I've never done anything like this before. But . . . I think I know where your missing woman is. Sarah Dresden."

"Uh-huh. And how did you come by your information, Miss . . . ?"

She swallowed hard, gathered up her courage. "I get . . . visions."

She heard his sigh, and realized she'd better talk fast before he hung up on her and filed her call away with all the other cranks he must receive. "Never anything this important. Actually, I've always wished . . . but it doesn't matter. My visions are always on the money. I swear."

"Look, lady, I don't have time for—"

"Sarah is twenty-five, a pretty brunette, a runner—"

"And all of that information has been covered by the local news, ma'am."

"She had a butterfly tattoo on the back of her neck, and was wearing red sneakers with white laces."

He paused for a moment. Then said, "I don't know if that's right or not. I'd have to check the reports."

"Check. I'll hold."

"All right." She heard papers shuffling. "Why don't you tell me where you think she is while I look?"

Maybe she had his attention. Maybe he was going to take her seriously now. No one in her life ever had. God, this could be a banner moment for her. If only the information she had to share were more positive. "I had a dream about her last night. She's not alive, Chief. Her body is in the river, snagged on some rocks underneath the Amstead Road Bridge."

"Uh-huh."

She swallowed hard.

"Ma'am?"

"Yes, Chief."

"It would give you considerably more credibility if you'd

give us your name. Not that we can't find that out anyway with the telephone system we have here, but—"

"Megan Rose," she said. "I live here in Pinedale, out on Sycamore Street. I own the Celestial Bakery in the village, corner of Silver and Main. And I'd appreciate your discretion about this. I'm not sure how my customers would feel about my calling you like this."

"I'm not sure that will even be an issue, ma'am."

"Excuse me?"

"I found the reports on the Dresden woman. She was last seen wearing suede hiking boots, not red sneakers. And there are no unusual markings on her body, no tattoos of any kind. Sorry, ma'am. It was a nice thought, though."

She felt her jaw drop and her head swirl. What the hell . . .? How could such a vivid dream be so wrong? God, would her so-called *gift* ever be of any use to anyone? She swallowed hard.

"You have a nice day now, Ms. Rose."

"Uh—Chief?"

"Yes, ma'am?"

She sighed heavily. "You left your headlights on when you parked your car this morning. You might want to check."

"I'll do that."

Megan hit the cutoff button and set the phone down, then leaned back against her headboard, and wiped the sweat from her brow. Damn, damn, damn. She thought she had finally seen something *important*. Something more than the useless tidbits her visions provided every day of her life. Something big.

No such luck.

The damn dream had started out as the same one she'd been having since she was twelve years old—the one where she saw the handsome man's face hovering in the mists and heard a voice telling her she was going to break a curse and save his life. Then it had taken a unique turn, and the image had changed to one of the missing woman, first smiling like in the photo on TV, and then lifeless and pale, her hair tangling around her face just below the surface of the Genesee River.

Megan licked her lips. Probably her subconscious had

heard the television news report talking about the missing woman. Probably her mind had woven what she heard into her dream, a bad case of wishful thinking. Not wishing the woman was dead, of course, but wishing she could help find her, and finally be believed.

She thought again of the man, the one she was supposed to save from some kind of curse, and she sighed. "Whoever you are, mister," she said softly, "my feeling is, you're doomed."

SAM Sheridan knocked twice before stepping into the chief's office. "Morning, Chief."

"Morning, Sam. How's your mother?"

"Mom sends her love and a slice of apple pie." Sam set the Tupperware container on his boss's desk. The older man had been an intimate family friend a lot longer than he'd been Sam's boss, and old habits died hard. "She says you're expected for dinner on my birthday and she won't take no for an answer."

The chief smiled, his wrinkles showing more deeply when he did. "You bet your ass I'll be there. Your old man would come back from beyond and knock me senseless if I missed it."

Sam nodded, a twinge of sadness twisting his belly, even though it had been twenty-seven years. Ed Skinner turned to move to the window, absently parting the drapes and looking out over the parking lot below.

"Listen, Sam, I wanted to talk to you about this Dresden case. There's—well, I'll be damned."

"Chief?" Frowning, Sam moved closer to the window.

"I left my headlights on," the chief said.

Sam smiled. "Old age creeping up on you, that's all. I'll flip 'em off on my way out if you want."

The chief let the drapes fall back into place, turned to face Sam again. "Where you heading?"

"Questioning some witnesses on the Sarah Dresden case. People who might have seen something in the area along the riverbank, where we found the body this morning."

The chief nodded. "Press hasn't been notified about the body yet, have they?"

"No, sir. Hell, she's barely been out of the water an hour."

"No leaks, that you know of?"

"None."

The chief pursed his lips. "Sam, I've got something else I'd like you check on for me."

Sam lifted his brows.

"Woman by the name of Megan Rose. Knows a little more about this case than she ought to."

Sam tipped his head. This was the first thing remotely like a lead they'd had in the series of rape-murders plaguing the small western New York town. "Like what?"

"Like where the body was. I just got off the phone with her."

Sam felt a little shiver go up his spine. "Did she say how she knew?"

"Yeah. Claims she's some kind of psychic."

Sam would have laughed if the topic had been a less serious one. As it was, he just shook his head. He didn't believe in that sort of garbage, despite the fact that his grandmother claimed a touch of E.S.P. herself. She'd never predicted anything beyond his own impending demise, and he wasn't about to give that any credibility.

"I'd like to find out how she really knew—and what else she might know," the chief said.

Sam nodded. "You want me to question her?"

"I'm thinking we might want a more subtle approach; we don't want to scare her off. Let me do a little checking on her first. Stay available. I'll let you know how I want you to proceed."

Sam nodded. "Whatever you say, Chief."

Chapter Two ⅀

MEGAN glanced into the rearview mirror when she heard the siren, and cussed to herself when she saw the lights. And now she understood her premonition that she would arrive at the bank three minutes after it closed, and that as a result, a check would bounce tomorrow. She'd left early to circumvent fate, and she'd driven fast to further ensure her success.

Only now she realized that if she'd never had the damned vision, she never would have been driving several miles an hour above the speed limit, and never would have been pulled over, and maybe, never would have been late. Was there such a thing as a self-fulfilling prophecy?

Not only was her gift of little practical use, it was often downright cruel.

She pulled off onto the shoulder and sat there, drumming her fingers and looking at her watch while the officer took his sweet time about doing whatever it was they did in their cars while the speeders sweat it out and everyone they knew drove past and saw them. She took her wallet out of her purse, slid her license out of her wallet. Might as well save whatever time

she could. She took the registration from the glove compartment, and rolled down her window. Then she drummed her
fingers some more as the seconds ticked away.

Finally, a cop came walking up alongside her car, uniform,
sunglasses, jack boots. He glanced inside, quickly into the
backseat, then leaned down.

"Li—"

"License and registration," she said, handing both to him.

He took them, peering at them through his sunglasses. "Do
you know—"

"How fast I was going? Yes. Forty-three. And yes, I know
this is a thirty-five-mile-per-hour zone. I won't even argue
with you. I was speeding, I admit it. Trying to get to the bank
before it closes, but I'm obviously not going to make it now."

"You always finish peoples' sentences for them?"

She looked up at him, noticed the line of his jaw, square
chin with a little dimple in the center. Something niggled at
her. The sunglasses hid his eyes. "Always."

"A little boy's dog was hit here last week. Kid cried for
three days straight."

She closed her eyes, nodding. "Point taken. Speed limits
are posted for a reason."

He nodded. "I'll go run this. It'll take a minute."

She looked at her watch. "It's too late to make the bank
now anyway. Tomorrow a check is going to bounce."

"You know which one?"

She glanced at him, frowning. "Yeah. Why?"

"Call whoever has it tonight, ask them to wait until noon to
deposit it, and then go to the bank in the morning."

She tipped her head to one side. His solution was so simple
she could not for the life of her figure out why she had bothered racing for the bank in the first place.

He tapped her license against his fingertips. "Be right back."

Something was off here. Why had her so-called gift bothered to warn her about making the bank on time in the first
place? Nothing all that earth-shattering was going to happen
and she could even avoid the bounced check.

She smiled to herself, shook her head at her own efforts to

force her premonitions to be useful, helpful, and how those efforts always backfired. "I suck," she muttered.

Then she closed her eyes, leaned back on her seat and waited for the handsome cop to come back. Just once, she thought, she would like to find a missing child, or identify a murderer or solve a bank robbery. Other psychics got to do dramatic, wonderful things like that. Meanwhile, she foresaw a "closed" sign in the bank window, and failed to see the speed trap until Officer Studly back there sprang it on her.

She smiled again, almost laughed at her own silliness. At least she'd got to meet the good-looking cop. She wondered if he was married.

He tapped her car door. She turned to see him holding her license and registration out to her. No gloves. No wedding ring either.

"You'll be glad to know you're not wanted for anything."

"Hey, I resent that remark."

The cop, stone-faced till now, smiled slowly as he got her joke. "I meant by the law."

"So did I," she told him.

His smile flashed then, full force and almost blinding and again something niggled at her. Something powerful. "I'm gonna let you off with a warning this time."

"Really?"

He nodded.

"Thanks, Officer. I appreciate that." She reached up to take the license and registration from his hand, but when her fingers brushed over his, she froze, as a flash of light and sensation hit her all at once. She knew her hand closed powerfully around his, and that her head slammed back against the seat and her eyes rolled. And then she was gone, down, down through a dark tunnel, until she emerged on the other side into the pouring rain and driving wind. Small green pup tents whipped, tore, stakes popping, cords snapping. Teenage boys huddled together, a canvas wrapped around their shoulders and mini rivulets running past their feet. A large tree. A creaking limb.

"Hey. Hey, come on, are you okay?"

His voice drew her back into the tunnel, back into her body, where she landed with the same thudding, jolting impact she always did. She felt warm pavement underneath her back, and a warmer hand cupping her nape. Her eyes popped open.

Her cop was leaning over her, a hand supporting her head, his face close to hers. He'd apparently pulled her out of the car when the vision hit. And no wonder. They'd never hit her so hard before, with such a physical impact.

She blinked her eyes clear and stared up at him. The sunglasses were gone, and she could see his eyes. They were deep brown, with thick dark lashes. And they were painfully familiar.

He was the man she'd been dreaming about from the age of twelve. She realized it suddenly and with a shock that nearly made her gasp out loud. God, she knew his face like she knew her own.

"There you are," he said softly. "Don't worry. You're going to be fine."

"I know I am." What on earth was happening here? Something . . . this was no accidental meeting. She blinked a couple of times, pressed a hand to her head. The rush was gone. She felt normal again—physically, at least. She sat up, but her cop pressed his hands to her shoulders, telling her to stay down. "I'm fine," she said. "Really. You didn't go calling for backup over this, did you?"

"I radioed for an ambulance when you passed out," he told her.

She blinked at him. "Cancel it, will you?"

"Are you sure?"

She nodded. "It's not the first time this has happened to me." It was the first time it had knocked her senseless, however. "And I didn't pass out."

"You didn't?"

She shook her head. "Can I sit up now?"

He nodded, extended a hand, and helped her into a sitting position. Then he tapped the microphone that was clipped to his collar, calling her attention to his corded neck, and spoke in cop jargon. She was pretty sure he was canceling the ambulance he'd ordered up for her.

She was getting to her feet, and he was still holding her, helping her. He said, "So if that wasn't passing out, what was it? Some kind of seizure?"

She studied his face. Hell, she was going to have to tell him. It wasn't life and death, or even minor crime solving— but then again, who was she to say? It could be important. He was the man of her dreams, after all. And it would be cruel not to tell him. "It wasn't a seizure. It was . . . a vision."

His brows went up. "A vision. As in . . . a psychic vision?"

"I get them sometimes. I think when I touched your hand . . ." She watched his face, waiting for one of the looks she had come to expect: the blatant disbelief of her overly critical father, who would call her a compulsive liar and probably punish her for it; or the horrified fear of her zealot mother, who would call her evil, offensive to God, and would probably punish her for that.

The man's face betrayed no emotion, neither skepticism nor fear. "So you're psychic, then?"

She swallowed her fears. "Yeah. Just not usually about anything important. I do have some advice for you, though."

"Really? For me?"

She nodded, staring into his eyes. She didn't tell him about her dreams, about her having seen his face in her mind for such a long, long time. She didn't ask him if he were laboring under any sort of curse that he knew of. No sense giving him further reason to doubt her sanity.

She wanted to see this man again. And she kind of thought she needed to. So she'd start him off easy. And even then he probably wouldn't believe her. No one ever believed her.

He walked with her the few steps to her car, opened her door for her, waiting patiently for her advice.

She stood beside the open door, lost in her explorations of his face. God, he was handsome. "You're, um . . . taking a group of teenage boys camping this weekend?"

He blinked, clearly surprised that she would know that. "Yeah. Over at Letchworth. It's a departmental program, and it's my turn."

"It's a very, very bad idea."

He frowned at her. "That's what your vision was about? My camping trip?"

She nodded. "I saw torrential rains, high winds, soaked, miserable kids, and tents getting torn to shreds." She frowned. "And I got a bad feeling—something about a tree. Big pine, lots of dead branches."

"The one where the vultures roost," he muttered.

"Could be. I didn't see any vultures. Still . . . if I were you I'd change the date."

She got into her car. He stood there, holding her door open, staring in at her. "You're not kidding about this, are you?"

"Nope. If I were making it up, I'd predict something much more important. I mean, this isn't earth-shattering, but you might stay drier if you listen." She shrugged. "I may not change the world with my visions, but I'm never wrong."

"Never, huh?"

"Well. Almost never," she said, recalling that she'd made a complete fool of herself with the chief of police this morning.

"Then how come you didn't know I was sitting here clocking your speed?"

She pursed her lips, saw the twinkle of humor in his eyes, and knew he wasn't ridiculing her—he didn't believe her either, but he wasn't being mean. He wasn't calling her a liar or a sinner. "I've been asking myself the same thing, to be honest. If I hadn't had the vision of getting to the bank too late, I wouldn't have been speeding. I wouldn't have been stopped. And I wouldn't have been late. As it is . . ." She shrugged. "I don't know. Maybe we were supposed to meet." That was it. She knew it the moment she said it, with a certainty she rarely felt about anything.

"You think?"

"I do." She stuck her hand out the window. "Megan Rose."

"So it said on your driver's license," he said. But he took her hand in his, and it was warm, smooth, and firm. "Sam Sheridan."

"Good to meet you, Sam."

He lifted his dark, thick brows, maybe a little surprised she had used his first name. He shouldn't be. The man belonged on a police-hunks calendar. And besides, she'd known him forever. It wasn't her fault he had no way of knowing that. He was far more stunning, she thought, in person.

"I hope next time it'll be under more pleasant circumstances," he said.

And there would be a next time, she had to make sure of that. "Will you do me a favor, Sam?"

"What's that?"

"A favor? It's something nice you do for someone else." He smirked at her, and she smiled in return. "If you should take my advice about camping this weekend, and something important results from it, would you let me know?"

He frowned at her, obviously unsure she was being serious.

She shrugged. "You never know, one of these days this so-called gift of mine might actually do something useful. So will you call if you get the feeling it has?"

"Sure I will."

She smiled, tugged a little card from her purse, and handed it to him.

He looked at it. "Celestial Bakery?"

"You were expecting me to tell fortunes for a living, I'll bet."

He shrugged, tucked the card into his pocket. "I'll call."

"I hope you do."

She pulled her seat belt on, put the car into gear, and pulled into the nearest driveway to turn around, since it was already too late to make the bank.

I'M never wrong. Well, almost never. . . .

Sam stood in the woods of Letchworth State Park, huddled with the boys currently enrolled in the Pinedale Police Department's Cop-Camp program. All of them were shivering and soaked to the skin. Their tents hadn't held up to the gale-force winds, and he doubted these trees were going to hold up against them much longer. He could have kicked himself for ignoring Megan Rose. Not that he thought her claims of psychic powers were anything. Hell, she could have figured this storm was coming from watching the Weather Channel.

Though the local weather reports had completely missed it.

Something creaked ominously overhead, and her voice whispered through his brain, yet again, the way it had been doing for three consecutive nights now.

And I got a bad feeling—something about a tree. . . .

He looked up at the tall, haunted-looking tree the kids referred to as the Vulture Roost, as the woman's words whispered through his memory.

Big pine, lots of dead branches.

A limb creaked and groaned.

"Everyone out from under the tree!" Sam shouted. As he said it, he herded the cold, wet teenagers out of the relative shelter of the woods and into the open, and the full fury of the storm. "Move it!"

They moved it. And when they were standing in the clearing that had seemed like such a perfect campsite, he heard a loud CRACK and saw the overweight limb crash to the ground right where they'd all been standing.

The boys and his Cop-Camp cocounselor, Derrick, were all staring at him. One of the kids said, "How did you know?"

"Heard the limb cracking," he replied, making his voice loud enough to compete with the storm. "What, you telling me none of you heard it?"

The entire group of males shook their heads side to side.

"Well, I heard it. Good thing, I guess."

"Yeah. Darn good thing," Derrick said. He was searching Sam's face as if he didn't quite believe him.

Sam looked away, recalling Megan Rose's warning. She couldn't have seen that limb breaking on the Weather Channel.

Then again, it wasn't that big a leap of logic. A storm, plus a forest, equals falling limbs. It was only common sense. Still . . .

"I think maybe we need to get out of here."

"What about the gear?" Derrick asked.

"Leave it. We can't protect it anyway. We'll come back when the weather breaks and grab whatever's left. I think the faster we get out of these woods, the better."

Derrick nodded in agreement. "You heard him, boys. We're out of here."

"I heard that," one of the teens said.

As soon as he managed to get warm and dry and stop shivering, Sam promised himself he was going to tell the pretty redhead that her warning had been dead on target. He supposed he owed her that much. And he had to see her again, anyway. Chief's orders. Though he kind of thought he'd have wanted to see her again even if that hadn't been the case.

There was something about Megan Rose that had brought his senses to life in a way he'd never ever experienced before. Which was not a good thing, considering that the chief suspected she was somehow involved with a murderer.

Chapter Three ⚬

S HE stood at the counter, blinking in surprise at the man
who stood on the other side.

He wasn't wearing his uniform, but that didn't interfere
with the instant recognition, nor with the tingling awareness
that came with it. He was still gorgeous. Still familiar. Still
important to her, even though it made no sense he should be.

She tipped her head to one side. "I wasn't speeding, I
swear," she said.

He smiled at her. "That's what they all say. How do you
know I'm not here for the doughnuts?"

She let her gaze slide down the front of him. "It doesn't
take a psychic to see you're not big on doughnuts, Sam."

He shifted a little, as if self-conscious under her stare, so
she brought her eyes up to his again. There was a hint of fire
there. "Actually," he said, "I'm here to keep my promise." He
shrugged. "Well, technically I guess the promise was to call if
anything happened, but I, uh—I don't know. I just decided to
come by."

Megan frowned, her attention shifting instantly from his
looks to his words. "Something happened?"

"Yeah. Something happened."

"Hold on a sec." She turned toward the kitchen in the back and called, "Karen, I'm taking a break. You okay by yourself?"

"Sure thing," Karen called as she came walking out of the kitchen, wiping her hands on a towel. Megan took off her apron as she came around the counter. "We can talk over here. You want some coffee?"

"No, I'm good, thanks."

She led him to one of the small, round tables. There were only a handful. Most people came here to pick up orders and carry them home, but now and then someone liked to just get a doughnut or pastry and relax with a cup of coffee.

"This is a really nice little place," he said. "You seem to be doing well."

"Yeah, yeah, enough with the small talk. What happened? Did you go on that camping trip?"

"I did. It's a program the department has for at-risk teens. Cops volunteer, take groups on camping trips a few weekends every summer. It's a good program."

"Sounds like. So what happened?"

He pressed his palms to the tabletop. "I don't even believe in this stuff. I mean . . . I never have."

She gnawed her lip and tried not to bark at him to get to the point already.

"It was just like you said it would be. A storm hit, even though the weather service predicted it would miss us by fifty miles. We had high winds, heavy rain, tents blowing all over hell and gone. Everyone was huddled near a copse of trees for shelter."

"Please tell me no one was hurt."

He looked her dead in the eye. "No one was hurt. It was close, though. I don't know what happened. All of a sudden I heard the limb creaking, and your voice was in my head, repeating what you said the other day. I got everyone out of the way just before the limb fell." He shook his head slowly. "It was huge. Came crashing down where we'd been standing. I have to tell you, Megan, if it hadn't been for your warning, someone could have been seriously hurt. Or worse."

She sat there for a long moment, just staring at him. "You're not just messing with me, are you?"

He lifted his brows. "Why would I do that?"

She lowered her head. Her father had pretended to believe her once, just to trick her into elaborating on what she had seen, so he could punish her for even more lies. And after her vision came true her mother had never forgiven her.

"We went back this morning," Sam was saying; she shook off her painful memories and focused on the present; ". . . to gather up the gear. Several trees had come down in our camping area. It was a real mess, Megan. Could've been a real disaster."

She let her lips pull into a smile. "I can't believe it. All my life, it seems, I've been waiting for this gift to be . . . useful. Helpful in some way."

"It's never been before?"

She shook her head. "It . . . tried to be once. But I couldn't make anyone listen."

He tipped his head, silently urging her to go on. But she shook her head firmly. "It doesn't matter. Ever since then it's been little things. I'd know when the phone was going to ring and who would be calling, or when the deliveryman was going to be late. I'd know which roads were going to be jammed with traffic and where to find a parking space. I knew Karen over there was going to get a puppy long before she ever thought about it, and I always know what people will order when they come into the shop."

"Doughnuts, right?"

She smiled at him. "Hey, you're psychic too?"

"Well, just so you know, this time you did some good."

She sighed in relief. "You don't know what that means to me. I'm so glad you kept your promise and let me know."

He nodded. She started to get up and he said, "So what now?"

Frowning, Megan settled into her chair again. "What do you mean, what now?"

"Well, I mean . . . this can't be it. The end of it."

She tipped her head to one side.

"Look, you said yourself you couldn't understand the vision that resulted in us meeting that day. That you would have made the bank on time, if not for the vision messing with your head, so you drove too fast and ended up with me stopping you, right?"

"Well, yeah. But—"

"But what? You said it that day. Maybe we were supposed to meet. And we did, and you wound up saving a bunch of kids because of it."

She shook her head. "Not necessarily. You said you heard the limb creaking."

"Yeah, but no one else did. I'm not even sure I really heard it, or just thought I did because of what you had said."

"Okay, maybe."

He nodded. "I've been thinking about this ever since that limb fell. And the more I think about it, the more I think it would be stupid not to see where this thing might lead."

Shaking her head slowly, she said, "I don't understand. What *thing*?"

"Us. Working together."

She blinked precisely three times. "Tell me you're talking about you coming to work for me at the bakery."

"I'm talking about you, working with me on crimes. One crime, in particular."

She closed her eyes. "Jeez, Sam, I'm nowhere near good enough for something that important."

"I think you are."

"Well, you think wrong. One time, I get a decent vision, and you want to turn it into . . ." She let her voice trail off, because she couldn't resist asking, "What crime, in particular?"

He lowered his head, she thought to hide a look of triumph, and a suspicion whispered through her brain. "A string of sexual attacks. All connected. The department is stumped."

"And?"

"And what?"

"What are you leaving out?" she asked.

He shrugged. "I'm up for a promotion. If I can be instrumental in solving this thing it will be in the bag."

She frowned at him for a long moment, feeling deflated. She'd liked him, at first. Thought he was genuine. Maybe, being psychic, she should have picked up on the fact that he was looking to get ahead, willing to use her to do it. It hurt that the first person to believe in her gift had to be so small-minded.

Pushing back her chair, she got to her feet.

He reached out and clasped her hand.

The flash hit her hard, snapping her head back with its impact, and sucking her out of her waking state, and into a vision that burned her brain with its brightness. Girls. No. Women. Two beautiful women, laughing and talking both at once, and him, Sam, right in the midst of them. And then there was something else. The dead woman, Sarah Dresden, the tattoo and the river.

The vision released her as if dropping her from a great height. She hit the earth so hard it jarred her teeth.

"Jesus, are you okay? Megan?"

She opened her eyes, found herself sitting back in the chair where she'd started out. He wasn't. He was kneeling close beside her, and across the room Karen was looking over the counter at her.

"Who are they?" Megan asked. "The women, the two women?"

He shook his head.

"All S names. Sabrina and She—Shelly?"

"Shelby. They're my sisters." He was looking at her as if she'd sprouted horns. "What did you see? Is something going to happen to them? Are they in trouble?"

She shook her head slowly. "They're fine. Who is your mother, anyway, Cleopatra?"

He frowned even harder. "I don't know what you—"

"You all look like you belong in the movies. Your sisters are as gorgeous as you—uh—as you probably already know." God, she hated the slightly stupid state in which that powerful vision had left her.

He was crouching there on the floor, looking up at her, the concern in his eyes slowly being replaced by amusement. "You're not too hard on the eyes yourself, Meg. You okay?

Better now?" He gently pushed her hair behind her ear, and she was surprised at how intimate the small gesture seemed, how right it felt, and how hard she had to fight not to lift her hand to cover his, and press it to her cheek.

"I'm okay," she said. "You lied to me, though."

"I did not. I really am up for a promotion."

"But that's not why you want to catch this guy. It's not about the job at all. It's about your sisters. They're local, I take it?"

"Local, single. Walk to their cars alone sometimes. Jog in the park. Used to, anyway."

"They even have S names. Just like Sarah Dresden."

He nodded.

"Did all the victims?"

"No. It's coincidence. But it still drove it home for me. How it could just as easily happen to one of them," he said. He averted his eyes. "The thought of that bastard going after one of my sisters—"

She nodded. "You want to protect them. And you feel for the victims because you see them as someone's sisters, too. You have a real empathy for them."

He frowned. "I'm not sure how much I'm going to like hanging out with a woman who can see through me that easily."

"Shouldn't be a problem, unless you have something to hide. Which you don't. Not anymore, at least."

"And what is that supposed to mean?"

She pursed her lips. "I heard on the news that Sarah Dresden's body was found."

"So?"

"But they didn't say where."

He didn't look at her. "We like to keep some information private, Megan."

"But you already know that I know where she was found. You know I phoned your chief and told him where that body was located, and that she had a tattoo, and I'd lay odds she was wearing red sneakers too."

He licked his lips as he moved back to his seat. "I'm not allowed to tell you any of that."

"You don't have to tell me. What I don't know is why your

chief denied everything I told him that day. Or why you're really here with me now. Is it because you really believe I can help you with this case, or do you suspect me of something?"

He lifted his head, met her eyes. "You were right about the body, the tattoo, the sneakers. The thing is she was found a couple of hours prior to your call. The chief isn't convinced there wasn't a leak."

"I see."

"Obviously I don't suspect you of anything, Megan. I like you."

She searched his eyes, looking for the lie, and found sincerity there instead.

"To be honest, I'm not entirely convinced you can help me on this case, but I'm willing to give it a try. If you are."

She lowered her head. "I don't know how much help I'm going to be. But yeah, I'll give it a try. I guess. Let me make some arrangements here. I can call some of my part-timers, see if they can take on full-time for a week. Will that be enough? A week?"

"We can work around your schedule. When you have time, I'll take you to some of the crime scenes, see if you can pick up on anything from them."

"Okay. All right. And maybe I could talk to some of the victims."

"He . . . hasn't left any of his victims alive, Meg."

She closed her eyes. "How many have there been?"

"You haven't been following the case on the news?"

She shook her head. "Not until this last one. Something about her . . ." She let her voice trail off with the thought.

"Thirteen so far," he told her.

She shook her head sadly. A little voice asked her if this wasn't exactly what she had always wanted. A big case, a chance to do some good. To prove herself.

No, she thought. Not like this.

But she knew she had to try. "So when do we begin?"

"Tonight."

"So soon?"

He smiled gently. "Tonight, I'm taking you out to dinner.

To thank you for saving those kids, and maybe me along with them."

She held his gaze and wondered if maybe she had fulfilled that part of her premonition—that of saving him. She also wondered if he thought he was going to have to romance her a little in order to ensure her continued cooperation.

She kind of hoped so.

Chapter Four

"So you're seeing her tonight?" the chief asked.

"Yes, taking her to dinner as ordered, but like I said, I think you're off base on this one." Sam sipped his beer and reached for a handful of pretzels. They were off duty, having a beer after work at the Cock and Bull Tavern. It wasn't an unusual occurrence.

"Come on, Sam. You heard the tape of her call to the tipline."

"I heard it. I just don't think it's all that incriminating, considering . . ."

"Considering what? Her so-called abilities aren't for real, Sam. She warned you about a storm she could have heard about on the Weather Channel, you said so yourself. She's no psychic. If she knows something about our boy, it's personal knowledge, not some crap she's getting from a crystal ball."

Sam lowered his head, shook it. "She's a nice person, Ed."

"Yeah. Prisons are full of nice people."

Sam didn't like what he was being asked to do, but he didn't have a choice. It was his job as a detective with the small city's police department. Pulling over speeders wasn't. He'd been in that borrowed uniform and cruiser for three days before Megan Rose had finally fallen into his phony speed trap. And he would have pulled her over whether she'd been speeding or not, which blew her theory, about her "vision" causing their chance meeting, right out of the water. No, he didn't believe she was some kind of psychic. He wasn't beyond crediting her with a sharper than average intuition, though.

"I don't want your opinion on this, Sam. I just want you to do your job."

"How did this end up being my job, anyway?" he asked the chief. "Was I chosen for my skill, my instincts, my record?"

Ed slapped his shoulder. "Your record—with women, that is. The ladies love you, Sam. God only knows why." He winked good-naturedly. "One-Night Sam, right? Once I found out she was in your age range and unmarried, I knew you were our best chance of tripping her up, getting her to tell us how she really knew the things she did." He tipped his head to one side.

"That's about what I figured." He sighed.

"Come on, Sam. It's in the line of duty, how bad can it be?"

Sam shrugged, thinking it wouldn't be *bad* at all. Just kind of cruel. But there wasn't much he wouldn't do for Ed Skinner, and he thought Ed knew it. That was probably a big part of the reason Ed had chosen him for this job. "How far do you expect me to take this thing, anyway?"

"As far as you have to, Sam. Date her, bed her, wed her if you have to, just get the information."

Sam rolled his eyes. Ed was being sarcastic. About the "wed her" part, at least. "All right. I'll stay on it. But you jot it down somewhere that I did so under protest, and that I'm convinced she's harmless and completely innocent. I know I'm right about this."

"You're psychic, too, huh?"

Sam made a face.

Ed shrugged. "Well, hell, maybe she is innocent. If that's the case, then you'll just get her to tell you who the killer is by using her *powers*."

* * *

SHE changed clothes three times while waiting for Sam to arrive to pick her up. The first choice, a slinky red dress, was too sexy. The second, an off-the-shoulder peasant blouse with jeans, was too casual. She finally settled on the standby little black dress, added an ivory lace shawl, and stood in front of the mirror wondering if she should put her hair up or leave it down.

The doorbell rang.

She swore and glanced at the clock. "Hell." He'd said six; it was only ten of.

Oh, well, she would just have to do. She went to the door, opened it wide.

He frowned at her. "Don't you think you ought to ask who's there before opening your door? Given the situation, I mean?"

She frowned right back at him, stepped back, and closed the door.

He chuckled softly, but he played along, and promptly rang the doorbell again.

"Who is it?" she called.

"It's Sam. Your date for the evening."

"How do I know it's really you?"

"You're psychic, remember?"

"Oh, yeah." She opened the door again. "Now perhaps you'd like to try again with your uh . . . greeting?"

He blinked, then he got it. He stepped back and looked slowly down her, all the way to her toes, and back up again to her eyes. "Wow," he said. "You look incredible."

"That's more like it."

"I mean it."

She smiled. "So where are you taking me?"

"That's a surprise. Got everything?"

"Um-hm."

He crooked an elbow, and she took it, pulled the door closed behind her, and double-checked the lock. He led her to his car, a hot-looking black Mustang, and opened the door for her. "Buckle up, now," he said when she got in.

"Buckle up, hell. I want to drive."

He smiled at her. "I've seen you drive."

She rolled her eyes at his little joke, then said, "You need to get the oil changed. It's past due."

He frowned and glanced down at his odometer. "Hey, you're right."

She shrugged. He closed her door and went around to his own side to get behind the wheel. And then he drove her to the best restaurant in town, fed her a meal that was so sumptuous it should have been illegal, and insisted on ordering a single dessert they could share.

As she spooned bites of luscious brownie sundae into her mouth, he watched her from the other side of the table. He picked up the white cloth napkin and dabbed something from the corner of her mouth, and said, "I think pulling you over that day was one of the best moves I've ever made."

She averted her eyes and felt her face color. "You're not getting any tonight, Sam. You can stop shoveling it on."

"I'm not expecting any tonight. And I'm not shoveling anything but the truth. I like you, Megan."

"Well, what's not to like?"

"Nothing I can find."

She put her spoon down, pushed the fishbowl-sized dessert away. "I can't hold any more of that."

"Me neither. I think we'd both do well to walk some of this meal off, don't you?" As he spoke, he waved at the waiter, who immediately appeared to take his credit card.

"You want to go walking?"

"Sure. The town park is just a block from here. It's a beautiful night."

"God, I haven't gone walking in the park since . . . since all this started."

"The attacks, you mean."

She nodded. Then smiled at him. "I'll be safe enough with my own cop in tow."

"Damn straight you will. How are you set for footwear?"

"Pumps," she said with a frown.

"You *must* like me, if you broke out the heels."

"You do have sisters, don't you?"

He nodded.

"Well, I only went for the two-inch ones. It is a first date, after all."

He grinned at her, flashing the dimple that made her stomach flip-flop. "Maybe next time you'll wear the stilettos?"

"You play your cards right, cowboy, I might even wear the open toes."

He sucked air through his teeth and pressed a hand to his chest.

She laughed out loud.

"My sister Shelby left a pair of flip-flops in my car," he said. "One size fits most."

"You're ready for anything, aren't you?"

The waiter returned with the credit card and the check. Sam added a tip, signed the bottom, and put the card in his wallet. Then he got up. "Ready to try on the new shoes, Cinderella?"

"Ready."

He cradled her elbow in one hand as he guided her around tables and waiters to the exit. The car was waiting out front, but he only opened the back door and fished out the flip-flops. She kicked off her pumps, realized she was wearing stockings, and got into the back of the car.

"What's wrong? Change your mind?"

"Stockings," she said. "They have to go. Flip-flops have that toe thing."

"Ahh." He stood there in the doorway, and she thought about telling him to turn around or close the door, but decided to play instead.

She slid her skirt up to the top of the stockings, and pushed them down her legs, one at a time.

He was mesmerized. She couldn't remember when a man had looked at her the way he was looking at her. And it wasn't all that revealing; the stockings only went to midthigh. She noticed he only took his eyes off her once, and that was to make sure no one else had the view he was so obviously enjoying. He blocked the doorway with his body. And he whispered, "You're killing me, you know that?"

"You'd see more than this if I wore shorts."

"Then next time, wear them." She left the stockings on the seat and slid the flip-flops on. He took her arm and tugged her out of the car, and this time, he held her hand as they walked down the block, around the corner, to the sprawling, grassy Pinedale Town Park. It was minuscule in comparison to the sprawling state park nearby, but perfect for an after-dinner walk with a handsome man.

They entered one of the walking trails and followed its meandering course through the woods, until they reached the park's centerpiece, a perfect little pond, currently home to several wood ducks and a pair of swans who were permanent residents. The moon had risen; it hung low in the sky, huge and lopsided, nearly full.

They moved to the benches near the pond, and Sam took off his jacket and slipped it around her shoulders.

She turned to face him. "This is nice. You're good at this dating thing."

"So I've been told." Did he look a little guilty when he said that? "You want to sit awhile?"

"No. I want to know if you're as good at first kisses as you are at first dates."

He held her eyes, slipped one arm around her waist, and cradled the back of her head with the other hand. It made her feel delicate and cherished. He pulled her to him, bent his head, and brushed his lips across hers lightly, softly, repeatedly, before finally parting them and covering her mouth for a kiss that took her breath away.

The flash hit just as she was starting to reconsider her earlier promise that he wasn't getting any tonight. It hit bright, hard, and fast. She went stiff in his arms. And by the time he lifted his head away, it was gone.

"What is it?" he asked.

"Two things. Most importantly—the killer. He's in the park—here, now. I saw you chasing him, wearing just what you're wearing tonight. So it has to be—"

Before she finished the sentence, the night was split by a woman's scream.

"Stay close to me," he told her, and, gripping her hand, he took off running.

SAM tugged her along behind him, and she surprised him by keeping up without any trouble, despite the flip-flops, the dress, and the darkness. It lifted her a notch higher in his estimation that she didn't stumble or complain or ask to stop. Though after that kiss, it would have been tough to lift her much higher.

He spotted the struggling couple in the wooded area off the trail: a larger form straddling a small one. The small one lay on her back, and the bigger one had her pinned and was pounding her face.

"Police! Get off her, you sonofabitch!" Sam veered off the trail and went crashing through the brush toward the pair. He pulled his gun, but the attacker was already on the run. The perp had rolled off his victim at Sam's first shout, sprung to his feet, and was racing through the underbrush.

Sam glanced back at Megan. She was already crouching beside the battered victim, her face stricken. She looked his way, as if feeling his eyes on her. Hers were intense, damp, powerful, and furious. God, she was something else.

"Stay here, stay with her," he said.

She nodded. "Go get that bastard," she said. "But be careful, Sam."

He didn't believe in her powers, he reminded himself. So why did that warning send a chill right up his spine?

Chapter Five ✍

MEGAN knelt there, half afraid to touch the young woman, but knowing she had to. The victim was frightened, traumatized, probably in shock. She needed to know someone was there, that she was safe, and Megan didn't think words alone could do the job.

She put a gentle hand on the trembling shoulder. "It's okay, the police are chasing him. He's not coming back. You're safe."

Her eyes—one wide with fear, the other split at the corner, swollen, and bloody—fixed on Megan. She couldn't have been more than twenty-five, probably younger. "H-h-he h-hurt me."

"I know. An ambulance is coming. You're going to be okay."

A twig snapped, and the woman's hand shot to Megan's like a cobra striking, and squeezed tight.

"It's just a bird. You're safe," Megan began, but then the flashes came, rapid-fire, blinding, far more vivid and potent than anything she'd ever felt before.

She was running, her feet hitting the path, a satisfying burn in her muscles and the rush of chilled air in and out of her lungs.

An arm like a steel band snapped around her neck from behind . . .

Can't breathe!

. . . yanked her off balance, slammed her into the ground. Something hit her face—her cheekbone exploded in pain. *What's he hitting me with? God, is it a hammer?*

But it was only his fist, again and again, while he fell atop her, knees on either side, groin grinding against hers, his free hand tearing at her spandex running pants, his white sneakers bright in the darkness.

Rapist! No. Fight, fight him. Don't let him—

She used her hands, pounding at her invisible attacker, clawing at his eyes, and kicking her feet, though they hit nothing. It was if he couldn't feel any impact, and with a few more of his blows to her face, she was fighting just to remain conscious.

Megan felt it all. The panic, the fear, the pain of every blow, the hot blood oozing into her left eye and burning there, the weight of him, the smell of his breath. She screamed.

"Hey, hey, come on, talk to me now!"

She opened her eyes, found she was lying on her back a few feet from where the victim lay. Paramedics surrounded the wounded girl. One was leaning over Megan, looking at her as if he thought she might be another victim. Beyond him lights flashed red and white in the darkness, painting everything in alternating strokes of color. She drew a breath, pushed herself up into a sitting position. "I'm okay, I was helping her, and I—I thought I heard him. I just panicked and, uh . . . fell."

The medic frowned, but then Sam was there, moving the man aside, crouching down and clasping her shoulders, looking at her with worry in his eyes. "What happened?"

"The usual," she said, holding his upper arms for support. He pulled her to her feet, but she didn't let go when she got her balance. If anything, she wanted more contact. To be wrapped up in him completely would be a good start.

"Did you get the guy?" she asked.

"No, he took off in what looked like an SUV. It was too damn far away and too dark for me to get a description, much less a plate number." He shook his head, leading her aside, away from the others. As he did, he slipped an arm around her shoulders and held her close to his side.

Better, she thought.

"You got another flash?"

"Man, did I. That poor woman is hurting. I think her cheekbone is broken, maybe her jaw too by the way it felt when he hit me. Hit *her,* I mean."

He stopped walking, frowned down at her. "You . . . felt it?"

She nodded. "As if it were happening to me. God, I've never felt that kind of fear in my life." She watched the medics lift the gurney and carry the woman to the clearing where the ambulance waited. "At least he didn't rape her."

"He didn't? You're sure?"

She nodded. Other cops were arriving now, securing the scene, stringing yellow tape. One carried a camera and began flashing photos.

Sam gripped her upper arm, suddenly animated. "Meg, I don't suppose you . . ." He bit his lip.

"What?"

"Well, did you see him? In the flash, did you get a look at him?"

She thought back. "I was too scared to try, it was happening so fast, you know? I was being pummeled, trying to avoid the blows, trying to cover my face and hit back." She narrowed her eyes, remembering the experience. "I think there were times when I could have glimpsed his face, I just wasn't thinking clearly enough to try. And I think he might have been wearing a mask of some sort."

He sighed. "That's all right."

"We have to get her address, Sam."

He looked at her, frowning as if confused.

She shrugged. "You know me. The most useful piece of information I got from touching that poor woman is that there's no one to go to her house and feed her cat. She was thinking that, as she lay there. 'If he kills me how long before someone knows I'm dead, and goes to my apartment to take care of Roderick? Will he starve to death in the meantime?' "

"I'll see to it the cat is taken care of," Sam told her.

She smiled a little. "I doubt he'd starve, he's pretty over-weight anyway."

Sam stared at her. "Don't tell me—the cat you can describe?"

She lowered her eyes. "Maybe it's because I have a cat of my own. Slender little gray tabby. Hers is big, long-haired, buff-colored, with one green eye and one blue eye."

"You're incredible," he said softly.

"Just not very helpful," she replied.

He swallowed hard. "You saved that girl's life."

"You did that."

"You knew the rapist was in the park."

"So did you, the second you heard her scream."

He shrugged. "So we were both instrumental. The fact is, we have a survivor now. If she got a look at him, we might finally have a description of our boy."

"I don't think she did, though. But . . . I hope you're right."

"Look, I have to go to the hospital." He clasped her shoulders, studying her face, really searching her eyes. He looked at her more deeply, more thoroughly, than anyone had ever bothered looking before. "Are you sure you're okay?"

"I'm okay. You have a job to do. I'm fine."

"I'll take you home on the way to the hospital, all right?"

She shook her head left then right. "Sure . . . but . . . it's just, I thought you wanted my help on this case."

"I do, but—"

"Then why not take me to the hospital with you?"

Sam seemed to consider that, then shook his head with real regret in his eyes. "The chief would never get it. He still thinks . . . not tonight, okay? I'll take you sometime when the place isn't crawling with cops."

By now they were nearing the restaurant and his waiting car. He flicked a button on the key ring, and the locks opened. Then he opened her door for her. She got in, then he did, and he started the engine, then paused.

"What was the second thing?" he asked.

"What?"

"When I was kissing you in the park—"

She smiled just a little, the warmth of that memory chasing away the chill that had settled over her.

"—you got that flash, and I asked you what it was. You said, two things, the killer being the most important one. What was the other?"

She lifted her brows as the warmth left her in a rush. "Oh. That." She looked him dead in the eye. "It was the clear message that you're still keeping things from me. Important things." She shrugged. "Go figure."

OF course he denied it all the way back to her house, tried to cover it, but she knew. She'd felt it clearly when he kissed her. It was lingering, lurking beneath the real passion, the heat that rose between them—there was a *reason* he was kissing her. A *reason* he was even with her at that moment, and that reason was *not* the one he was trying to make her believe.

He didn't want to date her, and he didn't believe in her visions.

She sighed, disappointed. It didn't matter. She had to stick with him, see this thing through, because she, too, had reasons for being with him.

The dreams.

Besides, there was something about him. Something she liked. Not the lying, though. She didn't like that at all. At least he didn't seem like any sort of a threat to her. He'd even given her a card with his cell phone number on it, in case she needed him. As if he were feeling . . . protective of her.

Megan dropped her coat on the back of the sofa and kicked off her shoes—belatedly realizing she still wore the borrowed flip-flops. Her pumps were in the back of Sam's car. She sank into her favorite chair, and Percy jumped into her lap, nuzzled her chin. She petted her cat, thinking of the other woman, and her own pet at home alone as she stroked soft fur. "What do you suppose that fellow's keeping from me, Percy?" she asked.

Percy purred and arched his back to her hand for more affection.

"Lot of help you are. Hell, I suppose being the psychic, I ought to know. Then again . . ." She glanced across the room, to where her computer sat collecting dust. "I suppose I could do a little research, couldn't I?"

She set Percy aside, ignored his mewling protests, and crossed the room to flip on the PC. A few mouse clicks later she was online, running a search on Samuel Sheridan. She was surprised at the number of hits that came up, news articles, mostly. Old ones.

Samuel Sheridan, Killed in Line of Duty.

Officer Shot Down in Robbery Attempt.

Hero Cop Gives All.

She clicked on the first link, which took her to a newspaper's Web site, but not to the article. So she went back to the search results and tried again, finding the same outcome every time. Frowning, she looked more closely at the links, each of which gave just a line or two of the accompanying story, and realized the links were more than a decade old.

Of the three newspaper sites, only one had a "Search the Archives" button, and she used it, relieved when the article actually showed up.

Whispering a silent thank-you to whoever had come up with the idea to put the last twenty-plus years of articles online, she read through the piece, and realized Sam's father had been a cop too, and that he'd died in the line of duty just a few days after his thirty-fifth birthday. This article was about him, not her Sam.

"Samuel Sheridan Jr. was shot at point-blank range when he attempted to foil a liquor store robbery in progress last night. Both suspects were also killed."

The article shocked her, but not so much as the line that brought her to a grinding halt.

It is a painful irony that Samuel Sheridan's father, also a police officer, was likewise killed in the line of duty at the age of thirty-five. In the elder Sheridan's case, death came by way of a high-speed pursuit that ended in a fiery wreck, in the fall of 1950.

She blinked slowly. Both Sam's father and his grandfather had been police officers, and they'd both died in the line of duty at the age of thirty-five? God, how awful. Sam couldn't have been more than a child when his father died. The story was published in 1977. How old could he have been then? He'd mentioned at dinner that he had a birthday coming up.

A low growl made her turn her head sharply. Percival stood on the back of the sofa, staring toward the front door, his back arched and the hair on the scruff of his neck bristling. His tail switched back and forth.

"Percy, what's wrong?" She looked toward the door too, suppressing a shiver.

Percy jumped to the floor and darted across the room, ducking through the slightly open bedroom door and out of sight.

As a guard dog, he left a lot to be desired.

Megan saved the article to her hard drive, then quickly clicked the disconnect button, got up, and walked to the front door. She hadn't locked it behind her when she'd come in, she thought. After what she'd witnessed tonight, that should have been the first thing she thought to do. She turned the locks now, even while peering through the glass panes, but they were more decorative than functional. Beveled and pebbled. Pretty, but useless.

She backed up enough to flip on the outdoor light, then moved to the nearest window to push the curtains aside and peek out.

She saw no one. Nothing. She thought she would have felt better if she had. A local dog trotting by or a neighbor out for a walk. Her cat had sensed something out there. But what?

A car passed by, and its lights fell on a solitary figure, standing across the street. A man. Just standing there, staring . . . at her house.

Megan jerked away from the window, swallowed hard, then forced herself to lean closer again, to take another look.

White sneakers.

The attacker in the park had been wearing white sneakers. It was the one thing she'd noticed, the way they stood out so prominently in contrast to the darkness of the night, and of his jeans.

Jeans. White sneakers and blue jeans. Okay, at least she had something to tell Sam.

What the hell was the killer doing outside her house? If it even was him. Hell, there were probably lots of men running around in white sneakers and jeans.

Not standing outside your house, kid. There's only one of those.

She reached into her pocket, pulled out the little card Sam had given her. Then she dialed his cell phone and prayed he would answer.

Chapter Six 🔊

S AM was leaving the victim's hospital room when his cell phone bleated. He answered it, then said "Hold on" while a scowling nurse told him to turn it off or take it outside.

"Sorry." He headed toward the elevators, noting the signs that told him not to use a cell phone inside the hospital, something he'd already known and just hadn't thought about as he'd rushed in here. When the doors slid closed on him, he brought the phone up to his ear again. "Yeah?"

"Sam. It's Megan. There's, um . . . there's someone outside my house."

He blinked twice, his brain quickly processing her words, weighing the fear in her voice, and spitting out an interpretation he didn't much like, and a rush of panic so overblown it bore further analysis. But later. "Where?"

"He's standing across the street. Just standing there . . . looking toward my house."

The elevator stopped and Sam stepped out of it, striding rapidly toward the exit doors and through them into the parking lot as he spoke. "Are your doors locked, Megan?"

"Yeah."

"You double-checked, all of them?"

"Yes, I did that. Windows too."

"Good girl." He hit the lock release button on his car, got in, and started the engine. "I don't suppose you're getting any flashes? As to who this guy is or what he's doing out there?"

"No flashes. Just a gut feeling. It's him, Sam. It's the killer, I know it is."

He pressed the accelerator to the floor, speeding out of the parking lot. "I'm on my way, hon. Five minutes, tops. I'm gonna click over and call nine-one-one, but I'll come right back on with you. All right?"

"I . . . guess so."

"Just for a second, I promise."

"I'm scared, Sam."

"I know. Jesus, I know. I'm coming for you."

He ran a red light while he manipulated the phone, hitting the flash key, getting a fresh dial tone and dialing 911. He hit the flash key again to bring Megan back into the call as he took a corner so fast the car rocked to one side. "I'm back, Meg."

The dispatcher's line was ringing, and in a moment he heard, "Nine-one-one, what's your emergency?"

"Hold on," he said. "Megan? Are you still there?"

No answer.

"Shit. Dispatcher, this is Detective Sam Sheridan with the Pinedale P.D., badge number seven eighty-five. I have a prowler—possible murder suspect—possible witness in danger—five-one-three Sycamore Street and I need immediate assistance."

"I'll send cars right out, Detective. Can you stay on the line?"

"No, I need the line open."

"All right then. I have officers en route."

She disconnected, but the line remained open. His call to Megan was still connected. "Meg?" Still no answer. His throat burned, and so did his eyes. He told himself he would be just as worried no matter who had been on the other end of that phone call, but he knew damn well it wasn't true.

There was something about Megan Rose. It felt as if she had sunk roots into his flesh, roots that had burrowed deep and twined themselves around his bones. He didn't *get* this way about women. In fact, he'd made a conscious decision not to. Not ever. It wasn't part of his emotional makeup and never would be. So then what the hell was this?

"Megan, for the love of God, answer me," he whispered.

Then there was the distinct sound of her phone hanging up. It shattered the silence on that line like a gunshot, and Sam's last ounce of composure with it. He slammed the accelerator to the floor, his heart pounding in his throat. God, he'd had no idea how much that redhead had gotten under his skin, until this very moment. It made no sense for One-Night Sam to feel this way about a woman he barely knew. And yet, he did. And there wasn't much point in fighting it.

MEGAN dropped the telephone when she heard rattling at her back door, then the sound of breaking glass. She was already racing for her front door when the heavy footfalls came from her kitchen toward her. Her hands shaking, she flipped locks, yanked the door open, and bolted outside into the night. She ran, damp grass and then cold pavement hitting her bare feet, cold air filling her lungs.

A car came speeding toward her, its lights blinding her, tires squealing as it skidded to a stop. There was one moment of sheer panic before she stepped out of the headlights' glare, blinked, and recognized the vehicle as Sam's Mustang. And by then he was out of it, running toward her. His arms came around her powerfully and instantly. He held her hard against him, his grip ferocious, his heart pounding wildly beneath her head, one hand in her hair. "What happened? Are you all right?"

She nodded against his chest, amazed at the power of his fear for her. Amazed at how odd it felt to have someone care this much, and at the way her own arms locked around his waist in return. As if there were something between them—as if they were important to each other. As if they had been for a very long time.

"He's in the house, Sam." She didn't want to say it. She

would rather have just stayed there in his arms until everything was all right again.

Gently, he pried her arms from around him, turned to face the house, and lifted the gun he had in his hand. God, she hadn't even seen in there. "Get in my car," he told her. "Lock the doors. Pull it off the road."

"Sam, I—"

"Do it now, Meg." He softened the harshness of the command with a tender look, a quick touch, his hand cupping her head briefly as his eyes compelled her to obey.

She drew a shaky breath, nodded, and got into his car, then sat there watching in panic as Sam moved toward her house, the gun leading him. This wasn't right. She was supposed to save this man, according to her recurring dreams. Not send him walking into what might be his death.

Sam went inside, and she swore part of her went with him. Belatedly, she put his car into gear and pulled it off the road. But she had no intention of staying safe inside it while he risked his life. Swallowing her fear, she opened the car door, got out, took a few tentative steps along the sidewalk toward her home. "Sam?"

No reply. She moved closer, turning now up the walk to her front door. Behind her, sirens wailed and lights flashed as police cars came screaming up her road. Doors slammed, but she kept moving forward, shaking. "Sam?"

A hand fell on her shoulder, stopping her. "Ms. Rose? You all right?"

She nodded. "Sam—Officer Sheridan, he's in the house. There was someone in there."

The cop turned, waving to others who were apparently awaiting his orders. He pointed to two and swung his hand in an arc, pointing toward the back of her house, then he pointed to another and nodded to the front door. "Sheridan's inside. Possible intruder as well," he said, his voice low but firm as the men moved past him to carry out their orders.

Before they got far, though, Sam was coming out the front door, his gun holstered once more. When she saw him, Megan's breath rushed out of her, and her muscles went soft.

"Forget it," he said. "Whoever he was, he's long gone." His eyes found Megan's, held them as he came to her. She barely restrained herself from wrapping her arms around him, she was so relieved to see him safe. It wouldn't look good, not in front of the other cops, she knew that. But Sam did embrace her, when he joined her there. He touched her with his eyes, with his serious but reassuring smile, with how close he stood, and his hand on her shoulder telling her it would all be okay.

"Chief," he said, nodding to the older man.

"What's the story, Sam?"

"Chief Skinner, this is Megan Rose. She was a witness to the assault in the park tonight. An hour later she called in to say there was a prowler outside her house. Apparently, he broke in before we got here."

The police chief glanced at Megan, and she at him, now that she could tear her eyes from her own front door, and from Sam's. The chief was an attractive man, perhaps fifty-something, lean, strong, with neatly cropped black hair that was graying at the temples, and friendly brown eyes. She knew that he knew who she was—the crackpot psychic he suspected of God only knew what.

"You were inside at the time?" the chief asked her. His concern seemed genuine.

She nodded.

"That must have been terrifying for you."

"It was. I heard someone trying to get in the back door. Glass breaking. Footsteps. I ran out the front."

He nodded, looking again at Sam.

Sam said, "Glass was busted out of the back door. Looks like he reached through and unlocked it, walked right in. We'll want to dust it for prints."

"Terry, get that scene secured," the chief said, sending one of the officers scurrying to obey. "I'm sorry you've been through so much today, ma'am," he went on, focusing again on Megan. "Did you get a look at the man, when you saw him outside your house?"

"No. It was too dark. He was just a shape. White sneakers,

jeans." She shook her head, belatedly skimming ground level, noting all the shiny black shoes running this way and that way.

"And what about the one in the park? Could you identify him?"

She shook her head slowly. "No, I didn't get a look at him. But apparently, he got a pretty good look at me."

"You have reason to believe it was the same man?"

Megan lifted her eyes, shifting her gaze to Sam's, then back to the chief's. "I don't have a reason to believe it," she said slowly. "But I believe it anyway."

The chief frowned. "Why? Is there something you're not telling me?"

She lowered her head, trying to come up with an answer that would sound logical.

Then he nodded knowingly. "It's that ESP thing again, huh?" His face bore that same look of blatant disbelief she'd seen so often as a child, in her father's eyes. Though his words were kind, and his expression tried to be, she knew that deep down he believed she was a fraud.

He did remember her name, though. She almost wished he didn't. She wished she had never made that phone call the other night. "It's nothing psychic," she said. "It's just a gut feeling. That's all."

The chief nodded as if he understood. "Is there somewhere else you can stay tonight, Ms. Rose?"

"Sure. I can go to a hotel for the night."

"You do that, then. You'll be safer, more comfortable, and besides, we'll need access to the house for the next couple of hours. Sam, why don't you take her inside to pack up a few things?"

"I can manage—" she began. But she didn't want to. She didn't want to get more than two feet from Sam's side right now, and frankly, the thought of spending the night alone in a strange, impersonal hotel room didn't appeal in the least.

Sam shook his head, and slipped an arm around her shoulders. "I'll go with you. We don't want you accidentally tromping on evidence, after all."

She let him guide her toward the front door of her house, belatedly turning back to the chief. "It was nice meeting you, Chief Skinner," she said, holding out a hand.

He had a notepad in one hand, and a cell phone in the other, but he gave her a nod, attempted a sympathetic smile, then moved toward his officers.

"Come on, Meg." Sam led her into the house, straight to her bedroom. He stood just inside the bedroom door, looking around. "Do you think he came in here at all?"

"I don't think he had time," she said. "Nothing's out of place. He was coming through the kitchen, maybe made it almost into the living room by the time I got out and ran. And then you were there. I imagine he went right back out when he heard your car."

"Thank God the hospital's only five minutes away."

"The hospital is fifteen minutes away, Sam." She tipped her head up to look at him.

"Yeah, well . . . I'm trained in high-speed techniques."

"You were worried about me."

"I was freaking petrified."

She smiled just a little. "Thanks for that."

He shrugged, averting his eyes. She decided to let it go for now, but God, it did her good to know he felt the power of this . . . *thing* between them as clearly as she did. She tugged an overnight bag from a shelf in her closet, tossed it onto the bed, then went to her dresser to open drawers. She pulled things out almost at random, her attention not on the job as she tucked items into the bag. In the end she didn't even know what she'd packed. She was too busy analyzing what was happening between her and Sam, wondering what her dreams had been telling her all this time, speculating on the killer's reasons for coming after her tonight.

"You need anything from the bathroom? Toothbrush, makeup?"

She nodded vaguely, realizing she had gone still with her hands buried in her top drawer. She shook herself, then went into the bathroom off her bedroom and gathered more items. "What do you think he wanted?" she asked.

Sam stood in the bedroom still, beyond her range of vision. "We don't even know for sure it was him."

"Of course we do. Your Chief Skinner does too. At least, he didn't disagree."

She heard Sam sigh.

"He seems nice, Chief Skinner. Even if he doesn't believe I'm for real."

"He's a decent guy. Taught me everything I know about being a cop."

She frowned, coming out of the bathroom with her hands full of things from her counter. Hairbrush, makeup, deodorant, toothbrush. She stood in the doorway, where she could see him. "I would have thought your dad would have done that."

He looked at her sharply. "You know about my father?"

She shrugged, moving to the bed to drop her collection into her overnight case. "I got curious. Did a little Internet research on you tonight."

"Why?"

"I told you earlier, I got the feeling you were being less than honest with me about something. I thought maybe I could find a clue what."

He sighed. "And I told you I've got nothing to hide from you, Megan. My father was killed in the line of duty. I was only a kid at the time."

She nodded slowly, bent over her bag to zip it up. "What happened to him?"

"Liquor store robbery. He and his partner showed up before the perps got out of the store. One took the back door, one the front. Bad guys decided to shoot their way out the back. Dad chose the wrong door."

She felt the heartache in his words, the loss. It still hurt. "I'm sorry."

"Skinner opened fire, got them both. Too late, though. Dad was already down."

"Skinner? The chief was your father's partner?"

He nodded. "It hit him as hard as it did the rest of us, I think. He took us under his wing after that. I think he felt like it should have been him, instead of Dad. He didn't have a wife or kids."

"Survivor's guilt," she said.

"Yeah, I guess so. He was there for us after that. Kind of stepped in, took care of things my father would have. My grandmother resented it, I think, him stepping into her son's place. But the rest of us were awfully glad to have him around."

"God, it must have been awful for your mother. How many kids did she have?"

"Three. My two sisters and me. And my grandmother, to boot." He moved to the bed, picked up her bag. "You ready?"

"I can't find Percy."

He frowned.

"My cat." She looked in all Percy's usual hiding places—under the bed, in the bathtub, in the closet—all the while wondering if she wanted to pry further than she had into Sam's personal history, and decided she might as well. "Your grandfather died in the line of duty too, the paper said."

He frowned at her. "You really have been snooping, haven't you?"

"The article mentioned it."

"Yeah, he died on duty too. Car wreck. Anything else you want to know, Megan?"

"Quite a lot, actually."

He watched her face, waiting, his own seeming clouded or angry or something.

"But not now." Did he seem a bit relieved by that? Hard to be sure. "The Windsor's right in town, ten minutes from here. I can get a room there. I'm sure they aren't booked this time of year." She looked around, but there was still no sign of Percy. "There's plenty of food and water here. I guess he'll be all right."

"I'm sure he'll be fine. But you're not going to the Windsor."

"I'm not?"

"No. I want you someplace safe, someplace this guy wouldn't think to look for you, just in case your hunch is right."

She blinked. "And what place would that be?" she asked.

He sighed. "Mine. I'm taking you home with me, Megan. And I don't want to hear any arguments, okay?"

"I'm not going to give you any." He looked at her, brows

raised. "Arguments, I mean." Hell, that didn't come out right either. "You know what I mean."

"I know." He actually smiled a little, and it lightened the somber mood brought on by what had happened tonight, and by her morbid, probing questions. "And I'm going to pry into your past to pay you back for prying into mine. Come on."

Chapter Seven

"DID you get to see the girl from the park at the hospital tonight?" Megan asked, probably to change the subject.

He glanced at her as he drove, decided to let the matter of her snooping go, for now. Hell, he had all night. "Yeah. Her name's Linda Keller. I didn't get much out of her, though. She didn't get a look at the guy, and was still too shaken up to give me anything helpful."

She swallowed hard. "Maybe . . . I could see her."

He blinked, looking at her face, her eyes. Still worried about trying to help, even after all she'd been through tonight. "I don't know if you noticed this, Megan, but being involved in this might very well have put you at risk."

"If I could talk to her, touch her hand again, I might be able to get something."

"You did that once. All it got you was knocked on your ass and feeling her pain. Not to mention a visit from the suspect."

"Maybe."

He didn't have much doubt himself. "Why are you so determined to help?"

She shook her head, shaking off his question. "I wasn't

expecting the vision to hit so hard last time. This time I'd be ready. I could look more carefully, see things I missed before. She might have seen things she doesn't realize she saw, or is too traumatized to remember."

His lips thinned. "All right. I'll take you to the hospital in the morning."

She nodded.

"If you tell me why you are so damned determined to do this."

She shrugged. "What makes you think there's a reason? Why can't it be something I just want to do?"

"Come on, Megan, I know it's more than that."

She closed her eyes. "You don't know anything about me."

"I know a lot about you, Meg. Way more than I ought to. I want to know more." He smiled at her. "Besides, I told you I was going to repay your prying with some prying of my own."

She drew a breath, sighed. "I haven't had a vision about anything this important since I foresaw my father's death."

He swung his head toward her, stunned by her words and the pain he sensed behind them.

"I saw it all. He'd been drinking, left the bar, got behind the wheel, went off a bridge on the way home. The car exploded. He was gone. I tried to warn him, he didn't believe me. Called me a liar just the way he always did when I claimed I had a vision. I got the back of his hand for this particular lie, and was sent to my room. Then my mother came in and made me kneel and pray with her rosary for nine hours straight. She believed visions like mine could only come from the devil."

"I had no idea. Meg, I'm sorry."

She shrugged. "When the vision came true, just the way I said it would, she was even more certain I was evil. Said I had caused it. She barely spoke to me after that, and eventually sent me to live with her aging aunt, where I basically became a caregiver. My mother died a few years later. For years after that, the visions just didn't come—except for this one recurring dream I could never understand."

She averted her eyes when she said that.

"What was the dream?"

"It doesn't matter, Sam."

"Okay," he said. "Okay, I won't push on that. But what about the visions? Why did they stop?"

She shrugged. "I don't know, maybe I suppressed them. Maybe on some level I believed I was to blame for my father's death. I don't know. But when they did come back, they came almost tentatively. Minor things, nothing big, nothing I had to prevent or change. This is the first time I've had a vision about something this important. And I guess I'm afraid if I don't do what I'm supposed to do, they'll go away again and maybe never return."

He nodded slowly. "You think you stopped having visions because you failed to save your father. And you'll stop again if you fail again."

She shrugged. "Maybe. Maybe saving this girl is part of my penance." She was silent for a moment. Then looked at him quickly. "If the killer is going after witnesses, Sam—"

"She's safe. We've got a guard on her hospital room door, and her house is under surveillance."

"And . . . what about her cat?"

Damn. He'd forgotten about the cat. "Tell you what," he said. "You and I will go by her place and feed her cat ourselves, all right?"

"That would make me feel a whole lot better," she told him.

He shook his head slowly. "All you've been through and your chief concern is still a damn cat."

She shrugged. "I like cats."

"Yeah. I kind of figured that out."

Sam wasn't 100 percent convinced they were going to find any cat at all, much less a buff-colored, overweight one with one green eye and one blue. But he phoned the hospital as he drove and asked a nurse to put him through to Linda Keller's room, but only if she was still awake.

She picked up the phone, and Sam had her put the cop who stood outside her door on the phone to verify who he was, just to put her mind at ease before speaking to her. When she came back on the line, he said, "I wanted to check in, see if there was anything you needed taken care of at your house while you're in the hospital."

"Is there any—have you caught him yet?"

"Not yet. But we will, I promise you that." He hated that he couldn't bring her better news, tell her the bastard was in custody and wouldn't be hurting anyone ever again. He hated it. "When we talked earlier, you said you didn't have any family or friends in town, being new here. I thought I should check in, see if there's anything you need taken care of at home."

"I'm . . . thank you. That's so thoughtful of you."

"It's the least I can do, believe me."

"There is something you could do for me, if it's not too much trouble. There's really no one else I can ask. . . ."

"That's why I called. And it's no trouble at all, really."

"I have a cat at home. I was out of cat food this morning, so he missed his breakfast, and if he doesn't have anything tonight he'll be just miserable."

Sam caught Megan's eyes, saw the knowing look in them. "I'll pick up some cat food and feed him for you. Is your house locked?"

"Yes, but there's one of those hide-a-key rocks near the front walk. Um . . . he likes Frisky Cat, the tuna flavor."

"Got it. Is there anything else I can do?"

"Yes, actually. That woman, the one who helped me in the park . . . is she all right?"

"Fine. She's with me now. Actually, this call was her idea."

"Thank her for me, will you?"

He glanced at Megan, a thought crossing his mind. "What does your cat look like?"

She seemed taken aback by the question, but answered after a brief pause. "Yellow gold. I guess you'd call him buff. And terribly overweight. He's got two different colored eyes, which makes him sort of bizarre looking, but I think that's what drew me to him in the first place. Why do you ask?"

A funny little wave of something washed through his stomach and head.

"I, uh—just curious. Listen, if you like, you can thank that woman yourself. She'd like to come by and see you tomorrow, if you're up to it."

"I'd like that," she said. "Yes, I'd like that very much."

"All right then. I'll see you in the morning."

"Thank you, Detective Sheridan. For everything."

"You're welcome."

He flicked off the phone, glanced sideways at Megan. "You nailed the cat. To a tee."

"You sound surprised." She tipped her head to one side. "You *are* surprised, aren't you?"

He shrugged. "I just—I'm not used to seeing this kind of thing in action."

"I thought you believed me about the visions, Sam."

"I do."

"No," she said. "I'm not so sure you do. I don't think you're sure you do."

She sounded almost heartbroken. Hell, he didn't want to hurt her. He cared about the woman way more than he ought to, and to be honest, while he'd never believed in this kind of psychic bullshit—had actively refused to believe in it—she had him wondering. Her childhood tale was goddamned heart-wrenching.

Unlike his chief, he didn't believe she had any real knowledge of or connection to the killer. He was on her side in that. And while technically, he was working here, getting close to her to get the truth out of her, the truth was, he was with her because he wanted to be. And he was starting to believe in her abilities.

"This kind of thing takes getting used to, Megan," he said, aware she was still waiting for him to reply. "It's never been a part of my experience. That's all."

He turned the car into the parking lot in front of a twenty-four-hour convenience store, and they went inside for the cat food. Frisky Cat, tuna flavor. Then they drove to Linda Keller's address, and he easily located the key in the fake rock. Too easily.

He picked it up, took the key from the compartment in the

bottom, then held the rock out to Megan. "This is way too obvious," he said. "She might as well leave the key in the door."

"Oh? Where do you suggest people leave a spare key?"

"In their pocket." He put the key into the lock and opened
the door.

Megan came in behind him, carrying the cat food. The
biggest cat he'd ever seen came bounding toward them with a
plaintive meow, and proceeded to rub itself against Sam's leg.
Megan located the cat's dishes, and promptly filled them. The
cat pounced on the food as if starved, though Sam estimated
he could probably live several weeks without a bite. She filled
the water dish too.

Sam saw the collar, heard the jingle of the tags that hung
from it, and out of curiosity, crouched down to take a look. He
read the tag with the cat's name, Roderick, engraved on it.
"Well, I'll be damned," he muttered.

"Got the name right, too, didn't I?"

He glanced up at her.

"Wish I could get the name of our killer that easily."

"So do I." The voice of reason, and force of habit, told him
it wasn't proof of anything. Hell, now that he thought about it,
the victim could have told her about the cat back in the park,
while he was chasing after the perp.

But he didn't really think so. "So are we set here?" he asked.

"Yeah." She squatted down beside him and stroked the cat.
"You'll be okay for the night, won't you, boy?"

A throaty purr that did not interrupt the feeding frenzy
was the beast's reply. She rose again, and Sam did too, walking to the door, pocketing the key. "We'll take this to her tomorrow at the hospital. Leaving it where it was is just asking
for trouble."

"You're the expert."

They walked out to his car, and he drove the rest of the way
to his home, a small, functional shoebox in a residential
neighborhood. He wasn't all that surprised to see the lights all
on, and three cars lined up along the roadside out front. "The
troops have arrived," he said softly.

"I thought you lived alone."

Was that a hint of disappointment he heard in her voice? He searched her eyes to see for sure, but there was too much going on in them for him to pick out or identify any one emotion.

"I try to live alone," he said, offering a smile to lighten things up. "With my family, it's not always easy. At least they left me a parking spot this time." He pulled into the driveway, which was only big enough for one car, and shut off the engine. Before they even got to the front door, it was opening and people were spilling out. Sam waved to them and tried to look happy to see them.

"Megan Rose, let me introduce my family. This is my mother, Evelyn, and these are my sisters, Sabrina and Shelby."

Evelyn smiled and nodded hello to Megan. "I'm sorry if we've interrupted a date, dear."

"Please, Mom," Sabrina said. "It would have been over in a couple of hours anyway. They don't call him One-Night Sam for nothing, you know."

He felt Megan flinch, realized he still had a hand on her arm, and promptly released her.

"It's not a date," Megan said quickly. "It's . . . business."

"Megan's a witness to a crime. Now do you mind parting the waters and letting us in?"

The women exchanged curious glances, but moved aside. Sam and Megan went in, and he saw that his grandmother was there as well, sitting in his favorite chair, watching a football game on his big-screen TV.

"Told you he was all right," she said, barely looking up. "Hello, grandson."

"Hello, Lily."

"These hens heard over the scanner that you were chasing after a murder suspect and got worried. I told them tonight wasn't the night."

"I'm fine, as you can all see." He frowned, sniffing the air, turning toward his mother again. "You cooked, didn't you?"

"Oh, just a little, dear," his mother said. "As long as we were here, you know, we thought it wouldn't hurt to toss a few potatoes into the oven."

"Smells like chicken," he said.

"Well, the oven was already hot. No sense wasting gas, you know."

"And cake?"

"I hate to leave an oven rack empty."

"Mm-hm. Nothing like a full blown meal at 11 P.M."

She smiled. "I'll just go set an extra place for your guest."

He closed his eyes slowly, then turned to Megan. "They're staying for a post-dinner dinner."

"I got that."

"You, girl!" his grandmother called. Megan turned her head sharply, and the old woman waggled a finger at her. "Come on over here and sit with me. It's halftime anyway, you may as well be polite."

Megan blinked in shock, sending a look at Sam. "Sorry," he whispered.

She smiled, an amused, indulgent smile, and went to obey his grandmother's summons.

Chapter Eight

MEGAN sat alone with Sam's grandmother, while his mother and sisters coerced him into the kitchen, obviously wanting to talk to him in private. The old woman had a face like aged leather and twinkling blue eyes. She had short curly permed hair, and wore a pair of faded jeans and a sweatshirt that was two sizes too big. It had a fat cartoon cat on the front, with the caption *Cats Rule. Dogs Drool.*

"I'm Lily," she said. "You're my grandson's flavor of the week?"

"I'm Megan." She offered her hand and the old woman took it, then paused, frowning, squeezing tight, and looking more closely at Megan's face.

"Megan," she repeated and released her hand. "They come and go so fast, I don't bother learning their names. Yours though, maybe I will. You have any pull with Sam, girl?"

"Pull?"

"Influence. Does he listen to you?"

"I really haven't known him that long, Mrs.—"

"Lily. Just Lily."

"Lily." Megan wasn't sure where this conversation was going, but the woman had her curious. "Why? What is it you would want me to . . . influence him to do?"

"Quit his job."

Megan blinked. "Quit the police department?"

"That's what I just said. And soon, girl. His birthday's next week, you know."

"I'm afraid I don't under—"

"His *thirty-fifth* birthday," she said, as if that were significant somehow.

"I didn't know. But I still don't see why—"

Lily leaned forward in her chair and gripped Megan's forearm, her clasp powerful. "His father—my own son—was a policeman, you know."

"I know. I'm so sorry for the way you lost him."

She shook her head. "We all lost him. That wife of his keeps his den like a shrine. Won't even let anyone in there. Hasn't changed a thing since he died." She sighed deeply. "Shot down in his prime, he was. The week of his thirty-fifth birthday. Just like my husband."

And suddenly the light dawned. Megan met the old woman's piercing blue eyes. "And you believe Sam will be killed as well?"

She nodded slowly. "I know he will. It's . . . it's some kind of curse," she said.

The word "curse" seemed to echo endlessly in Megan's mind. It made her knees go weak, and she sank into a chair near the older woman.

"If he doesn't quit that damnable job in time, I'm afraid we'll lose him too." Her lips thinned. "I'm a tough old bird, but I think it would kill his poor mother. And those sisters of his. It's not right they should suffer like that just because he's too stubborn to listen."

Megan licked her lips, understanding now why Sam's family tended to panic every time they heard what seemed like a dangerous situation on the scanner. "Have you talked to Sam about this? Maybe if you told him—"

"Talked myself blue, girl. He says he doesn't believe in curses, doesn't believe in any of that sort of hoo-ha. Much less my intuitions."

"You have . . . intuitions?" Megan asked, lifting her brows.

Lily nodded slowly. "I knew something bad was coming before my husband went to work that day. I had that same bad feeling the day Sam Jr. died, and I think he did, too, the odd way he'd been acting all week." She tipped her head to one side. "You get feelings too, don't you, girl."

It wasn't a question. "Sometimes. I . . . see things."

"You have the sight," she whispered. "I knew it. Felt it when I took your hand." She bit her lip, shaking her head slowly. "You're with my grandson for a reason, girl. God didn't send you to this family by coincidence, and I think you know it."

Megan drew a breath. Her gift had changed since she'd met Sam. The visions had grown stronger, more important, more frequent. And never before had they hit her with such crippling impact.

"You're the one who can break this curse and end this family's grieving once and for all. You can do it. You can save Sam."

Break the curse. Save his life.

Megan took Lily's papery-soft hand. "I'll try my best."

"That's all I can ask."

"What's all you can ask, Lily?" Sam said, coming in from the kitchen.

"I've just promised her my favorite recipe," Megan said, seeing the note of panic in the older woman's eyes and knowing, as Lily apparently did, that Sam would be furious if he knew what they'd really been discussing.

"You cook too?" he asked with a smile. "You're just full of hidden talents, aren't you, Meg?"

"She's a keeper, this one," Lily said. "And if this wasn't a date, then you're a damn fool. Now, are you people gonna put some food on the table before I starve to death or what?"

Sam shook his head slowly. "Dinner—or rather, an all-out Sheridan-family midnight snack—is served," he said.

* * *

THE meal was pleasant, which surprised Megan. She ate only enough to be polite, since she and Sam had already enjoyed one luscious meal tonight. Sam's mother, Evelyn, seemed naturally friendly, and the sisters dropped their attitude at a single, swift, meaning-laden glance from Lily. The old woman had apparently decided to view Megan as her ally.

When the meal was over and the dishes were done, they didn't linger. Just said their good nights, and left.

Sam stood in the doorway, waving and smiling until they were all out of sight, then he closed the door, turned, leaned back against it, and heaved an exaggerated sigh.

"Oh, come on," Megan said. "They're not so bad."

"They're not bad at all. Just a little . . . exhausting." He straightened from the door, looked at her, then beyond her, to where her overnight bag sat beside his sofa. "Hell, you didn't even get to settle in."

"From the sounds of things, none of your dates ever do."

He scowled at her. "I meant for the night."

"So they usually spend the night, then?"

"Megan."

"The way your sisters talked, I got the idea you hustled them out of here before the sweat began to dry."

"Oh, that's lovely imagery."

She shrugged. "You're the one they call One-Night Sam."

"This is pretty irrelevant."

"I don't think so. After all, I'm not *just* a witness to a crime you're trying to solve. You did kiss me in the park tonight. Or was that . . . part of whatever game it is you've been playing with me, Sam?"

He narrowed his eyes on her. "I kissed you because I wanted to kiss you, Meg. That wasn't part of anything, not the case, not your abilities. Nothing. I'm sorry if things my well-intentioned sisters said are making you have doubts about that, because I'd really like to kiss you again."

"Oh, I'd like that too," she said. "But I'd kind of like to know what to expect afterward."

He came to her, slid his arms around her waist, and tugged her close. "Haven't you ever heard of living in the moment?"

"Heard of it. Never practiced it much."

"No time like the present." He leaned closer, and she tipped her head up. He kissed her, slowly and softly. It was wonderful. It was also revealing. And this time the knowledge didn't come to her as a vision, and it didn't knock her off her feet or snap her head back. It just slipped gently from his mind to hers.

When he lifted his head away, she blinked up at him. "You don't get involved because you don't want to leave someone behind, the way your mother was left behind. And your grandmother."

He frowned down at her.

"The way you were left behind."

He shook his head. "Grams has been talking again."

"She believes there's a curse on the Sheridan men."

"It's silly superstition."

"But Sam, what if it's not? Don't you think you should . . . take some precautions, just in case?"

He released her, turned, and paced across the room. "She convinced you to try to get me to quit the force, didn't she?"

"Before your birthday next week, if possible." She smiled. "It's only because she loves you, Sam."

"Hell, I know that." He turned and sank onto the sofa. "Look, I don't even believe in curses. I'm certainly not going to start letting one dictate the way I live my life."

She nodded and crossed the room to sit on the sofa beside him. "You don't believe in psychism or precognition either, do you?" He opened his mouth to argue, but she held up a hand. "It's okay. I get it. It's tough to believe in one without believing in the other, and if you let yourself believe in the curse, you're faced with a terrible choice. Your life or your life's work. So you refuse to believe in either."

"Megan, it's not that I don't believe you—"

"No, I know it's not. Because you do. Deep down, you do. And you believe in the curse too."

He looked at her as if she were speaking a foreign language. "And how did you make that leap of logic?"

"Because you already are letting it dictate your life. One-Night Sam." She got to her feet, picked up her bag, and slung it over her shoulder. "So where's my room?"

"Top of the stairs, second door on the left."

"Night, Sam."

"You're wrong, you know."

She walked up the stairs, shaking her head. "No, I'm not. And you know it. And just for the record, that dream I've been having since I was twelve? It was about you, Sam."

SHE was wrong. Dammit, she was dead wrong. He didn't believe in the curse. He lived his life exactly the way he wanted to. Did exactly what he wanted to do, every single day. Lived every day as if it were . . .

"My last," he whispered, finishing the thought aloud.

Hell, what was it with Megan Rose, anyway? One date, and she'd turned him inside out, read his mind, met his family, and was spending the night. One date. Two kisses. Most women barely remembered his last name, after considerably more than a couple of kisses. Most didn't know or care what made him tick.

Most didn't touch him the way she did, either. He was so wrapped up in her he barely knew which end was up. Thinking about her every waking moment. Dreaming about her at night ever since the speed trap.

She claimed she had been dreaming about him for years. And hell, he was inclined to believe her. God knew there was something powerful between them.

She seemed able to look right inside his head—not only that, but she managed to see what was going on inside him . . . even more clearly than he did himself.

He closed his eyes slowly. Okay, so maybe she was right. Maybe he did believe in the curse on some level. That didn't mean he was going to surrender to it. It didn't change a damn thing.

So why was he having so much trouble sleeping tonight?

He'd done some paperwork, checked his e-mail, taken a

shower. It was 2 A.M. and he still couldn't shut off his mind. He rolled over, punched the pillow, laid on it a moment longer, and then finally gave up. He might as well get up. He wasn't going to sleep. He sat up in the bed, swung his legs around to the floor. Some of that leftover chicken might take his mind off things.

Damn Megan. He'd been perfectly content to keep this looming death sentence buried in his subconscious mind. Now it was right there on the surface. Three days. Three days left until he turned thirty-five.

A soft tap on his bedroom door made him turn his head sharply.

"Sam?"

Frowning, he said, "Right here, Meg."

She opened the door, stepped into his darkened bedroom, and then stopped. She was silhouetted by the light from the hall, which she must have turned on to find her way to him. Backlit that way, her white nightgown was virtually transparent, though he didn't suppose she would have any way of knowing that.

"I can't sleep in there."

He lifted his brows, saw her peering at him through the darkness. He sat there with nothing over him but a sheet, and he could tell her eyes were adjusting by the way she stared.

"I keep drifting off, but as soon as I do, I hear that glass breaking, the door opening, that man coming after me, and I wake up with my heart racing."

"Come on in, Meg. Stay in here with me. Maybe we'll both feel better, huh?"

She swallowed hard. "Maybe." She came in the rest of the way, closed the door behind her. He lost the luscious view, but could still see her form as she padded across the room toward the bed. She didn't go to the opposite side, though. She came to his side, instead. "How long until your birthday?" she asked softly.

"Three days. Why?"

She shrugged. He saw her shoulders move with it. "Because I don't do one-night stands," she said softly. And then she peeled the nightgown over her head and stood there, in the dark, waiting.

Sam stood up, took a single step closer, and put his hands on her shoulders. They were small and soft, her skin warm to the touch. She pressed closer, breasts to his chest, belly to his belly, hips to his hips. Her arms twisted around his neck, and she tipped her face up. Sam kissed her, letting his hands slide lower, tracing the gentle slope of her spine, the curve at the small of her back, and then lower over her rounded buttocks and lower still until he could cup them and hold her harder against him. He was hard, wanting her in a way that was new to him. Unfamiliar. Usually, at this point, the thing he felt himself wanting, yearning for, was sex. Release. Pleasure.

This time was different. This time the thing he wanted, craved . . . was her. Megan. He felt her mouth open beneath his, a silent invitation, and he slid his tongue inside, tasting her. He moved a hand lower, between her thighs from behind, and touched the wetness there. She moved against his hand, rubbing herself over his fingers, and when he slid one inside her she sighed into his mouth.

Turning her gently, he eased her onto the bed, never taking his body from hers. He slid his mouth over her jaw, down to her neck, over her collarbone, and lower until he captured a breast and sucked at the nipple. Her hands clutched his head as he worked her there. He slid around to the front of her, between them, touching her, finding the spot that made her squirm and pant. And then he felt her hand, closing around him, squeezing and rubbing.

She spread her thighs to him, guided him to her center. He moved his mouth to capture hers again, and pressed himself inside her. Soft, wet heat surrounded him, enveloped him, welcomed him. He moved slowly, carefully, until she wrapped her thighs around him and pulled him into her swiftly and completely.

Sam buried his face in her neck, overwhelmed with more than just passion. So much more. "God, Megan," he whispered.

She moved with him, taking him in a way no woman had

ever done. And the wonder he felt in this was rapidly overwhelmed by the tidal wave of passion that swept them both away in a frenzy of clutching, writhing, straining. Her felt her nails digging into his back and heard her cry his name as spasms of release racked her body, squeezing around him until he, too, found release. He came inside her, and it felt as if he were filling her with his soul as well as his seed. He held her there to take all of it, all of him as he drove to the hilt and stayed there, pulsing inside her.

Slowly, her body unclenched, relaxed. Slowly, his did too. He started to roll off her. She held him where he was, and when he looked into her eyes, wide and sparkling in the darkness, she whispered, "No." And she began to move again. "I need more of you than that, Sam. Much more."

He gave her what she asked for.

Chapter Nine

MEGAN woke in Sam's arms, rolled over, and found him staring at her. His eyes, roaming her face as if seeing it for the first time and trying to memorize every feature. When he realized her eyes were open, he smiled, and the solemn expression faded.

"Sweat's dry," he said, stroking a finger down her cheek. "I didn't throw you out."

"Good thing, I'd have been really pissed."

"Hungry this morning?"

"Starved."

"Take the first shower then," he said. "I'll make us some breakfast."

She shook her head slowly. "Shower with me. And we'll go out for breakfast."

"I like the way you think." He sprang from the bed without warning, came around to her side, and scooped her up in his arms to carry her to the bathroom. As he held her, he asked softly, "Will you tell me, Meg? About your dream?"

"There's really not much to tell. It's short, simple. I see your face." She lifted a hand, palm to his cheek. "Your wonderful face. I hear a voice. 'Break the curse. Save his life.' That's all."

"That's all?"

She shrugged. "Except that seeing that face of yours always does something to my insides. It's like every cell in my body recognized you as someone—important to me."

He lowered his eyes.

"You are, Sam. You are so important to me. I know it doesn't make any sense, but—"

He stopped her speech by lifting her head to his and kissing her deeply. She was utterly engulfed in him, held in his arms, possessed by his mouth, her head supported only by the strong, large one that cupped it. It was intoxicating. When he broke the kiss, she was breathless.

"I'll be damned if I'm going to let you get yourself hurt or killed trying to break some fictional curse, much less save my life. I'm a cop, Megan."

"Then maybe you shouldn't be."

He met her eyes, shook his head firmly. "Don't. Don't do that. Don't ruin this by making it about my job, Megan. It's not what I do. It's who I am."

She nodded gently. Getting him to give up his career was not the right approach, she decided. Especially not if it broke the spell between them. "I won't suggest it again," she promised.

"Good." He smiled, letting it go, set her on her feet, and reached past her to turn on the shower.

By midmorning, Megan was in Sam's car again, munching on a cheese Danish and sipping coffee from a Styrofoam cup, actively resisting the urge to talk more about what was going on between them. Where it could be going. She knew he didn't want to. She knew that her uncertainty about their future together—or lack thereof—was nothing compared to his uncertainty about his own future. He wasn't even sure he would be around next week, much less whether he would still want her by then. Besides, she wasn't naive enough to think that one night with her would alter his One-Night Sam persona. Though she liked to think it had. He'd silenced her with a kiss when she had brought it up before, and while she loved his methods, she wondered about his motives.

He stopped at a traffic light and looked at her. "What are you thinking about?"

"About Linda Keller," she lied. "I'm not sure what to say to someone who's been through what she has. Why, what were you thinking about?"

"I was thinking about whether you were going to come home with me again tonight."

She smiled at him, just a little. "Would that make me your first two-night stand?"

He looked at her steadily for a long moment, as if considering his reply. Finally, he said, "You're more than that to me, Megan. Whatever happens, I want to make sure you know that."

His words set her heart racing, both in delight that he seemed to be telling her she meant something to him—and in fear that he was expecting the worst. "Nothing's going to happen to you, Sam."

A horn blew. The light had turned green. He didn't reply, just put the car back into motion.

When they arrived at the hospital, Megan's earlier lie became true. She honestly didn't know what to say to the young woman. But as it turned out, she didn't have to know. When Megan walked into the hospital room, she was at first stunned by the bruises on Linda's pretty face. They hadn't been so colorful last night. Now they were vivid—deep purple, dark blue, nearly black in places. Her shock quickly turned to relief, though, when Linda smiled at her. She was sitting up, the bed in an upright position, one eye still swollen shut, but the other clear and brighter than before. She held out a hand to Megan.

"I'm so glad you came," she said.

Megan's tension faded instantly, and she went to the girl, took her hand, felt only genuine warmth. "I wanted to make sure you were all right."

"I am. I'm going to be fine." She looked down at her hands. "I've only just begun to realize how lucky I am. If this is the same man who killed all those others—" Then she shook herself and snapped her head up again. "But what about you? Are you all right?"

"Of course I am. I'm not the one who was attacked." Megan sat down in the chair beside the bed.

"No. But . . . *something* happened to you out there. When I took your hand, I felt it. Like a jolt zapping from my hand to yours. I know you felt it too. It knocked you flat on your back."

Megan glanced at Sam, who stood near the door. He gave her a nod, silently encouraging her to go on, to tell the girl the truth as she had planned to do. She took strength from his presence, and the look in his eyes—a look that could almost have been described as loving, though she told herself to stop thinking things like that. Then she told herself it was too late.

Megan said, "Linda, sometimes I get . . . well, visions."

"You're psychic?"

She nodded. "Yeah."

"So . . . when I took your hand, in the park, you had a vision?" Meg nodded, and Linda went on. "Wow. That's what knocked you flat? What did you see?"

"I saw what happened to you. Felt it, all of it, as if it were happening to me. Even down to you worrying about your cat."

The girl frowned at her, studying her seriously.

"It was so fast and so unexpected . . . I didn't see anything that could help us identify the man."

"If you were only seeing what I saw, then that makes sense," Linda said. "I didn't either."

"But it was the same for you, sudden, unexpected. And you were terrified."

Linda nodded, averting her face, failing to suppress a shiver.

"We don't have to talk about this now if you don't want to," Megan said.

The girl licked her lips, lifted her eyes again. "It sounds as if you think . . . there's something more you can do."

"There might be. I was thinking if I could hold your hand, and you could try to remember what happened, this time seeing it from a safe place, where you know he can't touch you, well, between the two of us, maybe there is something we can learn. To help the police catch him."

"Before he does this to someone else. Someone who might not be lucky enough to have you two close by to save her."

Megan nodded. "Yes. Yes, exactly that. I know it won't be easy, and that you'd probably rather not think about it at all, but—"

"I can't stop thinking about it. At least this way I can put those thoughts to good use, huh?"

"Maybe."

She nodded again. "What do I have to do?"

Megan got up onto the edge of the girl's bed, clasped both her hands between both of hers. "We need to go back there, together. In your mind. You talk me through it, everything that happened, and remember it as you do. I'll do the rest."

The girl closed her eyes as if searching inwardly for strength. "All right. All right." She took a breath and began, her voice shaky, but determined. "I was running. . . ."

And then Megan was there. Side by side, she and Linda Keller were running along one of the winding paths through the town park. Megan felt the night breeze on her face, the cool air in her lungs, the heat of her body, her own steady footfalls and the other girl's hand in her own.

"Remember, we're safe. This is over, in the past. Nothing can happen to us."

"I know. It's still so scary." The girl's steps slowed, and she came to a stop. "It's up there, right around that bend. He must be hiding behind that tree, there."

Megan strained her eyes, but couldn't see any sign of anyone.

The girl squeezed her hand. "Okay, here we go." And she began running again. They approached the bend, and her grip grew tighter. They started around it, and then Megan felt the powerful arm snap around her neck, jerk her backward to the ground.

"It's not real," she said, though her voice was strained. She was on her back now, and the man was straddling her. His weight on her made it almost impossible to breathe. Beyond the hulking form she saw Linda standing there, a petrified on-looker, still clutching Megan's hand. When the rain of blows fell, Megan's head snapped with every one and pain shot through her, and she heard the girl begin to cry.

"Megan, stop, it's enough!"

That was Sam's voice, and it was rough with emotion.

"It's all right. It's okay," she managed. "Slow it down, Linda. Remember it as if in slow motion."

"I'll try."

And the scene playing out slowed. Megan was able to look up at the dark shape that loomed over her. To see every blow coming at her before feeling its impact. He was bigger than Sam, heavier. She couldn't see his face, only the black ski cap that covered it. The blows came slowly, but she still felt the pain of them. She fought to stay as calm and as cold as ice, even when she felt his hands tearing at her clothes.

She was seeing through only one eye now, as he jammed a hand down her pants, and she gripped his wrist with one hand, just as Linda had, to stop him, touching not the glove he wore, but the skin above it.

Then Sam was there, shouting, and the man tore himself off her and ran.

SAM was on the floor beside Megan, and so was Linda Keller. They'd started out on the bed. Linda had been describing everything that had happened, while holding Meg's hand, but Megan seemed to be the one living it. When Linda got to the point where the man grabbed her from behind, Meg had come off the bed as if jerked from behind herself, hitting the floor back-first. Linda came off the bed with her, grappling to grab hold of her hand again, and Sam rushed to Meg's side, terrified of what he was seeing, Meg jerked her arms up over her face as if warding off blows, and then one hand shot down to clutch at something—at nothing. Just air.

"Megan, honey, come on, it's enough. You're killing yourself with this." He gripped her shoulders, shook them gently. "Meg, I mean it. It's enough, come back!"

Her eyes opened slowly. Sam was shocked to see a trickle of blood coming from her nostril. "Jesus, what the hell?"

She touched the blood, looked at it on her fingertips. "Your body believes what your mind tells it," she whispered. She took a few breaths, seemed to try to shake off the vision. "Mine thinks it just took a beating. This is a little more realism than I expected, but . . ."

He helped her sit up, realized he was shaking as badly as she was. It was as if he'd just witnessed an assault on her by some invisible force. And he realized she was hurting as if that were exactly what had happened. She held a hand to her jaw as he lifted her to her feet, then helped her to the chair. She sank into it.

The girl handed him a box of tissues, then got back up onto her bed. "Megan, did it work? Did you see him?"

Megan lifted her head, clutching a tissue to her nose, while Sam leaned over her, stroking her hair and back and shoulders. It tore him apart to see her going through all of this. He hated it.

"No," Megan said. "But I felt him. You touched him, grabbed his wrist to stop him from groping you. And so I did too. And I felt him."

Linda frowned, looking at Sam. "I don't understand."

"Neither do I," Sam said. "There was no skin under her nails, Meg." He looked at Meg, but she said nothing. "I'm sorry we put you through all that, Linda," he said, without taking his eyes from Megan. "I really think I should get her home."

"Me too," Linda said.

"Will you be okay?" Sam asked, forcing himself to look at the girl.

She nodded. "They're letting me go home today."

Meg came out of her thoughts, and smiled a little. "Roderick will be so glad to see you."

"I know. I miss him." Linda shifted her eyes to Sam's again. "Will I be safe there?"

He nodded. "We'll have a car watching the place, and set you up with a panic button. You hit it, and officers will be there within seconds."

She nodded. "Thank you again." Then she looked at Meg. "I can't believe you put yourself through that once, much less twice. Will she be okay, Detective Sheridan?"

"I'll make sure of it." Sam bent to scoop Megan up, but she shook her head. "I can walk. You go carrying me, they're going to want to check me in."

"Are you sure?"

She nodded, so he held her close, supporting her as they walked slowly out of the room. And then Meg said, "She called you Detective Sheridan. I thought it was 'Officer.'"

He closed his eyes. "It's Detective."

"I didn't think detectives routinely worked traffic," she said.

"They don't." He sighed, wishing this had come at a better time. "Meg, I'm not going to lie to you. The speed trap was a setup. No one believed you knew the things you knew about that last victim through ESP. I was assigned to get to know you, try to find out what was really going on."

She looked as hurt by that revelation as she had been by the attack she'd just experienced. God, she was barely holding her own weight. He felt like the meanest bastard in the world as she stared up at him, her eyes as betrayed as if she were a puppy who'd just been drop-kicked by her beloved master.

"That's what you were keeping from me."

"It doesn't matter, Meg. I believe you now. I do."

"Do you? Or is that just another part of your cover story?" She sighed, her eyes flooding. "And last night? Was that part of your investigation, too?"

"Meg—"

"Oh, God," she whispered, backing away from him as her tears spilled over. "I thought it was real."

"Sam, I need a word." Chief Skinner was in the hospital corridor, waiting for Sam when they came out of Linda Keller's hospital room, demanding his attention.

Sam gave Megan's hand a squeeze. It *was* real, he thought, and he hoped to God she could see his message in his eyes, even though he couldn't say it out loud, not with the chief standing right at his shoulder now. He willed her to see the truth in his eyes. But she only kept backing away, shaking her head from side to side. And then she turned and ran for the elevators.

Chapter Ten

H E was surprised she made it to the elevator without collapsing, and only the chief's firm grip on his shoulder kept him from racing after her.

"Jesus," the chief muttered. "What happened to her?"

Not sure how to answer without losing credibility with the man whose respect he valued above all others, he said, "She took a little fall, that's all. I need to go after her, Chief."

The chief nodded. "Yeah, I know you do. Thirty seconds, okay?"

Sam sent a worried look toward the now closed elevator doors.

"So, are you getting anything out of her?"

"No." He took a step toward the elevator.

The chief put himself right in Sam's path, blocking it. "Then she hasn't come up with anything on the killer?"

"No, nothing yet." It was all he could do not to shove the man aside.

"We didn't find any prints at her house," Ed Skinner said, shaking his head with regret. "Are you sure he was even there, Sam? Hell, she's the only one who saw him. For all we know she could have smashed that window in herself, just as an excuse to make you come running."

Sam frowned deeply, finally focusing on the chief. "She's not the kind of woman who'd do something like that. You don't know her, Chief."

"You don't know her either, Sam. You only met her a few days ago. She probably doesn't seem like the kind of woman who'd hang around with a serial killer either. But she must be, or she wouldn't know what she knows."

Sam licked his lips. "Chief—Ed, I know this is gonna sound crazy, but what if she really does have some kind of . . . ability? What if she's telling the truth about how she knew where that last body was found?"

"I don't buy it," he said.

"Apparently, the killer does. I think that's who was at her house last night. I really do."

"What makes you think so?"

Sam shook his head. "Instinct. And I know she hasn't come up with anything solid yet, Chief, but I think she's close. I think she might just come up with what we need to break this case."

"How? She know what the guy looks like?"

"No. She said she knows what he feels like, though."

"Feels like? I don't get it."

Just then, the elevator doors opened, and Megan came through them and walked up to stand beside Sam. "I was going to wait in the car, but . . . I forgot the keys," she said.

She didn't look good, worse than she had a moment ago, if that were possible. She was pale, and trembling. He reached into his pocket for the keys even as it occurred to him that wasn't why she'd come back. She'd come back because she was hurting bad, and because she needed him. She sagged a little, and reached out a hand to steady herself on the chief's shoulder.

"Hell, Meg, come here." Sam slid his arms around her waist, pulling her against him. "I gotta get her out of here, Chief."

"Yeah. Yeah, you go on," he said. "Feel better, Ms. Rose."

She lifted her head slowly, her eyes finding the chief's, just before Sam helped her back into the elevator. As soon as the doors closed, she slumped in Sam's arms and passed out cold.

He scooped her up, swearing, thought he ought to take her right back in and hand her over to the nearest nurse. But she wasn't suffering from anything physical, he knew that. Not really. She wanted to get out of here, and he was compelled to give her what she wanted. He knew she would be all right in a few minutes. So he ignored his practical mind and heeded his instincts, carrying her out of the elevator when it stopped on the ground level, and then out to his car. He lowered her onto the passenger seat, then knelt in the open doorway, pressing his hands to her face.

"Megan? Honey, come on, are you okay?"

She blinked her eyes slowly at him. "No. Far from it." She looked back toward the hospital suddenly, as if frightened, and he followed her gaze, only to see his boss, the chief, leaving through the same doors they'd just exited, heading for his car in some other part of the lot.

"Get me out of here, Sam," she whispered.

"Okay. All right." God, they had to talk. He had to explain himself to her, but he'd like her at least coherent when he did. And he wasn't even entirely sure just what it was he was going to say. "Do you want to go back to my place, or to yours?"

She stared into his eyes. "I need to see your grandmother."

Sam was tempted to check her for a fever, or ask how many fingers as he held a couple up in front of her. "I'm not following."

"Neither am I."

"You know something. Or you think you do. What is it, Megan?"

She swallowed hard, nodded slowly. "Chief Skinner—" she began. And as if saying his name invoked him somehow, the chief's car passed by on its way out of the parking lot, and Sam saw him staring at the two of them.

"What about him?" Sam asked as he waved at his trusted friend.

"He's the rapist. He's the killer."

Sam's hand froze in midair. He felt his face change with

the shock of her words, and quickly shot her a look of sheer disbelief. "Don't be ridiculous—hell, Megan, did you hit your head or something back there?"

"It's him. I touched him, and I saw it, felt it. It's him, Sam."

He swung his head toward the chief's car as the man drove away, and caught him looking back, his face troubled.

"No. No way, you're wrong. You're dead wrong about this, Meg."

"I know I'm right. And there's more, but I . . . I have to see Lily before I can be sure."

He shook his head. "He's been my mother's best friend since my father . . . I'm sorry, Meg, but I can't let you go making all kinds of crazy accusations to my family. He's practically a *part* of my family, for God's sake." Then he looked at her again. "It's Lily who put this crazy notion into your head, isn't it? She's never liked him. And now you want to go making some wild accusations that will convince her she's been right all along."

"Maybe Lily never liked him because she's slightly psychic herself. She calls it intuition. Whatever it is, somehow she knows he's rotten inside. Evil." She pressed a hand to Sam's face when he looked away from her. "Sam, look at me. You know I wouldn't repeat any of this to your family. And no, it isn't coming from Lily and I'm not going to make any accusations to her or to anyone else. Only you, Sam. I can't not tell you this. Not this. Because . . . because all of a sudden, I understand what it means."

"You're three steps ahead of me, then. What does it mean?"

She held his face between her palms. "There's no curse. There never was."

He was having trouble trying to follow her as her train of thought seemed to jump the tracks. And focusing on her words was damn near impossible when she was touching him, when her mouth was so close to his and her eyes were sparkling the way they were. "No curse?"

She smiled softly. "No curse." Then her smile died as she looked past him, and her eyes widened. "He's coming back."

Sam turned to see the chief's car rolling back into the parking lot.

"Sam, we have to get out of here!"

She was terrified, clearly, of his boss and mentor and friend. And it made no sense at all, but something wouldn't let him brush it off. He didn't believe any of it, but for Megan, he would give her the benefit of the doubt. Act as if there were some remote chance she could be right. Because he believed in her. "We're going," he promised. "Buckle up, Meg."

He closed her door, went around to his side, got in, and got going.

On their way out they passed the chief in his car. He watched them closely, didn't return Sam's friendly wave or his forced smile. Something was off, something was wrong.

"Sam, we have to keep him away from Linda Keller."

"He already knows Linda didn't see anything. Even if he was our boy—and I gotta tell you, Meg, there's no way in hell he is—but even if he was, Linda would pose no threat to him." He glanced back to watch the chief's car, in spite of himself. "And even if she did, he wouldn't do anything at the hospital. Not when she lives alone, and is being released today."

And yet he watched. The chief's car only circled the lot and left it again. "Look, he's not even stopping."

Megan was watching too. "He only came back to see what we were doing. He's checking up on us, Sam. He may realize we're on to him."

"We're not on to him."

"You're not. I am. And I think your father was, too."

"My . . ." He couldn't talk for a second. It was as if her words stole his breath. He managed to catch it and tried again. "You think my father believed this? Jesus, Megan, he was a cop. If he thought his own partner was a violent criminal he'd have turned him in, no matter how close they were."

"Yeah. Exactly. So Skinner would have made sure he never got the chance."

"No. No, no way was Ed involved in my father's death. They were like brothers, Megan."

"Lily said your father had been acting oddly for a week prior to his death. Don't you want to know why?"

He stared at her, and something icy cold seemed to solidify over his chest as he finally considered how easy it would have been. His father and Ed Skinner had been the only two cops on the scene of that liquor store robbery. And Ed Skinner had been the only survivor left to tell the story.

He tried to shake off the chilling feeling. "There could have been a hundred reasons for him to have been acting off-kilter that week."

"You're right. There could have been." She covered his hand with hers. "Lily told me your mother hasn't changed a thing in your father's den since he died. That it's like a shrine to him in there."

Sam nodded as he drove. "It was always off-limits to the rest of the family, that den. Mom still doesn't let anyone in there. Guards it like a lioness. She's the only one who can go inside. Says she feels closer to Dad when she spends time in the den."

"Has she ever let Skinner inside?"

He shook his head. "Never."

"Has he ever asked?"

Sam blinked, recalling how determined Ed had been to get into his father's private den right around the time of the funeral. Hell, it had been a source of added worry to his mother, and had infuriated Lily. He slanted a look at Megan. "Actually, he did. Right after Dad's death. Something about some missing files that pertained to a case they'd been working on."

"And did your mother let him go in?"

"No. As I remember it, she told him she had gone through the room from top to bottom and had boxed up everything that had to do with work. She gave that box of files to Ed." He tried to swallow but the memories seemed to be drying out his throat. "It was odd, he asked her if she'd read through them. He seemed almost—scared. When she said she had been a po-liceman's wife long enough to know better than to snoop through private files, he seemed satisfied, took the box, and as far as I know, he never asked again."

Megan nodded slowly. "I wonder if he found the evidence your father had on him in those files."

"Megan, this is all speculation on your part."

She held his eyes, and he thought maybe she could see that he was trying to convince himself as much as her. She didn't even waver. "We need to convince your mother to let us go through that room, Sam. I don't know how I know it, but I do. If there's anything to find, your father left it in there for us."

"She'll never agree to that," he said.

Megan lowered her eyes.

Sam drew a breath. Everything in him was telling him to trust her. To believe her. And he was damned if he had it in him to do otherwise. "All right, Meg. If you feel this strongly, we'll do it."

She looked up at him, an emotion he couldn't name shining from her eyes. "You believe me?"

"I trust you like I've never trusted anyone. If you say we need to check it out, we need to check it out, Megan." He saw the tears gathering, and then it hit him why she was reacting so strongly to him believing the unbelievable at nothing more than her word. "I'm not your father, Megan."

She smiled. It was shaky, unsteady, and wet. "No, you're not even close."

There was so much more to say, so much to explain. But she didn't give him the chance. "How are we going to get in if your mother won't agree to let us?"

He glanced at the clock on the radio dial. "She'll be out all morning. Volunteers at the Ladies' Auxiliary till noon. If we're lucky, Lily is with her. She often goes along."

He drove her to his mother's house, the house where he had grown up. And while he was at it, he phoned the hospital and spoke to the guard on Linda Keller's room, told him not to let anyone, including police officers, even the chief himself, be alone with her and to delay her release from the hospital until further notice.

Then he pulled his car into the familiar driveway. The house was a big old Victorian, and his parents had lived in it for as long as he could remember. It had changed very little over the years.

Meg seemed to have recovered, physically, during the course of the drive. Still, he held her arm as he led her up the walk to the front door. *She* might be feeling better, but he wasn't sure *he* was over seeing her take a phantom beating, and pass out like that, much less hearing the things she had to say afterward.

"Lily's not home, either," he said, deducing as much from the fact that the door was locked. "She refuses to live behind locked doors. If she were here, it would have been open."

Megan nodded, and he led the way into the house. He looked around first, making utterly sure they were alone, before leading the way down a hall, to a closed door. Then he paused, hesitated.

"It's not easy, is it?"

He turned to face Megan, saw her looking into his eyes. "Mom would consider it a betrayal, my bringing you here. Invading Dad's space."

"I wouldn't ask if I didn't feel it was vital, Sam."

He nodded. "I know that. And I wouldn't bring any other woman in here. Dad . . . Dad would be rolling over in his grave if I did. But somehow—I just don't think he'd mind so much with you."

"There's something in there he wants us to find. Maybe even needs us to find."

Sighing, Sam nodded and turned to face the door again. His hands felt clammy and his heart heavy as he inserted the key into the lock.

Chapter Eleven ❧

Sam opened the door to his father's den, and was immediately transported backward in time. He was seven years old again, tapping on the door of his father's inner sanctum, waiting without drawing a breath until that deep, powerful voice, laced with just a hint of laughter, called, "Hmm, if it's important enough to interrupt my quiet time, it must be pretty important. Come on in, then."

He looked at Megan, saw her watching him, feeling what he felt. "Dad usually stole a half hour a day in his den," he told her. "It was off-limits to us kids, to everyone except Mom. He didn't even bring his friends in here."

She nodded as if she understood. "It's okay, Sam. Take your time."

Stepping further into the room surrounded Sam in the very essence of his father. He could smell old cigar smoke, and expensive leather, and aging books. So much his dad, those smells. "God, no wonder Mom likes to come in here sometimes, just to sit alone."

"It's bringing back a lot of memories for you, isn't it?" Megan put a hand on his arm as she asked the question.

"It's like he never left. Like he could just walk in here like he used to, pick up where he left off."

"You loved him a lot."

He nodded. "Still do."

"He'd be proud of you, Sam. He is. I feel it."

He met Megan's eyes. Could she know what her saying that meant to him? Yeah, he thought. She knew. He'd never been with a woman who knew him the way Megan did.

"Sam, if he had kept anything related to work, private files or cases he was working on . . ."

"Mom found everything he had here, gave it to Ed."

She tipped her head. "Probably. But there's a chance she could have missed something. She must have, because I feel very strongly there's something here. So where would he have kept them?"

Sam shrugged and looked around the room. The big oak desk took up most of one wall, face out, a chair behind it, so his father could sit there and work and still see the TV set. It held an oversized IBM Selectric typewriter with the cover securely in place, a leather blotter, an earthenware mug full of pens and pencils, a stack of blank sheets of paper, a paperweight—clear acrylic with a forever-frozen spider inside, a Father's Day gift from Sam—and a couple of framed photos of the family, as they had been many years ago.

"I don't know. The desk I suppose." He moved behind his father's desk and opened its drawers. None were locked, but then there was no reason why they should be. He didn't find anything like what they were looking for in any of them, but the small center drawer's contents brought him up short.

It held his father's badge.

"I know this is hard for you, Sam. I'm sorry. God, I'm so sorry to put you through this."

"I know you are." He took the badge out and held it in his hands as he moved from the desk to the file cabinet, which was nearly empty. The badge was in a folder the size of a wallet, with his father's photo ID card on one side and his badge on the other. He couldn't stop looking at it as he searched the room. Within a few minutes, he realized Meg wasn't joining him in the search. Instead she was standing patiently aside, while he checked all the obvious places. She seemed engrossed in the family photos on the desk.

She felt his eyes on her and looked up, meeting them; she offered him a sad smile. "Your father was a handsome man. You look like him."

"Think so?"

"Mm-hmm."

"You can help me look, Meg."

"It feels like a sacrilege," she said softly. But she joined him in the search, even crouched down to look under the sofa and chair, while Sam checked beneath the cushions. He felt the backing and upholstery for unusual lumps or bulges. Nothing.

It was while he was performing that last little function that he dropped his father's badge on the floor. Meg was on her hands and knees peering under the chair, and it fell right beside her hand. Naturally, she stopped what she was doing and picked it up, looking at it, her eyes somber as she rose to her feet.

And then her head snapped backward so hard Sam thought she might have wrenched her neck. Her eyes widened and rolled back, and she staggered backward until her body slammed into the bookcase.

"Jesus, Megan." Sam went to her, reached out to her, but she spun away from him, her arms flailing and knocking books to the floor.

"Easy, Megan, easy."

"No, no, no!"

She wasn't seeing him, wasn't hearing him, he realized. She was seeing something else. Some vision brought on by the touch of his father's badge.

God, he was almost afraid to speculate. . . .

Meg backed into a corner and sank to the floor, curling her legs up to her chest, hugging them and rocking. Sam knelt beside her, touching her. "Megan," he said. "It's okay, baby, it's okay. I'm right here." He stroked her hair away from her face. But she didn't seem to feel him, didn't see him, was beyond his reach, and clutching his father's badge in a death grip.

He could do nothing but leave her alone until it passed. She seemed to need space to recover. So he backed off, turning to return the books to the shelf and minimize his mother's outrage at his invasion of what was, to her, sacred space. But when he lifted the first several volumes to the shelf, he stopped and just stood there, blinking.

In the space left by the fallen books, there appeared to be a false bottom on the bookshelf. He could see the fissures on either side of a short expanse of the wood. And when he gripped it and tugged, it came away, revealing a shoebox-sized compartment underneath. Inside that compartment was a manila envelope, folded in half, lengthwise, and tucked out of sight.

He gently pulled the envelope free, swallowing hard as he turned it over. But before he could examine the contents, Megan's blood-chilling scream split the silence.

MEGAN shook off the debilitating impact of the vision and shot to her feet when she saw Chief Skinner walk through the door into the room. She tried to form words to warn Sam, but couldn't seem to make her lips form anything coherent, and finally poured every ounce of energy she had into warning him in any way she could, clenching her fists, opening her mouth, forcing sound to come. The result was a scream.

Sam spun around, wide-eyed, an envelope in his hands, but it was too late. Skinner had already drawn his weapon and was pointing it at Sam. "I'll take that file, Sam."

"Ed, what the hell is going on here?" Sam asked.

The chief looked momentarily confused, then angry. "Trying to pretend you haven't already figured it out isn't going to help."

"No, it didn't help his father after all. Did it, Chief?" Megan asked from behind him. She'd found her voice. It was weak, shaky, far softer than normal, but at least she could put words together now.

The chief turned his head slightly. "Get over there next to him." He directed her with his gun.

She stayed where she was, lowering her gaze to the badge she held in her hand. "I know what you did that night at the liquor store. I saw it, all of it."

"You don't know a damn thing, Ms. Rose."

She looked past him, met Sam's eyes. "They got the call. Armed robbery in progress, and they went over there. To the liquor store. It was called Joe's Wine and Spirits. There were tubes of red neon in the shape of a giant wine bottle in the front window. I don't think it's there anymore."

"No. They closed it after . . ."

"Your father went around the back. Skinner went in through the front. The place was empty except for those two kids and the clerk, who was lying on the floor, unconscious, bleeding, maybe already dead. It was the perfect opportunity, wasn't it, Chief?"

"What did you do?" Sam asked.

"Pulled his gun and shot both of the suspects," Megan said softly. "Never shouted a warning. They didn't even know he'd come inside. Your father heard the shots, came in to help. He saw that his friend had it under control, and he lowered his weapon." She narrowed her eyes on Skinner. "That's when you took the gun from one of the boys you'd killed, pointed it right at your best friend, saw the shock and horror in his eyes, and shot him down. Pumped three bullets into his head."

"Stop it!" Skinner cried.

"Jesus, Ed," Sam whispered. "Why? My God, why?"

Skinner faced him again. "Because of that file you have in your hands. All this time, it never surfaced. I figured it never would. Your mother gave me everything that was in this room. When I didn't find the evidence there, I thought maybe I'd been wrong. Maybe he really didn't have anything on me after all. Maybe I killed him for nothing."

His eyes turned distant, pain-filled.

"And that's why you took care of us, stepped into Dad's shoes the way you did," Sam said. "It was guilt." He shook his head. "And you're gonna make the same mistake now that you thought you'd made then, Ed. Because I don't even know what's in this file, and neither does Megan."

He lifted his brows. "You really don't know?"

Megan could see Sam trying to inch his hand toward his gun. But he couldn't do it with the other man's eyes on him.

"Oh, come on, Sam," she said. "You can guess, can't you?" The chief turned his attention her way. "Skinner is the man who's been raping and murdering girls in town. And I suspect he was doing it long before the police realized they had a serial killer on their hands." She added, "He knew someone was on to him when I phoned the police with that tip on where the next body would be found."

"I still don't believe you have any so-called psychic powers. But I had to find out for sure," Skinner said.

"So you assigned Sam to get close to me, try to find out how much I really did know and how I knew it. That way you could keep an eye on both of us."

"None of this is relevant," Skinner said. He swung his gaze back to Sam's, held out his free hand. "Give me the file, Sam."

Sam held it out. Skinner reached for it, and seemed to realize at that moment that Sam's gun was no longer in its holster. "Don't, Sam!"

Skinner lifted his own gun higher, even as Sam brought his around from behind his back. It all seemed to happen in slow motion, barrels pointing, fingers squeezing, shots exploding, muzzles flashing.

Megan launched herself, hitting Skinner in the side just as his gun went off, so that he stumbled and fell. Rolling onto his back, he turned his weapon on her.

"No!" Sam shouted.

Skinner's gun bucked in his hand. The shot exploded in a deafening roar, and Megan felt the blaze of red hot metal slice through her midsection; she doubled over at the impact long before she felt the pain. She lifted her head, shocked, stunned. Skinner was taking aim, would have shot her again if not for the shot Sam fired that made the chief's head snap backward, leaving a neat hole between his eyes. His body went lax, his arm and gun dropping to the floor, and then he was still.

"For the love of God, what's going on?" someone cried. Megan heard feet crashing through the house, female voices crowding around her. But Sam was her only focus. He knelt beside her, his face stricken.

"Megan, hold on." Without looking away from her he told his mother, grandmother, whoever was within earshot, to call 911. "Tell them there's an officer down," he said. "It's the truth, and it'll get them here faster." He added that last with a meaningful look at Skinner.

Then he was leaning over her again, holding a hand to her belly, where she felt warmth and pulsing wetness. "Don't leave me, Megan. Hold on."

She smiled softly, staring up at him. "Guess I was another one-night stand after all, huh?"

"No. Not by a long shot." He held her desperately. "Jesus, Megan, you have to know I wasn't pretending. Not from the first second I set eyes on you. This is real, this thing between us."

Her hand closed around his. "I know that, Sam."

"The curse is lifted," Lily said in her raspy voice, from somewhere nearby. "The girl broke it, exposed it, took it upon herself."

"There was never any curse, Grams. Skinner killed Dad."

"And would have killed you too, if not for this woman and her gift." She knelt on Megan's other side. "Bless you, child."

Meg smiled, shifting her gaze from the old woman's back to Sam's again. "Finally did something important with my abilities. Finally got someone to believe me."

"Yeah. And I will never, ever doubt you or your visions, Meg. I promise." He leaned closer and pressed his lips to hers, and she kissed him back until the darkness swallowed her up.

Epilogue

Megan was in the darkness, and it occurred to her that she might be dead. Oddly, she felt no terrible grief or resistance to that idea. She had reached one of the most important goals of her life—she'd understood, at last, why she had been given these powers. What earthly use they could be to anyone. They had been useful. Vital. They had saved an entire family, broken a curse, of sorts, solved a string of murders, prevented who knew how many other women from being victimized by Ed Skinner. And maybe kept Sam Sheridan from an early death. God, that was worth anything, wasn't it?

He'd believed in her, in her gift. So had his grandmother. And so had she.

That was all she had ever wanted. Validation. Respect. And the chance to use her gift for something good.

"I love you, Megan."

No, not love. She'd never asked for that. Just to be believed, just to be useful, just—

"Do you hear me? I love you. I've never said that to a woman before, and I'm not about to lose the only one. I want you back. I want you to stay with me. Always."

Sensation seemed to return by degrees. She became aware of a warm, strong hand holding hers. And she opened her eyes, and stared up into a pair of familiar, loving ones.

"There you are," Sam whispered. "You gonna stick around, then?"

"I think so."

He squeezed her hand, and a vision flashed, making her suck in a breath and close her eyes, just briefly.

He frowned at her, his face filled with worry. "What is it, honey? What are you seeing?"

She drew her brows together, wondering if she should tell him what she had seen. The two of them in a photo a lot like the ones on his father's desk, with two little angels standing in front of them, golden ringlets and strawberry curls. A boy and a girl. She smiled and knew she still had a whole lot left to do in this lifetime.

"Meg? You gonna tell me what you saw?"

She blinked and met his eyes, saw the love in them, knew it was going to last. "You parked in a terrible spot. You're going to get a ding in the Mustang."

Sam smiled slowly. "That's my Megan."

"Yours?"

"Oh, yeah. And I'm not leaving this room, even if someone's going to total the Mustang."

"No?"

"No. And as long as you're still having visions, I'd like you to try one on for size, will you do that for me?"

"I . . . guess I could try."

He nodded, taking both her hands in his. "Look into the future, honey. See if you can make out a long and happy one— one you'll be spending with me."

"I don't need any psychic skills at all to see that, Sam. If we want it, we can make it happen."

"I want it, Megan. Do you?"

"With all my heart."

He leaned closer and pressed his lips to hers. "Then that's the way it's going to be."

Shocking Lucy

SUZANNE FORSTER

Chapter One ✑

"No, please! Don't touch that thing!" Lucy Sexton was only half-kidding as she scurried through the men's section of Blanchard's department store and seized the last attaché on the display. She'd been shopping all morning, searching for exactly this elegant Cavalli calfskin case. Now, finally, Frederick would be happy, and she could relax.

She hugged the case to her chest and nodded reassuringly at the shoppers who hazarded a glance her way. Probably thought she was crazy, but they didn't know how hard these cases were to come by—or how picky Frederick could be. No. Discriminating. Her fiancé was discriminating. And a very sweet man, really.

Still hugging her prize, she headed over to the counter to pay for it. And if a checkerboard pattern hadn't caught her eye, she might have made it there. The new Hermès ties for fall? Was that really a checkered Hermès on the rack? Frederick loved them, and this one was perfect for him. Black and silver, his favorite colors. If she bought the tie, she could slip it inside the attaché case when she gave him the gift.

Should she? They were so expensive.

She abandoned the attaché on the nearest counter for just a second to rub the cool silk between her fingers. She was already over her wedding budget, and she and her mom were footing the entire bill. She shouldn't be considering anything extra, even if it was her gift to Frederick. Her mother had recently made her a full partner to celebrate the success of their mediation company, but there'd been plenty of lean years when they didn't know where the rent was coming from.

She draped the tie around her neck and began to loop it into a knot. Did she remember how to tie these things? She peered into a countertop mirror. Over, under, and then what?

"Oh, excuse me!" she said as someone bumped her from behind. She turned to see an alarmingly tall stranger manhandling her attaché.

"Sir, I'm sorry. That's my case."

The man seemed perplexed. Lucy noted marine blue eyes and a flash of straight white teeth as he smiled. Rolled-up denim shirtsleeves revealed strong tanned arms. Chestnut brown. Outdoor work?

"Handsome is as handsome does," she murmured.

"Excuse me?"

"Oh, nothing." She shrugged it off. "Just something my mom used to say."

Actually, Lydia Sexton used to say it a lot. And mostly about men with dreamy blue eyes and heartbreaker smiles. Her mother would not have approved of this guy, just on principle. Still, Lucy was secretly glad she'd worn her wool jersey wrap dress today instead of her usual gray blazer and slacks. At Frederick's suggestion she'd been trying for a more sophisticated look, which included taming her unruly dark auburn waves with a no-nonsense claw clip.

"The case still has the tags on it," he said. "How could it be yours?"

"I picked it out. I was just on my way up to pay for it."

He turned the case over. "Doesn't look like it belongs to anybody."

Lucy felt a ping of exasperation. "It's a gift for my fiancé—my wedding gift to him—and he specifically asked for a Cavalli. Could I please have it back?"

The case ended up under his arm. "We may have a problem," he said. "I've been looking for one of these, too."

"You?" She raked him over with her gaze, inspecting him from the shock of dark hair that fell onto his forehead with reckless disregard for his vision to the scuffed toes of his work boots. Work boots? He was wearing torn jeans and a tool belt, too. You didn't see a lot of that in the men's section of Blanchard's. Too bad, she thought, resisting a smile. It was sexy as hell.

"Why would you need an attaché?"

"To visit my Swiss bank account. Never judge a guy by his tools." He returned her skepticism with a hint of amusement. "Why do you need a tie?"

"Oh!" Lucy pulled the checkered silk from around her neck and offered it to him. "I'll trade you," she said, boldly taking hold of the case's handle. "The tie for the attaché. Can I have it back?"

He held fast to the attaché. "This is for your fiancé?"

"Yes, please!"

"He doesn't need it."

"He doesn't? Why?"

"He has you. What else could he possibly want?"

His blue gaze was so intent that Lucy felt her stomach go hollow, and the attaché slip from her grasp.

"Thank you," he said. "That's very generous of you."

"No, wait! Frederick really wants that case. He even suggested this store."

"Tell Frederick I'll trade him." With that he gazed straight into her eyes, giving her a thrill that could have rivaled the explosion of confetti on Time's Square at New Year's Eve. If she'd let it.

"Trade him what?"

"The briefcase for you."

Lucy might have been shaking her head. She wasn't sure.

"No deal?" At least he had the decency to look disappointed

as he waited for her reply. "My loss," he said softly. With that, he gave her a nod, turned, and headed for the counter with her precious gift.

Watching him whip out a money clip brought her back to life. "You want him to trade me for a briefcase? Be serious."

He glanced at her, the heartbreaker smile tinged with irony. "Maybe I should sweeten the deal? How about an hour of your time?"

Lucy realized she was negotiating with a total stranger in the middle of Blanchard's. They were twenty feet away from each other—and miles outside her comfort zone.

"Never mind," she said, unable to disguise her sharp disappointment. "Enjoy your new briefcase." She turned away to begin the search for another gift. Frederick would just have to get over it. Maybe cuff links would ease his pain.

She was looking through the glass case at a pair of gold and silver links when she felt another bump from behind. She didn't excuse herself this time. A second bump turned her around, ready to give the rude person a stern look. *Excuse me? There's plenty of room in this store for both of us.*

"You?" she said under her breath. He'd been waiting for her to turn. She could tell by his expectant smile. "What's your problem?"

He held out a purple and gold Blanchard's bag. "I don't ever want to make anyone look that unhappy. That's my problem."

Lucy peeked inside the bag and saw the attaché. "Did you buy this?"

"Call it a wedding gift," he said. "Your fiancé is lucky to have someone who cares so much about him."

She took the bag from him, aware of his outstretched palm and how the purple satin rope handle dangled from his fingers. They were long and calloused at the tips, those fingers, as golden brown as toast drizzled with honey. You had to wonder about what those hands would feel like scraping your soft skin. You just had to.

"I'll pay you for it, of course," she said.

He shook his head. "Take it with my blessings. Be happy."

"Why are you doing this?"

"I told you. I didn't want to be the cause of your unhappiness."

"Would you like the tie?" Lucy didn't know what else to say.

"No, I'll live without the tie."

A subtle smile sent tension rippling through his jaw and made the blue of his eyes look smoky hot. Lucy watched the changes with fascination. He seemed to return her interest, and their gazes locked for long enough to make her want to look away. Instead she found herself smiling back at him as he nodded a good-bye and left her standing there with his bag. When he got to the door, he stopped and turned, as if for one last look at her. His expression seemed to say the tie was easy. It would be much harder living without her.

Now there was a fantasy. Where did she get *that* from?

Lucy took the case from the bag, wondering why she wasn't thrilled to have it. She ought to have run after him and insisted on paying him back. He couldn't just hand her an expensive attaché like this and leave. Instead, she watched him disappear from sight with a sense of loss that left her confused. Her thoughts were all aflutter. Her heart was pinging. This was the most excitement she'd had in ages. Really.

The case for an hour of your time?

What was he going to do with her for an hour?

Her mind started to run with that one, and she felt herself getting breathless just standing still. But within seconds she had talked herself out of any romantic notions. The man was a total stranger, and obviously some kind of rogue. Look at those eyes! In her mind they were still as bright as a sunlit bay. *Handsome is as handsome does.*

She had the case. She had Frederick. Of course she would be happy.

"YOU'RE all sparkly this afternoon. What's up?"

Lucy plunked her packages on the table and sank into one of the vinyl chairs, watching her mother make a fresh pot of coffee for the company lounge. "Really?" she said. "Sparkly? I've been shopping for Frederick."

"Oh, poor baby."

"Now, Mom, don't start that. In two weeks, Frederick will be your son-in-law."

Lydia Sexton looked around at her daughter, concern in her sapphire blue eyes. At fifty-three she was still strikingly beautiful—and ageless except for the pearl gray hair cut close to her head.

"I just don't understand what the rush is, Lucy."

"Rush?" Lucy blinked. "We've been engaged four years."

Lydia brought two huge mugs and sat down at the table across from Lucy. The steam pouring off the freshly brewed coffee was redolent of amaretto and cream, her mother's favorite flavor. A mug with the company logo came sliding across the table at Lucy. She caught it and knew without looking that her mother had a contagious smile on her face.

Lucy rolled her eyes, fighting an answering grin. She lost, of course. This was their ritual, and it had nothing to do with Frederick. Not so very long ago, Sexton Mediation Services couldn't afford personalized mugs or specialty coffee. They couldn't even afford an office. Now they had a suite of offices, a full complement of mediators, and a top-flight clerical staff—and, given her mother's penchant for it, probably every flavor of gourmet coffee known to humankind.

"Where is everyone?" Lucy asked, checking her watch. It was lunchtime, but some of the crew usually brown-bagged it and ate in the lounge. Lucy's assistant, Valerie, was one of those, and Lucy needed to ask about a rescheduled appointment for a divorce mediation.

"That training seminar on office communication," her mother said. "We gave everyone the afternoon off to attend."

"Oh, of course, it's Tuesday." Lucy slapped her head. She really was distracted.

"Lucy?" Her mother laced her fingers around the mug and leaned forward, a pleading tone in her voice. "Hold out for the man of your dreams, darling. Frederick doesn't make you sparkle, and he never will."

Lucy sighed. "Mom, I don't want to sparkle. I want appliances that sparkle. I want a kitchen that sparkles. Frederick can give me that."

"You can give *yourself* that. You just bought yourself a condo. Buy another one. You don't need Frederick for that."

"I don't want two homes. I want one home, one husband, and at least two children. I'm thirty years old and I want a family. But most of all, I want a husband who'll be there when his kids are growing up."

Her mother blew on her coffee. "No one understands that better than I do, dear. I just don't want you to make the same mistake I did." She brought the cup to her mouth and took a pensive sip.

Lucy wished there was something she could say to ease her mother's mind. Her parents had divorced when Lucy was eleven, and her mother had never remarried. Bart Sexton had betrayed his wife in so many ways, including stealing from the hardware store her father left her, that she was unwilling to let another man into her life.

Lucy had never blamed her for that, especially considering all the sacrifices her mother made. She'd gone back to school in her thirties, earned degrees in both communications and law, and started the mediation company. She'd thrown herself into it, working brutal hours to secure a better future for herself and her daughter. But sadly, now that she'd achieved success beyond her dreams, and brought Lucy in as a partner, she had regrets.

She looked up from her coffee. "I missed out on too much," she said. "But what haunts me most is that you grew up without a father and a stable family life."

Lucy's shrug said Look at me, I'm *fine.* "It doesn't seem to have done me any permanent damage. Hey, I just want the same things for my kids that you wanted for me. That's why I'm marrying Fred."

Lydia Sexton looked as if she might cry, which wasn't like her at all. "Lucy, are you certain he's the man you want to be with the rest of your life? If you are, I'll shut up. You have my word. I'll support you and Frederick one hundred percent."

Lucy reached over and gave her mother's hand a squeeze. "I'm not only certain, I can prove it to you. Give me a sec." She turned and started rummaging.

"You know, sometimes it's good to be a packrat," she said as she found her purse in the clutter of shopping bags she'd left on the table. She pulled out her wallet and retrieved a folded square of paper. "Came across this list in my college yearbook. I went through it to be sure I hadn't excluded any old friends from the guest list for the wedding."

Lucy waved the tattered notebook paper. "Tah-dah! Exhibit A. One dateless Saturday night, a few of my girlfriends and I decided to get even with all the campus zeros who hadn't asked us out."

Lydia smiled. "Really, and how did you do that?"

"By coming up with the top ten traits of the perfect male. Fantasy Dude, we called him. We each made lists and compiled the data. Very scientific, huh? Our perfect male had a great smile, a great car, a great job, and so on and so on."

"But that's not *your* perfect male," her mother pointed out.

"I know." Lucy carefully opened the folds and smoothed the paper. "What I have here is my original list. This is Lucy's Fantasy Dude. Ready?"

She ticked the first three off in a singsong voice. " 'Great smile, great job, great car.' Okay, so I wasn't an original thinker. But, listen to this. 'Urbane sense of humor, snappy dresser, good social skills.' That's Fred to a tee."

"Fred is snappy," Lydia conceded.

" 'Sweet and attentive,' " Lucy read in a bright tone. "Can't argue that."

"I could, but I won't."

"*Thank you.* These next two are body parts." She grinned. " 'Nice hands, cute tush.' Fred's tush isn't bad."

Before Lydia could comment, Lucy raced through the last three. " 'Good morals, values, and goals,' " she said, folding up the list with a pleased smile. "That's my Fred, solid as a rock. There's not a dishonest bone in the man's body. And more important, he's what I want. He's what I've *always* wanted."

"That's the whole list?" her mother asked, looking skeptical.

"Mmm, there's one more, but it doesn't count."

"What's that?"

Lucy wrinkled her nose and unfolded the list. "It's only on here because the other girls had it on their lists, and I didn't want them to think I was weird."

"What is it?"

"Great kisser."

"Nothing wrong with that. What's your definition of a great kisser?"

"I don't know. Someone who makes me shiver and gives me goose bumps, I guess."

"*Really?* Frederick gives you goose bumps?"

"No, but the Fantasy Dude does. Or would, if he existed. But it really shouldn't count. It's on the list under false pretenses."

Her mother had that look. "Has anyone *ever* made you shiver, Lucy?"

"*Mom.*" Lucy's mind paid an unbidden visit to Blanchard's, and her chance encounter with a stranger whose gaze had reached so deeply into hers that she'd felt "seen" for the first time in her life. Who was he, and why had he singled out her? The attaché couldn't have been the only reason. If it had, he wouldn't have given it back to her.

A sensation of cold made her clutch her arms. No, it was heat. Strange. Could you burn and freeze at the same time? Her stomach had that feeling of confetti being tossed high in the air.

Lucy felt her mother's eyes on her. She'd rarely been able to hide anything from the woman who raised her, but she had no intention of admitting these feelings. Her mother was at a different place in her life. She might even be ready to take some risks again, but Lucy wasn't. Her father's failings had devastated her—not because he'd let her down, but because she felt responsible. Once, in a fit of anger, he'd told her that she was an accident, and he'd never really wanted children. After that she'd always wondered if she was the cause of the troubles between her parents. It was a heavy burden, and she didn't want her own children to go through anything like that.

Frederick was nothing like her father, and if he wasn't spot-on the man of her dreams, he was close enough.

"Are you all right, Lucy?"

"Yes, why?"

"You have that secretive look about you again, the one I saw when you walked through the door. What's going on?"

"I probably need to visit the john. You'll excuse me." Lucy was tucking the list back in her wallet when her mother tweaked it out of her hand.

"Not so fast, child of mine." Lydia settled back in her chair. She looked over the ten traits with an air of perplexity. "It's a fine list, but everything on it is designed to make you feel safe."

"And what's wrong with safe?"

Her mother tapped a finger against her lips, thinking. "Nothing, as long as it doesn't smother the life right out of you. Did you catch the way you reacted when you read this last one—'Great kisser'?"

"Kissing isn't such a big deal."

"It is when his kisses make you shiver. A man like that doesn't make you feel safe, Lucy. He makes you feel alive."

Lucy tweaked the list from her mother's hand, plucked up her bags and her purse, and without another word, made her escape. Some people didn't know when to stop.

"Any chance I'm right, Luce? Hey, Luce Caboose? Think about it!"

Lucy was already out the coffee lounge door, but her mother's words followed her down the hall as she headed for her office.

You might be. You just might be. I met a man today who made me sparkle, and I didn't hate it. She was just grateful her mother couldn't see her smiling now.

Chapter Two

LUCY glanced over at the passenger seat of her Chevy Blazer, where the attaché sat, looking as superior as a piece of luggage could possibly look. She'd had a crisis of conscience this morning when she woke up. She couldn't give the case to Frederick as a gift. What was she supposed to do, pretend it was from her? She had to return it, but to whom?

Hopefully the clerk at Blanchard's would be able to hunt down the man who gave it to her and make arrangements to return it to him. Then Lucy could get on with her life. As it was, she hadn't thought about much else since the incident happened—and she had plenty of other things to think about. Maybe her period was due. She'd been feeling a little puffy, and that would explain why she was so flighty and distracted. If anything about her was sparkling at this point, it was her overstimulated nervous system. She just wanted to give the briefcase back and be done with it.

The digital clock on the dash said nine A.M. as she let herself out of the car and grabbed the attaché, along with the bag it came in. The mall had just opened, and the lot was nearly empty so things looked good for getting in and out quickly.

She had meetings stacked up with staff, as well as clients, plus an appointment with the wedding planner this morning.

She tugged down the skirt of her summery cotton sheath. Mid-September was a little late in the year to be wearing a blue and white plaid sleeveless dress, but the Indian summer weather called for it. The news that morning had forecasted mideighties, which sent Lucy straight to her closet, looking for something that said California girl and endless summer. Her shoulder-length auburn tresses and milky skin didn't exactly scream beach bunny—and the white T-strap high heel sandals she'd chosen were definitely not her usual work shoes, but they did amazing things for her calves.

Okay, confession time. It had occurred to her that she might run into him again. Actually, it would make things easier if she did. She could thank him politely, return the briefcase in person, and be on her way. No explanations necessary beyond that. The extra care with her outfit and her makeup was a little harder to rationalize, so she didn't try. It might even have given her some satisfaction to rivet that man's attention, even for an eyeblink. He'd certainly riveted hers.

The heels slowed her down. They weren't stilettos, but she wasn't used to the height or the clicking sound they made when she tried to hurry. Awkward going, to say the least. Once she got herself to the store, she explained her situation to the young male clerk at the counter, who called out the store manager. But neither could help her. Blanchard's didn't give out personal information on customers, the manager told her, and that particular customer had paid cash, so he couldn't be contacted. Lucy had been afraid of that.

Okay, she'd tried. She told herself that all the way back to her car. She'd done everything she could. Yesterday had happened. It had been one of those crazy days that you couldn't explain. She'd run into a kook, and for some reason, he'd given her an expensive briefcase. The rest of it was her imagination, and she had to let it go. There was no special significance to her meeting with this man, no special significance to anything he said. And it made no sense clinging to his every word as if there were.

She did not want to sparkle. Jewelry sparkled. Dishes did. Lucy Sexton didn't.

At least now she could check one thing off her To Do list and get busy on the rest of it. That would lighten her load, but as she drove back to the office, the sigh she let out had more to do with frustration than relief. Every stoplight on her trip seemed to turn red just as she got there, and the sky above was gray, which guaranteed she was going to freeze *and* be out of style today. She almost wished Cassandra, the radio psychic she often listened to in the car, wasn't so annoyingly upbeat. Lucy wasn't in the mood to hear romantic bliss predicted for caller after caller when she was feeling this low. Blue, actually, if she had to pick a color. She'd been working a lot of hours for a long time to get the mediation service going. Maybe she was just pooped.

She spotted a coffee shop and glanced at her watch, wondering if she had time to pick up a cup of chai tea. She hoped the spicy hot brew would lift her spirits and warm her up. Her endless summer outfit was a little chilly. A parking spot opened up right in front of the shop, which made the decision for her. She pulled in and let herself out, preparing to dash inside. But before she got to the coffee shop door, she noticed a man down the street who looked familiar. Blue jeans encased his long legs and a tool belt hung on his hips, clanking softly as he walked.

Was that him? The attaché guy?

He was a half-block away and headed in the other direction, but when he glanced across the street, Lucy got a glimpse of his profile.

"Wait!" she called, starting after him. If she got his attention, she could return the case and free herself. She broke into a run, hobbled by the heels and sheath.

"Hey, wait!" she called again, pulling up her skirt.

He didn't seem to hear her, but he stopped to look in a store window, and she poured on the speed. This was her chance. By the time she caught up with him, she was too breathless to speak, but apparently he heard her gasps. He turned and looked at her as if he'd never seen her before.

He hadn't. It was the wrong man.

"S-sorry!" She gulped air. "I thought it was someone else."

"Lady, you scared the hell out of me."

If she hadn't already felt ridiculous, his indignation would have fixed that. His eyes were close-set, his mouth thin. He didn't even resemble the attaché guy, except for his height and clothing. How could she have made such a mistake? She apologized again and headed back to her car, the chai tea forgotten.

This was it. The beginning and end of her fascination with tool belts and the men who wore them. Her twenty-four-hour detour into fantasyland was over. She needed to get back to business. She had a wedding to think about, a company, a future.

She kicked off her heels as she got into the car. The damn things were dangerous. With three inches of heel, you could floor the gas pedal and not even know it. No more short skirts, either. She was switching back to gray blazers and slacks.

"OUCH!" Lucy felt something cold thunk against her forehead and looked up to see an aluminum ladder looming before her. It looked like a giant silver letter of the alphabet shooting toward the lobby ceiling. She'd run smack into the spreader that braced the legs open, but hadn't even noticed the ladder when she walked into the building.

"Hello!" Lucy called up to the man balanced like a gymnast on scaffolding attached to the top rungs. He'd removed several ceiling panels and appeared to be working on the wiring. It didn't surprise her that he didn't look down.

"I work upstairs," she said. "No one mentioned anything about construction in the lobby. Shouldn't you have the area cordoned off?"

"It is cordoned off," he said, without bothering to stop what he was doing. "And there's a sign on the door as you're coming in. Take a look."

Lucy set down the shopping bag and her briefcase, then pushed open the entrance door, which was right behind her, and saw the handwritten sign taped to the glass. No question about what it said: MEN AT WORK. USE OTHER ENTRANCE, PLEASE. The cordage he'd mentioned was an orange ribbon, now draped around her waist and floating behind her. Apparently she'd taken it with her on her way in, like a runner crossing the finish line.

She went back inside and looked around the lobby, deeply chagrined. Luckily it wasn't the elevator that was under construction. She would have fallen down the shaft. Maybe she did have her powers of concentration back. She'd forced herself to think about an upcoming case—and nothing else—on the drive here. Obviously she'd locked in her target with such intensity she'd pushed everything else away, which was the point. But still.

A soft ping told her the elevator was operational. The workman was engrossed in his task and seemed to have forgotten she existed, so she grabbed both bags and carefully picked her way around the ladder. She didn't see any other construction going on anywhere, but the small lobby was empty of people. It was an older building with just the one car, so perhaps they were using the stairs. Even Burt, the burly security guard who made it his business to greet everyone in the morning, was nowhere in sight. With the lobby closed, he may have taken the day off.

Burt liked to operate the elevator, too. It wasn't strictly in his job description, but none of the women complained when he escorted them inside and gallantly delivered them to their floor. Now, the elevator sat open, as if waiting for Lucy. She actually felt some relief when she went inside and pressed the button. She was on her way to the tenth floor, just like every other weekday morning for the last several years. Life was back to normal. She would fix herself a cup of blueberry vanilla tea, water her philodendron, settle down at her desk to check her voice and e-mail, meet with her assistant, and prioritize the workload for that day. Yes, life was back—

"When *do* I get that hour of your time?"

Lucy's senses pricked at the sound of a man's voice. The question slipped through the closing doors of the elevator, and she craned to see who'd said it. There didn't seem to be anyone out there. *The attaché for an hour of your time.* Wasn't that what the alarmingly tall stranger had said to her?

Open the door, Lucy! She thumbed the button repeatedly, but it was too late. The doors sealed with a woosh. The elevator lurched and whirred, already on its way up.

Lucy gripped the safety rail with her shopping bag hand. High heels and a rocky elevator had made her unsteady on her feet. She watched the floors go by, her gaze frozen on the panel above the door. She had heard a man's voice. Maybe he hadn't been talking to her, but she'd definitely heard it. Crazy how her heart was pounding. It was probably nothing, a comment made to someone else. She had to get to work. She didn't have time to go in search of disembodied voices. She shouldn't even be thinking about things like that.

Two weeks, Luce. You're going to be Mrs. Frederick Anderson in two weeks. This is your dream come true. He's the perfect man, honest, solid as Gibraltar, and good to you. Good to you—and probably too good *for* you. You could spend the rest of your life and never find a guy like him. *Don't* blow this.

She hit 10, then immediately hit LOBBY. She was going back down.

"Lucy, shit!" It was a reflex! She hadn't meant to do that.

The elevator shuddered—and so did her heart. She was going to get stuck. As elevators went, this one was an antique. Burt seemed to know its quirks, but no one else did, and Lucy may have jammed the works. Just watch her get trapped between floors.

She kept her eye on the panel as the car continued up. Maybe it was going to ten before it went back down to the lobby. If she was that lucky, she would get out on ten, drop to her knees, and kiss the carpet.

But it didn't go all the way to ten. It went to the next floor and stopped. The doors opened, and Lucy stood there, torn. She could get out and take the stairs, or let the door shut and hope the car continued up. But why had it stopped?

The doors closed while she deliberated. The elevator lurched, and Lucy braced herself against the handrail. She was going down. She watched the floors slip by and realized

she was headed back to the lobby. She didn't dare punch another button, so there was no stopping this ride. She was cap-
tive to whatever awaited her.

By the time the car reached the bottom floor, her heart was
thumping. She chided herself for being a drama queen. No
one would be down there, certainly not him, if that's what she
was thinking. But as the doors parted, she found herself staring at eyes blue enough to dive into from a cliff. Crystalline
waters, those eyes. It was a moment before she could tear her
gaze away to verify that it was actually him.

She took in the jeans, tool belt, and enigmatic smile.
"You," she said softly. "What are you doing here?"

He cocked his head. "I could ask you the same question."

"This is my building. I work here. Lucy Sexton. Sexton
Mediation. You aren't following me, are you?"

She hadn't meant it to come out like that—accusatory, but
she was flustered. He had no way of knowing that she'd been
chasing down men who looked like him. At any rate, he didn't
seem to mind her tone. He answered with a shrug.

"I was just going up to the roof," he explained. "I have a
job up there."

"You do not."

"I do, too."

"You're working here? In this building?" She let go of the
safety rail and steadied herself on her feet. "Your being here
has nothing to do with me?"

He handed her a card that said HIGHTOWER ELECTRIC with
his name inscribed at the bottom: NOAH HIGHTOWER. But she
wasn't able to take it until she'd tucked her briefcase under
her arm. "I'm doing the wiring for the restaurant on the roof,"
he explained. "I was the guy on the ladder you ran into."

"Why didn't you say something?"

"I didn't see you until you walked away."

Lucy couldn't get over it. "It doesn't seem possible that
you were in the store yesterday and here today, unless—"

The elevator door tried to close, and he caught it with his
arm. "Unless I'm following you? Maybe you're following me."

Well, she had been, actually. "But you did say you wanted

an hour of my time, didn't you? Please tell me I'm not hearing voices."

He grinned, still battling the door. "I want much more than that, but I'll settle for an hour, and not a minute less."

Lucy had begun to wonder which of them needed a padded cell. "Why? Why should you want *any* of my time?"

"Why not? Life is short," He joined her in the elevator, apologizing as he reached in front of her. He hit a button that said SKY HARBOR LOUNGE and asked her what floor she wanted.

"Ten." Lucy pressed against the railing behind her, but the elevator didn't move. Nothing happened. No lurching, no shuddering. The doors didn't even close.

He tried again. Still nothing.

She could hardly contain the moan that welled up. "It's stalled. Burt is the only one who can fix it. There's a stairway," she suggested.

But he already had his tools out and the floor selector panel off the wall. She watched him work with multicolored wires and switches, wondering if he might be electrocuted at any second. It was a delicate process, and his fine motor skills were pretty impressive, but Lucy was particularly struck by the caramel tones in his complexion, and the way his skin glowed against the blue chambray of his work shirt. He spent time in the sun. That was evident from the amber highlights in his dark waves and the golden dusting of hair on his forearms. His hands looked powerful, yet sensitive.

She was reminded of a safecracker, listening to the clicks and caressing the locking mechanism, every sense pricked to the task. The image played and replayed in her mind, provoking an odd little thrill. But her fantasy was over too quickly. Within moments he had the panel in place and stood back to view his handiwork.

"Try your floor now," he said as he put his tools away.

Juggling all her burdens, Lucy reached around him to press the button. Somehow she brushed his arm with her breasts and felt a sizzling snap of heat. Already off balance, she bumped him again, and the sensation zinged through her like electrical current. It was hot enough to make her suck in a gasp. Fiery sharp and sweet, it sizzled and crackled all the way to her toes.

He'd given her a shock, she realized. Not one of those dry, prickly biting shocks. This was the real thing.

"Sorry," he said, "I tend to carry a charge."

"I noticed." Her fingertips were still tingling. The current had shot to her extremities as if it were searching for a way out of her body.

"Is that an occupational hazard?" she asked.

"It wasn't before today."

Was he kidding? Her eyes locked with his for a moment, and she felt another jolt, this one to her equilibrium. *All* she needed.

He pressed the buttons, and the doors closed. She braced herself as the elevator lurched, trying not to bump him again, but she wasn't anchored against anything, and he stood between her and the railing. The car lifted, and she swayed forward, just barely able to catch herself.

"Are you all right?" He gripped her arm and steadied her.

"I'm fine. I just need to put these bags down. And maybe take off my heels."

"Sexy shoes," he said, glancing down at them.

Lucy felt a moment's satisfaction knowing her beach bunny outfit wasn't totally wasted. Being off balance seemed a small price to pay for the pleasure his appreciative gaze brought. She didn't even mind that the elevator bucked when they got to her floor and sent her reeling. Right into his arms.

"I can't seem to stay on my feet," she said, allowing herself one delicious moment in the heat of his embrace.

"I'm liking those shoes better and better."

Her throat burned with pleasure, and she was glad he couldn't see her face. He felt safe, warm, solid, and she didn't want to tear herself away. She had to, but she didn't want to. He was better than the handrail any day—strong and warm, with a body designed to support her and arms that felt as if they could protect her from anything.

"It's my floor," she said in case he hadn't noticed. "This is ten."

She put a hand to his chest, but it might have been as much out of the desire to touch him as the desire to have him move. At any rate, he didn't release her. Instead he hit the DOOR CLOSE button—and drew her tighter. "Stay with me," he said.

"Stay with you? In the elevator?" Lucy's heart had begun to thump, a common occurrence when she was with him. She didn't know what to say, except, "I can't." But it came out so faint she could barely hear it herself.

The door closed and sealed. What was he doing? Taking her up to the roof? Her mind started to dart every which way, none of them good. Did he actually work up there or was this something much more sinister? Should she be frightened? What if he'd caused the electrical problems as a way to clear out the lobby so that he could trap her on the elevator? Had he been stalking her all this time just to catch her in a situation like this? Was she being taken by force?

"You'd *better* tell me what you're doing," she said, "and tell me now."

"It's a test."

"What do you mean, a test?"

He cradled her with one arm and pushed another button. But it wasn't the SKY HARBOR LOUNGE. It was DOOR OPEN. "Just making sure it works."

"What, the elevator?" She gaped at him while the doors opened like clockwork. "Are you going to let me go now?"

"Do I have to?" A smile touched his lips, but she wouldn't let herself smile back.

Dammit, heart, shut up. He'll hear you! "Please."

"I guess that's a yes?"

"That's a resounding yes. I'm very self-sufficient," she assured him. "I *can* take care of myself."

He released her and gallantly handed her over the transom. When she was safely on the other side, she turned and watched him disappear behind the closing doors. Good God, what a flight of fantasy that was. He seemed to have that effect on her. Her brain kept going off on tangents and whipping her into a frenzy instead of letting her do what she was supposed to—like return the damn briefcase.

Lucy glanced at the purple and gold sack in her hand. She'd found the owner, but she hadn't accomplished what she wanted to, which was to return the Cavalli. You might say she'd been left holding the bag.

Chapter Three

LUCY busily juggled packages and tugged down her skirt as she approached the reception area of Sexton Mediation Services. It surprised her to see her fiancé standing dead center in the large open room as she entered.

"Frederick? Is everything okay?"

His body language stopped her from going over to give him a hug. He couldn't have seen her encounter with the electrician; the reception area was down the hallway from the elevator bay. But something was wrong. His arms were folded, and he didn't greet her with his usual warm smile. Tallish and lean, Frederick could best be described as dapper. He even looked a little formidable in his double-breasted banker's suits and his perfectly trimmed graying-at-the-temples hair. Everything about him was perfectly trimmed and tidy, which was exactly what had attracted her. He was her ballast, her island of calm amid stormy seas.

He tapped his watch, as if he were dealing with a tardy teenager. "We had an appointment with the wedding planner."

"Right, at ten, and it's—" Lucy checked her watch, too. "Ten-thirty? Can that be right?" The receptionist wasn't at her

desk, so Lucy unloaded her packages there. She glanced around at the wall clock behind her, then pulled out her cell, which was always accurate. It *was* ten-thirty! She'd dawdled away more than an hour this morning.

"What are you doing?" Frederick asked.

Lucy tapped out the number for their wedding planner. "I'm calling Cheree. Maybe she can still take us. We'll dash right over there. I'll be a little late for my next meeting, but that's okay."

He walked over, took the phone from her hand, and closed it.

"What are *you* doing?" she asked as he handed the cell back to her. There were times when his quiet brand of superiority could be annoying, like now. But Mr. Frederick Anderson wasn't quite so perfect today, she realized. There was dandruff on his otherwise pristine gray flannel suit. She could see at least two flakes. She didn't tell him, but she was tempted.

"Cheree left fifteen minutes ago," he explained. "We were supposed to meet her here. You set the appointment up yourself, remember. It was the only way you could squeeze it into your schedule."

It all came back to Lucy in a woosh. She'd juggled everyone's schedule including hers, but this morning's distractions had completely thrown her off. That wasn't like her. She was usually great with scheduling, and she would never dream of inconveniencing people this way.

"I'll set something else up," she said. "Don't worry about a thing. I'll coordinate with your assistant."

She had her cell phone open, but he stayed her hand again. "Are you sure you're okay with all of this? Maybe the wedding is too much, too soon? We could postpone."

"Frederick! The invitations have gone out. We can't postpone now. Everything's in place."

She couldn't believe he would suggest such a thing at this late date. They'd been planning the wedding for months, and she'd known she was going to marry him within a week of meeting him at a gallery opening in town. That was four years ago, and she hadn't wavered in her conviction since. Frederick might have, but she hadn't.

"Do you want to postpone?" she asked.

His brows furrowed, hinting at exasperation. "Lucy, I'm not the one missing meetings. You were a no-show at your last gown fitting, too."

"I didn't miss it. I had to reschedule. Elsa is coming over here and bringing the gown with her. She'll do the alterations in my office."

The reception desk phone rang, and Lucy picked it up without thinking. When the receptionist took a break she switched on the voice mail service. No one needed to answer. Lucy jotted down a quick message for one of the paralegals, and as she hung up the phone, she saw that Frederick was watching her. His expression had softened.

"Are we okay?" she asked. Her wheedling tone seduced a smile out of him.

"Of course we are. But don't tell me not to worry about you, Lucy. You haven't been yourself, especially lately. You seem agitated."

"You call it agitated. I call it sparkly." Lydia Sexton breezed into the room, a steaming mug of Amaretto-scented coffee in her hand. She gave Frederick an obligatory nod and then focused her attention on Lucy. "Something's up with our girl," she said, "and she won't tell me what it is."

"Nothing's up, mother of mine. Brides-to-be are supposed to sparkle *and* be agitated. It's natural, pre-wedding jitters."

Lucy wanted no further talk of her sparkliness, but her mother had already turned her critical eye on Lucy's outfit. Lydia batted her eyelashes, as if surprised.

"Is that a miniskirt?" she asked.

Naturally Frederick had to check Lucy out as well. Under their double-barrel scrutiny, Lucy turned the hottest shade of pink there was.

"Why are you dressed like that?" Frederick asked, visually measuring the shortness of her skirt and the length of her leg.

Lucy shrugged her shoulders. "The weather. It's hot outside."

"It's hot inside, too," her mother said with a sly wink.

Lucy pretended not to have any idea what all the fuss was

about, and Frederick gallantly came to her aid. "I like the outfit. It looks—"

"Summery?" Lucy suggested.

"Very summery," Frederick agreed. He held out his arms,
as if to give her a hug, and Lucy felt a twinge of reluctance.
Normally, she loved hugging Frederick, but today it didn't
feel quite right. Guilt, maybe? She really hadn't done anything wrong. Confusion?

Thankfully, Frederick didn't seem to notice her hesitation.
He'd spotted the shopping bag on the receptionist's desk and
was craning around her for a better look at it.

"What did we buy at the Blanchard's?" he asked.

Lucy swooped on the bag, clutching it. "Uh—a gift?"

"For anyone I know?" he teased.

"I don't think so. But he's one terrific guy."

"Oh, really?"

He made a grab for the bag, and she snatched it away.
Clearly he took that as a challenge because he came for her
like a basketball guard trying to steal the ball. Lucy wouldn't
have thought Frederick capable of such antics, but she couldn't
let him get a look in the bag.

"Mom!" she shouted, lobbing the bag over his shoulder to
her mother, who caught it with one hand—and without spilling
a drop of coffee.

Frederick whirled, saw what had happened, and threw up his
hands. He wasn't going to mess with his future mother-in-law.

Lydia took a victory bow. She then snapped the bag open
and looked inside. A mysterious smile dawned, and she
glanced from Lucy to Frederick and back again. She said
nothing, but Lucy could read her expression. She just hoped
Frederick couldn't.

All this effort to hide a briefcase? Lydia seemed to be saying. What's the story, daughter of mine? You may be fooling
Frederick, but you're not fooling me.

"THE gift that keeps on giving." Lucy sighed and tossed her
pen down. She might as well hang the damn attaché around

her neck like an albatross. After the encounter with Frederick and her mother, Lucy had hooked the shopping bag on a coat-rack in her office, turned her back on it, and thrown herself into her work. Her paralegal had joined her and they'd prepped for that day's session with Lucy's new clients, which had gone reasonably well, considering there was a family business involved.

But now that the session was over—and in fact, the entire day was over—Lucy could no longer avoid the obvious. She still hadn't figured out what to do with the briefcase. She had some ideas, though.

Plan A was to reupholster the seat of her office chair in calfskin and park her fanny on it all day long. Plan B was to take it up to the roof of the building, give it back to the elec-trician, and if he gave her any guff, to toss it over the side, preferably with him attached.

How about that for conflict resolution? Plan B, definitely.

Moments later she was in the elevator, on her way up to the roof. She'd started the day off late, and there'd never been time to change from the sundress and heels. Such a mistake, that outfit. The weather had turned stormy and the temperature had plunged into the fifties. Now the sun was going down, and she had gooseflesh to add to her list of fashion faux pas. She was freezing! Nevertheless, she had a good feeling about her mission. She'd actually come up with a viable way to carry out Plan B. She was going to make the electrician an offer he couldn't refuse.

Please don't let him have left yet, she thought.

The elevator emptied directly into entry of the Sky Harbor Lounge and it surprised her that the restaurant looked ready for business. Construction had been going on for nearly a month, but with the top floor closed to the public, there wasn't any way to see what was being done. Between Lucy's work and her upcoming wedding, she hadn't been paying much at-tention anyway.

Rustling noises to her left took her down a flight of black marble steps and into what looked like the dining area. The large room curved like a discus, spilling out onto a wraparound patio, where wrought-iron bistro tables were shaded by bright cobalt blue-and-white–striped umbrellas. Massive ebony fans spun slowly from the vaulted ceilings. But what caught Lucy's eye were the floor-length white curtains, blowing like enormous flags. All the French doors and windows were thrown wide open, letting the wind whip through.

Lucy could see the storm gathering outside, but the man with his back to her seemed oblivious. It looked like he was packing up equipment, perhaps in preparation to leave. It was hard to see anything but his broad back and decadently lush dark hair. But as she drew closer, she noticed the initials T. H. carved into his leather tool belt, and the words, "Let there be light."

"Who's T. H.?" she asked.

He turned, and she forced herself to meet his gaze. Her smile was involuntary. She had absolutely no control over it. Thank God, he didn't know what was happening inside her, the riot of excitement.

"Now I know you're following me," he said, stepping back to look her over. "Did I mention those were great shoes?"

She glanced down, still smiling. "You did."

All her mind could see were his eyes, sapphire depths, deep seas. He was the sea, not the island, and the kind of storm he could create was already swirling around her. She had done her best to avoid storms of all kinds. It was too much like the chaos her father had created in her childhood.

"You didn't tell me who T. H. was," she said.

"My uncle, Thomas Hightower."

"He gave you the belt?"

He rubbed the worn leather with his thumb, smoothing a deep scratch. "I went to live with him and my aunt when my mother passed. He was a journeyman electrician, and a genius at lighting interiors. He taught me his trade and gave me his tool belt to get me started. It's been good luck."

Lucy could hear the genuine affection in his voice. She didn't ask what had happened to his mother. She'd already intruded enough.

"Do you still want me to spend that hour with you?" she asked him.

He hesitated and her heart wavered. Everything depended on his wanting that.

"Of course I do."

Good. "Then I have two things for you. The first is a question. The second is an offer."

"And the question is?"

The draft from the French doors was brisk. It sent the billowy white curtains flying. Lucy rubbed her arms in an effort to keep warm. "I don't understand your interest," she said. "Why do you want to spend time with me?—and don't tell me life is short."

"Life *is* short, but that's only part of the reason." He cocked his head, thoughtful for a moment. "The truth? You remind me of someone."

"Who?"

"Me, at a time when I was about to marry a woman I didn't really want to marry, only I didn't know it."

"And what did you do?"

"I married her and made her very unhappy. I haven't forgiven myself yet."

"So now you go around trying to stop people from making bad marriages? That's your atonement?"

He thought about that a minute. "Yeah."

"And that's why you want an hour of my time? To talk me out of my wedding?"

His blue eyes were unblinking. "I just want an hour of your time. Does there have to be a reason?"

His voice had dropped low, and the question took on a resonance that Lucy couldn't dismiss.

"No, I guess not," she said. Odd, though, for her there did have to be a reason, for everything. Her practical nature demanded that. Still, there was something about this man that elicited things she didn't expect to say, or feel. She wasn't sure anyone had ever spoken to her the way he just did, certainly not Frederick.

Across the room, an empty carton fell off a table, blown by the wind. She and Noah hurried to close the doors and windows. The sky was rapidly darkening outside, and by the time they had everything locked up, Lucy realized the dining room was glimmering with light. The walls glowed with amber fire, and silvery beams streamed from the ceiling, catching the room's rich teak furnishings in their spotlight. The lighting system must be computerized, and he must have done it.

"I think you're the genius," she said.

He didn't answer, and finally she got around to the point of her trip. "I still need to make that offer."

"I wish you would."

She held up the Blanchard's bag. "If I give you the hour will you take back this briefcase?"

"Absolutely."

"Great, let's do it."

He breathed out low laughter. "My thoughts exactly. When?"

"You choose the time and place," she said. "I'll be there with the merchandise." She waggled the bag and took a step back toward the elevator. She took another and another, waiting for him to name the date. Maybe he was thinking it through. But he was also watching her every move, and she was much too wobbly to walk backward on high heels.

She turned around and headed for the bay, delighted she was able to do it without dancing all over the place. Just as she got there, he said, "Tomorrow, the pier, nine o'clock."

"It's a date." The car doors closed on her secret smile. He was the sea. He was the storm and she was a girl who could barely swim. Why did she want to go there?

NOAH watched the elevator doors close and allowed himself a moment. The word *"yesss"* hissed softly through his lips. He'd just been propositioned by a leggy brunette, wearing stilts and sporting goose bumps. He wanted to savor this. She'd left him with a pleasant buzz in his head and a tight sensation in his groin.

Pretty sweet. Pretty bold.

Lucy Sexton, girl on a mission. Get married, have children, create the solid family unit she never had. The only thing she'd forgotten was matching blinders to go with her outfit. She saw what she wanted to see—what she needed to see—and very little else. It was a dangerous way to navigate through life. You could get blindsided.

How did he know all that about her? He just did. Call him the Marriage Angel. He wasn't out to create problems for her. He wanted to help prevent them. And he'd known she needed help from the moment he saw her in the men's store. She was asleep at the wheel and had no idea that she was about to crash the car. He'd been there, done that. Sadly, nobody got his attention in time to prevent the accident.

The table where he'd left his toolbox was cluttered with rolls of electrical tape, pliers of all kinds, wire caps, and a voltage meter. He scooped up an armful of the supplies and dropped them in the box. Within minutes he had everything packed and the restaurant locked up for the night. He took the steps to the elevator two at a time, hit the button, and drew in a breath, wondering if the lingering hint of fragrance he picked up was Lucy. It smelled like her, but it wasn't perfume. Vanilla, maybe?

The best part of her sudden appearance was the weather-inappropriate outfit she wore. If the gooseflesh on her arms was any indication, she was freezing to death. She didn't look terribly comfortable in the dress and heels, but he loved them. Nothing better for a lonely guy than watching a woman in ultrahigh heels who was unsteady on her feet. Better than ESPN any day.

Lucy Sexton, girl on a mission. She was about to make the most important decision of her life, and she was in an emotional coma. Sleeping Beauty had nothing on her. It wasn't his goal to steal her away from her fiancé. In fact, he might be the last kind of man she would ever be interested in. Still, saving her was not an entirely selfless act on his part. He couldn't help wondering what it would be like to be the prince who kissed her awake.

Chapter Four

TONIGHT Lucy was dressed for the weather in her favorite snug-fitting jeans, a black cashmere cardigan, two buttons demurely undone at the neckline, and Birkenstock sandals for comfort. She'd thought about restraining her dark auburn mane in a claw clip, but there was such a thing as too prim. When she wore her hair down, like now, the long waves tended to fall onto her face, veiling one eye like a thirties movie vamp. Naturally, her mother loved the look, but her mother didn't have to deal with impaired vision. Still, it did force Lucy to toss her head occasionally, and she'd heard men loved that.

Yesterday's winds had blown every bit of haze from the air, and the vast dark sky twinkled with fiery stars. It was a lovely fall night, cool, crisp, and clear. She didn't live far from the beach, but she seldom made the trip. She didn't do much these days that wasn't directly related to work or her marriage to Frederick. Those were her two main thrusts in life, and they seemed to consume every minute. Maybe she secretly liked it that way. At any rate, she had no time for distractions, which begged the question: What was she doing here?

Meeting a man on a pier for the purpose of giving him back a briefcase? That wasn't the reason, and both she and the mysterious Mr. Hightower knew it, which begged a second question. Where was he?

She'd walked almost to the end of the pier, but she didn't see him anywhere. A young couple came toward her, too involved with giggling and trying to feed each other catsup-smeared French fries to notice the woman wandering around all by herself and tossing her head to keep the hair out of her eyes. Lucy quietly moved out of their way. At the very end of the pier, where a take-out seafood bar stood closed for the season, several fishermen dangled lines in the water. None of them seemed to be catching anything. Apparently it was a quiet night for everybody.

Lucy heard footsteps on the pier behind her, and her heart rocketed. He had come after all. She turned and saw an older couple, out for a late-evening walk. Not him. There was still no sign of him, but the way she'd reacted forced her to face an embarrassing reality. She had really wanted it to be him. An image had flashed into her head of rich, dark hair, lit with honeyed tones, and those eyes. Bluer than blue, those eyes. She hadn't caught her breath yet. His height was nice, too. It was the first thing she'd noticed about him. Having to tilt your head back that far was a little disorienting, but she'd sensed that he would have caught her if she'd lost her balance. Definitely, he would have caught her . . . and who knew what would have happened then.

Something quickened in the pit of her stomach. The shivery sensation she felt made her want to sit down and cross her legs. Tightly.

Shivery was not good. How and when did she get hung up on this guy? It wasn't just his looks. That had never been her thing; well, not entirely. It was his manner, his easy confidence and penetrating comments.

She stopped for a moment, trying to decide what to do. Below her, the waves broke gently against the pilings, and each one sent up an explosion of tangy brine. A gull touched down on the railing next to her and immediately took flight again. Its cry was eerie and wild.

Her watch said it was nearly nine-thirty. He wasn't coming.

She'd been stood up on a date she hadn't even wanted to keep. How about that for a rejection? She started back toward shore, her sandals slapping against the wooden planks. An angry toss of her head got the hair out of her eyes, but not for long, she knew. She tucked the errant waves firmly behind her ears. Enough vamping already.

She had to be out of her mind agreeing to come here. She counseled people every day about rational decision-making. It was her specialty, and yet she'd been making nothing but irrational ones. Her compulsion to give the briefcase back to a near stranger made no sense. Who cared about the damn briefcase? Certainly not him. He was just using it to manipulate her.

The shopping bag bumped against the railing as she walked. She would give the attaché to Burt, the elevator man, and be done with it. As for the electrician, he could stick his finger in an open socket. She needn't bother even to speak to him again.

"DRIVING too fast, Lucy," she chided. She let up on the gas and glanced in the rearview mirror for any sign of flashing red lights. No point adding a speeding ticket to her already long list of screwups. She was on her way home to drown her troubles in a steaming hot shower and maybe something fast, unhealthy, and therefore decadent, like instant chocolate pudding with a big dollop of Cool Whip, but first she had to stop by the office.

She'd forgotten to take files that needed to be reviewed for tomorrow's mediation sessions, something she'd been doing like clockwork for as long as they'd had cases to review, which had been about five years now. Every night the next day's files came home with her, and she went over them in bed, making notes and sipping a cup of blueberry vanilla herbal tea. It was a ritual by now. That afternoon, she'd actually put the files in her doorway on the floor, so she couldn't miss them on her way out.

How did you step over a stack of files and not see them?

She glanced in the rearview mirror again, and frowned at her own reflection. You had a man on your mind was how. You looked at a pile of folders and you saw blue jeans, sexy narrow hips, and a tool belt.

As she pulled onto the street where her building was located, she noticed lights on the roof. They were like glittery white diamonds, blinking on and off. It reminded her of a Christmas display. She watched for a while, then realized the lights were spelling out something, one letter at a time: L. U. C. The next letter looked like a Y. And what came after that could have been a question mark. LUCY?

Her name? She watched as it appeared again, one letter at a time.

Lucy didn't know what to make of it, but she was going to find out. Her building had a porte cochere at the entrance, much like a hotel. She pulled in, grabbed the shopping bag, and left the Blazer there, hoping it wouldn't get towed. The lobby was empty as she burst in, which didn't surprise her. The night security guards patrolled only the exterior of the building.

The elevator seemed slower than ever before, but maybe it was her racing pulse. Anything would seem slow in comparison. She could have scaled the building. Finally, the doors let her out in the restaurant's entry. The dining area was dark this time, but she saw lights in the lounge to the right.

As she entered, the spacious room appeared to be nothing but windows, a vast panorama of glass overlooking the city and, in the distance, the twinkling coastline. Candle flame was the only light in the room, and it was flickering everywhere— on the tabletops, in the wall sconces and torchères, and especially in the graceful iron chandeliers that hung from the ceiling.

Lucy wasn't sure she'd ever seen more candles, even in a cathedral. It gave the dark room a hushed, magical effect.

"And where has Lucy been all day? Shopping again?"

Noah's voice. She couldn't see him. Her eyes hadn't adjusted. But he was nearby, close enough that she could hear the traces of sarcasm.

"Where have *you* been?" she asked him, searching the shadows. "I went to the pier. I've been there since nine, waiting for you."

The lights came up slowly. Recessed panels along the baseboard and the ceiling created a glow that gave the crescent-shaped room a sense of intimacy. A track of spotlights illumined the bar area and another lit a small bandstand at the opposite end of the room. The candles dimmed, and Lucy realized they weren't real. The electric flames had fooled her.

Noah was standing just across from her by the windows, a remote in his hand, from which he apparently controlled the known universe, not to mention the lighting in the room. She thought she heard music playing softly, strings and woodwinds.

"You were at the pier tonight?" He came closer, the lights illuminating his confusion.

"Of course, we agreed to meet at nine."

"Right, nine this morning."

She gaped at him. "Who goes to the pier at nine in the morning?"

"I did—and waited until noon for you to show up."

"You were there? You weren't just playing games with me?"

"Of course not. Why would I do that?"

She wanted to believe him. She really did. "I don't know. I'd begun to think everything about this situation was a joke. Are you sure someone didn't put you up to it? Like my mother?"

He smiled. "Am I sensing some mother-daughter friction? I can assure you your mother's hands are clean. I've never even met her. You have only me to blame."

She wanted to ask him all over again what his interest in her could possibly be, but he'd already told her. He seemed to think she was about to make the biggest mistake of her life, and apparently, he had some fantasy about saving her from herself.

"No one sent you?" she asked.

He looked around, as if to see whom she might be talking

about. "You mean like divine intervention?" he said with a glance at the ceiling. "No, I'm not an emissary from up above."

"Or down below?"

He laughed, but Lucy's shrug said Hey, it could happen.

She could feel herself relaxing. Now that the lights were up, she could see that the lounge was complete to the point of décor. It had been designed to take advantage of the view, with terraced rows of velvety black booths accented by white linen, calla lilies, and crimson anthuriums, which were either silk or someone had been watering them, she realized. The room was spectacular, but she wondered if anything was what it seemed. The stars twinkling outside? Were those real or something he created?

"How did you manage to do all this?" she asked.

"Most of it was done when I got here. I'm the bells and whistles guy. In this case, the owner wanted candlelight, but no candle wax, so I tried to oblige."

"It's a work of art," she said as she set the shopping bag on the table. "I didn't know you could do things like this with lighting."

Noah thanked her and looked at his watch. "You brought my Cavalli attaché. Does my hour start now?"

"Well, I guess technically it started ten minutes ago, when I got here." She smiled and left the bag behind, walking toward the windows—and toward him. But she was looking past him, outside.

"I thought I saw my name from the road," she said. "It looked like Christmas lights."

"I'm to blame for that, too," he admitted. "It's called an electronic billboard. My company makes them."

"How did you do it?"

He pointed to an exit doorway with a sign that said OBSER-VATION DECK. "It's out there. Come on. I'll show you."

She was curious enough to follow him outside, and was immediately glad she'd worn her cardigan. It had turned chilly in the last hour. He directed her to a platform that jutted like a diving board, from which she could look back and see the six-foot billboard lashed to the railing of the observation

deck. It was similar to signs she'd seen on the freeways, an-
nouncing traffic jams and accidents, but this one spelled out
her name, which was strange to see. She imagined it could
probably be programmed to spell things backward, forward,
and upside down.

"Curious about how I did it?" he asked.

"I'm more curious about why you did it."

"My motives were pure." He pressed his hand to his heart
as if he were about to take the pledge. "When I got back from
the beach yesterday, I went to your office, but you weren't
there. I didn't want to be indiscreet, so rather than leave a
message with the receptionist, I did this."

"Putting my name in lights on the roof is discreet?"

"I figured there had to be more than one Lucy in town, but
you were the only one who would know for sure that it was intended for you."

She couldn't help but smile and shake her head. Clever
beast.

He walked to the railing and joined her, looking out at the
sky and the sea. The music could be heard outside too, if it
was actually music. The silvery sighs and soft rustlings might
be the lullaby of ocean waves in the distance, ebbing and flowing. Lucy even picked up the wood smoke of beach fires.

She shivered. They were up high, and it was breezy, but
that wasn't why she had chills. She was touching shoulders
with a wildly attractive man.

Well, technically it was his bicep her shoulder touched.

"How tall are you?" she asked.

"I don't know. Maybe six feet four. Why?"

It wouldn't have been appropriate to tell him why, but in
all honesty when you had to tilt your head back to look at a
man, one of the things that naturally came to mind was kissing. Not him, necessarily, and not now, of course, just the experience of kissing someone so tall, and wondering what that
would be like.

"Interesting that you're looking at my mouth." His tone
was conversational, but his expression wasn't. He was searching her face.

"I wasn't—"

"Yes, you were. You still are. What's with that?"

"Maybe I'm interested in reading lips."

"Then read mine." He looked into her eyes and enunciated every word. "Maybe you're really interested in that *other* thing we do with our lips?"

She supposed it would be silly to keep denying it. "All right," she said, "it did cross my mind. I was just wondering what it would be like to kiss someone so tall."

"Is that right?" His smile was wicked. "I was talking about eating, Lucy. Food. That other thing you do with your lips."

"You lie!"

He started to protest, then laughed at the face she made. "Okay, maybe I had a fleeting thought about kissing you."

She turned her attention to the view, hiding her breathlessness. "Well, thank you for admitting it. And by the way, it doesn't mean anything. People are always thinking about things they shouldn't. It's human nature."

"I have news for you, Lucy. People who are madly in love aren't thinking about anyone's lips but their significant other's. Maybe you have some doubts?"

"About Frederick or you?"

"About yourself, smart-ass. About your feelings." He rested his elbows on the railing, staring out at the world beyond their perch.

"Everyone has doubts at this stage. It's jitters, perfectly natural." She took his silence for skepticism and plunged on. "At some point you have to take it on faith," she insisted. "Although no one seems to have any faith in my choice but me."

"You mentioned your mother. She hasn't given you her blessing?"

"I think she's finally accepted that I'm going to marry Frederick, but in her heart she wants me to hold out for the man of my dreams."

"And that isn't your fiancé?

"In her opinion, no, but Frederick meets all the criteria on my list except one—and don't ask me what that is."

"You have a list?"

She felt like taking the Fifth, but he didn't give her a chance.

"What kind of a list? The perfect man? Mr. Wonderful?"

"Something like that," she said, feeling the need to defend herself. "But I was just a kid when I made it up. What does an eighteen-year-old know about men? It's not really relevant now."

"In that case, you might as well tell me where Frederick falls short—if it's not really relevant."

He almost had her there. "You wouldn't be interested. The whole idea of a list—it's so immature."

"No one ever accused me of being mature, Lucy. I'm *interested*. So . . . Frederick leaves his clothes lying around, he snores, he isn't a good lover?"

She flicked the hair from her face and gave him a look. "Of course he's a good lover. He's a magnificent lover. He can't help it that his kisses don't . . ."

She hesitated, wanting to be accurate.

"Don't what?" he prompted. "Curl your toes?"

"Sounds painful."

"Make you swoon? See stars?"

"Yes, that's part of it." She sighed. "My mother and I were having this discussion the other day, and I couldn't put it into words then either. I guess the word I want is shiver. His kisses don't make me shiver."

"Like you're shivering now?"

"That's the cold."

"Lucy, I don't think so. I think you're shivering for the same reason you were looking at my mouth. You want that feeling."

"No, I don't. I want Frederick's mouth. He'll get it figured out."

"If it's not there, it's not there." He brushed errant tendrils of hair from her eyes. "The real question is why are you willing to give up something so important?"

"Kissing is not that important. It wouldn't even have made my list if I hadn't given in to peer pressure."

"You're not giving up kissing. You're giving up shivering,

a whole lifetime of shivering when the man you love touches you. Can you do that? Is it worth it?"

He made it sound as if it was the most important thing in the world. What was she giving up besides a few goose bumps?

After a moment, she said, "It has to be."

"Why?"

She looked at him for several tortured seconds, wondering if she could explain to him why she had to marry Frederick. "I don't need to shiver, Noah. I need to feel safe. Frederick can do that. He's a good man. He keeps his promises, and that's more important to me than anything else."

"Frederick doesn't hold the franchise on keeping promises. Lots of men keep them."

"My father never did, and I won't let my kids go through that. It's too heartbreaking to be let down again and again. It destroys your faith, little by little, until you don't believe in anyone anymore."

"So this isn't about you? It's about the children you haven't had? Maybe you need to take some time, get out in the world, do some reality testing, and figure out what Lucy wants."

"Lucy *knows* what she wants. And what's wrong with planning ahead? I want children, and it would be irresponsible not to think long and hard about who their father will be, especially when I know how much harm can be done."

Lucy had gone through her childhood thinking she was responsible not just for her parents' failed marriage, but for the kind of man her father had become. If she hadn't come into their life, he would have been happy with her mother, and he wouldn't have been driven to lying, cheating, and stealing. She blamed herself, as children often do when adults misbehave and marriages fail. She was the interloper. *She* had disrupted their relationship, and therefore deserved his callous, hurtful behavior.

Noah was quiet for a moment. "Do you think it's possible that you're planning ahead to avoid what you need to do now?"

"No!"

The force of her objection startled both of them, and she quickly apologized. "Noah, even if I were dying to find out what it would be like to kiss you, I can't. I can't be frivolous about something like this."

"Let's go inside," he said.

"So I can stop shivering." She laughed, but it was bittersweet.

Once they were inside, he gave her hand a gentle squeeze. "I shouldn't have pushed this, and I'm sorry if I upset you. I wish you well in whatever you decide to do."

"What are you doing?"

"I'm saying good-bye," he said. "That seems the best thing, everything considered."

"Everything considered," she echoed. What else could she do?

"Right, then, I'll leave you alone."

He went to pack his toolbox, and it hit home that she wasn't going to see him again. There was nothing to bring them back together now that the briefcase issue had been resolved. He would not be a part of her life in any way, and for some reason that was an unbearable thought to Lucy.

As he turned to go, she noticed the shopping bag. "Wait! You're forgetting the briefcase."

She picked up the bag, knowing she should give it to him. But she couldn't seem to let go of the purple rope handle. "You're leaving?" she said. "Just like that?"

"Yeah, I thought—"

"What about your speech about my not being committed to Frederick?" she blundered on, caught between needing him to stay and wanting to let him go. "I am, of course, but what if I wasn't? It would be important to find out, right? Important for me to know that I was doing the right thing, making the right choice? Maybe it is important to know rather than to wonder. Maybe—"

He cut her off midsentence. She hadn't seen him coming at all. She had her head down and was talking fast and clutching the bag, when suddenly he lifted her chin and bent as if to kiss her. The rope handle slipped from her fingers, and she swayed toward him eagerly, dizzily, touching his lips with hers, loving the heat and sizzle of his lips on hers.

It was a test kiss. Just a test.

She lifted up on her toes for another one. You couldn't be too sure, after all. But he stepped back and looked her over.

"So?"

"S-so? Oh!" She managed a little shake of her head. "No, nothing really. I'm fine."

"You're fine?"

"Yes, thank you, fine. But I'm glad we did that. It's better to know."

She made her way around him—and the shopping bag— and walked to the elevator in a daze. She really did feel fine as she approached the car and pushed the DOWN button. Steady as she goes. It was only as she stepped inside and the doors closed around her that she had the presence of mind to take hold of the railing. By that time everything had begun to tremble, and she could barely hold herself up.

What was happening? She would love to have blamed it on the creaky old elevator. But it was her this time. She was shaking to pieces. At this rate, there would be nothing left of her by the time she reached the lobby—and she did not want to think about what that meant.

Chapter Five 🔊

LUCY would never have described herself as beautiful. Not in a million years. Attractive, maybe. Even slightly sultry with the dark hair veiling her eye, but not beautiful. Her father had told her once that she wasn't a pretty child, and she'd taken it as one more reason that he seemed to resent her very existence. Now she knew that he was a profoundly self-centered man and an opportunist, who didn't want to share the stage with anyone, not even a baby daughter. But the little girl she'd been hadn't known that, and his words had cut deeply.

"He was wrong," she murmured, studying herself in the full-length mirror.

"Who was wrong? That handsome fiancé of yours?" Elsa, the alterations lady, looked up from where she was kneeling on the carpet, pinning the hem of Lucy's wedding gown. It was nearly seven on a Friday evening, and the staff had left for the weekend, so they'd decided to set up in one of the company's unused conference rooms, where they would have plenty of space.

Now, Elsa was beautiful, Lucy thought. She was a Swedish import, in her late twenties, and an aspiring designer. Except for the pin cushion attached with red ribbon to her wrist, she looked more like a streamlined blond supermodel than a seamstress.

"No one," Lucy assured her with a smile. "I was just thinking out loud."

"We're almost finished here." Elsa worked the pins as gracefully as any harpist plucking strings. "Once I have the hem done, I'll take a couple of tucks in the bodice, and the dress should fit like a glove. You're going to be a gorgeous bride."

"How could I be anything else in this gown," Lucy said, returning to her reflection in the mirror they'd borrowed from the ladies' lounge. "You've wrought a miracle, Elsa."

Lucy blinked away the threat of tears as she looked at herself. Her throat ached with the awareness that her father really was wrong. She felt like a princess in this dress. She knew that brides-to-be from time immemorial had felt this way, but she wasn't every bride, and she had never seen such radiance gazing back at her. The antique white satin fabric gave ocean depths to her blue-gray eyes and put a rose petal tint in her cheeks. It made her skin look like just-poured cream, and her figure both voluptuous and slender.

Frederick had actually found the dress at a local bridal shop, and with his usual eye, he'd known the fitted waist and princess lines would be perfect for Lucy. But the size was wrong, and it had needed alterations, so he'd found Elsa and hired her. Frederick could always be counted on to do whatever was needed.

Lucy didn't want to look away from the mirror. It was still hard to believe the radiant creature in the glass was her, Lucy Sexton. She didn't know whether the dress was responsible, or whether she had always looked like this but hadn't been able to see it until now.

Courtesy of her father, probably. She hadn't heard from him since he disappeared nearly twenty years ago, one step ahead of the law, and she had no idea where he was. But the sooner she shut the door on that part of her life the better. Just to declare herself felt good.

She heard noises in the hallway and looked at her watch. She'd thought everyone was gone. As she craned around to see who was out there, her mother walked in the door.

Lydia Sexton saw her daughter, stopped short, and whistled. "Wow," she said softly. "My baby's all grown up, and she's a knockout."

"Do you like it?" Lucy asked. "Tell the truth." She wasn't at all surprised that her mother was still in the building—or that she would be more than happy to weigh in on the dress.

Lydia cocked her head, scrutinizing Lucy from head to toe. After a moment, she said, "Want my honest opinion?"

"Of course."

She raised a motherly eyebrow. "Maybe a touch too much cleavage?"

Lucy glanced down at the lushness revealed by her gaping bodice and laughed. "Not to worry, Mother. Elsa has a couple of tucks planned. I'll be decent for the ceremony."

"No need to go *that* far," her mother said with a wink. "Farewell, my chickadee. You're stunning, and I'm starving. I'm going to hit a take-out place on my way home, and I'll see you tomorrow."

Elsa went back to pinning, and Lucy went back to daydreaming once her mother was gone. Guilt welled as she thought about the stack of work she had to take home with her tonight. She had a tough case coming up, and instead of staring at herself in the mirror, she should have been mentally planning strategies and thinking her way around the possible obstacles. But the pull of her imagination was strong, and it wanted nothing to do with conflict resolution.

She was in a dreamy mood, and that was rare for her. It was impossible not to imagine herself in the church at the moment the doors to the flower-adorned chapel opened, and the wedding march began to play. Her mother would walk her down the aisle, where her dashing groom awaited, fighting emotion as he realized that this day had really come, and what it meant, that his bride was giving not only herself, but two much more precious gifts: her love and devotion.

"Lucy? Where are you?"

A familiar male voice brought her back from dreamland.

"Frederick," she called out, "is that you? I'm down here in the conference room, but wait! You're not supposed to see me."

Lucy glanced back in the mirror and felt an impulse sweep over her. "Oh, come and look anyway," she said, giving her head a shake to discipline her hair. "Tell me what you think. Am I beautiful?"

She didn't hear his answer, but that didn't stop her. She wanted to share this moment, and she couldn't wait any longer.

"Just a minute, Elsa," she said, carefully extricating herself from the seamstress and her pins. Lifting her skirts, she picked her way over to the doorway and saw him at the end of the hall.

Was that Frederick? He seemed taller, but with the light behind him, she couldn't see his features well. Her heart went a little crazy as she stepped out into the hallway and faced him. Her feet seemed to want to move before she was ready, and she heard her own nervous laughter. This had to be how a bride would feel as she began her walk down the aisle.

Lucy's gaze was fixed on the dark figure, but as the angle of the light changed, she realized it wasn't Frederick. He was too tall, his posture too casual. She let out a soft gasp as she saw who it was. The man waiting for her at the end of the hallway was Noah, and she couldn't drag her eyes away from him.

Confusion made her blood rush. She felt light and unsteady, as if her feet had lost contact with the ground. The heavy satin of her dress became difficult to manage, but she continued her walk down the aisle that the hallway had become. Just moments ago she'd been lost in daydreams of her wedding ceremony, and it was exactly like this. But she hadn't clearly seen the man she was walking toward. Of course, she hadn't needed to see his face to know it was Frederick. Who else would it be? But now she wondered if in the back of her mind it could have been Noah she was imagining. Was it his image locked in her subconscious?

And was that why her heart pounded so hard now?

Frederick didn't make her heart pound. He calmed her flights.

She watched Noah's expression change from one of disbelief to an intrigued smile that was very sexy. There was awe and appreciation, too. In fact, there was everything she'd ever wanted to see in a man's face as she walked down the aisle toward him.

She felt as if she were floating. Her fantasies took on a strange reality, and by the time she reached the man at the end, she was dangerously close to believing that he was the one she wanted waiting for her at the altar. But she also knew that was ridiculous. She'd never had a crazier notion in her life. She had to marry Frederick. He was perfect for her. *He made her feel safe.*

Noah spoke first, his voice husky. "I stopped by on the chance you might still be here," he said. "I wasn't expecting a bride."

"I thought you were Frederick," she said, hoping to explain away the breathlessness. Surely he could see the stars in her eyes.

"You are beautiful, by the way," he said. "I don't think I've ever seen anything as beautiful as you in that dress."

"Really? Are you sure?" She glanced down at the gaping neckline.

"Oh, I'm *sure.*"

"Not too much cleavage? My mom thought there was too much cleavage."

Naturally, his gaze dropped to her breasts and she could see what the sight did to him. A muscle clenched in his jaw, putting an end to his smile.

"Obviously your mother and I place a different value on cleavage," he said, clearing his throat of its rasp.

Suddenly she felt very naked, but in a good way.

"You look nothing but ravishing," he added.

"Ravishing," Lucy echoed. Heat flashed toward her throat, burning a crimson path in its wake, and she realized she couldn't hide that from him either, not with all this skin showing. "I really can't look ravishing right now. I'm just not up to it. Besides, it's not me."

"Ms. Sexton? Can we finish?" Elsa had come out into the hallway, and she was calling Lucy back.

"I'll be right there," Lucy said, fixing her gaze on Noah. "Why are you here?" she asked him.

"I wanted to see you. Why else would I be here?"

Her voice dropped to a whisper. "That's exactly why you shouldn't be here. We put it to the test, and it didn't work, which only proves I was right. Frederick is the one."

"What didn't work?"

"The kiss. There's no chemistry."

He glanced at her lips and something inside her turned over and sighed. Her mouth had already gone dry, which it always did when she tried to tell a big fat lie. She was her own built-in lie detector. Her job might require her to bluff on occasion, but that was different.

He startled her by unbuckling his tool belt and taking it off. "I'd bet this belt on us, Lucy. If we don't have something—call it chemistry or whatever you want to call it—I'll donate this to a good cause."

"Don't be ridicu—"

"And keep this in mind," he said, cutting her off. His voice was low, challenging. "You kissed me. I didn't kiss you."

Now there was an argument she hadn't expected. It wasn't easy to force the shakiness from her voice. "Noah, I'm getting married next week." She lifted her skirts, preparing to turn around. "We can't see each other again. You can't drop by."

"No chemistry, huh?"

She swung herself around, managing to get out the word "None" as she did so. Elsa had gone back into the conference room, so at least Lucy didn't have to worry about trying to hide her ragged nerves as she made her way back.

She knew he was watching and she prayed for balance and coordination. *Don't let me trip.* Which of course, she did, almost immediately. It was just a little stumble, but she feared he might try to help her.

"I'm fine," she called out.

He didn't answer, which made her want to look over her shoulder to see if he was still there. What would she do if he wasn't? Run after him? Have another change of heart, the way she did last night? *Was he the one?*

"No," she said under her breath. No, he wasn't. She wanted the father of her children to be everything her own father wasn't: honest, compassionate, sensitive, smart, well-educated, and successful in life. He had to be a good role model and a man any child could look up to. Frederick was all of those things—and Noah? Noah made her sparkle. It was no contest.

She didn't look back. She'd given in to enough crazy impulses for awhile.

But as she marched up the aisle, going the wrong way, she had the strongest sense that this had something to do with the direction of her life as well. Was *she* going the wrong way? It weighed heavily on her that she might never see Noah again. *Would* never see him again. She'd made that clear to him. Now she had to stick to it.

But she already felt a void, as if something vital had been cut from her life and some part of her was in danger of dying off. But that didn't make sense. How could a man she barely knew have such an impact?

Was she supposed to disrupt her entire life because he'd come along and made her sparkle? The Fates were perverse in their timing, but she had a long-term plan, one she'd had since childhood, and she was sticking to it. There was a wedding next week, and she was going to be there, walking up the aisle the right way and joining in holy matrimony with the right man. Right? *Right.*

NOAH watched her go, wondering if she was going to make it in her beautiful boat of a wedding dress. He shouldn't have had a doubt. She had enough determination for a dozen brides. His sense of her was that she'd overcome a lot in her life, and this was just another hurdle.

He didn't like the idea of being a hurdle, however.

Maybe he had a fatal romantic streak, but the thought of being the prince who kissed Sleeping Beauty awake held much more appeal. Her test kiss hadn't been bad, but he hadn't had a chance to reciprocate. He wanted that chance. In all honesty he would have given almost anything for it, including his good luck charm, the tool belt. Since running into her in the store, he'd become pleasantly obsessed with the idea of having her come awake in his arms, realizing who she really was and what she really felt. Discovering how damn sexy she was.

He couldn't wait to hear the moans and sighs he knew were bottled up inside her. What a trip to uncork her and have her bubble all over him like champagne, her breath as sweet as strawberries, her lips as fiery as the wine. Sleeping Beauty coming undone in his arms. That was the fairy tale he wanted to come true. But she had no clue.

She also had no idea how sensual she was with her breasts spilling out of the satin wedding dress. He'd been getting ready to catch them if they fell.

Just the thought made his fingers tingle and ache.

He folded his arms and watched her disappear through the conference room door, his thoughts taking a turn toward the serious. The obvious hadn't escaped him. He was mucking in the lives of nice people, playing roulette with their futures. But was he changing what was written in the stars for Lucy Sexton? Or was he trying to help her see that she'd misread them? He honestly didn't know. He'd gone with his gut, and it had told him she was making one hell of a mistake.

Now he had to ask himself some questions and the answers would play heavily into what he did next. Did he go merrily on his way and let her make a mistake? He could easily make the argument that this wasn't a mission of mercy. What if he wasn't trying to save the woman from herself? What if he was trying to steal her for himself?

On that sobering thought he turned to leave and saw the surprise he'd set on the receptionist's desk when he came in. It was a gift to help Lucy with the goose bumps that raced up and down her arms. He considered leaving it for her, but that would have been *inappropriate* in her eyes, he was sure. He didn't give a rat's ass about being appropriate and never had, but clearly it was important to her.

He picked up the gift-wrapped box and tucked it under his arm. As he walked through the reception area, he ticked off all the reasons why he should keep going and never darken her doorstep again. Lots of people would be inconvenienced if she changed her plans; some would be hurt, like her fiancé. But was that a reason to sacrifice her life?

Not in Noah's mind. However, there was one reason he couldn't argue with. She didn't want him mucking with her plans. She'd just told him they couldn't see each other anymore, and she'd said it with conviction.

We can't see each other again. You can't drop by.

That was going to be a tall order, but he would have to carry it out. It wasn't like he had a choice anymore, he realized, surprised by the dawning awareness. What she wanted was the only thing that mattered to him.

LUCY needed an appliance exorcist. She'd just washed her hair, but she couldn't get the hair dryer to work. When she turned it on, her electric toothbrush sprang to life, vibrating madly in its ceramic holder, but the hair dryer just sat there. She'd also tried the bathroom's other two outlets, which had turned on her depilator and her curling iron, in that order. But no matter what she did, the dryer played dead.

She tried the bathroom lights a couple times as a test. There she was, staring at her own exasperated expression, flashing on and off in the mirror. Now you see the cranky lady. Now you don't.

At least the lights worked, but something was definitely wrong. It probably fell short of demon possession, but she had reason to wonder. With Frederick out of town on business, she'd spent the weekend alone, taking care of last-minute details for the wedding, and she'd had one minor crisis after another. Yesterday, it was the kitchen. Her dishwasher turned itself on and went into the wash cycle every time she used the microwave. The day before that the garage door had opened when her neighbor rang the doorbell. Fortunately, Lucy lived in a gate-guarded community.

She'd just bought the condo a few months ago, and she and Frederick were planning to start out here after they were married. It was the first home she'd ever owned, and she took real pride in that, but the downside was no apartment manager to call in a situation like this.

She gave the hair dryer a pained look. "What is your problem?"

Thank God, it didn't answer her.

The toothbrush was still buzzing away, so she turned it off, wondering if that might bring the dryer back to life. No such luck. Since she was headed for bed anyway and figured she might as well brush her teeth, she switched the toothbrush back on. Low and behold, the hair dryer began to hum.

Lucy quickly bent over and began working on her damp hair. As bizarre as this situation was, it didn't trump getting her hair dry, and she had no idea how long the dryer would hold out.

"Not long," she muttered when it snapped off just moments later. She caught the faint smell of something burning as she hit the ON button to restart the toothbrush. Big mistake. The lights began to blink and a crackling noise came through the walls. She toggled the toothbrush off, but it was too late. A series of tiny detonations sounded like fireworks. The room got very bright, and then Lucy was enveloped in darkness. The circuits had blown.

She let out a sigh that resounded in the silence.

Her kimono hung open, and she tied it tightly around her as she left the room, warding off the vulnerability she felt. She was surprised to see the bedroom lights still burning and the television running. Apparently the power had only been affected in the bathroom. She went to the bedside phone to call her mother.

"Ouch!" A hot bolt of electricity raced up her arm. She dropped the receiver and realized her own phone had given her a shock. It was a message machine with one of those plug-in units, and it must have shorted out, too. What was going to go next? She gave the rest of the bedroom a wary look. She should have taken care of this when the dishwasher started acting strangely, but she'd been too busy to breathe.

She grabbed her purse off the dresser and began riffling through it for her cell phone. She didn't find it in its zipper pocket, so she upended the bag and dumped the contents. When you were dealing with multiple pockets, compartments, and hidey-holes, a full-scale shakedown was the quickest way, she'd discovered. Once she'd found her car keys lurking in the satin pouch with her panty liners.

She retrieved the cell phone from the pile on her dresser and tapped out the number. Her mother answered on the second ring.

"What's up, Luce?"

Lucy rolled her eyes. Caller ID.

"My new house is possessed," Lucy said. "The appliances have gone bonkers. They turn on and off by themselves, and my telephone just gave me a nasty shock."

"Have you called George, the handyman?" her mother asked.

"It's nearly ten o'clock at night. I can't bother him now."

"Is it really ten? No wonder I'm sleepy." Her mother yawned and apologized. "Go through the Yellow Pages and call an electrician. They have people who make emergency calls at all hours. If that doesn't work, pack up and come over here."

She was not going to her mother's. She loved the woman dearly, but they were at odds right now, and the less concentrated time spent together the better. Her mother would only start probing about her and Frederick.

"Thanks, Mom. I'll call someone. It'll be fine."

Once they'd said their good-byes, Lucy sat down on the bed to go through the Yellow Pages. As she searched the book, she noticed a business card on the floor that had probably dropped out of her bag. She bent over and picked it up.

Hightower Electric.

Noah, the bells and whistles guy. She stared at the card and wondered if she was as crazy as her appliances. She hadn't seen him since the day she was having her wedding dress fitted—and she'd been fighting off thoughts of him since. She couldn't call him . . . even though he might be one of the few people with the chops to figure out why her appliances were acting like characters in a Disney animated feature. He was creative enough to have hot-wired the place himself, except that he didn't know where she lived. She'd never told him.

She didn't call George, either. He was retired and didn't deserve being dragged out on a Sunday night, especially on a job like this. She did call several of the electricians in the book, and got no answer. Not that she'd expected to. And she was going to bed anyway. It could wait until tomorrow.

Hopefully nothing would turn itself on during the night.

She closed her cell phone and set it by her bed, then wandered back into the bathroom, where one of her oversized T-shirts was hanging on a hook behind the door. She traded the kimono for the T-shirt, popped some pink Velcro rollers in her damp hair, and headed for bed.

The last thing she did before she turned out the lights was call the number on Noah's card just to see if he had a voice mail message. He did. And she shouldn't have called. His deep, resonant voice made her feel as if he could fix anything, any problem she had and might ever have, whether it had anything to do with her appliances or not.

LUCY'S eyes popped open to total darkness. She'd heard something. An odd creaking sound. There it was again. And again. Had one of her appliances turned itself on? She sat up, listening. The noises sounded as if they were coming from the kitchen.

She slipped out of bed and heard a click. This one had sounded like a door opening. Maybe the locks were unlocking themselves.

Her palms were wet as she picked up a heavy crystal paperweight from the dresser. She crept into the hallway and down its length. As she got to the kitchen, she saw that the door to the garage was slightly ajar. Someone was breaking into her house, and it was too late to call 911.

She moved up behind the door and waited for the intruder to make his move. As the door opened wider and the dark figure entered, Lucy reared up and cracked the lead crystal against his skull with all her might.

Chapter Six 🔊

THE intruder whirled, and Lucy screamed. She'd hit him as hard as she could. How could he still be standing? She swung at him again, but he blocked her and knocked the crystal from her hand. It hit something solid and shattered.

Lucy sucked in a gasp. Move, she told herself. Go for the eyes or the groin. The larger the target the better! She drove up with her knee, but he blocked her again, twisting so that she collided with his thigh.

He kicked the door closed behind her and backed her up against it, pinning her hands on either side of her head. He held the lower part of her body with his hips, so tightly that she couldn't move a muscle.

"Hey, hey, hey," he said under his breath, "what's going on?"

Between gasps, she got out, "Let go of me!"

"I'm not going to hurt you."

"What do you want?"

"I want you to calm down."

"Calm *down*?" she sputtered.

"Lucy, it's me."

His body was unyielding, but she knew that voice. "You?"

The kitchen lights came on. He must have reached behind her and hit the wall switch.

"Yes," he said, meeting her frightened gaze, "me. Noah."

His intense blue eyes and smoky eyelashes were all she needed to see. What was he doing here? Her legs would have dumped her on the floor if he hadn't been holding her fast.

"What are you doing here?" she said, echoing her thoughts.

"Trying to keep you from hitting me?"

He had the nerve to look amused by the situation. She really would have socked him, if she could have. Why was he still pressing her against the door with his hips and flooding her with his body heat?

She pushed back with her pelvis and realized it wasn't the smartest move. She bumped something she shouldn't have, and his eyes darkened dramatically.

It was almost impossible to ignore the warmth of his breath, with its hints of Scotch and wintergreen. He was much too close, and her body was responding as if she liked it. Her heart wasn't pounding just because he'd frightened her. "You broke into my house, and I'm not supposed to hit you?"

"I didn't break in. I pressed your doorbell, and the garage door opened. When I went to check it out, I found the door to the house open."

"Didn't your mother teach you to knock?"

"Didn't your mother teach you to lock doors?"

Her answer was a huge sigh. "Do you really need to keep holding me like this?"

He seemed to be giving some serious thought to the way he was holding her. His lashes lowered and his voice deepened as he met her gaze. "Yeah, I do."

"Well, I need you to stop."

He glanced at her lips and bent shockingly close to her mouth before releasing her hands. He stepped back, but not far enough for her to move, and she wasn't sure she could have anyway. He'd ripped the breath right out of her.

She ducked under his arm and escaped into the kitchen proper.

"I let you do that," he said.

Lucy groaned aloud. She'd just caught her reflection in the stainless steel refrigerator door. She looked like a Valley Girl from Mars. "I'm wearing a T-shirt," she groaned. "And big pink rollers in my hair!"

She pulled the rollers out of her hair and dropped them on the counter, wishing the T-shirt were a little longer—and that she'd worn some underwear to bed!

"Don't change for me," he said. "I think T-shirts are sexier than hell."

Her new kitchen had chrome appliances and a gleaming hardwood floor, all of which she had handpicked without the help of a decorator, but she hadn't realized how many reflecting surfaces she'd created until this minute. She could see herself everywhere—and so could he.

She moved behind the chopping block island in the center of the room, thwarting his view of her bare legs. "You're not for real, right? Tell me you're an actor and this is someone's idea of a joke on the bride-to-be."

"I've been called a few names, but never a practical joke."

"Then why are you here?"

He folded his arms, relaxing. "Because you called me."

"Called you?"

"Your number was right there on my caller ID log. You must have hung up without leaving a message."

"How did you know it was *my* number?"

"I didn't. I hit star sixty-nine and got your voice mail. I tried to call you back, but you'd turned off your phone, so I searched the Net and found your address."

The kitchen's recessed lighting began to flicker, and Lucy looked up. "Uh-oh, there go the lights."

"Aren't you lucky an electrician just broke into your house. Shall I go get my tool belt?"

"You planned this, didn't you?" *Easy, Lucy, that's a little paranoid, even for you.* But he had found her address and come over here on his own, which raised a few questions in her mind. She had no way of knowing if he was telling her the truth about anything, but she had many more pressing issues right now. She rattled off a list of the problems she'd been having all weekend, starting with her demon-possessed appliances.

"This was not caused by some random blown fuse," she insisted. "Somebody who knows what they're doing has been messing around."

He grew serious. "Do you have enemies who would go to this much trouble? Maybe someone who wasn't happy with the way their case was resolved?"

"Most people aren't, quite honestly. Mediation isn't a win/lose situation. It's compromise. In a divorce case, everybody loses in one way or another. I don't give out my home address, but you found it easily enough."

"Why don't you let me take a look around," he said. "I can probably get your appliances running again, and if it was sabotage, I should be able to tell."

"Of course, go ahead." She didn't have much choice but to trust him. She could call the police, but they wouldn't be able to help her with the electricity. "I'll go get changed in case you need me for something."

"I do need you for something, and you're not going to have time to change. I didn't bring my truck, and the only equipment I have with me is a spare tool belt and a couple flashlights. See if you can find some candles, lots of them, and quickly. I'm going to have to turn off the main breaker."

"The fuse box is in the laundry room," she told him. With that he was gone, and Lucy began to case out her kitchen. Candles? A client had given her brass candelabras and tapers for Christmas last year, and she had lots of beautiful candles in the living room and master bedroom. They were part of the décor. She'd never used them, and this wasn't quite the way she'd envisioned lighting them for the first time, but it couldn't be helped.

First, she checked herself out in the mirror her refrigerator had become, taking a look at her backside. The T-shirt hit midthigh, giving her pretty good coverage. He would be busy anyway. And the lights would be out. What was he going to see?

She found a box of long fireplace matches in her kitchen

drawer and set to work, lighting candles throughout the house. The candelabras she arranged on her glass dining room table, and she'd just finished lighting the tapers when he called to her from the garage. "Lights out! Are you ready?"

She shouted that she was, and the house went dark. The tapers flared, seemingly fed by the lack of light. It was eerie and beautiful. Her living room was ablaze, too, and the multitude of small fires created a sense of calm within her that was rare. She liked the feeling, which was probably why she liked candles, and darkness.

She heard footsteps and looked up to see a shadowy figure approaching. He carried a large flashlight that made her think of dark places, like coal mines and train tunnels.

He joined her, quietly taking in the scene. "You have a thing for candles, do you?"

"I like them, yes."

"I've been to Christmas Eve services with less candles."

"I like them," she intoned, "especially *real* ones. Do you mind?"

"Not at all."

He touched her arm and she felt a little shock that may or may not have been electrical. Given the way her hair stood on end, she hoped it was. Talk about tingling. She wondered if he felt it, but he didn't mention it as they walked to the laundry room, which was down the hallway and past the bedrooms.

The only light in the small dark room was the flashlight he handed her.

"You get to do the honors," he said. "I've already checked the fuse box. The problem isn't there, so I'm going to have a look at your master control panel. It regulates whatever's automated—porch lights that come on at dusk, coffeepots that come on in the morning. You may have some bad wiring or corrupted chips."

"Great," she said, "tell me how to help."

"Hit me with your best shot."

"Excuse me?"

The near darkness made his smile shadowy, sexy. "The flashlight. Put it where I need it, okay?"

Lucy moved closer to him, ignoring the quick little shiver that passed over her skin as she beamed the light on the control panel door. The bewildering array of wires, grids, and chips reminded her of a computer's motherboard, which it was, she supposed.

"No chemistry, huh?" he said under his breath. "Then why do you break out in gooseflesh every time we get near each other?"

"What makes you think I do?"

"I can see it, Lucy."

"Now? Here? In the dark?"

"We just came from the living room and that cathedral you created. I saw what happened when I touched you. You got goose bumps."

"You keep giving me shocks. Who wouldn't get goose bumps when you're around?"

"Sorry." Irony edged his apology. "I only shock people I really like."

Lucy was tempted to shine the flashlight in his eyes and make him blink those big baby blues. "We agreed not to see each other again," she reminded him. "It's not fair for you to take advantage just because I'm in trouble, and I called you."

"You're right," he conceded. "We did agree, and as much as I might love to take advantage, I won't. No more goose bumps. No more idle conversation, either, unless it involves possessed appliances."

"Thank you." Her sense of satisfaction didn't last long, however. He didn't have to give up *that* easily, did he?

The laundry room fell silent as he worked. Lucy concentrated on holding the light steady while he sorted wires and untangled circuitry. He seemed completely absorbed, which she found very sensual for some unknown reason. But it was the natural, sensual grace of his movements that held her attention. He had the precision of a bomb squad specialist. He knew exactly how to coax and cajole the tangled circuitry, how to tame the nest of wires. It was artistry, pure and simple. Seduction. *That's right, baby, come to me. Come to me. Give a little, just a little, that's right, let it go. Real nice, real slow . . .*

Seduction. And it was working.

She couldn't seem to stop fantasizing about the sensitivity of those hands in other situations, such as probing the tender mysteries of a woman's body. God, he had to be good. How could he not? She was getting jealous of the wires.

Another one of those sweet little shocks hit her, but this one was nowhere near her arm. It was a flash of pleasure between her legs that made her eyelids flutter.

The flashlight wobbled before Lucy realized she was moving. He didn't seem to notice, but she spoke up, mostly to distract herself. "What is it you find so sexy about T-shirts?"

"Nothing, unless you're wearing one of them."

"You can't be serious. I could be a half-naked bag lady."

"It's the half-naked part I like. Speaking of which, the one you're wearing could be a little shorter."

"Or have a V-neck to show off my magnificent cleavage?"

"Now there's a thought. Maybe you should ditch the T-shirt altogether. Think how inspired I'd be to get the lights back on."

Hysteria bubbled up inside her, causing the flashlight to dance. Clearly he'd never seen her nude self. She was not a hard body, and her breasts weren't the only pleasingly plump part of her five-foot, five-inch frame. Around her period even her ankles got chubby.

"You okay?" He hesitated in his work, as if waiting for the beam to stop gyrating.

"I'm fine." She tucked dark waves behind her ear, just in case he happened to look her way. "Such a nuisance, this hair. It's always falling into my eyes."

Of course he didn't look her way—and she wasn't certain what it would take to get him to do so. She'd never seen such focus. It was beginning to annoy her. He had way too much control. He obviously wasn't having any thoughts erotic enough to distract him, but why not? She'd love to shake him up a little, give him a few goose bumps. He'd shut off the circuit breakers, so it wasn't like there was any real danger in trying to get a charge of out of him, so to speak.

Just another test, she told herself. And she needed to do some reality testing. Noah had said so himself.

She mustered her courage as she watched him gingerly slide a wire back into place and then fasten it down with a screwdriver. Those agile fingers might be irresistibly sexy, but it was his ability to completely ignore her that finally spurred her into action.

"What's that funny red thing?" She sidled close to him and pointed out a flickering red switch on a grid.

"What?"

"That switch?" She leaned over him, as if to show him what she meant. "See?" Naturally she was brushing his arm with her breast. And quite openly, too. Why not, since he was so appreciative of her magnificent cleavage?

"It's a warning light to tell us the control panel is disabled, and the memory chip is running off battery power."

"Fascinating." Her tone was dry. How did he stay so oblivious? Was it a gift?

"Seems as if you've been at this for ages. Are we a little tight, maybe?" She switched the light to her left hand and smoothed her fingers over the bunched muscles of his shoulders and neck, feathering them as she went. "Ooo, we *are* tight. Does that feel better?"

She saw his eyebrows knit and wondered if it was her or the circuit he was working with. "I give excellent neck massages," she said, softening her voice to a purr. "It takes two hands, though. I'd have to set the flashlight down, and it might get a little dark in here."

"Think I'll pass," he murmured.

At least he was listening. "Are you sure?" She began to play with the dark hair that curled along the back of his collar. The soft, silky feel of it brought a little moan of appreciation to her lips. "Nice," she said as she swirled her fingers through it, working her way to the back of his ear. His lobes were soft, too.

"Doesn't that feel nice?" she asked.

He said nothing as she caressed the lobe with her knuckles, wondering what it was going to take to get his attention. Maybe if she stuck her tongue in his ear. Never going to happen, of course, but while she was contemplating the idea, she saw his bicep flex. And then his jaw knotted up, right before her eyes. Now that was interesting.

She dared to delve inside his ear, playing in the whorls. She seemed to have his attention now. At least he'd stopped tinkering with the wires.

"Lucy . . .?"

"Yes?"

"You have your finger in my ear."

"Oh, is that your ear?" Lucy was too embarrassed to defend herself. But then, thank God, fiery indignation came to her rescue.

"How did you know?" She set the flashlight down on the counter with a clunk. The man was impossible. Let him hold his own flashlight. She was leaving.

She heard noises, the control panel door slamming shut, a screwdriver hitting the floor, but she ignored it all. She was headed out of the laundry room when he caught her and turned her around. Once again he backed her to the door and pinned her there, but this time it was with the force of his gaze. And this time she let him.

Confetti. Her stomach was a blizzard.

No shivering, she told herself. *No gooseflesh. None.*

"Where are you going?" he asked.

"I'm getting out of your way. God forbid I break your concentration again."

"So you want to give me a massage?" A telltale roughness had sneaked into his voice.

"Uh . . . yes, sure."

"How badly?"

Not certain where this was going, she said, "Very badly?"

He took a deep breath. "What's this all about, Lucy?"

"Nothing, I was trying to be helpful."

"And you're trying to help me with *what?*"

Her flashlight must have fallen to the floor, but its beam ricocheted against the ceiling, throwing ghostly shadows.

"What's going on?" he pressed. "I'm trying to figure out what you want."

"N-nothing." She had to tell the truth. Her throat was drying up, and soon she wouldn't be able to talk at all. "I just wanted to get your attention."

"You have my attention. Now what are you going to do with it?"

She chewed on her lip. "Ask you a question?"

"Like?"

"Like when can we turn the lights back on?"

"Anytime you want. All I have to do now is flip the main breaker."

"Oh, that's great. Thank you. I really appreciate—"

"Lucy, do you want me to go or do you want me to stay?"

"Excuse me?"

"My neck, it's tight. I could use that massage."

She shrugged. "I'm really not that great at massages. Otherwise, I wouldn't have been messing with your ear, right?"

"Go or stay?"

She wanted him to stay. "Go."

He stepped back, and she was gripped with déjà vu. She'd done it again. He was leaving. Any opportunity of finding out what could have happened between them on this bizarre night was lost. He was leaving, and she wanted him to. He *had* to leave. It was crucial that he did, and yet confusion racked her. What *did* she want? Disappointment cut through any relief she might have felt. She wasn't glad to see him go, but she ought to be.

This is how it has to be, Lucy. This is the life you've chosen. One without storms.

She was still arguing with herself when he turned on the main breaker, and the condo sprang to life.

She tried to thank him, but he shrugged it off. "Not a problem."

The flashlight lay on the floor at her feet. They both reached for it at once, their bare arms brushing. Lucy expected a shock, but all she could feel was heat and hard muscle. There was no give to this man, even in his forearm. She didn't know if that was good or bad.

"I could let myself out," he suggested. "The way I came in?"

"No, come with me. The front door is closer." That wasn't precisely true, but she couldn't let him disappear yet. He wasn't coming back. The living room was dark as they entered, except for the brightly burning candles. She hadn't turned on any lights in there.

"Let's see if the porch light works," he said as they reached the front door.

Lucy couldn't think of any way to delay the inevitable. Silently she watched him open the door and then flip the switch. She started toward him, but what happened in the next split second froze her where she stood. A crackling sound filled the room. Sparks shot from the switch, followed by puffs of black smoke.

Lucy screamed as an explosion rattled the room, jolting Noah backward. He hit a small hassock on wheels that flew out from under him and threw him to the ground.

She couldn't move fast enough. He was out cold when she dropped to her knees beside him. "Noah! Oh, my God."

He had a pulse, but he didn't appear to be breathing. Terrified, she ran for the kitchen phone and found it dead. She couldn't find her cell in the darkness of the bedroom, and she knew there wasn't time to go back for a candle and continue searching. She had to get him breathing again.

She raced back to the living room, rolled him onto his back with great effort, and ripped open his work shirt. Buttons flew everywhere. As she unbuckled his tool belt, his words from last night flashed into her head. *I'd bet this belt on us, Lucy. If we don't have something, call it chemistry—*

She forced his voice out of her thoughts and concentrated on getting his jeans undone. She had no personal experience with CPR, but she'd seen it done on countless TV shows, and the rescue people always cleared the victim's air passage before they started CPR.

She opened his mouth and probed with her finger, but found nothing. Was he breathing? It was impossible to tell. His head rolled back, and she pressed her lips to his, blowing deeply enough to force air into his lungs. She held off a few seconds and blew again, continuing until she thought she felt him stir.

The sound he made could have been a cough, and his chest began to move.

Lucy wanted to scream for joy, but she kept going. Warm air streamed from his nostrils, but he still hadn't come to. Seconds passed, and it occurred to her to check his pulse again, but she couldn't find the beat this time.

Praying that he wouldn't stop breathing, she straddled him and began to push on his chest. Was she doing this right? Dear God, she needed help. How did she get his heart going and keep him breathing at the same time? She was just about to abandon her efforts and go search for the cell phone, when she thought she felt him stir.

"Noah?" she implored, leaning over him. "Please wake up, oh, please. I'll do anything!"

Chapter Seven

PLEASE, Noah, please, I'll do anything. . . .

Noah heard the woman's whispering voice and figured he had to be dreaming. But it was one hell of a dream. Somebody was touching him, kissing him, and pressing her hands to his chest, and it had to be her, the one who was whispering. When he tried to open his eyes all he could see was a beautiful blur. But it actually looked like the blur was sitting on him. She was straddling him, and he could feel her weight, her legs. Her hot, soft skin.

Was she naked? Was he?

God, what a dream. Now she was beating him with her fists, melting all over him in some crazy state of passion.

"Come on, Noah. Come on! Do it with me." She gripped his face and pressed her lips to his. Her breath rushed into him and then she broke away with a little sob of anguish. She was fiery hot all over, writhing and squirming.

"Do it," she pleaded, "give me something! *Breathe* with me."

His eyelids were too heavy to move. He couldn't open them enough to see more than a bobbing feminine silhouette, but he didn't have to imagine her naked body. He could feel it—the inside of her clinging thighs, the moist heat between her legs, the silky curls that caressed him whenever she moved. She was sitting on him, and she *was* naked.

Breathe must be a code word for making love, and it sounded like she desperately wanted him to do just that. Apparently she'd roused him from sleep for that reason, but he wasn't sure he could help her. His body was heavy and unresponsive. He found it hard to move a muscle. Except that one, which she'd had no trouble awakening. Already it was stirring, swelling, taking on a will of its own, and with each surge of energy, the pressure built. He wasn't naked. He was definitely wearing pants because it felt damn crowded down there, like seams were about to split.

Desire flared as she kissed him again, begged him again. He was waking up now. The tingling life that had invaded his groin raced through his entire body, and it felt incredible, although it didn't completely mask other sensations. For some reason, his shoulder ached, and his butt felt like someone had given him a good swift kick. It also felt like he was lying on the floor, which was odd. Then again, maybe not, given his dream lover's wild streak.

Little fires seemed to be flickering all around him, only he couldn't tell what they were. Gradually he realized he was in a darkened room, lit by a forest of candles. They were everywhere, like fireflies in the night. Even in his groggy state, he knew that candles meant romance and sensuality. The woman wanted to make love, no doubt about that. If this was a dream, he was going to make the most of it.

Once he was free of the jeans, they could drive each other as nuts as she was driving him now. He ached to touch her with his hands. When he'd had his fill of her soft flesh and lush curves—if that was possible—he would coax her to take him just the way she was now, sitting astride him like Lady Godiva. God, what pleasure. His mind could barely contain it. After that, he would roll her over, and they would take their sweet time, whispering and kissing, their bodies resonating with the pleasure they could give one another.

He wondered if he had the willpower to slow everything

down. In this heated rush of passion, it seemed decadent to casually brush his mouth over hers and watch her lids quiver, her breath catch. But that was exactly what he wanted, to let his lips wander over every delicate part of her, especially the secrets between her legs. What a thrill to watch those silken ruffles quiver and catch.

His fingers were hot, tingling with energy. He was coming awake, alive. He found her feet, which were tucked alongside his hips, and he began to explore them. Her legs were smooth and inviting. They coaxed him to follow their sinuous contours, but soon he was delving under a canopy of soft material.

So she wasn't naked. She wore some kind of small white tent, but he could change that. Beauty like this should be exposed to the night, the fireflies, the heavens.

"Noah?"

Her voice roused his senses. It pricked his memory. "Lucy?"

"Yes, it's me. Thank God, you're okay."

Okay? He was anything but okay. She was bending over him, stroking his face, and he could feel the feathery curls of her pubis tickling his skin with every move.

"Lucy," he whispered, "get me out of these jeans. I need to breathe. I need to breathe with you."

She seemed to hesitate, but he had no idea why. The flickering candles made it difficult to see anything. "Lucy, did you hear me?"

She didn't answer, and he fell back, exhausted, his mind swirling.

"Shhhh," Lucy whispered, trying to calm him. She'd heard him, but she didn't know quite what to make of his request. She was so crazy, out-of-her-mind thrilled to have him back—to have him *alive*—that she would have done anything. If he wanted out of his jeans, she would get him out of them. Maybe they'd twisted up and were cutting off his circulation.

"Just a minute," she told him, crawling backward down his body.

His anguished moan startled her. "Did I hurt you?" she asked.

"Wait!" He gripped her by the arms with surprising

strength and drew her back to him. "I can't let you go. Don't leave me yet."

"I'm not leaving." She hushed him, trying to soothe his fears. "You're all right. You're going to be fine."

"No, I'm not, Lucy. Not without you."

He caressed her face and lifted on one elbow to whisper something to her, but all she could hear was the rush of his breath as his mouth came perilously close to hers.

It felt as if they were kissing, the way their lips parted and their eyes drifted shut, kissing yet not kissing, playing with fire. God, how she wanted that. The kiss. The fire. She'd just had her mouth all over him, but that was different. This felt thick with promise, hot and sexual, and it gave her uncontrollable shivers. They darted like fireflies in the pit of her stomach.

She tried to pull back, but he wouldn't let her go. "Lucy, no, I need you."

He was making her flushed and dizzy. She needed some space. "Let me undo your jeans," she said.

He drew her against his mouth, moaning, and she wanted to fall into his arms and never fall out. Their lips touched, and she heard a tiny cry form in her throat. It nearly undid her, that utterance. She'd never made a sound like that in her life.

"Let me go," she said, dragging herself up.

He released her and she moved off him with an awkward lunge, thinking that she could help him with his jeans and be gone. Move away, out of the force field they'd created, run from the storm.

She had no idea that she would find him fully aroused. An enormous bulge had stretched his jeans tight. You could see *detail* through the material. "Noah, you're— I can't."

He pulled her into his arms, and they rolled over from the force of it. She landed on her back, with him looming above her. "I need you," he said, breathing the words. "I need to be inside you."

Her stomach clutched, and the fireflies swarmed, going wild. They were too bright to bear. Too sharp. That sound again. It quavered in her throat, and he heard it.

"Jesus, Lucy."

She reached up to touch his mouth, and air, warm from his lungs, flowed through her fingers. In that split second, she must have made a decision without even realizing she'd done it. She could run from the storm or let herself be taken by it. His kiss represented everything she feared. It was inviting disaster, a flirtation with death, and the only way she could come back to life. The alternative was limbo, and that's where she'd been since her father left.

She must have known that because when Noah tugged her to a sitting position, she met his gaze unflinchingly, and then she put her hands in the air. She raised them high, letting him strip her of all clothing, all protection.

A moment later, she sat naked in the candle flame, blushing under his gaze. She could feel the gooseflesh pricking her skin—and he could see it. Yes, he made her shiver. Yes, she wanted that feeling. But God, it was fierce. This was more than just pleasure. It verged on pain—and she felt completely alive.

Now the air was pouring in and out of him. He could have been breathing fire.

She fell back, throwing her arms above her head, and he moved over her like a gathering storm.

She was prepared for force and fury, prepared to be flung into the void, but he was astonishingly gentle. There was plenty of fury contained in his touch, but it was tempered with a reverence that brought a mist to her eyes.

"Now this is beauty," he told her, taking in her figure.

Stretched out in the firelight, she was a long, flickering flame. Her breasts gleamed like honey. "And these are sweetness," he said as he bent to taste them. His lips were like bees, drinking up the nectar. She wanted them to sting her and make her gasp. But he stopped too quickly, leaving her nipples wet and taut, aching for more. Still, it was good. This was what she had missed in her life, the lovely agony of needing.

She did nothing more than lie there, gazing up at him as he used his fingers to trace the golden contours of her breasts, one at a time, purling along the voluptuous outer curves. Odd that she felt it even more intensely when he stopped. Her flesh reached for him, yearning.

He left her long enough to slip out of his shirt and jeans. She glanced at his body in the firelight, but it was more than she could handle at the moment. Her own nakedness still shocked her a little. Her heart couldn't stand the impact of his, too. He was strikingly built, but she'd known he would be. She'd never seen longer, stronger legs. And his butt could have been sculpted from marble.

Noah noticed her looking at him, or rather, trying hard not to look, and once he had the clothes off he dropped down beside her to save her any more discomfort. She would become familiar with his body soon enough. He didn't want to frighten her, at least not in that way. Would he love to terrify her with the raw passion of their coupling? Would he love to terrify the hell out of both of them? *Yes*. And the way his heart was pounding and his muscles throbbing, it shouldn't be too difficult.

He captured her mouth with his and lowered his weight onto her. Her hands were already above her head, but he covered them, which gave the illusion of rendering her helpless. The way her eyes glittered told him she was excited. But the scent she gave off was tinged with fear and trepidation, all of it mingling to create an intoxicating female musk.

Her body was a mystery to him. She had secret places he'd never touched, never seen. He wanted to search out every one of them and shower her with pleasure, but the drive to be a part of her was too powerful. Especially when she dug her fingers into his flesh and urged him to enter her. Her legs surrounded him, gripping him tightly, and he was so hard, so ready, he ached.

If he didn't slow this down, he *was* going to be inside her, all the way inside, where everything was mindless bliss. At this rate it would all be out of his control.

He took the control back, lifting himself above her and extending his arms to their full length.

"What are you doing?" she asked.

"I don't want to lose my mind, not yet."

She reached up and raked his face with her nails. "We've both lost our minds. Maybe we're supposed to."

Her hand dropped to his shaft, stroking it and guiding it into her.

Noah groaned at the beauty of her touch, at the fire that blazed through his veins. His body was a live, hot wire. His penis throbbed. Nestled in her moist, sweet nest, it inched toward heaven with a will of its own.

He dropped to his elbows and thrust deep, deeper.

Lucy fell back, taking him, loving it. He kissed her mouth as he entered her body, and their breath mingled like wind and water. She choked back a sob. She couldn't have waited. She was too terrified that something might happen, she might change her mind. She'd been known to do that.

"God, I'm inside," he whispered.

"You're inside," she echoed. Joy coursed through her, deepening as he began to thrust. He was the storm. He was life, dangerous and sweet.

LUCY woke up to the realization that her ankles were freezing. She was lying on the floor on her side, her arm draped over her head, and her bare feet sticking out from under the covers. She didn't remember there being any covers when she fell asleep. She didn't remember falling asleep. Unfortunately, she did remember how she got on the floor.

"Oh, Luce," she whispered, her voice cracking, "what have you done?"

Probably no coincidence that she'd used her mother's term of endearment. She was in trouble. She wasn't clearheaded enough to grasp exactly how much trouble, but her thoughts were making her dizzy, so she pulled her feet back under the blanket and took a moment to get her bearings before doing anything else. She honestly had no idea what awaited her out there, and she'd had a tendency lately to cross without looking both ways, so she was taking it slow this morning. She didn't even know whether or not she had an overnight guest.

The house seemed unusually quiet, but maybe he was asleep on the floor behind her. She had an image of him sprawled naked in all his magnificence—and he had some of that going for him, magnificence. More than his share, actually. He'd taken her to places she'd never even dreamed of, the grand tour, and she hadn't wanted to come back. He'd be the perfect man to run away with . . . if only she were a woman who could run away.

She rolled to her back and looked around.

He wasn't lying next to her, behind her, or anywhere in the room that she could see. She was alone, but there was plenty of evidence that he'd been there. The overturned hassock, her discarded T-shirt, the array of candles, now dark. She hadn't dreamed about the laundry room experience or his near electrocution or any of the rest of it. The house still smelled of smoking wires and dripping wax.

She sat up slowly, drawing the blanket around her and wondering where it had come from. The soft claret-red material could have been cashmere. She spotted a label and took a quick look. It was cashmere—pashmina. The entire thing was bordered with a graceful red silk fringe that was extraordinarily long and dense. It wasn't a blanket, she realized. It was a very large shawl.

Wrapping herself in the deliciously soft cape, she went to get her T-shirt, then glanced around to make sure she was alone before she made the exchange. She slipped on the shirt and as an afterthought, tied the shawl around her waist, for modesty as well as warmth. Her ankles were still icy.

Not a fashion statement, she admitted. But at least she felt slightly more equal to dealing with the aftermath of . . . what? What did she call last night? An accident? A blackout in every possible sense of the word? Fate? She just didn't know, and his disappearance didn't help. They couldn't even talk about what it had meant.

Where had he gone?

She made a quick search of the house, but didn't find him. She didn't know how to feel as she walked back to the living room, but she found it damn hard to breathe. Only as she entered the room did she see the package that sat on the couch.

It was gift-wrapped, but looked as if it had been opened. The card lying next to it had her name inscribed on the envelope.

A thrill shot through her as she rushed to pick it up. She slid her finger inside the envelope flap and ripped it open. It had to be from him.

She read the note aloud, her voice unsteady.

> *A warm shawl and a decanter*
> *of French fire to help with those*
> *goose bumps.*
>
> *Love, Noah*

He'd handwritten a P.S. at the bottom: *I had an early call, but don't worry, your wiring's good.*

Love? He'd signed it love.

Now she knew how to feel. Giddy. Stupid. Happy.

Oh, jeez, she was *happy*. That was terrible. It required justifying and explaining. Tortuous soul-searching. How could she be happy under these circumstances? It was like trying to be happy about your toothache because you didn't want to go to the dentist.

Was that how she viewed her marriage, as a trip to the dentist?

She touched the cashmere wrapped around her waist. Noah must have opened the package before he left so that he could cover her with the shawl. A pretty sweet thing to do, she had to admit. The man was beginning to show some list potential. If she recalled correctly, "sweet and attentive" was number six.

She glanced at his note, curious about the second gift, French fire. A search through the popcorn-filled box turned up a bottle of aged cognac in a beautiful Limoges decanter.

"This is too much," she whispered.

When had he bought these gifts? Why had he bought them? She really didn't understand his motives, but maybe that wasn't the point. She needed to be questioning her own motives. Why was she making such crazy choices?

Clearly she'd given in to another impulse, but why had that

seemed like a good thing last night and a bad thing this morning? Probably because it wasn't her. Lucy Sexton didn't do things like that. She didn't make reckless choices. She always knew exactly what she was doing and why. She'd planned her life exactly the way she'd planned her wedding, with nothing left to chance.

She could have explained everything she'd done since the age of eleven to the satisfaction of anyone who cared to listen. She had reasons for what she did. But she couldn't explain this at all. It *was* a blackout. It negated everything that was normal and familiar to her. Was she trying to sabotage her relationship with Frederick? Did she want out of the wedding? If she was looking for an excuse, this was a doozy.

"What time is it?" She hugged the cognac bottle. "Too early for a drink?"

She heard a phone ringing faintly in the distance and wondered if she was imagining it. Why would anyone be calling her so early? It was the cell phone in her bedroom, and she dashed to answer it, but by the time she got there, she'd begun to suspect that it wasn't early. Her clocks were running, but they were hours late from having been off all night. Her cell—which was lying on the floor where she'd left it—said it was nearly ten-thirty. Cells didn't require electricity, so it was probably right, which made her all the more reluctant to answer the phone. The number in the display said it was her office calling, possibly even her mother.

Lucy was relieved to hear her assistant's voice.

"What's going on?" Valerie asked. "Why aren't you answering your phones? You have new clients due here in fifteen minutes!"

"I lost the cell last night, and the other phones haven't rung." Lucy checked to make sure her land line was on the hook. "I had a power outage. It probably knocked the land line out of commission. I'll have to reset the phones."

"Are you okay?" Valerie asked. "Can you get over here? I can stall your clients for awhile."

Lucy had poured her life into Sexton Mediation. She hadn't missed an important meeting since they started the company. Racked with guilt and remorse, she said, "I can't do it, Valerie. I'm not . . . well."

"You're sick? Lucy, you're *never* sick. What's wrong?"

"I don't know." She sighed. It was the truth. "Would you ask my paralegal to take my place at the meeting? It's a standard intake so there shouldn't be a problem. Anna's smarter than I am anyway. If she's not available, get Mom, but don't tell her I'm sick. I don't want her to worry."

"What shall I tell her?"

"You can come up with something, Valerie, *please*. Be creative."

Valerie reluctantly agreed, but as Lucy hung up the phone she felt like an escaped convict. She'd bought herself some time, but what was she going to do with it? Rethink her entire life? Frederick was coming back today, and she would have to face him sooner or later.

She pulled the shawl from her waist and wrapped it around her shoulders, then went back to the living room. Drawn to the place where she and Noah had been, she sat nearby on the rug, wrapped in her shawl and holding on to the bottle of cognac.

For the longest time she wasn't able to do anything, even think, but the fact that she had surrounded herself with Noah and his gifts to her told her something. Maybe she couldn't figure it all out. Maybe she would never be able to understand, but she couldn't dismiss what happened. There had been extenuating circumstances. She'd thought Noah was dead, and she'd been overjoyed when he took that first breath, but that wasn't the only reason they'd ended up in each other's arms. Something in her had wanted it, needed it, and allowed it. This wasn't really about Noah. It wasn't even about her relationship with Frederick. It was about Lucy Sexton. That's where everything began and ended. And that's where she had to look for the answers.

Some time later, it all began to come together for her. Still immersed in thought, she sat cross-legged on the floor, nodding her head at the idea that had taken hold. As much as it frightened her, she knew she'd hit on something significant.

And suddenly it was clear what she should do to resolve at least part of this nightmare. She just didn't know whether or not she could.

A sharp series of raps at the door brought Lucy out of her thoughts. She considered ignoring the insistent noise the way she'd been ignoring the cell phone all morning. She hadn't taken the time to fix the land line, either. She didn't want to talk to the office, her mother, or Frederick. Nor did she want to get another electrical shock. But mostly she was afraid it might be Noah, and she didn't know what to say to him. She was also a little worried about what he might have to say to her, maybe because she had no clue what that would be.

This could be him at the door. But she couldn't hide forever.

She was gathering herself to get up when she heard a key turn in the lock. She froze, staring at the door. Who had a key to her house? That could only be her mother or—

"Frederick?"

The door swung open, and her fiancé barged in, coming to a halt when he saw her. "Are you all right, Lucy? I've been try-ing to call you since I got back."

"I'm fine, Frederick." She rose, aware that she looked like a badly dressed gypsy. She didn't have the energy to explain her clothing—or lack of it—and it wouldn't matter anyway, not after what she had to tell him. Neither of them would care how she was dressed by the time she was through.

"Please sit down, would you?" She indicated the couch. "We need to talk."

"What is it?" He stayed where he was by the door, as if he sensed something was seriously wrong, and he wasn't sure getting involved was a good idea.

"I wish you'd sit down," she said imploringly. "There's something I have to tell you, and it may be the hardest thing I've ever had to do."

"What's this about, Lucy? Are you ill? I called the office, and they said you were out sick."

"No, it's not that. I'm not sick."

"Then what is it? Us? Next week? Something about the wedding?"

"Please, Frederick, don't play guessing games. I'll tell you if you'll just sit down."

He did as she asked, sitting on the arm of the couch. Lucy could see that he wasn't going to commit to anything more until he knew what was going on. He sensed bad news, and he was right about that. He didn't know how bad.

Her deep breath didn't help much. "I met someone," she told him. "It just happened. I don't understand it at all. I haven't been able to explain it to myself, but I had to tell you. I couldn't pretend. I couldn't lie to you, although I thought about it. I wanted to."

"You met someone? A man?"

"Yes—" Her voice broke as she realized how badly this was going to hurt him. How it was hurting her already. "He was working in the building, and things kept bringing us together. I'm not making excuses. I really didn't plan it."

Frederick was suddenly fiercely interested. "What's happened, Lucy? Are you trying to tell me you're involved with this man? Do you love him?"

"I don't know how I feel, but I did—" She held the ends of her shawl, tying them into knot after knot. "Or rather, we did—"

"You did what?"

"We made love." She blurted it out, and in the next breath, said, "I know, this is a horrible way to tell you, but I didn't expect you to walk in that way. God, you must hate me. I'm sorry, Frederick. We'll call the wedding off. You can tell everyone it's my fault. It is my fault. I'm so sorry!"

He went silent, bowing his head slightly.

She didn't know what to do. Should she go to him, say something? "Oh, God, Frederick, don't cry. I'll do anything to make it better. Tell me what to do."

When he looked up his eyes were dry. "I want you to calm down, Lucy. It's okay. I already knew."

"You knew I had sex with someone else?"

He rose from the arm. "No, but I suspected that you weren't really in love with me, and that it might be something else that was driving you to get married, like your need for a father figure . . . so I asked Noah Hightower to help me out. He's a client and a frat brother of mine from college."

"What are you talking about?" Lucy let go of the shawl and it dropped to the floor in a crimson heap. "How did Noah help you?"

He didn't answer, and she leaped to the worst possible conclusion. "You and Noah set this up?"

"Well, not like that."

He started toward her, but she backed away. "Don't," she said, "just tell me what you mean."

"We didn't plot against you," he explained. "I set it up so that you could meet someone else. Him, Noah."

"That meeting at Blanchard's was a setup? He wasn't there to buy an attaché?" She wouldn't have believed Frederick capable of this kind of scheming. She'd always thought of him as impeccably honest. Maybe she didn't know him at all.

His shrug was decidedly sheepish. "I called him that morning and told him you were shopping, and you'd probably show up there."

He'd been hinting around that he wanted a Cavalli briefcase, and he'd even suggested the store where she could find one. Lucy closed her eyes, dizzy.

"Dear God, Frederick, I had sex with the man!"

"Well, that's unfortunate, of course. That wasn't supposed to happen."

She couldn't believe any of this. "Get out of here," she warned him in a frighteningly soft voice. "Get out of here now."

"Lucy—"

"Get out of my house, Frederick. Go and don't ever come back. The marriage is off. We're off. Everything's off! If I had a gun I'd shoot you in the back on your way out the door."

Chapter Eight ✑

NOAH threw the last pair of jeans into his suitcase and zipped up the soft leather bag. Stepping back from the bed, he scanned the hotel room he'd called home for the last week. It boasted an ocean view, a whirlpool tub, and a well-stocked bar. Not a bad place as hotel rooms went, but he'd stayed in his share, and he wasn't sorry to leave. One final look around, and he was ready to go.

"Come on in," he called, responding to the sound of footsteps in the hall. He'd left the door ajar for the bellman.

Noah turned, stunned to see Fred Anderson walk into the room. His usually immaculate friend looked like he'd slept in his clothes. Fred was in shirtsleeves, his tie pulled loose, his hair rumpled, as if he'd been raking his hands through it.

"We have a problem, Hightower," Fred announced. "Lucy knows about our arrangement. She just threw me out of her house—and called off the wedding."

Noah felt as if someone had kicked him in the chest. Lucy knew? Noah was just headed over to her place to tell her himself. If she was furious at Fred, what must she feel toward him? *Jesus.*

"How did she find out?" Noah asked.

"I told her. Right after she told me that you two had sex."

"She told you that?"

"Lucy is honest to a fault. She couldn't stop crying and apologizing. She was distraught, and I was trying to make her feel better."

Noah felt as if he'd missed something. "Fred, you're not angry that Lucy and I made love?"

"Well, of course, I'd prefer you hadn't, but things happen, and I admit to feeling somewhat responsible. If her electrical system hadn't gone out, you wouldn't have been over there."

"Her electrical system?" Noah stared hard at his friend, not wanting to think what he was thinking. "How are you responsible for that? What did you do? Sabotage her wiring?"

"Me? No, of course not. I hired someone."

"Fred, for Christ's sake!"

Fred yanked at his tie, loosening it more. "How else was I supposed to get you two together? You told me she didn't want to see you again."

"Lucy and I *agreed* not to see each other again. She was committed to marrying you, you jerk."

"Right, I know, but dammit, Noah, you also agreed to help me find out whether she really loved me."

"So you arranged for her lights to go out, hoping she'd call me?" Noah started toward him, steaming mad. "Why the hell didn't you tell me what you were up to?"

"You would have said no!"

"You're damn right."

Fred had edged to the far side of the bed, as if that could buffer him from Noah. "Listen," he said, "we go back a long way. We've been friends for nearly twenty years—and fraternity brothers, don't forget that. I'm also the guy whose financial advice has helped you make some highly profitable business decisions over the years, right?"

"Cut the crap, Fred. I agreed to help you because you were a friend, and you were in trouble. I met Lucy at Blanchard's, and I did the electrical work at her building, all of which you arranged."

"*Exactly.*" Fred's nod was frantic. "I was getting married in two weeks, and I didn't know what else the hell to do. Lucy kept insisting she was madly in love and wanted to marry me, but she didn't act like a woman madly in love. What was I supposed to think? Her father walked out on her and her mom when she was a kid, and Lucy always felt responsible. I was afraid she saw me as a substitute father figure, so I called you."

"Maybe you should have told her the truth," Noah ventured.

"I did! I suggested we postpone the wedding, but she wouldn't hear of it."

"No, the truth, Fred—that you weren't ready to marry her. That is the truth, isn't it?"

Fred looked aghast. "And hurt her feelings? She would have been devastated."

"You don't think she's devastated now?"

"Oh, great, blame it all on me," Fred spouted. "You could have said no. You didn't *have* to get involved."

Noah shook his head in disgust. Fred wasn't ready to accept responsibility for anything beyond their arrangement, which Noah already regretted deeply. And maybe Fred did have a point. Noah could have opted out, but once he'd met Lucy he'd known right away that she was making a mistake. She was delusional on the subject of marriage and children. Delusional, absolutely. But damn if that hadn't enchanted him every bit as much as her inability to walk in high heels.

He'd never met anyone like Lucy Sexton, ever. And at some point he'd lost sight of his mission to uncover her feelings for Fred. He just wanted to know who this woman was.

Fred continued to pace the small room, raking his fingers through his hair and muttering. "What the hell am I going to do?" he said aloud.

"About what?" Noah asked. "There's not a whole lot you can do. What's the problem now?"

Fred halted. "The problem is I love her. I want her back."

Noah stopped dead. "Well, then you *do* have a problem, man, because I love her too." He stood his ground as Fred let out a roar of outrage.

"You don't even know her," Fred bellowed. "How could you be in love with her?"

Noah hadn't realized he was until that moment. "I know her a lot better than you do. Up until today, I may have known her better than she knew herself."

He shot Fred a fierce warning look. "You're the one who didn't believe she loved you. And now you know. She doesn't."

"That isn't true, Hightower. She's confused. And why wouldn't she be? You've been playing with her head, sneaking around and trying to seduce her."

"I didn't seduce her, you asshole. I can't say I didn't want to, but it didn't happen that way. I took a nasty jolt of electricity, *thanks* to you, and when I came to, she was giving me mouth-to-mouth. I thought she was kissing me. I thought we were making love."

"I don't care how it happened. I want her *back,* and since you caused the problem, you owe it to me to get her back for me."

"Now I owe you?" Noah wanted to laugh, but not as much as he wanted to hit the bastard. "Just answer me this. You weren't all that certain you wanted her before. Why now?"

Frederick hesitated, thinking about it. "There's something different about her lately. I'm not sure what it is, but she's lively. She sparkles. She's the Lucy I fell in love with."

Noah watched as Fred caught his own reflection in the dresser mirror. He checked himself out, rubbing his jawline, smoothing his hair.

"You selfish bastard." Noah had just begun to realize what a vain, self-involved man Fred was. "You want her because she doesn't want you. What is she now, Fred? Some kind of prize to be won? A trophy?"

Fred didn't deny it, and Noah fought hard to keep his aggressive impulses under control. He watched Fred clean himself up, straightening his tie and buttoning his cuffs, and wanted to mess him up but good. How about a broken nose to go with that smug smile of his? Let him clean himself up from that.

As Fred tucked his shirt in, he noticed the packed bags on the bed. "Are you going back to San Francisco?" he asked Noah.

"That's depends."

"On what?"

"Lucy."

"Lucy?"

It wasn't the answer Fred wanted. He glowered and his hand curled into a fist.

Noah braced his legs wide and folded his arms. He was about six inches taller than Fred, a whole lot fitter, and his stance said very clearly: Come on, *Fredericka,* come on, ol' buddy, make my day. Do your worst, but you ain't getting that woman.

"LUCY, are you absolutely sure?"

"Mother, I thought you didn't want me to marry Frederick."

"I didn't—and I don't—but this does seem a little hasty."

"Shooting him would have been hasty," Lucy muttered. "Castrating him, that would have been hasty. He set me up with another man to *trap* me. How despicable is that?"

Lucy pushed the hair from her eyes and swore under her breath. She should have tied it back. Better yet, shaved her head. Now there was a thought. Never another bad hair day. Never another man to wash out of her hair. It was symbolically perfect. Women everywhere should shave their heads in protest.

She'd forced herself to get dressed after the showdown with Frederick, and she'd come into the office, thinking work would distract her. Sadly she hadn't managed to do much but sit at her desk and rail under her breath about the false-heartedness of the opposite sex, starting with her father. Or possibly Cro-Magnon man.

"I think Frederick may have tried to talk to you, dear." Lydia had just come from an appointment and was nursing her usual cup of exotic-smelling coffee. This time Lucy picked up the essence of coconut and pineapple, which repelled more than it tempted. Her mother sat in the visitor's chair closest to Lucy's desk, her legs elegantly crossed and showing to good advantage the black pinstripe suit she wore.

Lucy felt frumpy in her everyday blazer and slacks. But then, she would have felt frumpy in anything today.

"Don't defend Frederick, *Mom*," she chided. "You're supposed to be on my side."

Lydia didn't have a chance to defend herself. Lucy's assistant, Valerie, appeared in the doorway. "Your clients are here," she said, speaking in soft tones. "Shall I entertain them for a while? I do a great Elvis impression, and there's no signing involved."

"Yes, Valerie, thanks." Lucy forced a smile that fooled no one.

"I'll handle it," Valerie said and was gone.

Lydia rose from the chair. "Luce, would you like me to take this session? I'm familiar with the case. I referred it to you."

Lucy nodded. She let out a deep, aching sigh. "I've failed utterly, haven't I? Failed at everything. My fiancé is so desperate to get out of the marriage he set me up with another man, my assistant is reduced to impressions to keep my clients amused while I wallow in pain and self-pity, and my mother has to rescue me by taking my sessions. Not one, but two."

Lydia had doubled up all day, rescheduling her appointments so she could fill in for Lucy that morning.

Her mother marched over and dragged Lucy out of the chair to give her a hug. "You are my brilliant and beautiful child, and I couldn't be more proud of you, especially at this moment. You haven't failed. You've made a choice, and it's the right one."

Lucy let herself be embraced, knowing she didn't have to do anything else at that moment, not even hug back. Thank God for mothers and assistants.

Her mother stepped back and smiled tenderly, brushing Lucy's hair from her eyes. "I know how badly you're hurting, sweetheart, but you'll be fine. Frederick isn't worth this, honestly."

Lucy nodded. This wasn't the time to tell her mother the whole story, that Frederick was only part of what was bothering her. "I will be fine. You go. The clients may actually like Elvis."

Her mother chuckled and was gone, leaving Lucy alone in her large, handsomely appointed office. She met here with clients for intake and individual sessions, so she'd designed the space to resemble a judge's chambers. The dark woods and leather upholstery had always brought her solace, but now, as she wandered amid the fine furniture and other signs of her success, trying to hang on to her mother's words, she still felt like a dismal excuse for a woman on every front.

She was falling apart, and she couldn't let that happen. She needed a plan.

She paced the office aimlessly until she realized that her wanderings were taking on purpose and direction. Maybe her anger was misplaced. Maybe she should be angry with *them*. Men. Her mother didn't seem to know it, but she may have made the right choice all those years ago. And if her mother was miserable now, if she regretted it, she could always find herself a guy and make herself miserable in a different way. It wasn't too late. Maybe the men her mother's age were tired of the game playing and ready to have a relationship based on honesty and trust.

Lucy nodded, relieved of her terrible burden.

A life without men sounded perfect to Lucy Sexton.

She wasn't absolving herself. She undoubtedly had seen Frederick as a father figure, and she probably had wanted to marry him for all the wrong reasons. One day she might be ready to accept that she was lucky this had happened now, before she made the mistake of a lifetime. For that she should probably thank Frederick.

But not yet. And not Noah. She wasn't sure she could ever forgive him.

"Oh, God," she whispered, pressing the heel of her hand to her chest. The sudden ripping pain didn't succumb to pressure. It left her fighting to breathe.

"Get to work, Lucy," she hissed.

She headed back to her desk as if it were the most potent pain pill on the market. She still had goals, dreams, and aspirations, things that were in reach, if she put her mind to it. *Things that could be controlled.* There was no reason she couldn't make Sexton the best damn mediation service in Santa Barbara, maybe the West Coast.

She pulled her chair out and sat, prepared to attack her work and keep attacking it until this terrible aching emptiness eased.

Frederick's deceit had shocked her. Noah's had hurt. To the core.

"I'VE been calling you for two days, Lucy. What's going on?"

Lucy nearly dropped the file she was holding. The angry male voice sent her pulse rocketing. Her palms were instantly damp. She set the file down carefully—and didn't look up until she could do it without anything visible shaking. Of course, her hair was in her eyes.

"Why won't you talk to me?" he said.

Noah in her doorway. Sexy beyond her wildest dreams. Blue shirt, tool belt, the works. What was she supposed to do now? Throw him out like she did Frederick? Fat chance.

"What is there to say, Noah? You conspired with my fiancé to trick and humiliate me."

"I never meant to humiliate you and neither did Fred, although I'm not here to defend him. I'm going to have enough trouble defending myself." He took a deep breath. "Lucy, he thought you were making a mistake, and after I met you, I knew you were."

"But you never felt the need to tell me that?" She thumped her own temple. "What? Am I some kind of idiot? You can't sit me down and tell me the truth. You have to deceive me for my own good?"

"Hey, you weren't easy to reason with on the subject. Ask anyone."

"I'm asking you." The words nearly died in her throat. "What did our night together mean to you? Did it mean anything at all?"

"Of course it did. That's why I'm here."

His features were shadowed with emotion, with contrition, but she didn't believe him. She wasn't going to let herself believe him. It hurt too much.

"I have your things," she said. "I want you to take them with you."

She opened the big drawer of her desk and pulled out the pashmina shawl and the cognac. She thrust the gifts at him, aware that the distress in his face gave her a sense of pleasure that was perverse and horrible. She hated taking any satisfaction from his pain. She just wanted him to go.

"Lucy, don't do this. At least give me a chance to explain, to apologize. I'm sorry. God, I am."

Emotion balled up in her throat. "I don't want the gifts," she got out. "I don't want anything from you. In fact, I don't want anything from anybody. I'm fine, Noah. I'm strong. I can do it on my own."

He folded his arms and stood back, all powerful shoulders and dark, thoughtful features. "I pity the people you resolve conflicts for," he said, "if this is how you do it, by telling them to push each other away."

The gifts ended up on her desk, unclaimed. "I'm damn good at conflict resolution, and don't you dare suggest otherwise. I know how to separate my life from my clients' lives. Besides, to be brutally honest, most people aren't paying me to resolve things. They're paying me to get them what they want—and right now what I want is to be left alone."

She sounded bitter. She was. Deeply. It went way back.

"I don't believe you," he said.

"About what?"

"Any of it."

She grabbed a pencil off her desk. "You think I'm not strong and self-sufficient? You're wrong. I have a thriving business and a beautiful office, filled with high-tech equipment that will do my bidding at the touch of a finger."

She waved the pencil as if it were a magic wand, touching each piece of office equipment that surrounded her. "A computer, a fax, a shredder, a phone that screens and answers my calls for me, and all at the touch of a button. If I want music to soothe my soul, I just touch a button. If I want to sharpen this pencil, I don't even have to touch a button. I just *insert* here."

She pushed the pencil into the mouth of the electric sharpener and let it grind away, waiting for a reaction that never came. He shook his head, not buying any of it.

"Men aren't even required to impregnate," she reminded him. "Women can be inseminated or adopt, which means your gender is all but obsolete."

"So you don't need anything?"

"Nothing, not from you."

She had no idea how he knew there was a breaker box behind her office door. She hadn't known it was there until he revealed it, pried open the panel, and flipped one of several black switches. The entire floor of her building plunged into darkness. Thank God, it was late and everyone else had gone home.

Seconds later, a flashlight beam hit Lucy between the eyes. "Maybe you're not so self-sufficient, even here in this fancy office of yours. Maybe you do need some help."

"Noah, turn the lights back on."

"You turn them on, Lucy. That's not a problem for you, is it? You don't need anybody or anything."

"Noah, you made your point."

"Did I? You mean all that technology you rely on won't run without something as basic and simple as electricity?

"Sleep warm," he said as he left the room, the flashlight beam proceeding him down the hall.

Lucy searched the darkness with her eyes, wondering how she was going to get out of her office. Did her phones work? Did the elevator? He'd made his point, but what did it matter? He'd just walked out of her life. And she had to let him go. She was much too hurt to do otherwise. But how could he not know that? How could he not see her bruised pride, the heart that ached with every beat?

Chapter Nine

NOAH shouted. He hit the door with his open hand. He butted it with his shoulder. And then he got serious. Curling his hand into a fist, he pounded hard enough to raise the dead, and he didn't let up until he saw lights click on inside the house.

Held by a security chain, the door creaked open a notch. "What are you doing here?"

"Open the door," Noah said. "I'm bunking with you tonight."

"The hell you—"

"Open the door, or I'll break it down."

The chain rattled and popped. The big door swung open, and Frederick stood there in his bathrobe, groggy and rumpled with sleep. "Why the hell should I let you stay here?"

"Because I'm not going back to a hotel tonight, and tomorrow you and I are going to resolve this mess with Lucy."

"How?"

"The only way it can get resolved. You'll find out tomorrow."

"I don't like surprises, Hightower."

"Then it shouldn't be any surprise that you won't like this one, either. Are you inviting me in?"

Fred slammed the door in Noah's face. Not ten seconds later he opened it again, and stepped back. "Get in here," he snarled, "before the neighbors call the cops."

LUCY brushed a piece of lint from the lapel of her favorite outfit, a double-breasted sharkskin pantsuit. She'd drawn her hair up into a sophisticated knot on top of her head and left a feathery bit of dark bangs to soften the look. The smoky gray cast of her eyes was due to lack of sleep more than makeup. It made her look a bit fragile and lost, but what could she do? It was all she had to work with.

It was all about morale today. All about fighting back. She was in one of the company conference rooms, waiting for Valerie to deliver her new clients. They should be there any minute. Otherwise Lucy would have been up and moving around, working off the jitters. She wasn't as nervous about the clients as about something much more intangible. Call it the uncertainties of life. Up until a few days ago, her future had been planned, the path clear. She'd known where she was going and with whom, and that had brought her great comfort. Now all she knew for certain was where she wasn't going.

She shook the bangs off her face, force of habit.

Noah had brought about the uncertainty. He was the land mine in her path. Nothing in her life made sense anymore, no matter how determined she was to regain her sense of direction. The same work that had once consumed her didn't. She wasn't feeling the deep sense of accomplishment and satisfaction.

"Come in!" she said, grateful to hear a knock on the door.

The door opened, and Valerie entered, looking concerned. "Your clients have been delayed, but there's someone else here to see you."

Lucy rose as the two visitors followed Valerie through the door.

She stepped back, bumping into her chair. It was Frederick and Noah, partners in crime. What were they doing here? No, she didn't want to know.

She was already shaking her head. "I'm sorry, I have an appointment. Valerie, would you show these gentlemen out?"

Noah came forward, holding Valerie off with a look. "Your assistant told us that your clients are going to be late. You have at least fifteen minutes to spare. Give us that much time, please. You owe it to yourself, if no one else."

Lucy was reluctant to give them fifteen seconds, but she was deeply curious.

She nodded to Valerie. "You can go, but buzz me when their fifteen minutes is up, please."

As Valerie left, Lucy invited the men to sit. "All right, what's this about?" she said, taking a seat herself. "I'll allow one topic. That's all we'll have time for in fifteen minutes. Who goes first?"

It was absolutely her intention to be abrupt and to take charge.

Noah spoke. "This was my idea. I'll go first. The topic is you, Lucy."

She sighed, but not in relief. "I thought as much. Proceed."

Noah walked to the table but did not sit, which put Lucy at a disadvantage unless she stood too. She decided against it. With his height, she would still be forced to look up at him. As it was she couldn't believe how easily he penetrated her defenses and held her gaze. Within seconds all she could see was hot blue eyes.

"Why are you here?" she asked.

"You're the conflict resolution expert," he said, "resolve this. Frederick and I are both in love with you."

"In love?" Lucy was stunned. "With me?"

"With you," Noah said softly. "I wish there'd been a better way to tell you, but this could be my only chance."

She didn't know how to respond. She was flustered, dammit.

Frederick didn't seem too happy at the revelation, either. He rushed forward. "I love you, too, for Christ's sake. That's why I'm here. You've known this guy for a week. You've known me for years. It's no contest. You can't choose him. I meet everything on your list, right? The top ten traits?"

She didn't even dignify him with an answer. She'd told him about the list the same day she'd found it, thinking it would reassure him that she was sincere in her feelings. A mistake, clearly.

"And you?" She turned to Noah. "Why should I choose you?"

"I don't meet anything on your list except the goose bumps. But I do love you, and I've never lied to you."

Her face flushed, but not with pleasure. Why was her heart drumming so ridiculously hard? It sounded like thunder. "Except perhaps lies of omission?"

He didn't argue, but she took little satisfaction in his silence. Maybe she wanted him to argue. Why hadn't he fought for her? Why wasn't he fighting now?

The heavy thud in her chest had become painful. She forced the emotion from her voice as she spoke. "The two most important traits on my list were honesty and trustworthiness. Neither of you have shown me those qualities. I'm sure you're both good men at heart, but you did conspire to deceive me, and I can't forgive that."

Noah's palm cracked against the table. "Just like you can't forgive your father? This is bullshit, Lucy, and you know it. The only thing I'm guilty of is harboring a romantic fantasy about you."

Her voice was gone, dry as dust. "What fantasy?"

"Forget it," Noah said. "That was stupid of me."

"No, please, I want to hear it."

He took a breath and glanced from the table to her face, as if trying to decide just how much of himself he should expose in this hostile setting.

At last he spoke. "You were in a trance," he said, speaking to Lucy, "like the princess in the fairy tale who couldn't wake up. Your eyes were wide open, and you were as busy as could be, making plans and getting fitted for your wedding dress. But you were dreaming the wrong dream, Lucy . . . and I wanted to be the guy who kissed you awake."

"Sleeping Beauty?" she got out.

He nodded, clearly a little embarrassed.

Frederick made gagging noises, and Lucy shot him a glare. "Shut up, Frederick. Shut up right now."

She turned to Noah, desperately glad that he couldn't see her arms. The fine hairs must be standing on end. "That was a very sweet thing to say," she told him, "but I believe it was me who kissed you awake, if you'll remember."

"Lucy, you can't be buying this fairy-tale crap," Frederick said. "That's not your thing at all. You'd be crazy not to choose me."

Frederick started around the table, and she sprang from her chair to stop him. "Stay where you are, Frederick! I'm not choosing either one of you. That's my decision, and it's final, so if you'll both leave, this conflict will be resolved, at least for me. The session is over."

Both men fell silent, and try as she might, Lucy couldn't bring herself to look at either one of them. It would have killed her to see the expression on Noah's face at that moment. They had to leave. *They had to.*

A buzz broke the silence. It was Valerie's signal.

"Excuse me," Lucy mumbled as she hurried around the table and out of the room.

Three weeks later

Lucy didn't pick Caspian Way as her route home because the scenery was better or the traffic lighter. In fact, the traffic was terrible. She did it for the billboard. Every night she tried to anticipate what the billboard might say next. And so did the rest of Santa Barbara. Tonight Cassandra, the radio psychic, was using it as her show's opening.

"Should Lucy forgive Noah?" Cassandra asked her listeners. "That's the question on everyone's lips these days. And tonight I'll give you Cassandra's answer. It might surprise you. Meanwhile, if you haven't seen the electronic billboard on Caspian Way and Dover, where a man named Noah is pouring his heart out to a woman named Lucy, take a drive by. Noah's doing a top ten list, and tonight is number one."

Lucy was about a block from the billboard as Cassandra went to a commercial break. Caspian Way had become so crowded since the board appeared that it had taken Lucy a half hour to get here from her office. Normally it was a ten-minute trip, but she would have driven any amount of time today. In fact, she hadn't missed any of the top ten except the first one. Her mother had spotted it and told her to drive by.

Lucy would never forget it. The sun had just gone down, obscuring the black background in darkness, and the bright letters seemed to be hanging in the night sky.

THE TOP TEN REASONS LUCY SHOULD FORGIVE NOAH

(10) He's got a great job and a great car. If he had Lucy, he'd have a great smile, too.

She nearly hit the brakes and caused a lovely pileup. Great smile, great job, great car? Those were the first items on her top ten list. Lucy looked around, sure the other drivers who'd seen it would be gawking at her, but no one had any idea that the Lucy of the billboard was in the lane next to them.

Every night after that there'd been another one. Number nine had been interesting: *He's not a snappy dresser, and he doesn't have an urbane sense of humor, but he'll let you play with his tools.*

Lucy had blushed purple reading that one. She'd already done some playing, and wasn't sure she appreciated the reminder. She had his card and had considered leaving him a voice mail, telling him to stop, but she decided that was probably exactly what he wanted. Still, she continued going home via Caspian Way. Every night.

Number five was her favorite: *He'd like nothing better than to spend the rest of his life being sweet and attentive, if Lucy would let him.* And number four had made her smile. *Nice hands? Noah would love to use his, to give Lucy a guided tour of the other body parts on her list.*

Lucy craned this way and that, trying to get a look around

the van in front of her. The billboard should be coming into sight any second, and she couldn't stand the suspense. She almost wished Cassandra had revealed what it was. And suddenly, there it was, hanging in the sky:

> *Lucy, meet me up on the roof, and I'll tell you*
> *Number One in person. Love, Noah*

Lucy made a U-turn at the next intersection.

As she stepped off the elevator, Lucy saw immediately that the dining area was dark, but the lounge glowed with light. She didn't take the time to steady herself or think through what she was going to say. She turned in the direction of the light, having no idea what to expect.

He was facing the doorway as she came through it. Facing her, his arms at his sides, his shoulders squared. She had the feeling he was no more prepared for this meeting than she was, even with the elaborate lengths he'd gone to in the last ten days. He looked vulnerable, despite his height and obvious strength.

"I didn't think you'd come," he said.

"You do realize you're tying up traffic on Caspian Way."

"All I realize is that you're here."

She was struck by the softness of his voice, by the harsh emotion. Honestly it felt as if her heart were going to break. Just seeing him did that to her. She didn't know how to be angry at him anymore. Or why she should be. He might not be any of the things on her list, but he was everything she'd ever wanted in her heart. She'd been terrified to love him because he had aspects of her father's wildness, but he wasn't her father. He wasn't, and she was just beginning to understand that.

She drank in the sight of his bronzed features and wavy dark hair. Sheened by candlelight, he was as striking as on the day he'd tried to snatch her prized briefcase. Although there was something different about him tonight, she realized. He wore the familiar denim shirt and blue jeans, but one thing was missing.

"No tool belt?" she said. "You must feel naked."

He patted his hip, where the belt would normally have hung. "I gave it to charity, the Big Brothers organization."

"Why would you do that?"

"We had a bet, and I lost."

"A bet?" She remembered instantly, and repeated what he'd said: 'I'd bet this belt on us, Lucy. If we don't have something—call it chemistry or whatever you want to call it—I'll donate it to a good cause.' "

He remained silent, and she began to shake her head.

"But you didn't really *do* that. You didn't give it away. When?"

"The day after the conflict resolution meeting at your office. There didn't seem to be much reason to hold out hope."

"Can you get it back?"

"No, Lucy, it's gone."

"Oh, my God, Noah, why?"

"Because I said I would."

She shook her head. "But I would never have asked you to do that. I know what the belt meant to you."

"I didn't do it just for you, Lucy. Some men do keep their promises, and I needed to keep this one."

Her throat had gone terribly dry, but it had nothing to do with telling untruths. It was raw emotion. Naked disbelief. Kindling hope.

"Noah," she whispered. She didn't know what to do.

Fortunately, he did. He closed the distance between them and took her by the hand, giving her a moment to feel his warmth and get accustomed to his nearness. She looked up at him and was immediately lost in the wild blue depths of his eyes. His lips touched hers, and his fingers held her face, exactly as he had the first time they kissed.

Not a test this time. The real thing. And so were her feelings. Hot and bright. Searingly real. Almost painful. God, was she awake, alive.

"Come here," he whispered. "Let me hold you."

Gladly she fell into his arms, warmed by blue denim and enveloping male heat. He seemed to need this as much as she did. He was holding her like she was something precious and irreplaceable.

As the moments flew by, she said, "By the way, what's number one?"

"Us," he told her, "if there is an us. That's number one."

She nodded against his chest, wondering if this was really happening. "I was wrong about you. Is there anything I can do to make it up to you?"

"I could compile my very own top ten list." Pretending to deliberate, he said, "Let me see. Number ten: Take the tucks out of that wedding dress?"

Lucy laughed and raised on her tiptoes to kiss him again, knowing her life was never going to be the same. Thank God. From now on there would be lots of laughing, lots of light, and a love that burned as bright as a forest of candles. And best of all, if she was lucky, she would be kissed awake by a blue-eyed prince, in the form of an electrician, each and every morning.

Midsummer Night's Magic

VIRGINIA KANTRA

In grateful memory to children's librarians Margaret Garwood and Jeanette Wermuth of the Ludington Public Library, who over the years introduced me to Andrew Lang and Georgette Heyer.

Thank you for making a difference.

AUTHOR'S NOTE

O I forbid you, maidens a'.
That wear gowd on your hair,
To come or gae by Carterhaugh,
For young Tam Lin is there.

I love fairy tales. The story of Tam Lin or Tamlane appear
as ballad 39A in *The English and Scottish Popular Ballads* edited
by Francis Child and is said to date from 1729. But the
legend is much older than that. You can find Child's ver-
sion online at http://www.tam-lin.org/front.html

Sexy, scary, and touching, the story has always seemed
timeless to me. I hope you enjoy this modern re-telling
as much as I did.

Chapter One ✑

THE entire evening had been a total waste of time, gas, and moonlight.

Not that librarian Janet Porter had much else to do with her Saturday night. She'd actually been pleased by Monica Randolph's invitation. A dinner party seemed like the perfect opportunity to do a little discreet fund-raising for the Poplar branch of the Wade County Public Library. She hadn't even minded the forty-five-minute drive out of town to the Randolphs' home, a half-million-dollar mansion perched, like a Swiss chalet on steroids, halfway up a mountain.

But Janet never had a chance to make her pitch for the library. Her hostess had been far more interested in Janet's failure to bring a date than in her lack of up-to-date computer equipment.

So Janet had written the evening off as a bad investment even before the squealing erupted from under the hood of her car.

She switched off the voices keeping her company on late-night public radio and glanced at the dash. Her stomach sank.

The engine light was on. That couldn't be good. She peered through the windshield, but it was too dark to see if the engine was smoking. Too dark to see much of anything, really, but tall black trees and humped gray hills and neglected white mile markers.

She tightened her grip on the wheel. If she could just make it to the next intersection . . .

The car shuddered and squealed again. And then the engine died.

Oh, please, Janet thought. The car rolled and bumped onto the soft shoulder as she braked, fighting to stay clear of the ditch. Not here. Not now.

But nobody listened, not the Fates or the fairies or the gods of Detroit. Her car lurched and stopped, nose down, under the trees.

Janet drew a shaky breath, still clinging to the wheel of her car. Her palms were damp. Her heart was thudding. Gradually, she became aware of other sounds stealing through the open crack of her window. Night noises. Insect noises. Rustling, whirring, buzzing noises, foreign and unfriendly.

So she wasn't nature girl. That didn't mean she had to sit here like a lump until the bats and mosquitoes swooped down to take her away. She was used to doing things for herself. When you were thirty-six years old and lived alone, it wasn't like you had a choice.

She wiped her palms on her skirt and got out of the car.

Her heels sank in the mud. Her feet tangled in the tall grass. Her clothes—long skirt, short jacket, tasteful earrings— were fine for dinner with a library patron. Not so good for poking around under the hood of her car.

She tottered around anyhow, not sure what she was looking for or even if she would recognize it if she saw it. At least she *could* see now. The moon, a clear, pale disk in the sky, shed silver light on everything.

She stared at the dark, greasy tangle of pipes and wires under the hood, fighting the curl of helplessness in her stomach. For one atypical year in graduate school, she'd actually lived with an engineering student; that didn't make her a car mechanic. Ross

MacLean had shown her how to change a tire and charge a battery. He'd taught her not to trust good-looking men who pretended to love her. He'd never informed her what to do about an engine that squealed and died.

She had her cell phone. What she didn't have was anyone she could call at eleven-thirty at night who would be willing to drive forty miles outside of town to rescue her.

She needed new friends.

No, she needed a tow truck. Or a North Carolina state trooper. She fumbled in her bag for her phone and pressed *SP to summon the state police. Nothing. Not a click, not a ring. . . . Maybe it was SP*? Or #SP? She tried them both without success. She was probably in some dead zone far out in the country.

The road curved into silence and shadow in both directions. Someone would drive by eventually, she assured herself. A farmer in a pickup truck. Or a pair of teens on their way to the local lovers' lane. A friendly trucker who wanted to stay off the main highway. A serial killer out trolling for victims. . . .

She shivered and looked over her shoulder.

Lights? Were those lights, twinkling through the trees?

Janet knew she wasn't brave. She didn't want to leave her car. But lights meant people, a phone, a farmhouse, safety.

She locked her car—leaving the hood up to attract any highway patrolman who might cruise by—and plunged off the road and over the ditch toward the lights. The bank proved to be surprisingly tough going. She had to brace her feet on tufts of grass and grasp at saplings for balance. Halfway up, the overhanging trees hid the lights from her view, and she almost gave up. But then she heard some kind of back porch music, fiddles and drums. A radio? So she went on.

At the top of the bank, she paused, panting. A low stone wall rode the crest of the hill, its outline gleaming in the moonlight. The sense of passing a border, a boundary, sucked at her feet and clutched her heart like the soft ground and the snagging branches.

Stupid. She threw her leg over the wall and ripped her pantyhose.

A lean, dark shadow detached itself from the deeper shadows at the side of the path and stood in her way.

"You're trespassing," the shadow said coldly.

Janet's heart rocketed to her throat. Her hand flew to her chest.

"I'm sorry," she said breathlessly, because the slog up the bank had taken it out of her and because, well, he'd scared her. He was very tall, whoever he was, and he'd appeared out of the dark like magic. Irritation flickered at the edge of her fear, like a line of flame on a piece of paper. Who did he think he was, skulking around, jumping out at people? Jerk.

"There wasn't a sign," she pointed out.

She thought he stiffened. She couldn't be sure. The moon was behind him, and she couldn't see his face, only the sudden tension in his broad shoulders.

But clearly he wasn't at all placated by her apology or her explanation. "You need to leave," he said. "Now."

Maybe it was the darkness that forced her to focus on his voice. It had a deep, low timbre that shivered her bones and stirred her memory.

Which was ridiculous, because she didn't know him. She couldn't know him. She didn't normally spend her time tromping the backwoods of North Carolina.

Although it was possible he'd visited her library. He could have come in to read up on bovine growth hormones or to borrow a government pamphlet on pesticides. Perhaps he was a student in town. Despite his height and his deep voice, Janet thought he was young. He had a young man's arrogant grace and long hair. Even in silhouette she could see it brushed his shoulders.

"I can't leave," Janet said in her best "Quiet, please" voice. "My car broke down."

He raised his head like a wolf scenting prey. "You're alone?"

Janet swallowed. He wasn't a patron. This wasn't her library. Maybe he was a rapist. Maybe, oh, God, maybe he was a lookout of some kind. Wild notions raged in her brain. She'd read her local history. Bad things went on in the woods at night. It wasn't that long ago that Klansmen ran in these hills. Moonshiners. Pot farmers.

"I have friends waiting for me," she said hastily.

"Right." He took a step forward, still in shadow. "Let's get you back to them, then."

Janet froze, her heart thumping like a rabbit's. She didn't want to go anywhere with him. But if she ran for the road, he would catch her. If she screamed, there was no one to hear.

"I think I'll wait here," she said.

He stopped, his tall profile blurred against the backdrop of trees. She wished she could read his expression. "You need help," he said flatly.

Well, obviously. But she hated needing help, and it didn't seem wise to admit a weakness. Not to him.

"I just need a phone," she said.

He shook his head. "You need a hell of a lot more than that," he said—amused? disapproving?—and slipped past her, down the hill.

He never brushed against her. In fact, he held himself carefully separate and turned his head away. But his movement stirred the air around her. His closeness made her tremble, and his scent teased her. He smelled like wild things, like night and smoke and some sharp, elusive memory.

She drew a shaky breath and held it inside as he disappeared in the direction of her car.

"Friend of yours, is he?" croaked a voice somewhere near her knees.

Janet's eyes popped open. Alarmed, she took a step back, trying wildly to locate the speaker. "I—no," she stammered. "He's taking a look at my car."

"Ah."

There. On a fallen log under the trees, a man hunched like a drift of leaves, like a lump of lichen. When she spotted him, he uncurled from his perch. And even though it was dark, she saw his smile gleam in the moonlight. His teeth were pointed.

"You're trespassing," he said.

Alarm made her cross. "Yes, I know."

"I don't mind," the man said peaceably, shuffling toward

her. He was short, and there was something peculiar about the way he dressed. Janet blinked. Were those *feathers* around his neck? "But *She* might."

"Who is she?" asked Janet. "Who are you?"

The man chuckled. "Now, that would be telling."

Had she stumbled on some kind of criminal activity in the woods? Or the Mad Hatter's tea party?

"You can't tell me your name?"

"You can call me Rob." The little man smiled at her, as if pleased with his solution. "Rob Goodfellow."

"Fine," Janet snapped, because she was having a bad night and she was nervous. "Rob. Can you tell me where I can find a phone?"

Goodfellow cocked his head to one side, as if he were listening. The music continued, faint and disturbing, like the bass rhythm on a stereo played in the next apartment. "You'll want to come to the Circle," he said at last. "It may be you'll find what you need there."

Great. The sooner she called a towing service and got back to town and normalcy, the better. She straightened her spine and followed him through the bare, dark wood, the ghosts of last autumn sliding and rustling underfoot.

She was looking for the warm yellow squares of house windows. Instead she saw red sparks sailing from an open fire toward the black and pewter sky. Silver points winked from the branches overhead like Christmas decorations or lights strung at a party.

A party. Janet's mouth dropped open as she tottered from under the cover of trees. Not a Klan meeting. Not a drug rendezvous. She had stumbled on a party, one of those Renaissance fair thingies or maybe a Mardi Gras festival, with people in costume and music and dancing. She saw feathers, she saw flowers, she saw velvet and fur. A woman with a face like an angel whirled by in the arms of a man wearing a horned satyr's mask.

"What—Where are we?" she asked.

Her escort watched her with shrewd black eyes like a bird's. "Those who live around here call it Carter Farm."

She squinted. It was hard to focus beyond the flickering fire and shifting dancers, the bright skirts and bare feet, the pale arms and glittering eyes, but she thought she could make out the pitched roof of a house, a stone well, a weathered barn. All dark, all deserted.

Janet glanced uncertainly at Goodfellow, the call of the pipes swirling in her ears and the rhythm of the drums louder than her heartbeat.

"You said there would be a phone," she said slowly.

He grinned at her. His teeth were very pointy. "Did I?"

"What are you doing?" It was the deep voice again, the voice of the tall man who had stopped her by the wall, only now he didn't sound cold at all. He sounded angry. "You shouldn't have brought her. She doesn't belong here."

Janet blinked, dazzled by the dancers and the light of the fire. She knew she didn't belong here. She had to get back to . . . Well, she'd sort of lost track of what she had to get back to, but she was pretty sure she was supposed to be someplace else. Still, the dark man's insistence that she was out of place among the dancers and the music hurt.

He shoved beside her, turning his back on her to confront Goodfellow. They were arguing, but she was distracted from what they said by how good the tall man smelled. His scent, raised by the heat of the fire, was compounded now by leather and engine grease.

Something about that smell woke a memory. Raised a ghost. But before she could identify it, he pivoted to face her.

"Are you wearing stockings?"

The fire was behind him. His broad shoulders, his dark head, were lined with flame.

Janet swallowed. "What?"

"Your fan belt is broken. If you're wearing stockings, I can rig something that will get you to the nearest service station."

"I have on pantyhose."

"That'll do. Take them off."

"You're in a mighty hurry to get rid of her," Goodfellow said.

The dark man turned his head and spoke over his shoulder. "Stay out of it, Puck."

Janet's breath caught in her chest. She could see him now, his profile lit by the blaze behind him. He was dressed in clothes less bright but no less exotic than the dancers'—black leather pants and black leather jacket and a T-shirt so dark a green it was almost black. A gold chain rested heavily around his strong, brown throat. He should have looked like a gay biker. But he didn't. He looked barbaric and dangerous and achingly familiar. In fact, he looked a lot like—

He looked exactly like—

Her hand covered her mouth.

Ross.

As if she had called his name aloud, he turned back to her and frowned. "You have to go now."

He couldn't be, Janet told herself even as her eyes strained to search his face. Ross MacLean would be her age by now. Old. Thirty-six. And except for the shoulder-length hair, this man—this boy—looked exactly like the lover who had left her fourteen years ago without even a good-bye. The same moss green eyes, the same angled cheekbones, the same *age.* . . .

He was too young. He couldn't be Ross. But he looked enough like him—like a dream come true, like the ultimate do-over—to make her heart hitch, all the same.

"Who are you?" she whispered.

His face was grim. Nothing like the boy's she remembered at all. "Nobody you want to know," he said.

Janet wasn't so sure. He was certainly more exciting than the majority of her library patrons. And there was that eerie resemblance to Ross. . . .

She didn't want exciting, Janet reminded herself. Exciting was disruptive. And Ross had broken her heart.

She cleared her throat. "You said you can fix my car?"

"I can't fix it. But I can get it to take you another ten miles. Is there still a garage in Miles Cross?"

"Still"? Didn't he live here? Shouldn't he know? But maybe he traveled with the fair. Maybe he only came through every few years or so.

Maybe she was overanalyzing.

She tried to remember if she'd passed a service station earlier that evening. "I didn't really pay attention," she confessed.

She thought his hard face softened. One corner of his mouth quirked in a smile. "No, you wouldn't," he said. But maybe the amused, tender look was only a trick of the fire, because the next instant he added brusquely, "Come on. Let's get you out of here."

Janet stumbled on the walk back to the car. The shadows seemed darker, the footing more treacherous. The trees closed in around them, blocking the light of the sky, sending roots snaking across the path.

He wasn't having any trouble, Janet noticed resentfully. Her escort moved silently and easily a pace or two ahead. But when they reached the low stone wall, he stopped as if he'd been shot. In the moonlight his face looked bleached.

Unwillingly concerned, Janet risked a touch on his arm. "Are you all right?"

He shook off her hand as if it burned. "Fine."

He drew a deep breath and stepped over the wall.

Fine, thought Janet, hiding her hurt. And I hope you slide down the bank and break your neck.

But he didn't. She jumped and slithered in his wake, grateful for the full moon that lit her footing.

The hood of her car was still raised. He leaned over the front bumper and then ordered, "Right. Take off your stockings."

Janet hesitated, reminded again that she was on a deserted road with a man she did not know. "Are you sure that's necessary?"

"Your fan belt is broken. Since you don't carry a spare, I can rig a substitute by threading your pantyhose around the pulleys on the engine and water pump. But you need to strip."

Her heart pounded. She stopped with her hands on her hips. "Could you turn around, please?"

His eyebrows raised. "You're joking."

She sniffed, a sound that echoed with more authority in her library than here by the side of a ditch. "I certainly am not."

"It's not like I haven't seen it before, babe."

Seen it. Seen . . . her? Her chest felt tight. Was it possible after all that—

"When?" she asked breathlessly.

"You really want me to tell you the last time I watched a woman take off her pantyhose?" He sounded as if he couldn't believe she'd asked such a question.

Neither could she. Deflated, embarrassed, she reached for her hem.

"Never mind," she mumbled.

He turned his back.

Janet appreciated his restraint. She did. Only as she fumbled her pantyhose past her hips, she thought miserably he probably wasn't exercising much restraint at all. He was young and gorgeous, and she was . . . Well, she was clearly no temptation.

She slipped the nylons down her calves and stepped out of her sensible heels. The ground was cold. Little stones pricked the bottoms of her feet as she balanced first on one and then on the other.

Wordlessly, she held her stockings out to him. And he wasn't peeking, either, because he didn't turn around.

"Uh . . . here," she said.

He pivoted. His face was set. Janet bit her lip. Had she offended him?

Not that he didn't deserve it—*It's not like I haven't seen it before, babe*—but, after all, he was fixing her car. The least she could do was be polite.

He plucked the nylons from her hand, stretched them once or twice, and started to twist them into some kind of rope.

Janet watched, her indignation leaking through the cold soles of her feet.

He slammed the hood of the car. "That's it," he said. "You can go now. Don't drive too fast."

"No," she said stiffly. "I won't."

He shoved his hands in his pockets. He looked very tall and alone standing in the moonlight. She made no move to get in the car.

"I—thank you," she said.

His shoulders hunched. "No big deal."

But she still felt there was something she should do or say.

"Can I pay you?" she asked impulsively.

He laughed, but there was no amusement in the sound. "No. Just get out of here."

Well, that was clear. But the niggling feeling that he wanted something, was waiting for something, wouldn't go away. Janet dug in her purse. "Here's my card," she said, thrusting it toward him. "In case you, uh, need to get in touch with me."

He stared at it. The small white card trembled between them.

Janet almost groaned. What must he think of her, a thirty-six-year-old woman pressing her phone number on an obviously reluctant young man? But she didn't pull it back.

Finally, he took it. "Thanks," he said roughly.

Janet climbed into the driver's seat. The engine started right away. With a little sigh—of relief? or disappointment?—she turned on her headlights, shifted into drive, and eased her car forward onto the road.

She only looked back once.

Her rescuer was still standing by the side of the ditch, watching her drive away.

SHE had changed. Aged.

The man who had been Ross MacLean didn't have to remind himself it had been fourteen years for her. The evidence was on her face. There were laughter lines at the corners of her big brown eyes and a new softness to her body, a curve to her hips and a swell to her belly, that fascinated him.

Even though he'd never been able to convince her of it, she had always seemed beautiful to him. Now she looked warmer. Rounder. Comfortable.

Human.

The gold chain burned around his neck. He closed his hand tightly around the little white card in his hand until the edges stabbed his fingers.

She was gone. Safe.

And while he had learned a dozen years ago not to hope, not to thank the God he once had worshipped, he was glad. He watched her red taillights disappear toward safety while the shadows crept out and plucked at his boots and the legs of his pants.

He was still standing there when the *sidhe* came to take him away.

Chapter Two ✑

JANET wasn't holding her breath waiting for the phone to ring.

Which was a good thing, because almost two months had passed since her odd, moonlit encounter with the young Ross look-alike. If she *had* been holding her breath, she'd be dead by now.

Janet paused by the children's corner to scoop a crumpled tissue from the floor, rescue a book flat on its face, and brush crushed Cheerios from the carpet. She never minded the mess the children left behind. It was careless adults who disappointed you and broke your heart.

She'd listened for the phone fourteen years ago. She'd waited, first with anger and then with disbelief and then, as the days passed without a word or sign from Ross, with sick worry.

Not this time. Janet sat on the floor in her long, full skirt and began to shelve the picture books alphabetically by author. She had no real expectations this time. Hot young traveling carnies didn't hit on middle-aged small-town librarians.

"Janet?" The woman's voice grated slightly, like the very finest sandpaper. "Where are you?"

Janet lurched to her feet. "Back here!"

A trim blonde rounded the low stacks. Monica Randolph could still pass for forty, if the lighting was right and she had her makeup on. Which she always did.

She took one look at Janet and raised her eyebrows. "Oh, my dear. Is that your *Sound of Music* look?"

Janet winced and brushed at her skirt. "We had story hour today. This outfit is good for getting on the floor with the kids."

"How very practical," Monica approved. "And I suppose it doesn't matter that the skirt makes you look the weensiest bit wide."

Janet adjusted the book display on top of the shelves, reminding herself that Monica gave generously to the library. Although Monica chose her charities the same way she selected her accessories: to make her look good.

"I don't think my Toddler Timers really care how I look," Janet said.

And neither do I, she wanted to add, but the truth was she did. She did.

"A man would," said Monica.

"I don't need a man."

Well, not often, anyway.

Monica sniffed. "You could have used one the other night when your car broke down. I told you you should have brought a date. Men are useful for things like that. And sex. Honestly, it's about all they are good for. But I suppose you handle things yourself."

Which things? Janet wanted to ask, with a spurt of rebellious amusement. Car repairs? Or sex?

But she didn't have the courage to ask.

One of the library aides appeared at the end of the aisle. "Call for you, Janet."

Janet propped a crowned frog beside a book of fairy tales. "Who is it?"

Her assistant twinkled. "He didn't say. Line two."

But there was no reason for that sparkling look, Janet thought. She excused herself and headed for the circulation desk. Her mysterious caller was probably only a parent demanding a copy of the sixth-grade reading list or a patron requesting authorization to keep her overdue books another week or . . .

"Janet Porter," she said crisply into the receiver.

"We'll be back this weekend." The voice was deep and male and had haunted her dreams. "I want to see you again."

Janet's heart tripped. She tightened her grip on the phone. "Who is this, please?"

The man on the other end of the line laughed. Not meanly, but as if he were genuinely delighted. "You know who it is," he said. "There's a full moon Saturday night. Will you come?"

Her palms were sweating. She should say no, Janet thought. She didn't know anything about this man except that he'd fixed her car and bore an aching resemblance to her long-lost lover.

She cleared her throat. "What time?"

There was a pause, long enough for her to panic. Had she sounded too eager? Didn't he want her to accept after all?

"Let's say nine o'clock your time," he said at last, slowly. "Carter Farm. Will you remember?"

She wasn't likely to forget. She wouldn't be able to think about anything else for the next four days.

"Nine o'clock, Saturday, Carter Farm. Yes, I probably can remember that much."

He laughed again softly. "Good. I'll be waiting."

"Where?"

But only a click and a hum answered her.

Janet's breath escaped like the air from a leaking balloon. He'd hung up.

Her assistant gave up pretending to scan returns and regarded Janet with bright, encouraging eyes. "Well, that sounded promising. Who was it?"

Janet opened her mouth to tell her.

And then realized she still didn't even know his name.

JANET wasn't abandoning her car by a ditch and scrambling up the bank this time. A farm had to have an access road. A carnival needed parking. She was sure she could find both.

Of course, her task would have been easier if she had dared ask for directions. But just the thought of approaching Sheriff Harris or Ed Grumbly at Grumbly's Gas and Eats made her hot with embarrassment. She really didn't want to explain why on earth the town librarian was traipsing around the countryside late at night after a bunch of fair folks.

Instead she dug through the library's collection of old county plat maps until she found one that showed a Carter Farm ten miles outside of Miles Cross. She was feeling fairly confident as she exited the highway and bumped down a rutted, moonlit road seeking the fair and adventure.

Her headlights caught a square white sign jutting from a tangle of trees. Wasn't that . . .? Yes, Carter Farm, and the gate stood open, white against a dark hedge. Encouraged, Janet turned onto the gravel drive. Her car lurched as the tires left the pavement.

The jolt woke all her doubts. What was she doing, driving to a rendezvous with tall, dark, and mysterious? At her age, too.

But she kept going. Anyway, there was probably room to turn the car around ahead. Trees pressed close on either side, but at the end of the long, leafy tunnel, she could see lights twinkling and the red glow of a fire.

There didn't seem to be anyone collecting money, so Janet nudged her car down the lane, looking for parking. Old-fashioned shrub roses, ghostly in the filtered moonlight, lined the track, and daylilies, their trumpets shut like spears. She was a little surprised the fair organizers had chosen such an out-of-the-way spot for their festival, but it was certainly very lovely.

Unease fluttered through her when the way widened and she saw how few vehicles were actually parked under the trees. The long silver hood of a classic automobile gleamed under the moon. Several horses tossed their heads in a tethered line, looking like circus ponies with long manes and decorated bridles. A row of motorcycles leaned together, black and sleek and wicked with chrome.

Janet frowned. Was this a Renaissance fair or a bikers' convention? And where was everyone?

She sat inside her parked car with the doors locked and the

windows rolled up, trying to summon the nerve to get out.
With the engine and the air-conditioning off, she could hear
that music again, pipes and fiddles and drums, evocative har-
monies with a heady beat. Her foot tapped the floor of the car.
Her hands twisted in her lap.

On impulse, she flipped down the visor over the driver's
side and peered at her reflection. She looked . . . nice, she decided, with an unfamiliar flare of hope. Her long hair was
down, and she was wearing more makeup than usual. Remembering the dancers' dress-up costumes, she'd paired her long
skirt with a slim-fitting top that showed off her arms and more
of her bosom than she was used to. The night was hot, so she'd
left off her pantyhose. Her bare legs made her feel cooler and
vaguely daring.

Would he think she looked old?

Janet blew out her breath and slapped the visor up. One
thing was for sure. She wasn't getting any younger sitting
here. Before she could chicken out, she threw open her door
and climbed from the car.

A warm breeze swirled her skirt. Leaves dipped and
swayed. A cloud scudded across the face of the moon. It was
as if her action had set everything else in motion, Janet
thought fancifully.

And when the cloud passed and the moon shone bright, he
was there, tall and lean and dark, one more shadow among the
shadows of the yard. He was all in black, his face barely dis-
cernible by the moon's glow, but she knew him. She knew.

"Hi." Janet was so relieved to see him—to see anyone,
actually—that her smile was genuine. She gestured around the
surprisingly empty yard. "Am I early or late?"

"You shouldn't be here at all." His voice was harsh.

She quailed. But having come this far, she refused to back
down. "You invited me."

Ross MacLean was furious.

He'd made the big sacrifice, damn it. He'd let her go. Hell,
he'd helped her on her way.

She had no business showing up now, tempting him, putting herself in danger, ruining his brief and bitter pleasure that this once he had done the right thing.

"The hell I did," he growled.

"You did," Janet insisted, but her voice wobbled. "You called me."

Panic struck him. She wasn't going to cry, was she? He'd never been able to resist her when she cried.

"Look," he began desperately, "I don't know what you—"

"Take it easy on the girl." Puck materialized from a shaft of moonlight. A pony snorted and pawed the line at his sudden appearance. Ross glared.

"She did get a phone call." Puck grinned, showing his teeth. "Lucky for you, her leaving her card behind like that."

Janet stood by her car, twisting her fingers together. Her ringless fingers, Ross noted, and was ashamed of the hot, deep flare of satisfaction he felt. If she heard his conversation with Puck, she gave no sign. Well, she wouldn't, if Puck didn't want her to.

Ross reached for his pocket. His empty pocket. "You bastard," he said slowly. "*You* called her."

The little man cocked his head, mischief gleaming in his eyes. Or was it sympathy? "She's your last hope, boyo. Do you really want to send her away?"

Not his last hope, Ross thought. He had no hope.

But it might be she was his last chance. A chance to feel something human, to feel human, to feel.

Ross let himself drink in the sight of her, her cloudy dark hair, her soft, bewildered eyes, her tender mouth and determined chin. Memory, desire, and despair stopped his breath and hollowed his chest.

"It's not like you don't want her," Puck observed slyly from beside him. "And she's willing, so why not?"

"I won't use her that way," Ross said fiercely. "I'll be damned first."

Puck chuckled. "You're damned anyway, boyo. Might as well make the most of it."

Ross turned on him.

But after fourteen years, the *sidhe* knew the limits of the human's temper. Or maybe Puck had already said what he came to say. He vanished, leaving Ross and Janet alone in the moonlight.

"Obviously, I've made a mistake," Janet said. Her voice was stiff with rejection. Hurt shimmered in her eyes. "I . . . Good-bye." She turned jerkily and reached for the handle of her door.

Way to feel like a dirtball, MacLean.

"Wait," Ross said.

Janet sniffed. "For what?"

Oh, God, she was crying.

"For . . ." His fists clenched. Why should she stay? How could he bear to let her go? "You just got here."

Okay, that was lame.

But she stopped fumbling with the door handle. "And I'm just leaving."

He could let her go.

He should let her go. Now, before she recognized him. Now, while there was nothing to hold her here.

But he couldn't do it. He couldn't let her walk away believing he didn't want her. Again. He had left her once. Betrayed her once. Let what should have been a stupid, patched-up lovers' quarrel turn into a fourteen-year exile because he'd been unwilling to give her everything she had the right to expect from him.

He had little enough to give her now. Only tonight. Only one night, instead of the lifetime they'd once dreamed of. But for one night, at least, she would know she was wanted. She could feel she was loved.

I'll be damned first, he'd told Puck.

You're damned anyway, boyo. Might as well make the most of it.

He took a step toward her. "Don't go," he said, his voice low.

Her neck was bent. Her hair veiled her face. All he could see was the tip of her nose and her unsteady hands, clutching her keys.

Tenderness for her welled in him. Tenderness and desire.

He crossed the moonlit yard until he was right behind her rigid back, close enough to feel the mortal warmth of her body, to hear her sudden intake of breath and smell the simple, ordinary scents that clung to her, the scents of soap and human skin.

He wanted her so bad he was shaking.

"Don't go," he repeated.

She kept her face turned from him, her keys tight in her grasp.

"I should," she said.

With the back of his knuckles, he brushed aside the heavy curtain of her hair, exposing the soft curve of her cheek, the pure line of her neck, the skin as delicate as a child's. He fit his mouth to the pulse beating in her throat, tasting her rising excitement.

"Not yet," he whispered.

He rested one arm on the roof of her car and pressed the other against the door, so that she was trapped between the cool metal and his hot body. He nuzzled her neck again until she shivered and swayed. He felt the soft brush of her buttocks against his heavy erection.

In fourteen years' captivity, he'd learned a lot about seduction.

She didn't stand a chance.

Chapter Three 🐦

JANET knew better.

Really, she did.

This hot, young Ross look-alike could only have one motive, other than pity, for asking her to stay. He thought she was easy, a stereotypical small-town librarian flattered by attention and hungry for adventure.

And she was.

She still clung to the metal door handle. She ought to climb in her car and drive away.

Except his body was hard and close. His voice was low and sincere, and his scent, that potent combination of warm male and engine grease, evoked a response in her blood and her brain. It was as if she knew him, remembered him along her nerves and in her bones.

And he . . . Well, if the thick rod prodding her behind was his only motive, it was a pretty good one. At least it seemed genuine.

So Janet let herself be— Not seduced, she decided. Persuaded.

His mouth was warm. He kissed the hollow of her neck,

making the muscles there loosen and tension coil tight in her belly. Her heart pounded with fear and anticipation.

Was it so bad, that he only wanted one thing from her, if it was what she wanted, too?

He kept on kissing her, using his teeth and his tongue, taking tiny, tasting bites of her throat and shoulders. His hair was thick and soft, brushing her neck. His breath rasped in her ear. He reached down, his warm hand searing her bare arm, and uncurled her death grip on the door handle. Lacing his fingers with hers, he raised her arm and flattened her palm on the roof of the car. The touch of cool metal made her shiver.

He crowded her against the door, widening his stance so she could feel all of him, his hard, broad torso against her back, his heavily muscled thighs on either side of hers, that thick, hot ridge riding the cleft of her buttocks. Dimly, she could hear the music, the pipes rising and falling, the drums driving like a heartbeat.

She should tell him to stop. She would tell him to stop. In a minute.

With her arm raised, there was nothing to block his hand from exploring her body. He palmed her breast, weighing and shaping it through her shirt. The nipple poked shamelessly against the thin cotton, and when he felt that, he murmured in satisfaction, tracing the shape of it through the fabric. Janet opened her mouth to breathe. His long, clever fingers played with her, stroking, squeezing, teasing.

She wanted to turn in his embrace, to feel him, to touch him, his soft hair and his hard muscles. But he wouldn't let her. He held her in place against the car with his strong, corded arms and the press of his lean body, while his hands roamed at will.

There was no breeze under the trees. No air. Janet gasped as her lover stroked her, his long-fingered hands blunt-tipped and sure, sliding over her blouse, rubbing her through her skirt. She was hot. Really hot. She should take off her clothes.

She frowned. No, she shouldn't. She should—

Gently, he bit the side of her throat, and she moaned and dropped her head back against his shoulder. He rocked against her, the hard thrust of his body making her melt. Her insides were molten, her knees wax. His cool hair brushed the side of her jaw. He slid one hand inside the low vee of her blouse while the other glided over her clothes, stroked over her body, kneaded her stomach and thighs. She felt the harsh intake of his breath, the heady heat of his body. *She* did this to him. The knowledge gave her a rush. The tension in her belly coiled tighter and tighter.

He eased his hand under her bra, closing his hand over her breast, making her entire body pulse with need, wilder than the music, more compelling than the drums. The stars whirled and spun. Dizzy, she closed her eyes and let the dark wash over her as he flattened the folds of her skirt with his hand, as he rubbed and plucked, as he made the darkness surge inside her, made it move and swell to his rhythm, made her shudder, made her come.

Janet cried out.

He held her while the aftershocks shook her, his chest and thighs hot and solid, his hands warm and reassuring. His jaw brushed the side of her face. He kissed her temple.

He still hadn't kissed her mouth.

Janet quivered against him. Her senses shivered and sang while her mind tried desperately to grasp what had just happened here. Had she really let this beautiful stranger touch her, grope her, make her come—against her *car*—while they both were still fully dressed?

Yep, her body told her smugly. Sure did.

As soon as she could think, she was going to feel horribly embarrassed and guilty. As soon as she could move, she was going to leave.

He turned her in his arms. Her breasts squashed against his chest. His shirt was warm and damp. She couldn't look at him and squeezed her eyes shut.

"Dance with me," he whispered against her lips.

It was so not what she was expecting that her eyes popped open. "But you didn't—"

"No," he said. "And you shouldn't let me. You don't know me, what I've done, where I've been."

That was for sure.

"I'm not sure I know myself tonight," Janet confessed.

In the darkness, she thought she saw him smile.

She sighed and rested her head against his chest. The night wrapped itself around them. The stars wheeled overhead. The music, in rhythm with his heart, thudded against her ear.

A thought insinuated itself into her brain. She raised her head.

"You don't have anything, well, contagious, do you?" she asked.

"No!" he said, so automatically she believed him.

Janet frowned. "Then, why—"

He kissed her.

To shut her up? Janet wondered, and then the heat and the darkness surged into her again, and she didn't care. She raised on her toes to kiss him back.

His arms tightened around her. She had time to register that he was still fully, heavily aroused before he gripped her upper arms and set her away from him. Her body protested the loss of his.

"We're going to dance," he said firmly.

Janet blinked. Her eyelids felt heavy. Her whole body felt heavy, and her head was strangely light.

"Do we have to?" she said.

His laugh sounded strangled. "Yeah," he said. "Or I'm going to kiss you again."

She watched him pluck a rose from the hedge and strip it of its thorns.

"Would that be a bad thing?" she asked.

He tucked the rose carefully behind her ear. Its stem was scratchy, its scent wild and sweet. Her heart swelled at the tenderness of the gesture.

"For you," he said.

Did he mean the rose? Or the kiss? A kiss would be a bad thing for *her*?

Janet was still wondering when he took her hand and led her toward the lights and music.

The trees drew back, revealing a motley ring of dancers

and a bonfire shooting sparks into the night. Why anyone would want to build a six-foot fire in the middle of June escaped Janet, but there was no denying the curling, leaping flames were pretty.

And the dancers didn't seem to mind the heat. They circled, stepped, and swung, their calm faces an unsettling contrast to their restless feet and outrageous costumes. Janet stumbled. They looked even more bizarre than she remembered. Or maybe she saw them more clearly this time, her eyes more accustomed to the dark? Some wore masks or crowns of jewels or flowers on their flowing hair. Some wore velvet and fur. Some wore leaves and feathers. And some wore . . .

Janet blinked. Some wore next to nothing at all. No wonder they didn't mind the fire.

The fiddles scraped. The drums rolled. But under the driving beat of the music, the gathering was oddly silent. The dancers seldom spoke, and their bare feet made no sound. It was like watching *Riverdance* with the volume turned down.

Janet's lover tugged her hand to lead her forward.

She hung back. "I can't do this."

He raised an eyebrow. "You can't dance?"

She looked at the swaying, bowing crowd and shook her head vigorously. "Not like that."

He didn't release her. "It's like square dancing."

"I haven't square-danced since fifth grade," Janet muttered, but he only smiled at her and held out his other hand.

Janet felt a quiver of panic in her stomach. She still wasn't sure she hadn't made a fool of herself back there by the car. Now he expected her to hop and twirl in front of a bunch of strangers?

But his smile, his gaze, his hand never wavered. The music skipped and swirled, beckoning. Beguiling.

Janet gulped, and took his warm hand, and let him lead her into the dance.

And it wasn't so bad. She didn't utterly suck, although she suspected her partner kept his steps simple for her sake. His hand splayed on her back. He held her close enough that her breasts brushed the wall of his chest and his thighs slid against hers. She could feel his rhythm, anticipate his moves, and inside she loosened, relaxed. Her body was soft and ready for him. Her heart was turning to mush.

Up close like this, she could smell his musky, male scent and see the faint prickle of beard along his jaw. Sweat sheened his upper lip. Against the harsh planes of his face, his eyelashes were dark and impossibly long.

Like Ross's.

Don't think about that, she ordered herself. Don't think about him. Don't think.

To distract herself, she stopped gazing at him, stopped watching her feet, and began to look around. Beyond the flickering ring of the firelight, she could see the low roof of the farmhouse and the hulking shadow of the barn. But no booths. No rides. No stands or stalls or anything to suggest what these people were doing here in the middle of nowhere in the middle of the night.

She turned her face up to her partner's. "So, what is this?" she asked.

The arm around her stiffened, but his voice was mild. "What do you mean?"

She smiled, hoping she wasn't spoiling the mood with her curiosity. "Well, it's too late for Mardi Gras and too early for Halloween. So, why the big deal with the costumes and all? What's the occasion?"

She thought for a moment he wasn't going to answer her. In the shifting red glow of the fire, his eyes were oddly blank, his mouth hard. But then he said, "Summer solstice."

She digested that as he guided her through another movement of the dance, turning her to promenade beside him.

"And before?" she asked, when he spun her again in his arms so that they were face-to-face. "When I was here before, what was it?"

"Beltane." He hesitated. "May Day, I guess you'd call it."

"Beltane?" Janet stumbled and stepped on his foot. Wordlessly, he caught and supported her.

"Sorry," she apologized. "But isn't that, like, a witches' holiday?"

He didn't say anything.

Unease ran over her skin like the tall grass tickling her ankles, like moth's wings brushing her cheek in the dark.

She laughed a little breathlessly, trying to make a joke of it. "You're not a witch, are you?"

His gaze met hers, dark, implacable. Her heart thumped.

"No," he said finally, briefly. "I'm not a witch."

Right. Janet swallowed. All right.

But the feeling of disquiet didn't go away. It followed her like a touch on the back of her neck, as if she were somehow being watched, weighed, judged.

She turned her head; twisted in his arms.

Someone *was* watching her.

There, at the edge of the circle of dancers, caught between the fire and the moon, a woman watched and waited. How had Janet missed seeing her before? Even in this exotic company, she glowed. Her skirt was red as flame, her skin gold as honey. Her breasts were heavy, dark-tipped, naked.

Janet's mouth dropped open. She craned her neck. She couldn't say if the woman in red was beautiful or not. She was simply the most striking, compelling person Janet had ever seen, with a figure that would stop traffic and a face to make women whisper and men groan.

And she watched them, a faint, knowing smile on her full lips, her black eyes at once indifferent and hostile.

Janet shivered.

Her partner felt her tremble. He turned his head to see what had caught her attention, and swore.

"Who is she?" Janet asked.

"It doesn't matter." His arm tightened around her waist. His hand gripped hers. "She doesn't matter."

But Janet knew he lied. Her confidence and pleasure leaked away. Under the weight of that coal black gaze, she felt awkward. Unfeminine.

"I don't want to dance anymore," she said.

He squeezed her hand. "Okay." His tone was gentle. "Let's go."

Tucking her against his side, he guided her out of the

glittering, weaving circle and into the shelter of the trees. Janet bumbled along beside him, grateful for his warmth and supporting arm. It was cold away from the fire, and she couldn't see her feet.

"Where are you taking me?" she asked as they made their way through the trees.

"Back to your car."

She dug in her heels. "No."

SHE didn't want to go.

Just for a second, Ross warmed himself with that thought, let himself enjoy the weight of her, soft and solid against his side, let himself imagine she could stay.

But only for a second.

Because now that Lilith had seen her, Janet needed to go. He had to get her out of here. Fast.

"It's late," he said.

Time didn't mean anything to him anymore. But he remembered it had been a big deal with Janet. It used to frustrate him, her awareness of clocks and calendars, her insistence that commitment required a timetable. As if love proceeded according to some kind of freaking schedule.

He understood her better now.

Oh, yeah. Now that it was too late for them, for him, he understood her fear and frustration perfectly.

Her shoulders drooped. Her resistance deflated.

"It *is* late," she admitted. "I guess I was having so much fun I didn't notice."

"It's not fun," he told her harshly. "It's—"

Magic.

But the *sidhe* collar burned around his neck, cutting off his air, choking his explanation in his throat.

"Maybe not for you," Janet said. He could feel her shrinking under his arm, withdrawing into herself, and he wanted to howl with frustration.

"But I had a very nice time," she continued, painfully honest and oh-so-polite. "The dancing and the . . . The dancing and everything."

He had to swallow before he could get the words out. "I had a nice time, too."

She didn't answer him. She continued to walk beside him, matching her steps to his, her head bowed. She wouldn't even look at him.

"I did," he insisted.

She shook her head. Her hair smelled like wood smoke and shampoo. "You don't have to say that."

"I mean it." His voice almost cracked with desperation, but he could tell she wasn't convinced. She was stiff. Dejected. Disbelieving.

He tried again. "Being with you . . . I want to be with you, Janet. I love being with you."

I love you.

She sniffed. "Sure you do. That's why you're rushing me to my car."

Anger burned inside him at her lack of belief in him. In herself.

"Stop," he ordered.

She stopped obediently, but there was stubbornness in the set of her shoulders, challenge in the lift of her chin.

He wanted to shake her. He wanted to laugh. He wanted to go down on his knees in gratitude for her hurt and humor and humanity that almost made him feel human again.

Instead, he kissed her, a deep, warm kiss with a lot of tongue and feeling behind it, and she—oh, man, she kissed him back like she'd been starving for the taste of him, like she couldn't get enough. Her mouth was open and eager, her body melting against his. She licked him. Fed him. Consumed him.

A wave almost of despair washed over him. It shouldn't be this easy. She shouldn't be this easy.

So he kissed her harder, thrusting his tongue deep in her mouth, rubbing himself roughly between her legs, against her heat, making it brutally clear what he wanted from her.

Only instead of pushing him away and yelling at him to

stop, Janet murmured encouragement and locked her arms around his neck. Her body wriggled as she sought to fit her soft curves to his greater height.

He could take her. The awareness beat in the back of his head like a throbbing tooth. She was ready.

But he wouldn't. Not the way she wanted him. Not the way he wanted to. Lilith had destroyed his self-respect, but she'd also taught him self-control. In fourteen years, he'd learned to draw out his pleasure and his partner's until they both shuddered on the point of pain, until every muscle begged and every nerve screamed for release.

So he could control himself now. He could control Janet and her response to keep her safe. To bring her pleasure.

He drew back his head. Janet's eyes were closed, her lashes spiky. Her lips were swollen and pouty from his kisses.

She touched his cheek. "Ross," she whispered.

And any hope he had of resisting her, of protecting her, went up in smoke.

Grabbing her elbow, he dragged her into the bushes.

Chapter Four

SHE'D called him Ross. How stupid. How rude. No man wanted the woman he was with to confuse him with another lover.

Janet stumbled, clumsy with lust and mortification. Branches scratched her arms. Thorns snagged her skirt.

He jerked to a halt, his hand hard on her elbow.

Janet's heart thudded against her breastbone. They stood at the edge of an old farm field overgrown with grass and wildflowers and silvered with moonlight. The scent of roses drifted from the broken hedge.

And maybe he hadn't heard her call him by another man's name, after all, she thought hopefully. Or maybe he didn't care. Because he didn't *look* angry.

In the stark light of the moon, his face was hard and intent. His eyes were dark. Dilated. But not with anger.

Janet's breath shivered out. Her nipples tightened.

"I won't stop this time," he warned her.

A rush of excitement weakened her knees.

"No," she said, accepting.

But even then, his hand, which had lifted to cup her face,

paused. Janet leaned into him, seeking his warmth, craving the fit of his palm against her cheek.

"No?" he repeated huskily.

Oh, God, she'd said the wrong thing. Again.

"No, I mean, yes, I don't want you to. Stop, I mean. I—"

His mouth came down on hers, cutting off her nervous flow of words. What a relief.

He kissed her with a kind of ferocious purpose that should have scared her and instead made her dizzy with heat. He hauled her against him, his body hard and heavily, gloriously aroused, his tongue penetrating her mouth.

And it wasn't enough. It wasn't nearly enough.

Janet shuddered and reached for him, her arms twining around his shoulders, her hands grasping his hair, as if she could hold him, have him, pull him into herself.

He dragged her down with him onto the ground, flattening the tall grass around them, and fell on top of her.

That was better. She relished his weight on top of her, his body long and lean, muscled, his angles squashing her curves. He levered up, raising himself on his elbows, and she made a soft sound of protest.

But it was all right, because he didn't leave her. He pushed up her skirt. He yanked down her panties, and she lifted her hips to help him. He thrust his knee between hers, making a place for himself between her thighs, and an instant of hesitation tightened her belly.

You don't know me, what I've done, where I've been.

But she wanted him.

She was ready for him. She had been ready for him since he'd trapped her against her car and touched her through her clothes. The memory made her squirm.

He choked out something—her name?—and jammed his hand between them to adjust his own clothes. She felt the brush of his knuckles and raised herself, reaching, seeking more. She was slick and soft with wanting him. He grunted with satisfaction as he filled her with his fingers.

It still wasn't enough.

She tugged at him. His shoulders were smooth and hot, his

chest rough with hair. The texture tickled a memory deep below the surface of her mind, down in the secret places where dark and slippery things dwelled.

Ross. She bit her lip to keep from saying the name out loud.

His chest shuddered with his breath. She felt him, blunt and hot and hard, searing her body's entrance. Pressing her feet flat on the cool grass, she lifted to take him. His weight shifted. His head blocked the stars. And then he thrust himself inside her, all the way inside her, deeply, thickly inside her, again and again.

Her head reeled. She contracted around him, everything inside her spiraling, tightening to a point. Their bodies strained together, sleek and sweaty.

"Janet." Her name on his lips was a groan. A plea. A prayer. "We shouldn't— I have to . . ."

His muscles bunched. She felt him withdrawing and jerked in protest. Instinctively, she clung to him, twisting to keep him with her. To keep him inside her.

His fingers pressed into her buttocks. He rocked against her harder, faster, his rhythm overtaking and controlling them both.

Janet arched. She was almost there. Almost . . .

He gasped. "I can't—"

"You have to," she cried, frantic. "Ross!"

He pounded into her; quaked and convulsed in her arms. She felt the quick, hard shudder of his release and it started her own rippling through her like rings of water in a pond. Stirred to the heart, shaken to the depths, she sucked in her breath and went under.

THE flowers stared up at the sky with innocent white faces. The stars looked down.

Janet floated somewhere in the middle, grass sticking in her hair and to the small of her back, every muscle limp with gratitude. The scents of summer grass and roses mingled with the smells of sweat and sex. She closed her eyes and inhaled, holding the moment inside her as long as possible.

At some point, they'd reversed position so her lover laid beside her, his shoulder hard against her cheek. His heart pounded under her palm.

His voice rumbled from his chest. "You called me Ross."

She started guiltily. Oh, dear. This was one of those awful lovers' etiquette moments, like using the bathroom after sex, only worse. Why couldn't she have cried out "darling" or "sweetheart" or even "Oh, my God" instead of another man's name?

"I'm sorry," she said. "I—"

"When did you know?"

Sex must have made her stupid. "Know what?"

"When," he said with exaggerated patience, "did you recognize me?"

Janet's breath whooshed out. Slowly, she lifted her head from his shoulder to stare.

He watched her, his long hair spilling on the ground that pillowed them both, his lashes thick and dark above angled cheekbones. In the dark, it was impossible to see the color of his eyes. But she knew his face. She knew.

"Ross?" she whispered.

One eyebrow lifted. "Yeah?"

A weight pressed on her chest. She couldn't breathe. Couldn't think. Couldn't—

"You can't be," she blurted.

His mouth quirked. He reached up to tuck a strand of her hair behind her ear, and the rose she wore tumbled to his chest.

"I think we just proved I can. Anyway, you knew."

She shook her head, rejecting the possibility. Rejecting responsibility. Rejecting him. "No."

He frowned. "Sure you did. You might have changed some, but you're still not the kind of girl who puts out on a first date."

But she was, Janet thought with a terrible clutch at her heart. She had. He didn't know her at all.

And she didn't know him.

"I have changed," she said. "I'm thirty-six years old. You're . . ."

Hot. Young. Incredible.

Impossible.

"Still twenty-two?" he supplied. His tone was dry, but his eyes were wary.

"Yes." She seized eagerly on the number as if, by sticking to the facts, she could somehow make them all add up. "Ross MacLean would be in his thirties now. You haven't aged at all."

He shrugged, but the casual gesture didn't hide the tension she felt in his body. "The *sidhe* don't age. I can't either, as long as I'm with them. But time passes, all the same, Janet. Years of it. Years of *them*." His tone turned slightly bitter. "I don't feel twenty-two. I feel about a hundred."

She didn't want to feel the tug of sympathy. What he was saying, what he was asking her to accept, was just too bizarre.

"What are you talking about? What—who are the shay?"

"Shee," he corrected her. "The ancient ones. The people of the hills, whose world intersects with ours at times and places when we're most vulnerable."

She stared at him, her mouth ajar.

"Oh, Christ, Janet," he snapped. "The fair folk, okay? I was abducted by the fucking fairies."

He rolled to a sitting position. Janet was left on the ground, feeling as though the earth had suddenly shifted off its axis.

Which it pretty much had, if she accepted even part of what he was saying.

"We had a fight that night. Remember?" the one-who-could-not-be-Ross asked over his shoulder. "You were upset because you thought I'd paid attention to some girl at a party, and I got mad because you didn't trust me. So I got on my bike, figured I'd ride around until we both cooled off some."

"That wasn't it," Janet whispered. There was a bitter taste in the back of her throat, like bile or disbelief. "I needed to hear the words. After four months, it wasn't too much to expect the man who was sharing my bathroom to tell me he loved me."

"Maybe," he acknowledged. "And maybe I thought I'd make you miss me. Or make you sorry. Maybe I would have wised up and apologized. Only before I got smart, I stumbled onto them." He stared out over the field, his profile bleak in the moonlight. "The equinox gathering of the *sidhe*."

Janet's head throbbed. Her brain couldn't absorb what he was telling her. She rose cautiously to one elbow, afraid if she moved too quickly, she would throw up.

"I was still sore over what you said," he continued softly. "And just pissed off enough to fall for their whole line. Never grow old? Sex without commitment? It sounded pretty good at the time. And Lilith knew it, damn her. No." He shook his head. "Damn me."

There was so much quiet self-loathing in his voice that Janet shivered in sympathy. The temptation to comfort him scared her.

"I don't believe you," she said flatly. How could she believe him? "You're not Ross."

He looked at her then, his eyes burning. Dark. "Then who am I? How do I know about us? About that night?"

"I don't know. I don't care. I can't *think*," she burst out. "But you can't make me believe that fourteen years ago my college boyfriend walked out on me and never came back because he fell under the spell of—of— Who is this Lilith, anyway?"

He exhaled. "She's the ruler of the *sidhe*. Their queen."

It was too much.

"You want me to believe you were kidnapped by the *queen* of the *fairies*?"

He winced. "Yes."

"Right." Janet stood, shaking out her skirt. Oh, God, where were her panties? "And I'm Sheena, Queen of the Jungle."

His shoulders shook. If he didn't look so miserable, she would have thought he was laughing.

And maybe he was.

The thought was like an arrow to her heart. If this wasn't all some elaborate con, he had to be laughing at her.

She scooped her underwear off the grass and balled it in her fist. "What do you want?" she demanded.

He stood, too, uncoiling his long body until he towered over her. "What are you talking about?"

She gestured impatiently with her free hand. "There has to

be some reason for this . . . this charade. You must want something to make up such a stupid story."

He looked down his nose, his expression so much like Ross's that her breath abandoned her. "Honey, what I want from you, I already got. I don't have any reason to lie."

She was confused. Her head pounded.

"What you want . . .?" she repeated blankly.

His gaze dropped briefly to the panties in her hand. He didn't say a word.

Her flush burned all through her body and flamed in her face.

"I'm going back to the car," she said.

He let her go two steps, three, before he started after her. "Janet—"

Turning, she kicked him in the shin as hard as she could.

"Ow." He stopped. "Honey, be reasonable."

"Be reasonable?" Her voice rose to a near shriek, and Janet, who prided herself on her library-quiet tones always, didn't even care. *"Be reasonable?* You dupe me into having sex with you and then make up some cockamamie story about the queen of the fairies, for crying out loud, and you expect me to be reasonable?"

She was shaking, bitter, blinded with tears, deafened by the crashing of her foolish hopes and the breaking of her stubborn heart.

"Stay away from me, Ross. Just stay away."

This time, she was the one to leave.

This time, he let her go.

Ross bent under the hood of the 1936 Auburn Speedster he was restoring. Life as a sex slave actually came with a lot of downtime. Especially after the first seven years or so, when the novelty wore off and escape attempts mostly ended in frustration and refined torture.

Besides, Ross liked cars. Cars didn't have emotions. Cars didn't make demands. Compared to the shifting shadow world of the *sidhe,* mechanical engineering was simple. Concrete. Manageable.

He listened to the engine. One, maybe two, of the pistons wasn't firing correctly. He'd have to adjust the timing. He reached to test the spark plug connections.

A voice broke into his concentration. "Shouldn't you be smiling?"

Ross straightened and smacked his head on the edge of the hood. Turning, he glared at Puck.

"Shouldn't you be minding your own business?"

"You are my business, boyo. And you've been mighty poor company lately." The little man hopped off a stump and shuffled forward. "I thought it was because our Lilith had lost her taste for you. But now you've had a tasty morsel of your own, and you're still gloomy as a man who's missed his dinner."

Ross leaned over the Auburn's engine. He was not discussing his sex life with the *sidhe*. He was not discussing Janet. He didn't even want to think about her. About last night.

Puck cocked his head. "Wasn't she any good?"

Ross threw a wrench at him.

Puck skipped out of range. "So, she was good," he said with satisfaction. "What's your problem, then?"

Ross went back to checking spark plugs. "I don't have a problem," he said through his teeth.

"She's going to help you?"

"No."

"Did you *ask* her to help you?" Puck persisted.

"I don't want her involved."

The little man clucked like a bird. "Bit late for that now."

Ross's fist clenched on the metal frame. Too bad he'd already thrown the wrench. He'd like to bury it in Puck's skull.

"That's your fault," Ross said. "You're the one who called her."

"I'm not the one who shagged her," Puck pointed out smugly, and Ross winced.

Okay, so it was all his fault. Mostly his fault. He should have resisted her. He should have protected her. He should have pulled out.

He thought of Janet, warm and wet and straining under him, and reached blindly for the distributor cap. It burned his hand.

Swearing, he jerked back. "It doesn't matter," he said, sucking his knuckles. "She won't come back."

"Sure of that?" Puck asked.

"Oh, yeah," Ross said grimly. "I made sure of it."

"Then you've screwed her twice, boyo. And yourself. You're not likely to save yourself that way."

Not himself.

Her. He'd save her.

Ross ducked under the hood again and began testing the cables that led from the distributor cap to the spark plugs, one by one.

THE farm looked different by daylight. Shabbier. Decrepit.

That was good, Janet told herself as she nosed her car down the rutted lane. She needed to see the farm and its inhabitants in the bleak and bracing light of day. She wanted to prove to herself that whatever she'd felt or been tempted to believe two nights ago was only a trick of moonlight and music. Once the carnival was exposed as the trumpery thing it was, once she accepted her one-night stand as the tawdry thing it was, she could put both behind her and get on with her real life.

Such as it was.

The thought left a flat taste in her mouth, like soda when the fizz was gone. She tightened her grip on the wheel.

The lane was empty. Were they gone? The farmyard was deserted. Had she missed him? Janet switched off her engine, feeling her resolution sputter and die.

Get over it. Get on with it.

She looked around. Despite the general neglect, she didn't see any fair debris, no overflowing trash bins, no crushed cans or blowing papers. Only a rusting car on cinder blocks and a well choked with weeds. The farmhouse stared at her through dirty panes of broken glass.

Slowly, she climbed out of the car, feeling as empty as the house. As abandoned.

Stupid. He got what he wanted from her, didn't he?

I don't have any reason to lie.

Or to stay, either.

The bonfire site was cold. When Janet stooped to touch the circling rocks, the blowing ash got in her eyes. Blinking, she straightened. The carnival had moved on.

Bereft of her target and her purpose, she wandered through the trees, finding her way at last to a break in the hedge. Taking a deep breath, she pushed through the bushes.

The sun beat down on her head. Insects droned and whirred from the trees. The field was silent. Empty. A lark darted against the blue bowl of the sky.

There was nothing to show that Janet had ever been here before. No evidence that anyone had ever been here.

Except there. Her heart beat faster. Below the nodding heads of Queen Anne's lace, a crimson splash against the flattened grass.

A rose.

The rose from her hair.

Janet bent and picked it up with trembling fingers. The red petals glowed in the sun, unwilted, unwithered, unfaded, as fresh as the moment when Ross had plucked the rose from the hedge to put it behind her ear.

What had he told her? *The sidhe don't age. I can't either, as long as I'm with them.*

Janet stood in the warmth of the sun, the rose quivering in her hand, and shivered with fear and possibility.

Chapter Five

T HE moon was a glowing sickle against the velvet sky, like the eye of a napping cat.

Janet heard the music before she saw the lights. Hope fluttered beneath her rib cage like the tiny heartbeat of an unborn child.

The ancient ones, Ross had called them. *The people of the hills, whose world intersects with ours at times and places when we're most vulnerable.*

Well, she was plenty vulnerable now.

She stumbled down the dark lane, awkward with anticipation, trembling with fear. Because if one part of his story were true, then couldn't it all be true? *Fourteen years ago my college boyfriend walked out on me and never came back because he fell under the spell of—of—*

The fairy queen.

Janet shivered.

Three months had passed since she'd danced with Ross in the fairy circle and made love with him under the stars. For three months, the rose remained beside her bed in a crystal bud vase, as fresh and bright as it had bloomed the night Ross stripped it of its thorns and tucked it into her hair. Its wild, sweet fragrance filled her empty apartment, teasing her to hope. Tempting her to believe.

In magic.

In Ross.

In love.

The memories of that night pervaded her heart the way the rose's perfume permeated her apartment. For the past three months, Janet had haunted the farm on her days off, a pathetic ghost searching for . . . Well, she wasn't sure anymore what she hoped to find. Closure?

Or a second chance?

In the shadows under the trees, outside the circle of the fire, she stopped. They were there. They all were there, the *sidhe,* dancing to the music of the pipes and drums. They glittered, they flowed in the figures of the dance, too beautiful to be borne and too numerous to count. She caught her breath, watching them. How could she have mistaken them for anything but what they were? For their grace was not mortal, and their silence wasn't anything human.

She wondered suddenly how Ross had endured it, fourteen years without the sound of a human voice.

The music sobbed and sang. But tonight her feet did not twitch, her breathing did not quicken to the rhythm of the fair folk's dance. Straining her eyes against the fire's glare, she searched the motley, whirling crowd for one tall, dark head.

She did not see him. Anywhere. Disappointment made her sag.

But he had to be here. He'd danced with her. And that first time . . . Janet bit her lip, remembering. The first time, she'd met Ross in the woods. He hadn't been dancing at all.

She edged through the trees, scuttling beyond the reach of the light like a cockroach. Compared to the scintillating dancers, she felt dark and small and plain. They whirled by, bright with gems and flowers, rich with velvet and fur.

What would happen if she were seen? What would they do to her if she were caught?

Better not to find out.

Janet slunk deeper into the shadows, testing her footing with each step, intending to circle the farm buildings and make her way through the woods to the stone wall above the road. A light, an honest yellow glow like lamplight, slid beneath the closed barn doors. Janet's heart tripped faster. Holding her breath, she tiptoed to the barn and eased one door open, her palms flat against the weathered wood.

He was there. Ross, his lean back bent over an engine the way she'd seen him hundreds of times, except now he was in silk and leather instead of jeans and an old T-shirt, and the car was a doozy, long and sleek, gleaming with paint and chrome. It looked wickedly expensive and at least fifty years old. Janet had doubts, big doubts, about her ability to compete against the fairy queen. She didn't stand a chance against this car.

She cleared her throat anyway.

Ross must have heard her, because he turned. His eyes widened. Whatever else he felt at that moment, Janet's biggest doubts disappeared. Because his face made it clear he was very glad to see her. He took a step toward her.

And with as little hesitation as a bird returning to its nest, Janet flew across the barn and into his arms.

He kissed her, her hair, her cheek, her throat, and finally, at last, her mouth. He smelled like engine grease and leather, like wood smoke and Ross. Janet clung to him and cried with worry and relief, so the honey of his kisses mixed with the salt of her tears.

"Are you okay?" he asked, his arms hard around her. He needed a shave. And then, sharply, "What are you doing here?"

After his "boy am I glad to see you" kiss, the edge to his tone cut her to the quick.

She stuck out her chin to hide her hurt. "Looking for you, obviously."

"Why now? Why tonight?"

Oh, dear. She wasn't ready to admit her belief or confess her hope. Not yet. Not without some encouragement from him.

"Well . . . You said you were taken at the equinox gathering of the *sidhe*. Tonight's the fall equinox. I looked it up," she explained, when he continued to stare at her blankly. "On the Internet."

"Smart girl."

She shrugged. "It was that or come back every hundred years, like in *Brigadoon*."

His laugh made her bold.

"What are *you* doing?" she asked, as if she had a right to know.

He narrowed his eyes. He didn't like questions, she remembered. Well, tough. If she could stand the answers, he could deal with a few questions.

He jerked his chin at the car behind them. "Working," he said.

"Not dancing?" With effort, she made her tone light.

"No," he replied shortly.

There was more to this reticence than male stubbornness, she saw. This was a wall, put up between his private self and hurt. His moss green eyes were dark with pain and pride and frustration.

She put her hand on his muscled forearm. "Show me," she invited quietly.

She felt the tension in his arm. But he guided her beside the long car, its hood gleaming with maroon paint and topped by a wicked, winged creature in chrome.

"The '36 Auburn Speedster," he said, "with a straight-eight supercharged Lycoming engine. Over three hundred horsepower—the fastest production car at Bonneville the year it was produced."

Janet nodded.

As Ross got into his subject, his voice warmed. The muscles in his arm relaxed. "It's got a great design. The blower system runs off a timing chain that forces more oxygen into the carburetor. Other manufacturers just made the engines bigger trying to get the same kind of power. If you look here at the pipes coming out of the side . . ."

She looked. She listened, impressed by his knowledge and his passion. He was talking now about adjusting the air/fuel mixture setting, of checking the ignition timing, but it wasn't his subject that captivated her. It was Ross himself: the intensity in his lean body, the focus in his eyes, the enthusiasm in his voice. She could have listened to him for hours.

Once upon a time, she remembered, she had.

"Did you do all the work yourself?" she asked.

"Yeah." His mouth twisted. "I had the time."

"It looks wonderful," she said sincerely. "Like a million bucks."

Ross shrugged. "It's probably worth a tenth that. More or less, depending on the buyer."

Janet peered inside to admire the leather upholstery. "Will you sell it?"

He crossed his arms and leaned against the hood. "How?"

"Well, you . . ." Janet straightened, feeling her cheeks flush. Caught up in his enthusiasm, swept back in time, she had forgotten where they were. What he was.

"If—if you leave here," she said. "You could sell it then."

"I can never leave," Ross said flatly.

The pain was back, lurking in his eyes. It deflated her spirits. It touched her heart.

"Sure you can," she said in the voice she would have used to encourage a dispirited six-year-old to read. "If you want to."

"If I *want*—"

He broke off. Grabbed her, whirled her around, and pressed her against the car. Her pulse spiked. Excitement ran under her skin.

"I'll show you what I want," he said thickly, and crushed his mouth to hers.

His kiss was deep, dark, and desperate. He kissed her as if his life depended on it, held her as if he would never let her go. Janet clung to him, too dazed, too delighted by the need that pumped through him to push him away. He wanted her. He wanted this. His body was hard against hers. Her nails raked over his shirt as he kissed her again, violent, raw. Arousing.

She gave him what he asked for and more. She was willing to give him everything, there on the straw of the barn, but he dragged his mouth from hers. Gripping her wrists, he put her away from him. His breathing was uneven, his eyes turbulent.

"I can never leave," he repeated heavily. "And you have to go."

She blinked, bewildered and near tears. "Why?"

A new voice curdled the tension in the barn. A female voice, cold as a silver knife and rich as cream.

"Because it is dangerous for you here," the voice said.

Janet jerked.

Ross stiffened and turned, putting her behind him. "Leave her alone," he said to whomever had followed her through the wide barn doors. "She's nothing to you."

Janet craned to see past his shoulder. His arm was hard against her cheek.

A lady stood on the dusty straw, the yellow lamplight pooling around her like water. Her stiff, dark skirts gleamed. Jewels glittered from her neck and in her hair. But the brightness that clung to her did not come from the lamp or her clothes, but from the lady herself. Her skin glowed. Her eyes burned. In the shadow of her robe, Puck crouched like Ignorance haunting the Ghost of Christmas Present.

The lady—Lilith, Janet thought with sudden, awful certainty—turned her magnificent head to Ross. "And to you? What is she to you, manling?"

He met her gaze steadily. "Nothing."

And despite Janet's belief that he was only protecting her, despite the kisses they had shared, she cringed inside.

She drew a shaky breath. Right. Like cringing was going to get her anywhere with these two.

She sidled from behind Ross's back. "I have the right to be here," she said bravely.

Lilith regarded her with coal black eyes, and Janet almost stepped behind Ross again.

"You have no rights here," the fairy queen said. "And your hold on him cannot compete with mine."

That was for sure.

Janet stuck out her chin. "At least I'm not trying to hold him against his will."

"You lie," the queen said. "The child in your womb binds him."

Janet felt as if Lilith had just hit her on the side of the head with a magic two-by-four. "My what?" she croaked.

"You're pregnant?" Ross demanded.

"I . . ." She saw stars. She had to sit down. She groped her way to a bale of hay and sat, trying to breathe, trying to think back over the past three months. "I guess I could be."

It was as good an explanation as stress or early menopause.

"Am I the father?"

Hurt shimmered through her that he felt the need to ask. She was very aware of the queen standing by the door, watching them both with an enigmatic expression.

Ross knelt in front of her, taking both her hands in his, willing her to look at him. "Janet, it's important. I have to know. Am I the father?"

"Yes." She blinked rapidly. "But I'd never make you do anything you don't want to—"

He dropped her hands. "That's crap. I have a responsibility, same as you."

"You have a choice, the same as I do."

His eyes narrowed. "What does that mean?"

"I just meant . . ." Janet floundered. What did she mean? What did she want?

"Would you choose that one over this?" Lilith's voice flowed through the quiet, lamp-lit barn like poison, smooth and insidious. "Are you so eager for age and pain and the chance to spawn?"

Ross shrugged. "It's like they say. Getting old sucks, but it beats the alternative."

Janet couldn't follow their conversation. She was still stuck on all that "child in your womb" stuff. *Pregnant.* She pressed her hand to her stomach.

"Do you really believe you are worthy of her?" Lilith continued. "Of either of them?"

"This isn't about what I deserve."

"Then consider what the woman deserves. Would you condemn her to your fate?"

Ross shivered like a horse tormented by flies. "No."

Lilith's smile was a terrible thing to see. "No," she agreed softly.

She turned and swept from the barn, her skirts brushing the floor. The shadows rustled in her wake.

Janet's heart threatened to pound its way out of her chest. She looked to her lover for help, for guidance, for an explanation. "Ross?"

But he did not—would not—meet her gaze. His lean, dark face was tortured as he spoke to Puck.

"Don't talk to her," he ordered. "Don't tell her."

He was leaving. He was leaving her. Again.

The bastard.

"Ross!" Janet cried.

His fists clenched. His shoulders hunched. And without another word, he walked out on her to follow the fairy queen.

Puck whistled and rubbed his hands together. "Well, now, that was a show."

Janet could barely speak past the bitter grief in her throat. "Be careful, you'll get in trouble. You're not supposed to talk to me, remember?"

The little man cocked his head. "That wasn't for my sake, poppet. Or for his. No, his care was for you. He would not want me to tell you how you could win his freedom."

Ross was already free of her. Of their child. Of all responsibility. He must be so happy.

But his face, as he left her, had been miserable.

I have a responsibility, same as you.

"What did you say?" Janet asked Puck.

"I said, you could free him." The *sidhe* eyed her slyly. "If you dared."

Her breathing hitched. "How?"

"On Samhain the court will ride by Miles Cross," Puck said. "Look among the riders nearest the town, for those once were mortal. As we pass the churchyard, watch for your love by the queen's side. For if you pull him down and hold him, hold fast, it may be he will live to be the father of your child. But you must hold on, whatever happens."

"I won't hold Ross against his will," Janet said stubbornly. "You must."

Pride and anger, sorrow and hope churned inside her and burst out in one great, "*Why?* Give me one good reason why I should fight for a man who doesn't want me."

Puck rubbed the side of his nose. "It's every seven years on Halloween we pay our tithe to hell." He smiled, exposing pointed teeth. "And this year, I fear young Ross is to be our sacrifice."

Chapter Six ❧

HALLOWEEN ought to be safe and fun.

There was nothing fun about standing in a church-yard after midnight, waiting for the queen of the fairies to ride by with her court.

It didn't feel safe, either.

Janet shivered, despite her long skirt and a sweater decorated with happy pumpkins and friendly ghosts. The lights of the town, spread below her, seemed very far away. The squat brick church tower with its spindly white steeple loomed to her left. The hills rose at her back. Between the church and the hills lurked the graveyard, its shadows stark in the light of the waxing moon.

She hugged her elbows and watched the road. She was going to be fine. Everything was going to be fine. The brisk young obstetrician who was taking over from old Dr. Abercorn had assured Janet that at four months pregnant, she could engage in most normal activities without any risk to herself or her unborn child.

Pull him down and hold him, Puck had told her. *Hold fast. . . . You must hold on, whatever happens.*

Janet drew a deep breath. She'd been waiting for hours.

What if she was too late? Or in the wrong place? What if Ross was sacrificed to hell because she'd picked the wrong church-yard to keep vigil?

On Samhain the court will ride by Miles Cross.

Her heartbeat rang in her ears. She trembled with cold and fear. But that ringing, that faint ringing, wasn't all in her head. It sounded like . . . bells. Sleigh bells? Bridle bells, Janet decided. And that growling vibration, that wild undernote to the night, sounded like an engine. Engines. Not coming from the town, either, not rumbling on the road, but behind her, a muted roar like off-road vehicles racing.

She turned and watched them come.

The riding of the *sidhe* was like a hometown parade gone terribly wrong, an azalea festival mixed horribly with a Mad Max motorcycle rally, filmed in flickering black-and-white and projected against the dim backdrop of the hills. Janet pressed one hand protectively to her stomach as she watched. Beauty queens on horses pranced beside road warriors on Harleys. Men as stately as the hills, women with the grace of trees, loped or swayed forward with a rushing sound like the woods in high wind.

There were other things, too, unrecognizable in the shad-ows, things that made her glad she could not see. Things with horns and claws and wings and multiple legs, riding or being ridden. Dread dried her mouth. Some carried torches with red flames and black smoke. Some shone with their own silver light, some with the phosphorescence of things long under-ground. She saw the gleam of spears and skulls, the glitter of gems and chrome, and her breath coagulated in her chest. Her knees refused to move.

Look among the riders nearest the town, for those once were mortal.

Her heart quailed. She was too far away. The fair folk were on the other side of the cemetery, following a track in the hills that probably existed before the Cherokee. She would never reach them in time.

As we pass the churchyard, watch for your love by the queen's side.

No. She was too late. She was too afraid. She couldn't possibly . . .

But she was already running over the sunken ground of the graveyard, dodging to avoid the humped headstones, the obelisks shining in the moonlight. Her heart pounded. Her breath escaped in gasps. She ran, one hand flattened to the curve of her stomach, as if the danger were at her heels instead of riding to meet her on the other side.

When she reached the low brick wall bordering the churchyard, she slipped in the fresh dirt piled by the wall and had to steady herself against a monument. Her ankles hurt. Sweat trickled down her back and between her breasts.

She squinted toward the beautiful, terrible, motley procession winding past the graveyard.

Her racing heart mocked her. *Too late, too late . . .*

Her breath caught. *There.*

Lilith shone among her court like a red coal at the fire's core. The silver light turned her gown the color of dried blood and her face as pale as the moon. She rode a shaggy pony. It should have been funny, the sight of the tall, strong queen on that short, sturdy mount, but it wasn't. Muscles rolled beneath the pony's shaggy coat. Rocks rattled under its small, round hooves. It was black, all black, without a whisper of white, and its eyes were the eyes of a goat.

Janet tore her gaze away before she fell under the spell of those golden eyes.

And there, at the queen's side, just as Puck had said he would be, was Ross.

Janet nearly wept with relief.

He rode a black and silver motorcycle, idling the engine. His long legs were encased in black leather. His dark hair flowed loose around his lean face. He didn't seem frightened, like a man dragged to sacrifice, or despairing, like a man who had lost the love of his life. His expression was flat. Wooden.

If you pull him down and hold him, hold fast, it may be he will live to be the father of your child.

Janet gulped back a sob.

She had always blamed him. For leaving—God, she had

blamed him for that—but also for not loving her enough, for not giving her enough, for not making the commitment she wanted.

She crouched in the shadow of a monument, and the crack that opened in her heart almost swallowed her whole. What if Puck was wrong? What if Ross didn't want to spend the rest of his life with a thirty-six-year-old pregnant librarian?

They were close enough now that she could see Ross's knuckles, white on the throttle, and the unbearable beauty of the queen's face.

Janet drew a shaky breath. She wasn't going to be pregnant forever. In five months, she would have a child. In five years, that child would ask questions: Who is my daddy? Where is he?

She had always blamed Ross. It was less painful somehow than accepting responsibility for her own failure to tell him what she wanted, what she needed.

She'd been afraid, then, of his rejection.

She was afraid now.

But there was no way she was explaining to their child that Mommy let Daddy go to hell because she was too big a coward to take a risk.

The riders were almost even with her hiding place.

Pull him down and hold him . . .

Oh, right. Panic sputtered through her. How *did* a five-foot-four pregnant woman pull a much larger man off a really big motorbike without killing them both?

She looked around wildly for inspiration and spotted a shovel stuck into the pile of dirt under the wall. Okay, if inspiration failed her, at least she had a shovel.

Grabbing it with one hand—it was surprisingly heavy—she swung a leg over to straddle the wall and practically fell off at the queen's feet.

She was right there. Lilith, passing on her pony, dragging the scent of old, slow, growing things after her like a cloak. The ground shivered under the pony's hooves.

Janet flattened herself to the top of the wall and turned her face away. Her cheek ground against the rough brick. She squeezed her eyes shut. She was pretty sure she'd stopped breathing, but her heart thundered in her ears.

Oh, God, they would hear her, they would see her, they would *smell* her and drag her down. . . .

Nothing happened.

Cautious seconds later, she opened her eyes. An engine growled by her ear. Turning her head, she saw the black and silver wheels of Ross's motorcycle glide by.

She had no time to think. She barely had time to act.

Flinging herself from the wall, she stumbled forward, the shovel in her hand. With all her might, she thrust it into the rear wheel of the bike.

Metal crunched and screeched. The shovel ripped from her grip, dragging her forward onto the ground. Pain lanced her shoulders, speared her knees and elbows. The rear of the bike slid away in a shower of sparks. The ground pitched and shrieked. The bike tilted.

Janet watched, wide-eyed, as time stood still and the front end of the bike torqued toward her head. She was going to die.

The engine roared in her ears. Its hot breath blasted her cheek. Ross's boot slammed in front of her face. He wrestled the bike away using his own body as a pivot. And then the motorcycle skidded across the grass, and Ross pitched off and fell heavily on top of her.

They both grunted. She grabbed him with a fist in his shirt and a hand on his thigh.

Everything got quiet. For a second Janet dared to hope that was it. She was done. He was safe.

But it wasn't that kind of quiet.

This was the awful, restive hush that seizes the air before a storm, the shadowed silence that waits for you at the top of the stairs. Janet struggled to her knees to meet it, clenching her hands in Ross's shirt. He lolled half across her. A gash bled blackly across his forehead. His eyes were dazed and dark.

Please, she caught herself praying, although it had been years since she'd prayed outside of church. *Please.*

The fairy queen's voice rattled into the silence.

"It's mine," she said like an imperious child. "Give it back."

Janet gaped at her across Ross's body, almost relaxing her hold in surprise. She tightened her grip. "No."

"He does not want you. Why do you want him?"

"Why do you?" Janet asked. Her shoulders hurt, and she was pretty sure her knees were bleeding. They stuck to her skirt.

The petulance left the queen's face. She drew herself up on her shaggy pony, and the look she gave Janet should have turned her to stone.

"My reasons are mine. As he is and has chosen to be."

Hard to argue with that.

Janet glanced down at Ross's white face streaked with blood. His lashes were dark against his gaunt cheeks. *I'm sorry if this isn't what you want,* she thought at him. *I'm sorry if I'm not what you want.*

She looked back at the queen. "He can't choose anything now. I've got him and"—she drew a deep breath—"I'm keeping him."

A sigh rippled through the assembled fair folk like wind through the grass.

"Let's see if you can hold him, then," said Lilith almost casually.

And with no more warning than that, he changed in her arms.

Instead of a man, Janet held a copper snake with moss green eyes that writhed and slithered in her grasp. Shock made her scream. Fear almost made her fling it to the grass. But she seized it behind its broad, flat head and supported its twisting body with her arms, and after a while it coiled around her forearm and was still.

Janet shuddered with relief.

The *sidhe* sighed again and swayed closer.

The snake turned into a red-tailed hawk that beat her with its wings and raked her with its claws and screamed in rage. Blinded, buffeted, Janet grabbed a taloned foot with one hand and shielded her eyes with the other. The hawk almost fought free. But she yanked the hem of her skirt up over its head and talked to it softly until it subsided sulkily against her breast, its hooked claws drawing blood from her arm.

The fair folk whispered and rustled together.

Not good, Janet thought.

The bird burst into a blue flame that crackled and blazed and seared her hands with terrible pain. Janet gasped. But she was prepared this time. Although the fire scorched her face and scalded the tears from her eyes, her skin did not blacken or blister. If she held on now, if she held on just a little longer, she would have Ross always. Ross and her baby. And she twisted her fingers in the fire and breathed through the pain until she couldn't feel it anymore.

The ring of *sidhe* pressed nearer. If she looked up . . .

But she didn't look up, and the flame melted to water in her hands. Janet was shaking so hard she was afraid the water would run away before she could catch it. But she cupped her palms and held them low and close over her lap, and every drop that trickled through her fingers she replaced with a tear.

The *sidhe* crowded at the corners of her vision.

Janet flinched in anticipation. Her shoulders ached. Her hands burned. Her arms were bleeding. She thought of the baby curled under her heart and squeezed her fingers together. They couldn't take much more.

From the water in her palms rose a mist that floated and formed above the ground. Janet held her breath. How could she hold on to a mist? But the cloud gradually took on the shape of a man; and the man was Ross.

Janet cried out in gladness and flung her arms around him.

He turned his head and looked at her with hatred in his eyes.

Chapter Seven

"YOU lose," Lilith said.

Janet waited for Ross to say something, anything, to allay the loathing in his eyes, but after that one brief, searing glance he wouldn't even look at her. He watched the queen like a dog waiting to be let out.

Janet's heart shattered.

"Release him," Lilith ordered, and the fair folk murmured and shifted in their circle. "He has made his choice."

She sounded so sure Janet almost obeyed. Ross's skin was warm where it pressed against hers, but his face, in profile, was distant and cold. The gash on his forehead had stopped bleeding. It was shrinking, healing, even as Janet watched.

The queen could do that for him. Could make him forever whole, could keep him forever young. What could Janet offer to compete with magic except her love and their child?

And he didn't want either one. Didn't want *her.*

A sob, dry as despair, swelled in her chest.

The *sidhe* watched and waited.

Movement crept in the corner of Janet's vision. She didn't dare take her eyes off the queen. But if she turned her head just a little she could see Puck, there in the circle, huddling between two tall tree people as if hoping to escape notice. When the little man saw her, though, he rubbed the side of his nose and nodded. To acknowledge her? Encourage her?

It's every seven years on Halloween we pay our tithe to hell. And this year, I fear young Ross is to be our sacrifice.

Janet swallowed hard. Okay, so Ross didn't want her. She could live with that. She could live without him. But maybe, just maybe, he wouldn't live without her.

Even if he never loved her, she could not let him die and be damned. Because she loved him.

Lilith sat her sturdy pony, her face a mask of triumph, unshakable as the earth in her feminine power.

Janet stuck out her chin. "Go to hell," she said.

Her words rippled through the *sidhe* like stones cast in a pond. Janet held her breath.

The queen's expression never wavered. But the air around her thickened, and the ground cracked beneath her pony's hooves. The chain slithered from around Ross's neck and fell gleaming to the grass.

He turned his head and smiled wryly at Janet. "You've done it now," he said.

She gawked at him. Something was different. He looked different. His forehead was bleeding again. "Done what?"

He shook his head. "Let's go."

"Go where?"

Lurching to his feet, he held out his hand to help her up. "Come on, honey. Move it."

The night eddied around them. The fair folk stirred restlessly.

Bewildered, Janet put her hand in his.

As if that were some kind of signal, the *sidhe* gathered themselves like the sea and flung themselves forward in a wave, whooping, cawing, rushing, roaring.

Janet stood transfixed, waiting for the flood to crash down on her.

"Come *on*," Ross said through his teeth, and yanked on her arm and dragged her after him.

The fair folk swarmed behind, banging and yammering.

The church wall bought them a little time. Ross half lifted, half threw Janet over. She landed in a pile of dirt. Ross grabbed her arm again and they scrambled over the bumpy ground as the fair folk's charge broke against the brick and swirled back uselessly on itself.

Janet didn't get it. She could see how the wall would stop the motorcycles. But the others . . . The queen's pony could have jumped the low barrier in one bound.

Lilith spoke. She wasn't yelling, but her voice shook the earth. The ground hunched like a stretching cat, and the wall tumbled down.

The *sidhe* rushed through the gap.

Janet ran. She had a stitch in her side and she stumbled into things—trees and headstones—but Ross kept pulling her arm, urging her on. Toward the church? Wherever he was going, he could have gotten there a lot faster without her. But he never left her side.

The fair folk clamored behind them, no longer a procession but a hunt. They were in the sky now, too, fluttering and swooping like kites, diving through the dark-leaved magnolias.

Janet stepped into the hollow over a grave and turned her ankle. She fell, right onto her bleeding knees, and that hurt so much she almost threw up.

Ross grasped her elbow. "Come on, honey. Almost there."

She couldn't get her breath to answer him. The night whirled sickly around her. Even with her eyes closed, she saw stars.

Ross picked her up—not a gentle lover's hold, either, he threw her over his shoulder like a bag of fertilizer—and ran with her, his shoulder bruising her stomach, his hard arm clamping her thighs, her head bouncing dizzily over his back.

But she could see their pursuers now, and that was enough to make her hang on for dear life. Compared to *that,* the jouncing was almost bearable.

Ross's gait changed. Hanging over his shoulder, Janet saw brick steps under his feet. Somehow, they had reached the church. Ross dumped her on her feet in the shallow archway that shielded the entrance, and she gasped in pain and clutched him for support. Her ankle throbbed. Propping her with his body, he reached past her to open the tall double doors.

They were locked.

Janet's heart plummeted to her stomach. Of course they were locked. No parish administrator would leave a historic church open to vandals on Halloween.

Ross turned, putting her behind him. He was breathing hard—well, it couldn't have been easy, lugging her through the graveyard—and his shirt was damp with sweat. Janet pressed her cheek to his shoulder blade and felt the faint tremor of his muscles. He was afraid. He had to be afraid.

But he faced the *sidhe,* for her sake, and his voice was firm and calm.

"Go back," he said. "She won me. I'm free now."

All the whooping, all the racket, all the clamor died. In some ways, the silence was worse than the noise, a heavy, breathing, waiting silence.

Janet peeked over his shoulder.

Lilith strode through the circle of the *sidhe* in her blood red dress, terrifying in her beauty, confident in her power. Her face shone like the moon.

She stopped at the bottom of the steps. Maybe it was a trick of the light, but it seemed to Janet she was somehow taller. Her head was almost level with Ross's.

Her black gaze bored into his. "If you go with her, man-ling, I will be in your every thought." Her voice was deadly. Low. "When you sleep beside her, you will dream of me. When you make love to her, you will see my face. You will never be free of me."

It was all horrible and horribly convincing. Ross shuddered and Janet closed her eyes in despair.

And then he laughed, the sound young and amazingly care-free. Janet started. Alone before the church steps, the fairy queen stiffened in surprise.

"No," Ross said. "You lose. Go away."

He turned his back on Lilith, turned his back on them all, and took Janet in his arms.

She touched his face in wonder. He looked different. Older.

Lines crinkled the corners of his eyes and creased his forehead. He seemed more solid, broader at the waist and shoulders.

"How do you know?" she whispered. "How can you be sure?"

Ross grinned at her, and his grin was the same, confident and young. Her heart stuttered crazily.

"Like I'm really going to think of her when I've got you," he said.

Janet was concentrating so fiercely on his face that she didn't spare a thought for the fair folk behind him, fading away like streaks in the sky.

"I was afraid," she confessed. "Fourteen years is a long time. It would be perfectly natural for you to—to think of her sometimes."

Ross shook his head. "How can my head be full of her when my heart is filled with you? All I can see when I close my eyes is you." He spread his hand over her stomach. "You and our baby. No, what worried me was that you wouldn't see through her last illusion."

Janet thought back. "When she changed you into water?"

"No. When she changed *me*."

"Because you're older? Younger? What?"

"The mist-to-man thing. Remember?"

She remembered that. Oh, she remembered. "You looked at me like you hated me."

"That was the last of Lilith's deceptions. I was afraid you wouldn't see through it, that you wouldn't believe I loved you."

Behind his head, the sky was lightening to a faint pearl gray like hope. It was almost dawn.

"Do you?" She knew now how to ask for the words. "Do you love me?"

His expression turned suddenly serious. "I always have. And I always will."

He bent his head and laid his lips on hers, kissing her long and sweetly.

Joy seeped inside Janet until she overflowed. She laid her head against his chest, listening to the strong, sure beat of his heart.

"What now?" she asked eventually.

"We ought to get you home." Ross frowned. "I've got a car, but we're a couple of miles from Carter Farm. You won't make it far on that ankle."

"We can take my car," Janet said. "I'm parked in the church lot."

"Okay," he said. "But tomorrow we go out to the farm and pick up the Auburn. Selling it should give me enough capital to start my own business."

She loved that he was thinking ahead, planning for a future. With her.

All I can see when I close my eyes is you. You and our baby.

"What business is that?" she asked, looping her arms around his waist.

"Classic cars. Rebuilding them. Restoring them. There's a real market out there." He helped her down the steps. "And I've learned a lot in the past fourteen years."

"I bet you've learned a lot about a lot of things," she said, daring to tease.

His slow grin liquified her insides. "Honey, I can't wait to show you."

They hobbled down the brick walk to the parking lot, leaning on one another.

As they drove home, dawn stippled the east in pink and gold. Dreaming beneath the cover of fields and trees, the hills rested.